Captured by the Pirate Laird

~ Book One: Highland Force series ~

by

Amy Jarecki

To my good friend and inspiring author, Jen Greyson. Thank you for being there. It's wonderful to have a friend who understands the peaks and valleys of this industry. Also, many thanks the very talented and generous author, Grace Burrowes, who spent an entire holiday season helping me edit this book.

Chapter One

England. Portsmouth Dockyard, 25th March, 1559

Anne resisted the temptation to turn and flutter one last wave at her mother. The Countess of Southampton had said goodbye on the pier and would not wish her daughter to exhibit additional emotion. Wearing a blue velvet gown, her hair coiled under a caul net and veil, Anne played the part of baroness with no outward sign of the storm roiling beneath her skin.

Clutching Anne's arm, Hanna walked up the gangway beside her. "I still cannot believe he wouldn't allow me to escort you all the way to northern England. Heaven's stars, you'll be alone."

"I'll be fine." Anne gave her serving maid a squeeze. "But I shall miss you most of all."

"If you need me when you reach Alnwick, ask the baron to send a missive and I'll come straight away."

A vise clamped around Anne's heart. "I know you will."

They neared the galleon and a sailor reached for Anne's hand. Hanna released her grasp and gestured forward. "Milady."

Anne stepped aboard the *Flying Swan*—the ship that would ferry her away from everything familiar. Hanna wrapped her in a warm embrace. "A baron who won't pay for a single serving maid to accompany his new bride doesn't deserve her—at least not a lady as gracious as you."

Anne closed her eyes and squeezed them, trying not to tremble. "Everything will be fine. I shall write often and plead with the Lord Wharton to send for you." She pulled back and held Hanna at arm's length. "You shall see. His lordship will be generous. He merely doesn't know me yet—doesn't know our history."

Anne watched her maid, her dearest friend return to Mother's carriage. Alone she stood, abandoned on the deck of the galleon. Five days it would take to sail to the mouth of the River Aln where she would meet her husband for the first time. *Five days without a serving maid?* Anne still did not understand the baron's reasoning.

She glanced at her gloves, covering the bare ring finger and shuddered. *He's how much older?*

Anne could see only the top of the carriage as it wound through the busy dockyard, and she reached her hand out as if she could touch it one last time. But the countess's carriage turned and disappeared behind the stone wall of the Fox and Hounds Inn.

Anne gripped the rail and craned her neck, but Mother was gone—Hanna gone—Anne's life winding away, like the wheels that rolled back to Titchfield House without her. Her heart gripped her chest like a musket had blown a gaping hole through it. There she stood, like a pawn to the highest bidder.

Anne's eyes drifted to the boisterous scene on the pier. Men loaded barrels onto carts pulled by big draft horses and merchants argued. She searched for a familiar face, and the hole in her heart enlarged when she recognized not a single person. She squared her shoulders. *I'd best become accustomed to it.*

Behind her, the quartermaster shouted the command to cast off. She leaned over the rail to watch the ship ease away from the pier with the water's swirling torrent. To jump now would be certain death, having never learned to swim. For a second, she contemplated it. Death *could* be better than sharing a bed with a husband older than her own deceased father.

Captain Fortescue moved in beside her. "May I show you to your quarters, Lady Anne?" He smiled, wearing a feathered cap and neat black beard, fashionably groomed to a point and highlighted by the white ruff of his collar. His dark eyes reflected a glint of humor—he smirked. How comical it must be to escort a lady to a husband whom she had never met.

"Thank you, sir."

"You will be under my protection until we meet the baron. If you should want for anything, please ask."

"That is very kind of you," she said, though the humor in his eyes was not kind in the least.

"'Tis nothing. You are a guest aboard the *Flying Swan* and with good wind, we should reach your new husband in no time. She's a grand ship, none faster."

The deck swarmed with able-bodied sailors, swinging from the rigging as the wind slapped and ballooned the giant sails.

While the quartermaster bellowed orders, Captain Fortescue led her aft to a narrow corridor. He used a key to open her cabin door and stepped aside. "I must apologize. I'm sure there is not as much space as a lady of your stature would be accustomed."

The tiny room held a small bed, leaving room enough for a narrow aisle between the cot and her luggage, which lined the far wall. A wooden chair, a round table, a bowl and ewer with a looking glass bolted above it—crude accommodations by anyone's imagination. "This will be fine." Anne squeezed past the captain, bumping her hip on one of her trunks.

"Very well." He reached for the latch. "My officers and I would be honored if you would dine with us."

"I'd like that. Thank you." *Perhaps they'll serve a draught of hemlock.*

"I shall knock on your door when it is time." He moved to pull it closed, but stopped. "'Tis best to keep the door locked when you are within."

Anne turned the lock and then covered her face with her hands. Only now did she allow the tears to come.

Lord Wharton, first Baron of Wharton, had seen her once at Queen Elizabeth's coronation five months ago. A hundred times, Anne had filed through her memory of that visit to court. She and her sisters had met so many people, so many grand men had kissed her hand and introduced themselves, but she could not place the baron—a grey haired man, no doubt—if he had hair. Anne staggered to the bed, buried her face in the pillow and surrendered to her silent sobs.

Since the day her uncle had come to Titchfield House and revealed she had been wed, Anne needed smelling salts to keep her wits. She hadn't taken to her bed with a bout of melancholy because her marriage had been performed by proxy. The age of the man mortified her. At eight and fifty, Lord Wharton was a widower with four children who were all older than Anne—past her prime at nine and ten.

She sat up with a jolt and slammed her fist into the pillow. She would have to meet those children. Would she ever be able to look them in the eye when they referred to her as stepmother? The pillow dropped to the floor. *Surely there are grandchildren as well.*

Anne pressed her knuckles against her temples and fought to regain control. She would overcome this. She would prove herself worthy to the baron's estate just as she had done at Titchfield House. His lordship might be old, but he'd discover he had married far more than a pretty courtier. Anne steadied her breath and repeated her title, "Baroness of Wharton." Married to a stranger nine and thirty years her senior.

***

Calum MacLeod stood on the deck of the *Sea Dragon* and peered through the spyglass. Just as his informants had advised, the new English racing galleon had set sail. The ship was bound for the north, laden with grain and cloth—all things his people on Raasay desperately needed. Things his miserly brother, living off the fat on the Isle of Lewis, refused to part with.

Calum intended to seize it for them. His father had gone to great lengths to separate the clan and secure a charter to name him laird over the Hebridean isle. Yes, it was insignificant compared to Lewis, but his clansmen were fighters. The people of Raasay fought through the eight months of winter, raising their bairns as they ploughed the rocky soil, more often frozen than not. Calum aimed to remedy their plight by building their wealth or dying in the process. On one thing he was firm, he would not recline in his keep while his people starved.

He salivated, admiring the galleon's sleek lines. With three masts and a trim hull, she could outrun any ship in Her Majesty's fleet, including Calum's own carrack, his beloved *Sea Dragon*.

"She's a beauty." John Urquhart, cousin on his mother's side, quartermaster, and Calum's closest friend stood beside him.

"Aye, and her cargo will keep us fed until the harvest."

John didn't have quite as much height as Calum, but they shared the family's tendency toward auburn hair and blue eyes. "I'm thinking more of the riches we'll gain once she's ours."

Calum lowered the spyglass and grinned. "Our people will prosper and then we can kick our heels up and enjoy the spoils."

"Do ye think ye can ever walk away? The sea's yer mistress."

"True." Calum watched the sun kiss the western horizon. "We'll not have time to think on it until the keep is finished and our clan is strong."

"I still dunna understand it."

"What?"

"Why yer father commissioned ye Chief of Raasay, but kept all the riches in Lewis."

"'Twas not me place to question Da's decision—only to honor it."

"Aye, but he just kicked ye out to make a go with the poor souls on the island."

"He gave me his trust." Calum ran his hand along the worn rail of his ship. "Besides, I received a fair bit more than a second son could hope for."

"If we dunna starve, 'twill be a blessing."

"If we plunder that ship, we'll no' starve."

***

The tap on her door roused Anne from sleep. "Supper, my lady."

The thought of food brought on a heave. She gulped back burning bile and tottered across the floor. Cracking open the door, she tried to focus on the captain, but his smile rose and fell with the rolling waves. Swallowing, she leaned heavily on the latch. "I am afraid I have not yet found my sea legs. Will you consider it discourteous if I excuse myself?"

"Your color is a bit pale. It can take a few days for a land maiden to gain her legs." He bowed. "I shall have my cabin boy bring you a tray."

"Thank you."

Anne lay back on her bed and stared at the wooden rafters. The swells of the ocean had increased since she'd cried herself to sleep. She hugged her pillow and closed her eyes, trying to will away the sickness.

Anne sat up when the boy unlocked her door and pushed inside. He set a silver tray on the table and lit the lamp on her wall. "Ye might want to eat quick, milady. The sea's angry tonight and your meal's likely to skip over the table lips and fall to the floor."

"My thanks." Anne eyed the latch. "Pardon me, but does everyone have a key to my stateroom?"

"Just the captain. He gave it to me to fetch your meal."

When the boy left, she locked the door and stared at the delightful prospect of overcooked vegetables and boiled fish. The ship listed starboard, then to port, and the tray crashed upside down. Crouching to tidy the mess, she pushed the tray up against the wall, but eyed the wine. Still corked in a small glass bottle, Anne pulled out the stopper.

She scrunched her face when she held it to her nose. The sharp bouquet indicated its cheap vintage. She looked at the goblet that lay on its side, covered with white sauce. Shrugging, she held the bottle to her lips. *'Tis only me and perhaps it will take the edge off the sickness.*

Anne took a sip and let the tart liquid slide across her tongue. The wine tasted better than it smelled—though not a vintage Titchfield House would serve. Imagining she would need to become accustomed to a great many new experiences, she tilted the bottle and drank again. In no time, the wine warmed her insides and numbed the pain, both in her gut and in her heart.

When the bottle was empty, she managed to remove her stomacher and untie her stays. It would be a long voyage without Hanna. Anne ran her fingers along her unbound ribs and shook out the skirts of her shift. Free of binding laces, she could finally breathe and crawl under the warmth of woolen bedclothes. She willed sleep to take her to a place where earl's daughters were not traded for riches and lands.

***

Anne's eyes flew open when a blast shook her awake. She swiped a hand across her forehead. *Am I dreaming?* The ship's floorboards groaned, followed by a raucous thud and a shout. "Fire!" A roaring boom shook the galleon.

Cannons.

Hurried footsteps clamored overhead. The quartermaster bellowed commands, his voice high pitched and quick, like a rooster with its head on the block.

Her skin prickled, she couldn't breathe. The walls closed in.

A cannon blast shook her bed. Heart hammering, Anne threw back the bedclothes and raced for her cabin door. She stumbled into the empty corridor. The ship rocked as she staggered toward the main deck. She braced her hands on the wall to keep herself upright.

She pushed the outer door, but it held fast. Leaning her shoulder into it, she shoved. A harsh gale caught it and flung the door open, sending her sprawling onto the deck.

Blinking, Anne steadied herself on the rail. Raindrops splashed cold on her skin. Her shift clung to her legs like a flapping sail. Shivering, she pushed the hair from her face and peered into the darkness. Sailors scurried in every direction while the quartermaster delivered a ceaseless barrage of shouts. "Climb the crows nest with your musket, Davey boy…Ready your cutlasses men…Unfurl the jib…"

Her heart nearly burst through her chest when an earsplitting boom lit up the sea less than a league away. She crouched and threw her arms over her head. A cannonball careened into the water mere feet from where she stood. Anne looked across the rail and ice filled her veins. A carrack bore down on them, flying a Jolly Roger—the unmistakable skull and crossbones of a pirate ship.

Captain Fortescue barreled down from the quarterdeck and threw an arm around Anne's shoulder. "Get back to your cabin. Lock the door. Open it for no one."

She leaned into his warmth. "We're under attack?"

"We'll outrun them."

"But they're on a course to cross our bow."

The captain's thin lips told her he was well aware of the pirate ship's strategy. Outrunning the heavier carrack would not be an option. He strengthened his grip and led her back through the corridor. "Remember what I said. Lock. The. Door."

He pushed Anne into her stateroom with such force, she stumbled against her trunk. She reached out and turned the lock with trembling fingers, then wrapped herself in her dressing gown, damp shift and all.

The galleon rocked beneath her feet. She turned full circle and hugged herself. Each breath shuddered. Being locked in her stateroom was far worse than standing on the deck. At least out there she could *see* what was happening. With every earsplitting blast, the ship quaked. Her trunks jostled. Water slapped against the hull, and her blood ran cold. She honestly could not swim.

How could the baron abandon me on a galleon with pirates sailing these waters? He most certainly has not appraised well in my eyes. The gutless miser will have much to answer for when I reach Alnwick. Leaving me alone without Hanna. And then there's my uncle, the mastermind of this whole marriage scheme—curse him too!

A cannon boomed. Anne's entire body jolted. She dashed to her bed, her heart pummeling her chest.

What if the brigands took the ship? Anne darted to her smallest trunk and threw back the lid. She pulled out an ornate wooden box and opened the hasp, then dumped the contents on the bed—her decree of marriage and the few precious jewels she owned. Using her fingernail to locate the string hidden in a groove, she pulled away the false bottom. Pushing aside the shillings, she stared at the ivory handle and slim blade of her father's dagger.

The cannon volley reverberated through the ship. The acrid smell of sulfur wafted into her chamber. Anne's stare shot to the ceiling. Feet pounded the floor above. Men screamed in agony.

She folded the marriage decree and replaced the false bottom, then shoved her precious keepsakes on top and stuffed it under her mattress. Jumping at an explosion that sounded like a cannonball crashing through the deck, Anne snatched up her knife and crouched upon the corner of her bed. Her gaze fixed on door, her seasickness replaced by uncontrollable trembling as the battle raged around her.

Surely I will die this eve. Dear God, have mercy on my soul.

***

The unending night wore on with sounds of battle that Anne had only heard tale of, tucked away in Titchfield House. How she wanted to be back there now, in the arms of her sisters and Hanna.

When the echoes of fighting stopped, an eerie hush filled her chamber. Anne sat up, gooseflesh rising on her arms. The knife in her hand slipped against her perspiration and she tightened her grip.

Footsteps plodded down the wooden planks of the corridor. They stopped outside her door. The latch moved. Anne did not mistake the hiss of a sword being drawn from its scabbard. She drew in a ragged breath.

Something slammed into the door. Her heart flew to her throat. Another thud. Anne pressed her shoulders into the corner and steadied her knife. The door bowed and groaned against a clashing blow. Hinges gave way and the door clattered to the deck.

A rugged man stared through the dimly lit doorway. Sword drawn, with a cropped copper beard, he glared at her with fierce, steely eyes. She was certain he could kill her with that look.

Anne held up her knife, shaking like a sapling in the wind.

"Holy Mother Mary." He clattered across the door and sheathed his sword. "What in the blazes are ye doing here?"

She clasped her free hand over her knife to steady the trembling.

His shirt splattered with blood, his face dark, he took another step toward her, holding her gaze. "I'll no' hurt ye, lass."

Anne tried to push herself deeper into the corner, but the walls trapped her. He moved closer, his eyes searing into hers. She glanced beyond him, breaking his stare. His powerful legs strained against his red plaid kilt with one more step. Over the scents of sweat and blood, she caught the whiff of rosemary.

"What is yer name?"

Name? What should I say? "A-Anne."

"Just Anne?"

She pursed her lips, unwilling to give him the satisfaction of knowing her true identity.

"We-ell you're no' Anne Boleyn, that's a certainty. She's dead and her daughter's on the throne." His eyes glanced to the dagger trembling in her hand. "Ye think ye can take the likes of me with that wee knife?"

He towered over her little bed and Anne craned her neck. Her stomach squeezed. Those piercing eyes stared down at her from shoulders as broad as her largest trunk. He held out his hand. "Now be a good lass and give it to me."

She licked her lips and stared at the blood staining his outstretched hand. Anne could *not* surrender without a fight. Gritting her teeth, she launched herself forward, aiming the dagger at his heart.

He snatched her wrist faster than she could blink.

A sharp pain wrenched her wrist and the knife dropped to the floor. The Highlander shoved her back onto the bed and shook his head. "Now what did ye have to go and do that for? I told ye to hand it over." He bent down and picked up the blade, turning it over in his hand appreciatively. "If you're going to be hostile, I guess I'll have to put it in me sporran for safekeeping."

She glanced down to the white fur pouch he wore across the front of his kilt, watching as he slid her father's dagger inside. "W-what did you do with Captain Fortescue?"

"The former captain of *this* ship?" The Scot patted his sporran as if the pelt were ermine. "I'm afraid he's on a wee boat headed back to shore."

"Of all the lawlessness. You mean to say that you tossed him overboard in a skiff?"

"Aye. At least I didna kill the bastard. He was a darned bit ornery 'bout it too."

"You say that as if pillaging and casting the captain overboard was a minor inconvenience."

A shadow darkened his face. "Oh no, 'twas not minor at all."

Anne stiffened her back. All her life she'd heard "my lady" when addressed, but then, she hadn't informed him of her title.

"Actually, *you're* the inconvenience."

"Me?"

His finger twitched across the hilt of the gargantuan sword strapped to his hip. "Ye see, we've launched the skiffs and I'm at a loss as to what we should do with ye."

Anne's mouth grew dry. Would he make her walk the plank? Would he take her to the hold and tie her down to be gnawed to death by the ship's rats? A clammy chill swept over her skin. Surely, he would respect her virtue…wouldn't he? "I-if you return me to Portsmouth, I should be able to find my way home." She most assuredly was not going to continue on toward Alnwick or the baron.

"Portsmouth, aye?" He took a seat at the end of her bed, putting Anne at eye level. "You would have us sail back into the mouth of the dragon herself, would ye?" He threw his head back and gave a hearty laugh, unlike someone bent on murder. "Nay. Ye will have to stay with us unsavory privateers for a wee bit longer."

Anne clutched her dressing gown tighter around her neck. *Privateers? He's a filthy pirate and a devilish one at that.*

A tall man in a dark green and blue kilt appeared in the doorway and spoke in a foreign tongue. *Gaelic.* She knew a little Gaelic. His eyes drifted to Anne and back to her captor, who responded in the same guttural tones—*they're talking about me.* The pirate's gaze softened when he turned to her. "John will see yer door is repaired." He surveyed trunks that lined her wall. "I suppose all of these are yers?"

There rested the entirety of her possessions. "Yes."

"It looks like ye were planning to stay—wherever ye were going."

Anne stared at her hands and whispered, "Yes."

The scent of rosemary grew stronger when the Highlander leaned in and eyed her. His rough fingers brushed a bronze brooch that clasped his plaid at his shoulder. "I take it ye weren't too happy 'bout it."

Anne chose not to reply to the gentle tone in his voice. Her happiness was none of his concern, though in truth this diversion postponed wedded bliss with her antiquated baron.

"Either way. Ye'll be delayed for a bit."

He headed toward the doorway, and she reached out a trembling hand. "Wait."

He stopped.

"Where are you taking me?"

"Northwest."

Of course he wouldn't be specific. "What should I call you?"

He turned, his powerful frame outlined in the doorway by flickering firelight from above. Those blue eyes as fierce as they had looked when he first knocked down the door. "Captain."

Dear God in heaven, praises to you that Hanna was not forced to endure this nightmare.

Anne slipped back into her corner and clutched the pillow while he walked over the door and clomped though the corridor. The pirate did not have the decency to tell her his name. But then, she hadn't been exactly forthcoming about hers either.

What was she to do until her door was repaired? She tossed the pillow aside, and levered the door back into place. Using all her strength, she pushed and shoved one of her trunks until it blocked the entry. It wasn't ideal, but would suffice to hold through the night. At least the racket would wake her if anyone tried to enter.

Chapter Two

Calum pushed through to the captain's cabin and turned full circle. The English hadn't spared any expense on this new ship. A row of five leaded glass windows looked over the ship's bow. In the center of the room stood a walnut table with six chairs upholstered in red with gold embroidery. A desk sat starboard with a thick leather-bound log atop. Port side, a bed hugged the dark paneling to hold firm during rough seas. Brass oil-burning lamps hung from the rafters to provide maximum light.

Calum strolled to the aft windows and peered through one of the small glass panes. The sun touched the eastern horizon in violets and pinks. Soon they'd turn north for the journey home, but first they must make a wide berth around English waters. Once the captain and crew were found, there would be retribution. Of that he had no doubt.

He rubbed his eyes, unable to remember when he'd last slept. But sleep didn't matter. He had secured the galleon, and its bounty would supply his people for months to come. The manifest of the cargo contained more than he'd dreamed with food aplenty, sheep, ponies and milking heifers, as well as fine cloth and a cache of hardwood for building.

The only thing he hadn't counted on was Anne, a beautiful woman, truth be told. Expecting another fight, he'd nearly hurtled into her room and started swinging. Never before had a woman stopped him cold, but those almond-shaped eyes shone cobalt blue, just like the sky in the hour before night falls.

She'd looked fierce as a baby badger crouched in the corner of her bed holding that ridiculous knife—it was nearly too small to be called a dagger.

Wrapped in a red dressing gown, her honey-blonde mane had partly shrouded her face and cascaded all the way down to her enticing hips. Calum hadn't been able to stop himself from mentally undressing her in that moment. Her hair draped across one eye gave her the appearance of a woman ready to be bedded. Fortunately, he'd recovered his wits when she tried to attack.

Calum chuckled.

He needed only to look at the collection of trunks to know she was a lady of stature, and her accent had confirmed it. He groaned. Plundering a ship was one thing, but plundering a ship and kidnapping a highborn lady would buy him more trouble than he cared to bargain for. *Anne*. He must find out who she was so he could ransom her, and fast. A beautiful woman amongst his men would cause mayhem.

At a rap on the door, Calum turned. John entered holding the manifest. "All accounted for, m'laird."

"Excellent. And the lady's door?"

"The carpenters are working on it now."

"Very good."

John placed the paperwork on the table. "Who is the woman?"

"She would only say that her name is Anne. But she's English nobility, there's no question."

"Have you checked the captain's log?"

Calum strode to the ornate desk and opened the large volume, thumbing the pages until he found the last entry. *25th March, Year of our Lord 1559. Set sail mid-afternoon. One passenger, Lady Anne, daughter of Lord Southampton, destination the River Aln. Clouds rolling in from the west. Rain likely.*

John peered over his shoulder. "Southampton—he's an earl, no?"

"He's a dead earl. I think his heir's but a child."

Calum pulled out the map of England and rolled it open on the table. "She's headed toward the River Aln." He ran his finger along the east coast until he found the said river and found the closest town. "Alnwick."

"The seat of the Earl of Northumberland," John said.

"The plundering bastard and his murdering sheriff, the Baron of Wharton."

John leaned in and studied the map. "Ye wouldn't think she'd be tied up with the likes of them?"

"And why not? Her da's an earl."

"Bloody hell. The last thing we need is Wharton and his henchman bearing down on us."

"'Tis a good thing our plaid looks like the Stewart's. That'll confuse the English until we can arrange terms for her ransom." Calum rolled up the map. "I'll have Lady Anne dine with me tonight to see what more I can pull from her."

John waggled his eyebrows. "Aye, and feast yer eyes no doubt."

"Don't let your shameless mind consider it. If she weren't worth a farthing, I'd bloody well throw her arse over the side of the ship."

"Aye, Laird Calum, Robin Hood of Raasay—always willing to drown a lady in distress."

"She's no lady to me. Be gone with ye."

Calum turned his back and closed his eyes. His palms perspired as he pictured the voluptuous Lady Anne, her full red lips trembling—undeniably kissable lips. He rubbed his palms against his plaid. Surely she would not be as alluring once she'd donned a proper gown and headpiece.

***

Anne stared at the door with its new hinges—and a lock she could not turn as before. Now a prisoner, she paced the room still wearing her shift and dressing gown. The night had been endless and carried on into a day trapped within. She'd heard about Scottish pirates who preyed on Her Majesty's ships. Even one of her family's cargoes of grain had been plundered by pirates. Whether it had been Scots or not, no one knew, but pirates were a thorn in England's side, not only to the crown but to every landowner who shipped their goods abroad.

At the time, she'd reported the incident to the Privy Council and they assigned Captain Hawkins to the task. *Hawkins*. He was a known pirate himself.

Anne balled her fists. The business of running her family's estates was no longer her concern. She needed to find a way off this ship and back to her family. No—her mother had made clear, she must honor the contract of marriage. She must find a way to her husband. Thomas Wharton had earned his barony by his shrewd talent for law enforcement. Once the baron learned that his new wife had been captured by Scottish pirates, he would surely not rest until the savages were brought to justice.

Aside from being much older, Anne knew little of her new husband, but one thing was certain—he hated the Scots. News of his raids into Scotland had even reached Titchfield House.

Her door opened with a light tap. "Excuse me, milady. The captain would like ye to dine with him this evening." John, the second-in-charge, who'd repaired her door, wore a green and blue plaid opposed to the red and black the captain and the cabin boy who'd brought her food had worn.

Anne lifted her chin. "I would prefer to take my meals in my stateroom."

"*Trom féineil nighneag,*" he cursed under his breath.

"Pardon me, but I am neither selfish nor burdensome."

Anne enjoyed watching the shocked bulge to John's eyes when she translated his Gaelic. He fumbled with the latch. "I'll be back to escort ye to the captain in an hour. I'd think with all these trunks ye would have more than a dressing gown to wear over yer shift."

He closed the door and the lock clicked.

Anne rushed forward and jerked on the handle. *Blast them for caging me like I'm the one they cannot trust.* When the pirate had first kicked in the door and entered her room, she'd been terrified, afraid he would kill her—a big man with a big sword, splattered with blood. Well, she knew differently now. The captain wanted to dine with her? *Fine.* She would use his misplaced hospitality to uncover more about him. Any information she could gather would assist Lord Wharton to capture the plunderer and his men.

She would dress the part for this *meal.* If the captain saw her in a gold silk gown—fabric reserved only for baronesses and above— he'd think twice about taking her back to Portsmouth.

It took three times as long to dress without Hanna. Turning in front of the dingy looking glass, Anne inspected her handiwork. All ribbons were tied, though she'd had to lace up her stays in the front, but no strings stuck out. While she secured the matching headpiece in place, a knock sounded.

"Yes?"

Opening the door, John appraised her with a half-cocked smile. "Och. Looks like I'll no' have to strong arm ye to the captain's cabin."

"You are brash, sir." She stood as tall as her frame would allow. "I would still prefer to dine in my quarters."

"'Tis fortunate ye've reconsidered." He offered her the crook of his arm. "Ye look lovely."

She glanced to the mirror and caught a rosy flush crawling up her face. "I presume you're expecting me to thank you."

"A lady generally does when a gentleman pays her a compliment."

"So you're a gentleman now that you've pillaged the ship?"

She placed her hand on the elbow he'd offered and inclined her head toward the door.

"We're no' as bad as ye think."

John ushered her into the captain's quarters, lavishly inlaid with the rich warmth of walnut wood. The captain stood with his back to them, staring out the windows behind the table, elegantly set for two. He'd tied back his dark auburn hair and wore a clean linen shirt. Anne had forgotten how enormous he was—his broad shoulders tapered down to his waist, supported by slim hips beneath his red and black plaid.

John bowed. "Her ladyship, m'laird."

The captain turned. Anne's breath caught. He'd cleaned the soot and blood from his face, but his eyes still bore through her like an arrow. She scarcely heard the door close behind her. He approached, his frown replaced by a smile, displaying a row of perfectly straight teeth.

Anne forced herself to breathe. She wanted the dirty face with the scowl back—it was easier to detest *that* pirate.

"Thank ye for coming, milady."

Anne's hands trembled as he neared. No man had ever made her hands shake like that. She clenched her fists to stop the tremors. "My lady?" she asked. "I did not tell you I was nobly born."

"Nay, but the captain's log did."

The log? "Oh? And what did Captain Fortescue note about me?"

Anne could not ignore how his muscles stretched his hose when he sauntered to the sideboard and poured two goblets of wine. "Ye can read it there on the desk if ye like, but he said you're the daughter of Southampton, bound for the River Aln."

"I see." She walked over to the bound volume smoothed her hands down the coarse velum. The entry made no mention of her marriage by proxy. *Interesting.*

He handed her the goblet. "Wine?"

She looked him in the eye and her heart stuttered. Gold flecks danced around rims of blue. She snapped her gaze to the goblet. "Thank you."

He pulled out a chair. "Please, sit. I trust ye have been treated well since our last...ah...encounter?"

She stepped toward him and ignored the chair. She caught the familiar bouquet of rosemary soap, though not mixed with blood and sweat this time. "If you call locking me in my stateroom good treatment, then yes."

The narrowing of his eyes reflected annoyance, but he politely bowed and gestured for her to sit. "Apologies. Your confinement was more for yer sake than to keep ye imprisoned."

When he helped her push in her chair, his hand brushed her shoulder. A tingle trickled down Anne's spine, though she suppressed her gasp. Her gaze drifted to his hand—large, strong, sprinkled with coppery hair. He was quite unlike what she'd imagined for a pirate captain.

He took his seat at the head of the table—a foot away, close enough for her to touch him. He smiled again, white teeth, fetching as the devil.

She studied the silver salt cellar and nervously tapped it to the exact center of the table. *Why does he have to be wickedly handsome?* On the few times Anne had been to court, there had been good looking men, but none so imposing as the captain. He had lines at the corners of his gold flecked blue eyes, as if he often squinted directly into the bright sun. His nose was not subtle, but the size and slight hook to it suited him. The nose alone announced this was not a man to trifle with. And his hands…They were large and powerful, but the nails were now clean and neatly trimmed, and in his hands, an elegant brass goblet was held utterly secure.

Her gaze trailed down to the laces of his shirt and tight heat coiled deep inside when she spied the auburn curls peeking just above his neckline. For no reason at all, she had an urge to touch him—to discover if those curls were as downy soft as they looked.

"Is my appearance displeasing?"

"N-no." Anne glanced behind her, hoping the food would come soon so this meal would be over and she could escape back to her chamber.

"I will see to it ye have leave to walk the deck."

She nodded, not trusting her voice.

She sipped her wine again and studied the ruby liquid within. She could feel his boring eyes upon her, assessing her as she had done him. She dared glance at him and those blues caught hers. He smiled. Again, her cheeks burned.

"Am I making ye nervous, milady?"

"Yes…er, no." *Where is the food?*

As if answering her thought, the side door opened and the cabin boy brought in pewter plates filled with roast meat and vegetables.

"Thank ye, Bran."

The boy bowed. "Will there be anything else, m'laird?"

The captain arched his brow her way, and Anne shook her head. "That will be all for now. Go eat yer supper, lad."

He reached for a basket of bread and offered it to Anne.

"That is the second time I've heard to you referred to as laird."

"Aye, 'tis what me clansmen call their chieftain."

"Chieftain?" She grasped a slice of bread. "So you *are* a Scottish laird?"

"Aye."

"Of which clan?"

"Ah, milady, I cannot say."

"Must I always call you Captain? I find it quite uncivilized that I am sitting at the table of a man whose name I do not know."

"Calum."

"Calum?" She liked the simplicity of it. "Is that all?"

"For the moment." He leaned toward her and winked. "Now ye have to tell me something."

Anne cut a small bit of meat and savored it in her mouth. But chewing was nearly impossible. That rakish wink sent her insides aflutter yet again.

"Why were ye bound for the River Aln?"

Anne studied the stern countenance that had now lost its jovial teasing. If she told him, he might ransom her on the spot— but that's what she wanted. Wasn't it? *Yes.*

"Lady Anne?" He persisted.

"I was to join my husband in Alnwick."

"Husband? But ye wear no ring."

She covered the naked finger. "The ring is with him."

"Odd." Calum pushed his chair back a bit, as if distancing himself from her. "The journal said nothing of yer husband."

"Captain Fortescue was well aware of my proxy marriage to Lord Wharton."

"Wharton?" Calum's chair screeched across the floorboards. "That ruthless son of an ill-breeding dog."

She sat erect. "Pardon me?" But she knew the Scots hated Thomas Wharton. He'd devastated them at the battle of Solway Moss, where he'd earned his barony.

"How could ye be married to the likes of him?" Calum stood and paced the room, then turned with his fists on his hips. "A fine lot ye've got us into."

"Me?" A sharp twist of her gut replaced her unease with unabashed disbelief. "I'm not the one who plundered this ship."

"Ye were no' supposed to be aboard."

"Tell that to my husband. He paid my fare." She assumed he had. Anne watched Calum pace. "Am I to eat while you walk the floor like a brooding tyrant?"

The deadly glare she'd seen when he kicked in her door returned. He dropped his hands and plodded back to his seat. He didn't touch his food, but guzzled the goblet of wine. Anne waffled between fear of the man and pity. That she chose pity shocked her.

She wrung her hands. Presently she knew more about the Scot sitting across from her than she did Baron of Wharton, and that was very little. Calum reached for the ewer and refilled his goblet, his face unreadable.

Anne wanted to say something, but no words came. Her concern for Calum's plight came as a surprise and toyed with her sensibilities. She turned her attention to her meal but she couldn't eat. He'd cursed her husband. Did that mean he felt the same contempt for her? She pushed her plate away. "I should like to return to my stateroom."

Calum didn't respond immediately. He swirled the wine in his goblet and then looked up with eyes that had no resemblance to the friendly blues that had greeted her when she entered the room. A tempest brewed behind his eyes. Deadly as nightshade, he watched her as he swallowed and placed the goblet on the table. "'Tis best." He stood. "I'll escort ye."

He said nothing as they walked the few feet to her stateroom door. Calum used his key to open it and bowed. "Milady."

She thought to thank him, but held her tongue and strode into her room. Turning, she saw only the door close. The latch offered a soft click against the creaking of the wooden ship.

Blessed saints, she'd practically swooned at the sight of him. Blast her betraying heart, and blast Calum's wayward charm.

***

Anne was already up when a knock sounded on her door. "Come in."

Bran, the cabin boy who had served dinner peeked in. "I've brought ye some porridge and bread, milady."

She gestured to the table. "I was wondering if the captain would see fit to feed me today."

"What? Ye think he would push a crust of bread and a jug of ale under yer door?"

"Possibly not the ale."

"Ye've got the laird all wrong. If it weren't for him, the people of Raasay would have starved last winter."

"Oh? Is that why he plunders ships? To feed the poor?"

"We-ell, aye, truth be told." He reached out and dropped a key in her palm. "This is for yer door. The captain says you're free to come and go."

"How generous of him. I can now leave my stateroom and consort with pirates."

"We're no' all that bad, milady. Just trying to make a go of it just like any other scrapper out there."

Anne studied the boy. As friendly as a Spaniel puppy, he was as tall as she with dark brown curls. "How old are you, Bran?"

"Two and ten."

"Oh my, you're quite tall for your age."

Bran ran his fingers along the plaid that crossed over his shoulder and stood a bit taller. "Calum's training me to be a knight."

"Honestly? That is quite a great responsibility at two and ten." She reached for the bread and broke it in half. "Where are your parents?"

He kicked a floorboard with the toe of his boot. "Me da's dead but me ma works in the kitchen at Brochel Castle."

"Brochel? Is that your clan's keep?"

"Aye, milady. 'Tis on the isle of Raasay."

Anne lifted her spoon. "And to which clan do you belong?" Hmm. Gathering information would be easier than she thought. She only need ask the right person.

"MacLeod." The boy rubbed his arm and grimaced.

Anne studied him furrowing her brow. "Are you injured?"

"'Tis only a bruise, milady."

She stood and folded her arms. "Show me."

Bran's gaze shot to the door. Biting his bottom lip, he reluctantly rolled up his sleeve. "'Twill be right in a week."

Anne swallowed her shock. The boy's whole arm was purple from the wrist right up to his shoulder. "What happened?" She inspected it for swelling. "This should be immobilized. It could be broken."

"I took a tumble off the rigging." With effort, he flexed his muscle. "See. I can move it."

"I'm not convinced." Anne pulled her bundle of healing essences from her trunk. "First, I shall rub a salve into it and then we'll put it in a sling."

Bran stepped back. "I cannot work with me arm bound up."

Anne made him sit in the chair and carefully smoothed in a salve of houseleek and St. John's wort. "It will not heal properly unless you take care of it."

She fashioned a sling from a piece of linen and tapped his nose. "Rest it as much as you can. Do you understand? 'Tis very important."

"Aye, milady. Thank ye."

"Bran," a deep voice bellowed from the corridor.

The boy blanched. "'Tis Master John. I must away."

***

When Anne finished her breakfast, she picked up the key and swung her cloak around her shoulders. She wished she had her dagger. She wasn't quite sure what she'd find out on the decks, but she couldn't hide in her stateroom forever.

Slowly opening the door to the main deck, Anne listened for any sign of improper behavior. Sails flapped in the whistling wind, men worked together mending the rigging above and when she stepped out, she saw John manning the wheel. *Rather a peaceful setting for a band of pirates.*

Scanning the deck for Calum, Anne pulled her cloak tight around her shoulders and walked to the rail. The dark sea rolled and foamed white in the ship's wake. Water stretched in every direction. Refreshing, salty wind caressed her face.

Footsteps tapped on the stairs leading from the quarterdeck above. The captain stepped beside her with that fetching grin of his. "Good morning, milady. I trust ye slept well."

She hoped her sudden queasiness had been caused by the rolling of the sea. "Reasonably well, considering I have no idea where we are headed or when I'll see my blessed England again."

Calum's lips thinned. He rested his elbows on the rail and looked out to sea. The wind blew his hair away from his face, unveiling the attractive and angular lines to his jaw.

Anne followed his gaze. "Where are we? There's no land in sight."

"We're giving England a wide berth. Once we cross into Scottish waters, ye'll see the coast."

"And what am I to do until then?"

"Whatever baronesses do, I suppose."

"I expected you to force me to swab the decks or mend the sails."

"Would ye like to mend sails?"

She cleared her throat. "I'm your prisoner. Of course you might do all sorts of horrible and vile things."

"Mending sails is vile?"

Anne looked skyward. "Saints preserve me."

Calum rubbed his palm over a belaying pin, which supported a coil of hemp rope. "I could set up a surgery. Half me men asked to rap on yer stateroom door to show ye their battle wounds—fix them up as ye did Bran."

Anne wrung her hands. "Are there many injured?"

"A few scrapes and cuts."

"Of course I'll tend them right away."

Calum grinned—almost laughed.

"They do need my assistance do they not?"

"Mostly no', but I'll have John ferret out the ones who do and ask him to bring them to ye."

"Very well." Anne smoothed her hands over her skirts. "And in the interim, I'd be much obliged if you would determine how you'll return me to England as quickly as possible."

Calum bowed, his eyes sparkling in the sun. "As you wish, milady."

He sauntered away, whistling some jaunty ditty, while Anne stifled the urge to giggle—for no reason. Queen's knees, he toyed with her. He probably flaunted his good looks before every maiden who struck his fancy. She could risk her reputation by befriending him. Heading back to her stateroom, Anne vowed Calum MacLeod would *never* charm her into believing him well-mannered and chivalrous.

Chapter Three

Calum didn't blame Lady Anne for holding him in low esteem. He would feel the same if he were in her predicament, though he wished it could be otherwise. He'd searched the seas for a woman like her. Upon his first glimpse, an inkling twitched at the back of his mind. Could she be *the one*? Bloody dreamer, he was.

Over the past few days, he'd ducked out of sight whenever she made an appearance. Though he watched with great interest when she set her basket of herbs on the deck and tended his men as if they were her kin. He needed her off the ship before she made them all soft.

After learning she was Wharton's bride, he'd thought of little else but Anne. Memories of the terrified waif cowering in her stateroom under that wild mane of blonde curls made his pulse race, but he couldn't assuage the grotesque image his mind conjured of Anne in Wharton's arms. Fortunately, the thought put a damper on his lustful urges.

However, he now feared for her, which was a miserable state of affairs for a privateer and his hostage, whom he must ransom. If only he could protect the lass.

The baron's legacy followed him. Wharton had been successful in the battle of Solway Moss back in 1542, when Calum was just a lad. His clansmen still spoke of it. The English raided Scotland and seized James V at Lochmaben. Even after the English council disapproved of Wharton's action, he pushed on and burned Dumfries. There, he beat the Scots down and took many a noble Scotsman prisoner. Calum's father had escaped with his life and little else. Wharton raided again in '47, and two years ago he'd joined Northumberland against the Scots. Calum got his taste of battle then. Wharton took no prisoners—hung them all.

Many MacLeods lost their lives, and bloody Wharton led the lot—
her husband.

Calum pressed the heels of his hands to his eyes and stood at
the helm. Twilight, he shed his thoughts and enjoyed a rare
moment of calm seas and clear skies. They would reach Raasay on
the morrow and his life would return to normal, running the keep,
solving problems.

Wearing a red gown with a low square neckline that accented
her lily white breasts, Anne stepped onto the deck below and
walked to the rail. His gut flew to his throat as if he'd jumped off a
cliff. He considered ducking into the navigation room, but
stopped.

The breeze picked up her hair from under her veil, and golden
strands fluttered proud as a flag. She moved with grace, reminding
him of a swan swimming upon a still pool. Facing the sea, Calum
admired the way her shoulders tapered to a waist so tiny, if he
grasped it with both hands, his fingers would touch. He tapped
them together, imagining how her waist would feel with his hands
upon her.

Bran tottered up, wearing that sling he'd become outrageously
proud of, and engaged her in conversation. Calum rested his elbow
on the rail and cradled his chin, completely enthralled. He watched
Anne chat easily, comfortable with the lad. Though Calum held her
captive, she maintained her regal refinement. If she was afraid, she
had not shown it since that first night. He'd never encountered a
woman like her—petite, totally in control, perceptive with
unfaltering manners. How could she have become entangled with
Wharton?

Calum would send the ransom note once they arrived on
Raasay. The missive would be carried to Edinburgh by one of his
men and passed to an English runner there. Calum watched Anne,
wishing he'd been six stone heavier and thirty or so years older—
like bloody Wharton. What he wouldn't do to lie in her arms for
just one night. If only he could run his fingers through that tangled
mane of silken tresses, caress the tops of her breasts with his lips.
But a liaison with such a lady could never be. Calum blinked and
shook his thoughts away.

Soon she would know where his keep hid in the cove on
Raasay. He couldn't kill her nor could he keep her.

If he ransomed Anne, she could tell Wharton how to find
them, but Calum's spies would see the blackguard coming days
before he reached Raasay. That wouldn't stop the battle, but it

would give Calum a chance to prepare—mayhap even send the bastard to his grave.

Would he have a chance with the widow when Wharton was dead? *Baa.* She thought him an outlaw. No highborn, beautiful woman like Lady Anne would give a man like him a second thought.

Though he'd tried, he had yet to find a woman to share his keep—a strong, capable, beautiful woman. No one on Raasay had laid claim to his heart and his bed remained cold—lonely even.

She turned and caught him staring. He bowed and his heart melted when she smiled—a smile with dimples that could light up the horizon. He half expected Lady Anne to turn up her pert little nose and head the other way.

Before he could persuade himself otherwise, Calum pattered down the steps and stood beside her. She watched the sunset and her warmth pulled him close to her like a magnet.

"'Tis beautiful," she said when the sky shone with violet and pink, highlighted against the strips of clouds that sailed toward the ship.

He inhaled. Her scent ever so feminine, Calum inclined his head to capture more of it. "Aye, milady."

She placed her hand on the rail. Again his reflexes took over and he rested his palm atop it. Calum expected her to snatch it away, but she did not. Her fingers lay cold under his touch, and he held his much warmer hand there as a comfort. They stood in silence as the sun dipped low, glowing orange-red on the horizon. He wanted to stand there forever—touching her. Barely breathing, he watched the sun disappear and held his hand still, unwilling to move it. Fresh air made pure by the salty sea filled his nostrils. The sounds of rigging flapping above, the sway of the ship—everything in this moment embodied perfection.

Darkness replaced the sun. Lady Anne slipped her hand out from under his, and the dark of the evening took up residence inside him. She was not his to lust after. "May I walk you to your stateroom?"

"Yes." Her voice sounded husky. Had she felt the connection too? *Of course not.*

Calum offered his arm and that same small, cold hand grasped it. "We'll arrive at Raasay in the morning."

"Our destination?"

"Aye."

"Bran told me."

Secrets were impossible to keep on a ship. "I will send a letter of ransom to yer husband upon our arrival." He didn't like how that sounded—*ye are my prisoner until Lord Wharton pays for your release.* But that's how it had to be. If he sailed up the mouth of the River Aln, he would incite yet another war between Scotland and England, and this time his countrymen might side with the enemy.

When they stepped into the corridor, warm air relaxed the tension in his shoulders.

Anne stopped outside her cabin door, breasts straining against her bodice with every breath. "I've never met him."

Calum forced himself to concentrate on her face. "Who?"

"Lord Wharton."

"What? How?"

"We were wed by proxy. My uncle made the arrangements."

Ah Jesus. Calum understood the way of highborn marriages, arranged for the trade of lands and riches. "Ye ken he's old enough to be yer father?"

"He's three times my age plus one year to be exact. His children are older than I."

A hundred questions flooded his mind. "Why?" he clipped with shocked disbelief.

Anne nodded as if fully understanding his monosyllabic inquiry. "I'm told the baron fancied me from across Westminster Abbey during the queen's coronation."

"No." *She doesn't even know the bastard. That's why she wears no ring.*

"Yes. My uncle said he kissed my hand, yet so many lords greeted me on that trip to London, I'm at a loss to place him."

The despair in her lovely eyes twisted around his heart. "Mayhap ye will remember if we playact it." With a halfcocked grin, Calum reached for her hand. His mouth went dry when her silken skin met the rough pads of his fingertips. Though a grown woman, her fingers were fine and delicate.

When she didn't pull away, he moistened his lips and bowed. Hovering above her hand, the soft scent of honeysuckle mixed with her—the unmistakable scent of woman now more captivating than it had been on the deck—ignited his insides as if she stood naked before him. Closing his eyes, he touched his lips to the back of her hand and kissed. Anne's sharp inhale made his skin shiver with gooseflesh. She did not try to pull away but remained so still, her pulse beat a fierce rhythm beneath.

Calum held his lips there longer than necessary. He wanted this moment to linger. He wanted a memory he could cherish long after she was gone. As he straightened, his eyes locked with hers.

Her lips parted slightly, almost as if asking him to kiss her mouth, but he knew she wouldn't want that.

He stood for a moment, not saying a word. She did too.

"Any recollection?" His voice rasped.

"No." Her voice low, she then blinked as if snapping back to the present. "You mustn't ever do that again."

"Forgive me, milady." Grinning, he opened her door and bowed, though he did not regret her lack of recall.

Anne stepped into her stateroom. Calum could not pull his gaze away until the door closed and blocked the bewilderment reflected in her sapphire eyes. Calum stared at the hardwood door—the same one he'd kicked in five nights ago. What the hell was he doing?

He ground his teeth and headed back to the quarterdeck. He needed the lady out of his life. She was not his to care for. Worst of all, she had wed the enemy.

***

Standing behind the closed door of her stateroom, Anne held up the hand that he'd kissed and brushed it against her cheek. Such a simple gesture—how did he make it so *impassioned?* She could still feel his lips searing into her flesh. She pressed the hand to her mouth and kissed it—kissed the very spot where his lips had been.

Anne held out her open hand and watched it tremble. How could *he* inflame her insides and captivate her thoughts? He was a pirate, an outlaw. She closed her fist over her heart. After their argument, she'd avoided him for days, tried to forget him. She nearly had except during the night.

The dreams tortured her. She'd barely slept in the five nights of this voyage. Every time she closed her eyes, she saw him—the powerful shoulders, the chiseled features, the penetrating eyes that could turn her insides molten.

Oh how sinful her thoughts had been when she lay in her bed at night. Calum's infectious smile, his playful banter, and mostly, her dreams fixated on the virile man presiding over the helm of the ship—a figure of command and power. Anne clutched her fists against her stomacher. She should not allow herself to entertain scandalous thoughts of Calum. The Church taught that a person could sin with thoughts alone. She fanned herself. Oh no, she mustn't allow him to touch her again.

What a precarious situation this had become. Without Hanna to console her, Anne wanted so desperately to be loved. Lord Wharton's impersonal marriage left her feeling like chattel. The baron had never held a chair for her, never enquired as to how well she'd slept or held her hand and watched the sun set on the horizon. *Perhaps he will one day—and be gentle like Calum?*

Anne groaned, certain her mind had strayed due to her fear of meeting Lord Wharton—*grandfather Wharton*. Calum had said he would ransom her. *Ransom?* Seek payment for her, no less. Was that an act of an honorable man? *Undeniably not.*

Anne hoped Calum would send word to the baron soon, for she could not bear to remain among these outlaws much longer. Their unsophisticated ways brought out a restlessness she did not know existed within her.

Always the solid daughter in her family, Anne's priorities were firmly grounded. She must not allow these impulses to overrun her sensibilities. She was a married woman. The reservations she had about her husband must be buried. She had a responsibility to her family to protect her virtue and serve the lord who'd asked for her hand in marriage and expected her to honor him.

Anne rubbed the back of her hand against her palm and wiped away the searing kiss. She would block it from her mind. Calum's heart could not have possibly inflamed as hers had. He was so adept at courting, he must be well practiced—most likely trifled with *thousands* of unsuspecting women.

She sighed and sat on the edge of the bed. Calum was going to ransom her—he'd get his money and he would move on to the next unsuspecting passenger when he plundered her ship. Anne's stomach churned when she considered there could be another woman like herself in his future. *Would she be married by proxy too?*

Anne shook her head. Once the ransom had been paid, she had little doubt Lord Wharton would seek revenge. After all, the baron had been the Sheriff of Cumberland and now maintained order for the Earl of Northumberland. *Thomas. The name is so unfamiliar to me.*

"Calum." Anne spoke aloud, the L rolled off her tongue as she hummed the M. She liked the sound of it.

Would Thomas see him hanged? She pictured Calum's powerful neck swinging in a noose and nearly wretched. A stream of cold sweat slid down her forehead.

Chapter Four

Lord Wharton washed his breakfast down with a draught of cider, feeling giddy for the first time in…well the first time ever. Any day now, the ship should arrive with Lady Anne, his new bride. He rubbed his fingers in a circular pattern across his palm, imagining her young flesh. He had worked hard all his life. He deserved this. Yes, he'd put on a stone or two and his body didn't respond as quickly. But Lady Anne would grow to accept him. After all, she had been cloistered in her father's estate. Her uncle had assured him that she knew nothing of men. A welcomed thickness spread across his groin. Having raised a family himself, he was the perfect man to show the sweet virgin a wife's place.

Of course, he would have preferred to take Lady Anne to his estate in Healaugh, but momentarily he was engaged with the Earl of Northumberland as warden of the region. The earl had given him use of the manor on the castle grounds as part of his service. It had been the earl's idea to marry by proxy and have Anne sail to the River Aln. When she arrived, the Lord Percy would host a feast to honor the Baron of Wharton and his new baroness.

Though the manor was nowhere near as grand as Alnwick Castle, it was solidly built—a fortress in itself, a home in which any baroness would be proud, even the second daughter of an earl.

His manservant, Samuel, leaned down to pick up his tray. "Will that be all, my lord?"

"Leave the ewer." Thomas looked at him with a twist to his gut. "Any word of the *Flying Swan?*"

"Not yet, my lord. I could send a messenger."

"No. The lookout will come when she's spotted."

"Very well, my lord."

Thomas waved the man away with a flick of his wrist and belched. Since he had returned from London five months ago, he'd been absorbed with negotiating the terms of his marriage. He would never forget watching Lady Anne from across the aisle at Westminster Abbey. She stirred a longing deep within, a feeling he'd not experienced since his years as a young man when he courted his first wife, Eleanor. *God rest her soul.*

Wharton had patiently waited until the crowd dispersed and then introduced himself. Lady Anne had looked past him when he kissed her hand. He expected that. After all, he was nearly three times her age. *Young women always think they want to fall in love with a younger, less experienced man. What they need is a learned man, aged by war and time, to guide them through the complexities of life.*

He poured one more goblet of cider and gazed out the window. Dora skipped into view carrying a bucket of chicken feed. His tongue shot to the corner of his mouth when the wind picked up the servant's golden hair from under her white coif. It was the color of Lady Anne's. Wharton rubbed his hand across his crotch. Dora smelled a bit too strongly of tallow, even when naked, and though she meandered beyond the glass, he could smell it. Perhaps her scent lingered from last night's interlude.

A rap on his door brought him back to the moment. "Come."

Samuel stepped inside and presented a missive on a silver platter. "From Captain Fortescue, my lord."

"Fortescue? It must have been dispatched before the ship sailed. Odd." He slipped his thumb under the wax seal and read. A lump formed in his throat. He tried to swallow, but the thickness stuck there along with the cider, turning to fire his belly.

He slammed the missive on the table and glared at the weathered face of his servant. "Where is the messenger who brought this?"

"I sent him to the kitchen, my lord."

"Bring him to me at once, and fetch Master Denton."

"Yes, my lord."

The table upended when Wharton pushed away. He growled and kicked the heavy thing aside with his heel. Grinding his back molars against the pain, he paced. His mind raced through the half-dozen people who knew of his marriage. He'd kept it quiet. Had a missive been intercepted? Where was Lady Anne? He'd fled Wharton Hall because of enemies hell bent on destroying him. Now they had pillaged the ship and the only soul not accounted for was his wife?

A young man appeared in the doorway, holding his cap. "You wanted to see me, my lord?"

Thomas whipped around. "You delivered the missive?"

"Yes."

"How was it handed to you?"

"I am Captain Fortescue's First Mate. I watched him pen the letter and seal it."

"Did anyone else read it?"

"No, my lord. Fortescue directed me to deliver it with haste."

"You were on the ship when it was attacked?"

"Yes."

"What happened?"

"We sailed into a squall. The night was black and the carrack dark. We didn't see her until she was crossing our bow flying the Jolly Roger."

"Pirates," Thomas said, thinking aloud. "Spaniards? Dutch?"

"Scots."

The baron's full belly churned, threatening to heave. With a rolling belch, he swallowed. The Scots—his fiercest enemies. "I knew it. Those murdering bastards will never rest. England will not be at peace until every last one of them is dead and their seed is snuffed out forever."

The boy nodded, his mouth drawn in a frown. Wharton wanted to slam his fist into his young face. "How could you lose my wife? Where is she, damn you?"

He stammered. "My lord?"

"What has Fortescue done to…" He clenched his fists and shook them. "Get. Her. Back?"

"He's gone to London, sir—reported it to the Royal Navy. Th-the queen is very upset indeed."

Wharton paced the parlor. *Imbeciles.* On his third trip past the incompetent first mate, he shoved his finger in the man's sternum and shouted, "I trusted you and your crew to bring her to me safely. Now all are accounted for *except* my baroness?"

The young man backed a step. "Yes, my lord."

Wharton glared at him—the young face of ineptitude. "Get out," he roared. "Be gone, or you'll feel the cold steel of my sword." Wharton grasped the hilt and yanked the cutlass from his scabbard while the man fled.

I should have been there. If I had traveled to Southampton to fetch her, none of this would have happened. I should have never relied on someone else. Scottish barbarians? Only I know how to quash the miserable Scots— Fortescue would have been beat before the battle began.

The lean figure of Master Denton appeared in the passageway. His eyes drifted down to the sword in Wharton's hand, and he brushed his fingers across his own hilt. "You sent for me, my lord?"

Wharton eyed his henchman and shoved the sword back in its scabbard. Though Master Denton had always been a most loyal and trusted servant, his appearance gave Thomas pause. With hair black as coal framing his gaunt face, Denton looked like an executioner. Wharton half expected him to carry a headsman's axe. Tall, lanky, the man's black eyes appeared to have no capacity for sympathy, and that's how Thomas wanted it. Never had he seen Master Denton look at a woman, or a woman look his way for that matter.

"Scottish pirates plundered Lady Anne's ship. It appears they have taken her prisoner." He looked away and lowered his voice. "Or worse."

"The Scots again?" If Denton had felt any remorse for the baroness he didn't show it.

"I want you to go to Portsmouth. Find out everything you can. Were there Scots hanging about the alehouses before the *Flying Swan* sailed? What colors did they wear?"

Denton nodded.

Thomas lunged in and jutted his face under Denton's nose. "I want that pirate captain's head."

"Understood."

"And you can give Fortescue a taste of my dissatisfaction while you're at it."

The corner of Denton's mouth twitched. "I'll see it done."

"Good. Leave now. I want word dispatched within the fortnight."

Wharton stepped to the window and watched Denton trot through the gates on his black steed. If anyone could dredge up information from the back alleyways of a dockyard, it was he.

Sickly dread stabbed Thomas in the gut. He envisioned a pirate with his kilt hiked up around his hips forcing his maiden bride. It blinded him with rage. He wanted to know who this pirate was, damn it. His fists clenched. *When I uncover his identity, he will rue the day he was born. And if he defiles my wife, I'll make the rutting bastard gag on her blood before I carve out his bowels and hang him.*

***

Anne clutched the bedclothes under her chin. The air had turned markedly colder on their voyage north. She'd heard about the bone-chilling wind from the North Sea. Now March thirtieth, she expected a bit more warmth, but the gooseflesh on her skin hinted that it might even snow. She shivered.

She wished she could pull up her feather duvet and go back to sleep, but that luxury remained behind, still covering her bed at Titchfield House. From the hurried footsteps clamoring above, she could tell that the morning's work had begun. The anxious voices told her this wasn't just any morning and curiosity took hold. She threw back the bedclothes and wrapped her woolen dressing gown around her shift.

Footsteps clomped down the corridor followed by a tap on her door. "Time to break yer fast, milady."

"Come in."

The tray jostled in Bran's hands, reflecting his excitement. "We're rounding Trotternish on the Isle of Skye. We'll see Rona and then Raasay within the hour."

Anne settled her hand on the boy's brown curls. He reminded her of her brother, Henry, but there was a world of difference between the two. Henry had succeeded her father as Earl of Southampton, and Bran stood on gawky legs in a moth-eaten kilt, his face caked with dirt and sea salt. He looked happy as a puppy, but he wasn't wearing his sling. "How is your arm?"

He stretched out his hand and jiggled his fingers. "All healed, milady. Yer ointment fixed me up like new."

"I still want you to be careful for at least another week." Anne pushed up his sleeve and examined his arm for bruising. The swelling had gone down and the purple was fading into an ugly yellow—an unattractive, but sure sign of recovery. "Are you excited to return home?"

"Aye, milady. It's been a harsh winter and the clan's starving." He straightened the plaid across his shoulder and looked up with a twinkle in his hazel eyes. "I cannot wait to see the look on me ma's face when she sees the *Flying Swan* and her cargo."

Anne wanted to share in Bran's excitement, but these were stolen goods. Arriving in Raasay filled her with the same trepidation as the thought of arriving at Alnwick. What would Calum do with her once they arrived? Would she be safe? Would they take her trunks and divvy out her clothing amongst the heathens?

After she'd eaten and dressed in her most modest gown—a woolen frock that showed as little cleavage as possible, she pulled a cloak around her shoulders and ventured out to the main deck. The brisk wind cut through her multiple layers of clothing, took hold of her silk veil and snatched the coronet off her head. With a squeal, she chased after it. The headpiece was amongst her favorite and seemed to grow a mind of its own, spiraling across the deck like a blue rogue sail.

A large hand reached out and stopped the coronet before it flew over the rail and into the sea. Anne's eyes trailed up the arm to a pair of broad shoulders. Calum wore his dark auburn hair loose. It shimmered with copper as the wind tossed stray strands across his face. White teeth flashing with his grin, he pushed his hair aside.

The wind swirled in puffs across Anne's skin, leaving a tingle behind. She reached for the rail to steady herself. Calum had shaved his beard. If anything, his smooth, square jaw brought more prominence to his raw masculinity. She wished she could reach out and brush her fingers across his unblemished skin.

Why did he have to be so rakishly good looking? Curses, every time she looked at him, he seemed more handsome than the last. Her heart fluttered. She clasped her hand over it to quash her reaction.

He clutched her coronet with both hands. Anne took a step toward him and blinked rapidly, the heat of her cheeks being the only warmth she'd felt that morning. She broke the tension by glancing down at her wayward headdress and held out her hand.

He casually handed it to her. "'Tis a bit too dainty for a ship's deck. Ye need a woolen bonnet in these waters."

"Unfortunately, I didn't anticipate a detour to the Hebrides when I packed."

He leaned against the rail with a hand on his hip. "We mean ye no harm."

"No?" Anne rubbed her upper arms. "And just how long will I suffer your *hospitality?*"

"No longer than necessary—a month, mayhap two."

"I did not ask for this," she said through clenched teeth.

"Nor did I, but you're here just like that cold wind that's cutting through yer dress." His eyes trailed down the length of it and back up again. "We have naught but to make the most of things."

A fireball ignited in the pit of Anne's stomach, flaring and melting away the cold. He looked at her with eyes an intensity that took her breath away. No man had ever made her insides sizzle and ache—as if he were the devil himself. Calum was a rake, a thief, and there was every possibility he would hang for his crimes. She would die if he ever discovered the effect he had on her sensibilities. She must cling to her resolve.

She twisted the headpiece in her hands. "How long do you think you can carry on, plundering Her Majesty's ships before you meet your end?"

His face turned dark and he stepped toward her. "Ye do have a quick tongue for a noble lassie." Anne inhaled—sea salt, musk and danger. He leaned in, his lips an inch from her ear. "I like that."

With a gasp, Anne faced him. From the flash of the gold flecks in his eyes, she knew she'd hit a nerve with her terse remark, but she wouldn't allow him to think he'd charmed her with his devilish smile and powerful shoulders.

"Rounding Raasay, Captain," John called from the deck above.

Calum rolled his arm in an exaggerated bow. "Lady Anne." He marched up to the quarterdeck leaving her alone at the rail.

Bran skittered past. "Come, milady. Ye'll have a better view from the forecastle."

Bran tugged on her hand and led her forward up the steps to the bow of the ship. He ran to the forward rail and beckoned her with a wave of his arm. "There she is—Raasay."

The island loomed like a dark shadow wedged between the shores of the Scottish mainland and the Isle of Skye. Spindly birch trees jutted up between the rocks, bent as if old before their time. As the ship sailed south, the terrain became lusher with bracken ferns shaded by healthier trees than she'd seen to the north. Ahead, verdant pastureland touched the shore of a beach covered with layers of smooth stone.

Bran pointed. "There it is—Brochel Castle."

Sitting atop a stony crag, the fortress walls extended skyward. Outer bailey walls surrounded a single square donjon tower that peaked above a ring of mist, as if separated from the earth. Anne spotted guards between the crenel notches. A bell sounded, and the beach erupted with activity as people ran to the shore. Waving their arms, their indiscernible shouts carried away by the wind.

"See the tower?" Bran yanked on her hand. "'Twas a broken shell when Calum came. We carted the stone from the north of the island and built it sturdy."

Anne admired the pride written across the boy's face. "It sounds like hard work."

"Aye, and it took an eternity, but we've a fine keep now."

"Where did you live before the repairs?"

"There are long houses at the back of the battlements. Some clan families still use them."

Anne stole a look across to the quarterdeck. Calum stood at the helm, taking charge of the ship's anchoring. The men jumped to his every command without question. His hands on his hips, he surveyed the scene as if he were born to captain a ship. His gaze snapped up, meeting Anne's. She quickly averted her attention back to Bran, giving a nervous laugh and hoping Calum didn't think she'd been watching him all that time.

Bran peeled away from the rail and danced around the deck. "We'll have a grand gathering tonight!"

The boy's antics made her laugh. Anne wished she could celebrate, but a cold shiver shot up her spine instead. The dark grey walls of the castle were archaic, far less refined than Titchfield House. She fixed her gaze on the tower. Would Calum lock her in a room at the top until her ransom was arranged? Her head swooned. The tower was the highest point in sight. It precariously ruled over the pasture and beach as if it teetered on the brink of collapse.

Anne crossed her arms and grasped her shoulders. She'd reached the next stage of her misadventure. Her gaze fell to the dark swells of water below. There was no need to dip her fingers in the sea to determine it was cold. The chill wafted up on the salty air.

Watching the men lower a skiff, she let out a breath. She looked behind her at the mainland across the sound. Would she find a chance to steal away?

Chapter Five

Anne hurried back to her stateroom. Locking the door behind her, she pulled her treasure box out from under the mattress. Calum's men would offload her trunks. God only knew what they would steal. She quickly removed her shillings and jewels and jammed them in her pockets.

She jumped at a knock on her door.

"Are ye ready to disembark, milady?"

"A moment." She closed the lid and fastened the buckles.

When she opened the door, she couldn't breathe. Clad in a kilt of fine wool with his red plaid draped across his shoulder and a massive claymore swinging from his belt, Calum looked the ideal laird. How could any woman not be enchanted by his blue eyes, glittering from a face so wickedly handsome? One eyebrow arched with the up-ticked corner of his mouth. The laird had thought to escort her ashore himself? Possibly his manners were genuine.

"My lord, I thought you'd send Bran or John to collect me."

"And trust my most precious cargo to another?"

Anne laughed at the devious smile dancing across his face. "Your charm is futile with me, laird Calum." So she wished him to think.

He held up her father's dagger. "I believe this is yers."

She plucked it from his fingers, a confusing concoction of resentment, surprise and appreciation caught her off guard. "You trust me then?"

"I think we can agree to a truce." His muscles rippled as he stepped forward and offered his arm. "Are ye ready, milady?"

She placed her hand in the crook of his elbow. He looked past her and assessed her trunks. "The men will see to it your things are delivered to your chamber."

"My chamber? And where might that be?"

"I planned to have Mara prepare the guest room for you."

"Guest room?" She touched her hand to her chest. "I thought you might lock me in the tower."

"I would have you comfortable during yer stay." He ran a finger across the gold brooch that clasped his plaid. "Unless ye would prefer to be treated as a prisoner."

"Are your guest quarters in the tower?"

"Two floors above the great hall. The clan guard occupies the floors above that." He gestured to the door. "Shall we?"

When they walked onto the deck, Anne thought she would die when Bran held out a rope harness fashioned with a board barely wide enough for her to sit upon. Swallowing hard, she climbed into the contraption. Dangling from the web of rigging above, they lowered her to the skiff. Anne shut her eyes and swallowed her urge to scream. Didn't they know she couldn't swim? Where was the pier?

Anne was sure the small boat would capsize as John Urquhart, Bran and Calum followed her, making use of the same harness as if they were swinging from a grand oak tree with lush grass beneath. When Calum took the seat beside her, Anne fastened both hands around his arm. When faced with an icy death in the Sound of Raasay, or clinging to a pirate, she threw her misgivings aside and opted for life.

His muscle flexed beneath her grasp. Surely he was hewn from iron. "Yer no' a seafaring lass are ye?"

"I cannot swim, and even if I could, these skirts would drown me. Why have you no pier?"

"I'll have to add that to the agenda for discussion at the next clan meeting. It can follow healing the sick and feeding the children."

Anne detected a note of sarcasm in his voice, but nothing could have prepared her for the scene on the beach. Yes, she had seen poor people on the streets of Portsmouth and Southampton. She had even opened her kitchens to the local crofters at Titchfield House. None of her tenants starved. She had seen to it.

Though there was laughing and dancing, the children were dirty and gaunt as if they hadn't a decent meal all winter. Their clothing was tattered—hardly warm enough for the cold north. Anne wondered how they could be so happy. They seemed to be teetering on the brink of death.

As they marched up the beach, an old man with a woolen blanket pulled about his shoulders coughed. Anne leaned in to study the pink rims around his eyes. He smiled, revealing a single tooth in the front of his mouth, and said something in Gaelic—spoken so fast, Anne couldn't make it out. Pleased with himself, he threw back his head and laughed, bringing on a fit of raucous coughing.

"What did he say?" Anne asked.

She could have sworn Calum turned red right up to the tip of his ears. "He's just a silly old man."

Anne noticed the others lining the shore were laughing too. "Well, whatever it was, they certainly thought it terribly funny."

Bran leaned toward her. "He asked Calum if he captured himself a wife."

Anne covered her mouth to hide her astonishment and hurried ahead. These people couldn't possibly think the captain had a romantic interest in her. Heaven's stars, she was a married woman. At a split in the path, she took the right.

Calum cleared his throat behind her. "This way, milady."

Anne glanced over her shoulder to see who had noticed. Everyone. With quick step, she fell in line behind Calum, climbing a zigzag path up to the castle. The monstrous gates to the outer bailey were opened wide, welcoming them. Inside the castle grounds, people lined the path to the tower, shouting friendly cheers, reaching their hands out to touch Calum. Fingers strayed to Anne and brushed her velvet cloak. She gasped when tiny palms found their way to her waist. A toothy smile of a small girl gazed up, her eyes wide with wonder.

Without a second thought, Anne picked her up. "What is your name?"

"Isabelle." She stuck a finger in her mouth. "Are ye a princess?"

Anne whistled. "No. I'm merely a lady lost at sea."

Anne kissed Isabelle on the cheek and returned her to the outstretched arms of a woman who must have been her mother.

Calum pushed through heavy oak doors into the great hall. A young woman with her hair tucked under a linen coif scurried into Calum's outstretched arms "*Fàilte mo laird*—greetings my laird."

Anne understood that.

"Ye must use your English, Mara." He gave her shoulders a squeeze. "This is our guest, Lady Anne from, ah, Southampton. Take her to the guest room."

Mara pushed a stray lock of auburn hair under her white linen coif. "The guest room?"

He winked. "Aye—ye ken—where the Chief of Lewis stays when he pays a visit."

Understanding lit up her face. "Of course." Mara looped her arm through Anne's—an inordinately familiar gesture for a serving maid. "Come with me, milady. We'll make ye right comfortable."

Anne let Mara pull her up the winding stone staircase. A few inches shorter than Anne, Mara's acorn eyes filled with excitement. "Ye must tell me what happened, milady. The whole castle was agog with news of your arrival afore ye made it up the hill."

"I'm afraid I was a bit of unexpected cargo on the *Flying Swan.*"

"Oh me heavens."

"Well, at least the captain didn't see fit to toss me overboard."

"Calum? He would never do that." Mara brushed the idea away with a flick of her hand. "And how long do ye think ye might be staying?"

"Until the ransom can be arranged with my husband."

"So you're married, then?"

"Yes. Somewhat."

"How can anyone be 'somewhat' married?"

"I suppose I'm legally married—on paper, anyway." Anne bit her bottom lip.

Mara stopped and gaped. "That makes no sense at all."

Anne shouldn't have spoken so freely with the maid. They'd barely met. But she asked so many questions, and her face looked as friendly as a kitten's, reminding her of Hanna.

Mara opened a door into a spacious chamber with a huge, but tattered mahogany bed with torn red canopy drapes. She gestured to a large stone hearth. "I stoked the fire when word came the ship rounded Skye."

"You did? I thought this was the guest room."

Wide eyed, Mara covered her mouth with both hands. "Apologies. I'm very bad with secrets."

"This is *his* chamber, is it not?"

She cast her eyes downward. "Aye, milady."

"Where does Calum sleep when the Chief of Lewis visits?"

"He takes one of the smaller chambers above. 'Tis no trouble—Please don't tell him I told ye, he'd be awful sore with me."

"And where is the laird's wife? Am I also imposing on *her* hospitality?"

"Calum has no wife."

Anne turned to examine a tapestry, afraid Mara might be able to sense her thundering heartbeat. Studying the exquisite needlework of the family crest with a sun encircled by a leather belt, Anne could not fathom why her insides flipped upside down at the news. But the fact Calum was unwed was most interesting indeed. She ran her finger around the circle which bore the Latin words, *Luceo Non Uro*. "I shine not burn."

"Pardon?" Mara asked, turning down the bedclothes.

Composure regained, Anne stepped to the other side of the bed to help—something she did with Hanna, though her mother never knew. "Is the laird promised?" She feigned her most blasé expression and fluffed the pillows while watching Mara out of the corner of her eye.

"Nay. He's been too busy trying to keep us fed. The cargo of the *Flying Swan* will be put to good use indeed." She giggled. "When we saw ye clutching his arm in the skiff, we all thought ye were *the* one."

The one? Heaven preserve me.

Mara walked to the door. "Is there anything else ye'll be needing milady?"

"Just my things. I suspect the men will bring them in due course."

"Very well. The dinner bell rings at dusk."

***

Calum couldn't draw his eyes away from the graceful sway of Anne's bottom as she ascended the stairs with Mara. When she'd clutched his arm in the skiff, he sensed a slight crack in her stately façade. He hadn't expected his body's response when she placed her hands upon him. He was certain she could hear his heart thundering against his ribcage. Blast it all, Calum should have asked her to sit beside Bran or anyone else.

He turned to his fair-haired younger brother, Norman, who held the keep during Calum's absences. A few inches shorter, Norman closed his gaping mouth, shook his head and looked toward the ceiling. "Ye only have to look at her to ken she's nobility. Ye want the entire English navy to come blow us to hell?"

Calum hated the way his younger brother jumped to conclusions. "'Tis good to see ye too, Norman." He led him and John aside. "We had no choice in the matter. The skiffs were launched before we found her."

"What do ye aim to do with the lass?"

"Ransom her to her husband."

"What? Is he the Duke of Norfolk or something?"

"Thomas Wharton—the Baron of Wharton after his attack on Scotland at Solway Moss."

Norman blanched. "Christ, Calum. Wharton? Do ye ken what he'll do if he discovers it's us who've absconded with his wife?"

"Aye—no more than if the English learn it's us who've plundered their ship." Calum's fists moved to his hips. "How much do ye think we should ask for her?"

John leaned in and kept his voice low. "Too much and he'll hunt us down for sure. Too little and he'll no' take us seriously."

"A thousand pounds." Calum looked between the two men. Both frowned but neither objected. "A thousand pounds it is. I'll write the note. John ye'll leave on the morrow. In Urquhart plaid, no one south of Inverness will tie ye with the MacLeods."

John nodded. A pang of guilt crept up Calum's nape. He knew John wanted to tarry longer with his new wife, but love would have to wait. Cousin and loyal friend, John would swim the frigid Sound of Raasay and back if Calum asked. As an Urquhart, he was the best man for the job—and they all just might return Lady Anne to her life without getting their necks stretched on English gallows.

Friar Patrick MacSween pushed his way into the hall, the hemp rope wrapped around his portly waist swinging against his brown robe. "Praise the good Lord ye've returned in one piece."

Calum smiled at the healer not only of souls, but the friar had a good knowledge of herbs as well. "I couldn't very well leave ye alone to twist the minds of me kinsfolk."

"Ye heathen lad." The big man pulled Calum into a welcoming bear hug. "And how are things with the English?"

"They're down one ship and its cargo." Calum nodded toward John and Norman. "We'll have to start refitting the *Flying Swan* as soon as she's offloaded—cannot take a chance on having it spotted by English spies."

"Are there any new medicines in the hold?"

"If there are, I'll wager ye'll sniff them out."

The friar was always anxious to find any new remedies from the south. With ships traveling to and from the West Indies, new herbs and medicines were coming to England all the time. It could take years before they made it to Scotland and even longer to reach the Hebrides. The *Flying Swan* was a Godsend for the entire clan.

Calum took John up to the solitude of the solar and penned a missive. Since discovering Lady Anne's identity, he'd carefully considered how he would make the transfer. There was no way he could invite Lord Wharton into Scotland, and yet traveling to

England was fraught with danger. In the end, Calum chose Carlisle. A small border town, he could slip into the area rather easily. The problem would be getting out.

Wharton was a snake. Calum had no doubt the baron would be well armed. Calum would need to receive the ransom first and then deliver Lady Anne. His mood darkened as if the grim reaper had walked across his soul. He dreaded the thought of releasing Anne into the hands of Lord Wharton. If she could have married any other Englishman, it would have been preferable. And if the marriage decree had not been executed, he would consider laying claim to her himself. But Calum would *never* take another man's bride, even a man as vile as the baron.

He folded the missive and dribbled a blob of red wax and sealed it with a blank. "Take this to Edinburgh. Have a runner pay an Englishman to deliver it to Wharton."

"Have ye decided how ye'll do it?" John asked.

"Aye." Calum handed him the note. "But I'll keep it to meself until your return."

John clamped his mouth shut and gave a quick nod. Calum hated to be tight-lipped, but the less his quartermaster knew when he traveled to Edinburgh, the better. Calum placed his hand on John's shoulder. "I can trust only you with this. Ye are closer to me than my own brother."

"I'll leave at dawn."

"Good. Now go find that bonny wife of yers."

"I'm afraid Mara has her hands full with the cargo."

"Tell her I said she can tend to it on the morrow. I'll see the cooks have supper ready and our guest is settled."

John shook his head. "Ye ken, Mara's a headstrong lass. I'll be dragging her away by her hair."

"Then get to it." Calum burst out with a rolling laugh. "If that's what it takes to plant a bairn in her belly."

Calum left John to his business and headed to the castle stairs. He hesitated on the landing. One floor up was his chamber, presently occupied by Lady Anne. He wished he had time to march up and tell her what a fool she'd been for marrying that codfish. Calum would take her in his arms and ravish those sweet red lips with passionate kisses—crush her voluptuous breasts against his chest. Christ, the lass had probably never been kissed by a man who could show her the heat of passion a man and a woman could share merely by the joining of lips.

He placed his foot on the first step and held it there. With a groan, he resisted the urge to follow after her. *Best let her settle first. Besides, she'd sooner see me swinging from the gallows.*

Trotting down the stairs, he refused to allow thoughts of Lady Anne or her ransom to further cloud his mood. He had a ship's cargo to unload, and a celebration to begin. Calum marched down to the shore. Everyone was working, carrying something, even the smallest children.

"'Tis a miracle, Calum," said Sarah, Robert's wife.

Calum had thought her pretty before this voyage. Now she seemed plain, though he cared for her no less. Sarah carried her bundle with a light step, her three bairns waddling in line behind her like a family of ducks.

He hefted the youngest onto his hip. "We'll have a feast tonight to celebrate our bounty."

The tot clapped her hands against his cheeks. "Och aye!"

With a squeeze, he set her down and surveyed the beach. These people were his sole concern. He could never cast aside the honor or the responsibility.

He glanced up to the window of his chamber. Was Anne watching? That she might filled him with vim. He wanted her to witness the teamwork of his clan—to see the harmony that existed between his people and the unity with which they bonded under his leadership.

***

A breeze tickled Anne's face when she pushed aside the heavy furs that shrouded the narrow window.

Calum strode onto the beach and she leaned forward to watch him. No others came close to matching his broad shoulders and imposing height. He walked with powerful confidence, and all heads turned to him while he made his way to the shore. Though the whistle of the wind and roar of the sea filled her ears, she could hear him in her mind, managing the cargo disposition, pointing in every direction, helping with heavy loads, patting his clansmen and women on their backs.

Bran ran up to him with his arms flailing, clearly ranting about a monumental problem. With a wide stance, Calum put his hands on his hips and listened, then grabbed Bran round the shoulders and ground his knuckles into his mop of brown curls.

Anne laughed out loud then looked over her shoulder to ensure no one had heard. Of course she was still alone. The entire clan was on the beach hauling grain, or shepherding sheep and cattle off to the paddocks. She caught sight of one of her trunks being lowered to a skiff and wrung her hands. Calum bounded into the surf with foaming splashes spraying around him.

How could he rush into that frigid water as if it were summer?

Once her trunks lined the shore, he organized a crew to haul them up the winding path to the keep. A sharp wind slipped through her gown and she rubbed her hands over her arms. Calum was down there in a soaking kilt, hauling her things about as if he were a servant. *The chill must cut to his bone.*

Calum's wet shirt clung to his chest. Even from the window, Anne could see his muscles straining against the sheer fabric. The last trunk was the heaviest and his arm muscles bulged under the strain. Her eyes trailed downward, but her blasted trunk blocked her from seeing more. She folded her arms and stepped away. It was just as well. How on earth could she allow herself to ogle the enemy?

By the time a knock sounded upon her door, Anne had pushed away the images of Calum in his wet shirt—until she opened it.

Calum may as well have been naked from the waist up. He seemed not to notice his shirt clung to his chest and arms like a second skin. Anne let her eyes drift down to his abdomen, which heaved with exertion, hard as…

"We brought your things, milady."

Her gaze snapped up and she caught his sly grin. Stepping aside, she gestured into the room. "Thank you. Please put them in the corner where they'll be out of the way."

Bran strained to help Calum maneuver her heavy trunk. "Hello, milady."

Calum tarried in front of the fireplace while he supervised the others, and then dismissed them. Last out, Bran closed the door. Anne found it necessary to study the tapestry and repeatedly interpret the four words there.

I shine not burn.

"The fire feels warm." Calum's deep voice flowed like thick sorghum.

"You must be chilled." Anne headed to the bowl and ewer to fetch a drying cloth and her toe caught on the edge of the rug. Her arms flung out and she fell straight into Calum's chest—the very thing she was trying to avoid. His arms slipped around her waist and stopped her tumble.

"Pardon me." Anne placed a trembling hand on his chest. His heart hammered against her palm. "I-I am so very clumsy."

"Are ye all right?" He clasped her hand. Oh dear Lord, he was soaked through, yet his hands were warm. She cast her eyes down to keep from staring at the transparent linen stretched across his muscled chest. The smell of sea salt and musk washed over her as if she'd been struck by a frigid wave herself.

"I trust everything in your trunks is secured just how ye packed it. I didna want anyone to rifle through your things by chance, so I had them brought up straight away."

She dared to glance at his face. Mistake. His penetrating blue eyes met hers. The hunger in his stare made her step into him. He strengthened his grip on her hand ever so slightly.

Anne fixed her gaze on the large calloused fingers wrapped around hers, terrified her eyes would betray her heart thundering against her stomacher. "You best remove those wet clothes before you catch your death."

His rough thumb brushed over her fingers and his gaze dropped. Anne swore it stopped at her breasts, but it continued downward as he bent to kiss her hand. His breath was warm against her fingers and Anne inhaled as the gooseflesh raced from her hand to the tips of her breasts.

"I must apologize. The warmth of the fire felt so good, I hadn't a mind to move." He took a step toward the door. "We will sup soon. I'll fetch ye at dusk."

"W-why you? Why not Bran or Mara? Surely you have your hands full."

Hurt flashed across his face. "As you prefer."

The door banged closed. Anne groaned and pressed her face into her hands. She could not allow him to come for her. Every moment in his presence had become pure torture. Each time he touched her, the tingling would linger. Her own flesh had betrayed her upbringing and breeding. Anne imagined the countess's dour frown. Mother would lock her in her chamber for a year simply for looking at a man like Calum MacLeod.

Chapter Six

"Ye look like a queen." Bran held out his elbow and puffed his chest. "Calum sent me to fetch ye."

"Thank you, Master Bran, but I'm a lowly maid in comparison to Her Royal Majesty, Elizabeth." Anne had chosen a blue gown with gold embroidery and wore her hair pulled back by a matching coronet and veil. "Does the laird always work beside the people as he did today?"

"Aye, none has a stronger back than Calum MacLeod. 'Tis why his da made him laird of Raasay."

"He was not heir? Who was laird before him?"

"We were annexed to Lewis, but the people of Raasay were starving. They needed a leader. So the big chief sent his son to help us."

"I see. Is Calum's father still living?"

"Nay. His heir, Ruairi, is the Chief of Lewis now."

"How interesting." Anne had never considered that Calum might be a younger son.

"If ye ask me, Raasay got the better end of it. Laird Ruairi is a tyrant. He pays no mind to us—would no' even help us when the frost came early and killed our crops."

"How did you survive?"

"Herring and seaweed." Bran scrunched his nose. "I dunna recommend it."

Voices rumbled from below. As they rounded the steps into the great hall, Anne gasped at the enormity of the crowd. Rows of wooden tables stood around the hall, pushed together and lined by benches. Men wore plaids pinned at their shoulders and the swish of the women's straight-bodied kirtles hushed across the floor.

She spied Mara sitting on John's lap, gazing into his eyes as if no one else existed. John covered her mouth with his and devoured her. His hand slipped to her breast and rested there for a moment before Mara pushed it away. With a gasp, Anne quickly averted her eyes. *What heathen place have I come to?*

As Bran led her toward the far end of the hall, Anne wondered how it would feel to have Calum place his hand on her in such a way. The friction of her nipples against her stomacher rasped as if they'd become the most sensitive flesh on her body. A flicker of heat twisted deep inside and her palms grew moist. She swallowed. Hard.

The crowd filled hall made it toasty, warmer than the crackling blaze in the hearth. Calum sat at the head of the table with a man she didn't know to his left. She turned to her escort. "Where are we going to sit?" She could bear to sit next to Calum if Bran were there to distract her.

"Why, Calum wants you to dine beside him, milady. It's only appropriate for our guest to be seated in a place of honor."

"Will you be joining us?"

"Nay. I've been gone for weeks." Bran pointed across the hall. "Me family's here. Besides, sitting at the head of the table with the laird is too serious for the likes of me."

Anne wished she could be in Bran's shoes, flitting about chattering with everyone—with no concern as to whether or not someone would place his large, masculine hands on her. She looked toward Calum and caught him staring. The image of his hand on her breast invaded her thoughts again. A tingle of longing shot to her core. Here she was a married woman, yet had not experience of a man's touch. *If only Bran could sit between us, my mind would be free of these sinful thoughts.*

When climbed onto the dais, Calum stood and reached for her hand. "Lady Anne. You are stunning this eve."

***

Calum didn't hear a word Norman said when young Bran entered the great hall with Lady Anne on his arm. Her ornately embroidered gown accented the rose of her cheeks and complimented her honey-blonde hair. But most of all, the deep blue brought out the glittering color of her eyes, fanned by long, dark-blonde lashes. She reminded him of a brilliant sapphire in a setting of gold.

"Don't ye think?" Norman asked.

"Aye." Calum had no idea to what he'd just agreed, nor did he care. At that moment, he also did not care that the woman walking toward him was married. He would put that misfortunate fact aside and enjoy the celebration.

When he stood and took her hand, their eyes met. He caught a flicker of longing in those deep pools of blue. There was no mistaking it. He bent down to kiss her hand. When he straightened, the desire he'd glimpsed had been replaced with a cool façade—the same one he'd seen many times since he kicked in her door on the *Flying Swan.*

"Please do me the honor of dining at my table." He gestured to the chair beside him. Anne sat with such grace, he imagined she'd practiced that move in her etiquette lessons a hundred times. He pointed to the man on his left. "This is my younger brother, Norman."

Anne leaned forward and nodded. "You have your brother's eyes."

"Aye." Norman pointed to his bright red mop of hair. "But I've a fair bit more upstairs, unlike me swashbuckling brother."

Calum laughed. "Don't let him fool ye, milady. Norman can be as shrewd as any other MacLeod."

Norman batted the air with his hand. "Baa."

"Me elder brother sent Norman from Lewis so I could teach him some refinement."

Anne's jaw dropped. "You?"

Calum sat back. "And why not me?"

"The plunderer of English ships? The pirate who kicks in a lady's stateroom door?"

"Aye, but I didn't ken ye were within. Had ye made some noise, I might have been a bit more genteel."

Anne's quick tongue had a maddening way of raising his ire—made him want to show her exactly what a true plunderer could do with a woman. Holy merciful God, what he could do with her. She tempted him, blast it all. And must she wear those damnable gowns that revealed her bosoms aplenty? Every man in the hall could view her ample breasts peeking above her bodice. She'd soon have them all breaking down her chamber door.

It was a good thing a trencher of roast beef was placed in front of him. Calum snapped his mind from its wayward thoughts.

"A welcome change from herring," Norman said.

"Aye, and with the heifers from the ship, we'll see a good deal more beef come next spring."

Norman speared a slab of meat with his eating knife. "And lamb."

"Where are yer manners, brother?" Calum snatched the trencher from Norman and held it out to Anne. "Milady?"

"Thank you."

Calum watched her daintily select a small slice of meat with her ivory handled knife that she pulled from somewhere in the folds of her gown. Her clothing was much different from the simple kirtles and bodices the highland lassies wore over their shifts. In English style, her gown pushed her breasts above a stiff stomacher, filling the neckline with lovely silken mounds of lily white flesh—*too much for this raucous crowd*. He resisted the urge to reach out and brush a finger across her breasts, though he ached to feel their softness yielding to his touch.

Anne cleared her throat.

Calum's gaze snapped to her face. "M-milady, I was admiring your gown—such expert needlework is rarely seen in the Highlands."

An adorable blush crawled up her cheeks. "Thank you."

Calum reached for his tankard of ale. He needed to fixate on something other than the lady's breasts. Then his leg brushed against her gown. He drew in a sharp breath and downed his pint.

Calum used his side vision to watch Anne eat. Everyone around him tore at their meat with their teeth, but Anne cut hers into small bits, placed them in her mouth and chewed delicately, as if she were handling a flower.

She caught him watching and raised an eyebrow. Calum cut his meat into smaller portions and pulled a piece off his knife with far more care that he had ever attacked a slab of meat in his life.

"I saw that Mara was quite friendly with Master John," she said, lifting her tankard.

"Aye, they were married only a month ago."

Understanding crossed her face.

"John is leaving for Edinburgh on the morrow."

"Oh? Why must he leave so soon?"

Calum adjusted in his chair. "He's carrying a missive for Lord Wharton." He couldn't bring himself to say, *your husband*.

Disappointment flashed across Anne's face so fast, Calum thought he'd misread it. But he realized Lady Anne had mastered covering her emotions. He could look her in the eye and have no idea how she felt. He'd thought she resented him for capturing her ship, but he picked up on little nuances—flashes of looks or words that told him all was not as it seemed with Lady Anne. He wondered if she had trepidations about her marriage. *No. She married Wharton. She must have loyalty to the cur. And who am I, a lowly Scot trying to make a go of it on this tiny island. No, no, no. A woman such as Lady Anne is far too refined for a life on Raasay.*

She toyed with the handle on her tankard. "I apologize for putting you out of your chamber. If there is a more suitable room…"

He should have known he couldn't fool her. "It is no great thing. We have been rebuilding the keep, and 'tis the most fitting chamber for a lady of your station."

"But it isn't right. You are laird."

He held up his hand. "I'll hear no more on it. Ye are me guest."

When the meal ended, the fiddler hopped up onto the dais and launched into a foot-stomping ditty with the piper following his lead. Tables were quickly pushed aside at the far end, and the hall erupted into a sea of dancers. What his clansmen lacked in technique, they made up for in exuberance with the men swinging the lassies by the crooks of their arms.

Bran sidled up to Lady Anne, doing his own rendition of a gawky lad's hornpipe. "Will ye dance with me, milady?"

Anne pointed at Mara and John who were swinging in a circle with their arms locked at the elbows. "Do that? 'Tis nothing like a volta."

As she faced him, Calum caught a hint of lovely honeysuckle bouquet. He leaned in closer than decorum allowed, just to sample it once more. "Aye, but 'tis every bit as vigorous."

Anne clasped her hands under her chin. "I'm not sure I would be able to…"

Bran tugged on her elbow. "Ye dunna need to ken how. Ye just need to have a bit 'o fire in yer belly."

Anne glanced at Calum. "The boy isn't going to allow me to say no."

He waved toward the dancers. "Go on. Ye'll have fun for a change."

Anne gaped, but had no time to fire off a rebuke. Bran yanked her arm and dragged her to the dance floor so fast, she nearly stumbled over her skirts, but she brushed herself off with flair. Calum laughed out loud, though would have to have a word with the lad on controlling his high spirits.

Calum reclined in his seat. He afforded himself few luxuries, but he did sit in a red-velvet upholstered chair in the great hall. It was from there he heard issues and petitions from his clansmen and where he took his meals. His father had done the same on Lewis. Though Calum's lairdship did not encompass the same great number of people, there were still some two hundred souls under his protection.

Calum nursed another tankard of ale while he watched Bran spin Anne around the floor. She tried to keep up as best as she could. Even Calum would have difficulty keeping time with the lad, though Anne's smile lit up the room. She threw her head back and laughed as Bran kicked out a leg and spun her in a circle. When she stumbled a bit, Calum sat forward, ready to spring off the dais and cross the floor, only to ease back when she gracefully recovered and giggled pressing her fingers to her lips.

It pleased him to see her having a good time. He wanted her to accept him, accept his clan. It shouldn't concern him, but for some reason Calum cared a lot about what Lady Anne thought of him. And he wouldn't allow a young lad to overshadow him on the dance floor.

Calum waited until the tune was nearly over before he pushed back his chair and sauntered around the room to where Bran had absconded with the lady. When the dancers applauded at the end of the reel, Calum made his move and tapped Bran on the shoulder. The lad frowned, but knew better than to argue with his laird.

Anne's chest heaved as she caught her breath. Calum held out his hand and she placed her dainty fingers in his palm. "My heavens, I'm nearly out of breath."

Calum tried not to notice the rise and fall of the breasts which teased him over her bodice. "I shall endeavor to be a bit more genteel, milady."

Anne bowed her head and curtseyed. Och, every bit of her filled his senses with woman. He felt like a stag tracking a doe during the mating season. Calum took in a deep breath to clear his head. *What the hell am I thinking?*

He led Anne in the dance with as much grace as the vivacious fiddling would allow. When the music stopped, the fiddler announced a strathspey. Calum took Anne's small hands and leaned his mouth close to her ear so he could be heard over the crowd. "Ye'll like this one. 'Tis a bit slower."

They stood across from each other with a line of men on one side and the women on the other. The dancing had piqued the color in Anne's cheeks and she looked as fresh as dew, sparkling in the glory of a summer's sunrise. She gazed across the open space between them, her eyes alive with anticipation of yet another dance with unfamiliar steps. There was no need for her to worry. He could guide her through every footfall.

The music began and Calum stepped forward, grasping her hands in his. By the suppleness of her movement, he could tell that she'd been trained to follow a man's lead. She responded to every twist of his hand and turn of his foot as if she could predict each move. He would expect the daughter of an earl to have mastered grace and she followed well.

He sashayed in a circle holding Anne's hands. Her skirts tickled his calves. Anne's sapphire eyes slid up to meet his. He swallowed. It was time to return to the line. His insides tightening, he didn't want to release those rose petal soft fingers, but the music demanded it.

Anne again stood across from him. The music and step sequence forced them to move sideways. He beheld another face, friendly, but not intoxicating like Anne's. He locked arms with Sarah. They spun in a circle—Anne circled with Adair behind him. Calum wanted Anne's hands back in his. He got his wish and her eyelashes fluttered with her giggle.

This time he grasped her possessively. He wanted her to himself and when they sashayed, he could see no other face but hers. The music in his ears dimmed to a low hum. His breath loud in his ears, he pulled her in for the spin and the sweet bouquet of honeysuckle and woman flooded his senses. In that moment, time stopped. He stood motionless and held Anne inches from his body, staring into those eyes. She gazed back at him with an expectant fire.

Adair tapped him on the shoulder. Calum begrudgingly released his grasp and turned to Sarah. The music came flooding back. He glanced over his shoulder and watched Anne as Adair whisked her in another circle. If only they could dance alone.

Calum wished the fiddler could play a volta, then he would have an excuse to wrap his arms around her without bringing attention to his deep-seated desires. But this was not England, thank God. Calum picked up his feet and danced to the music of his kinfolk. That's how he wanted it. Seeing Anne's face smiling up at him while he took every care to swing her around the floor, filled him with desire aplenty. Hell, if he danced a volta with her, he'd have to go down to the beach and throw himself into the icy sea to cool off.

To his surprise, when the music ended, Friar Pat tapped him on the shoulder. If it had been anyone else but the kindhearted friar with his careworn face, Calum would have told him to go jump in the bay, but he couldn't very well say no.

Anne's eyes popped when she looked at his brown habit—fortunately the reformation hadn't reached the island. "'Tis good to see the people of Raasay have a spiritual leader."

The friar took her hand and waggled his eyebrows. "Aye, milady. 'Tis a difficult job indeed, bringing the word to a heathen like the laird."

Calum looked toward the heavens. The friar had obviously had a few too many pints of ale and by his color, possibly a cup of whisky or two.

Nursing a tankard, Norman watched Calum return. "Ye've got eyes for her."

"What the blazes are ye talking about?"

"Ye like the sassenach wench."

Calum's hand shot out and gripped Norman's collar. He twisted it taut and muscled his face to within a hand's breadth. "Watch your mouth." He released the shirt with a shove.

The wee blighter huffed, rubbing his neck.

What business was it of Norman's how he felt? Calum reached for the pitcher and poured himself another drink. "John leaves on the morrow with a missive for her husband."

Norman folded his arms. "'Tis no' soon enough."

Calum took a long draw from his ale and slammed his tankard on the table. "Keep your mind on yer own business, brother."

Norman shoved his chair back. "Her beauty has half the men in the room wanting to bed her. She's a temptress. She's no' meant for the likes of you."

"Don't ye think I ken?" Calum scowled into his drink. *She's no' meant for the likes of Wharton either.*

However, Norman's words struck a nerve. It seemed every man on Raasay wanted to dance with the beautiful and refined English lass. When Anne finally returned to the table, her coronet had been knocked from her head, her tresses hung loose around her shoulders—she looked wild and wanton. She could seduce the Holy Father with that wild mop of thick tresses flowing everywhere.

Calum groaned.

"Are you well, my lord?"

Calum leaned back in his chair, his knees parted to the sides. "I'm fine, but it seems ye've lost a piece of yer costume."

Her hands went to her head. "Oh dear. It fell off a dance or two ago." She stood. "I must go fetch it."

Calum gestured to the chair beside him. "Nay, stay and drink a pint of ale. Ye must be thirsty after having the entire clan spin ye around the floor."

She giggled and pressed her hand to her chest—just above those creamy breasts that had managed not to burst free. Calum swiped his hand across his mouth and forced his gaze away.

The dance and the drink cast aside the stone façade the lady had worn earlier. Calum watched her, chatted with her, while his heart swelled with desire. Norman was right. The sooner she left Raasay, the faster he could return to the way things were—the way things *ought* to be.

When the hall began to empty, Anne glanced toward the stone tower stairs. "I think I'd best retire."

Calum stood. "I shall escort ye."

"That shouldn't be necessary."

"I insist." He didn't want to admit it could be dangerous for a stunningly beautiful woman to climb the stairs of the keep alone after the entire clan had partaken in a feast. Whisky had a way of pulling away men's inhibitions where the lassies were concerned. That's why Calum stuck to ale.

Anne accepted his arm. The stragglers watched him lead her to the staircase, whispering behind their hands.

"It seems we're making quite a spectacle."

"Pay them no mind. They're not used to seeing a fine lady like yourself in the keep."

"I saw a number of pretty girls dancing."

"Pretty, aye, but none have yer refinement." He grasped a piece of her blue damask fabric between his fingers. "Or a gown as fine as this. 'Tis never seen in these parts."

"Ah. I am a bit out of place."

Calum clamped his jaw shut. She shouldn't be there at all— Brochel Castle was no place for an English maid—*matron*. His heart thundered against his chest He walked the lady to *his* chamber, fighting an internal battle. How could he convince her to allow him inside—and how the hell was he going to resist if she did? The offending chamber door came all too quickly. Anne stopped and lifted her chin to face him. His stomach squeezed when her stare met his in the dim shadows of the landing. A slow burning torch danced shadows over her. A strand of blonde hair covered her sultry face. Heaven help him, he wanted to ravish her.

"We made it the whole two flights without mishap." Her eyes flickered in the light reflecting her amusement. She offered him a teasing smile.

"Aye, milady." His voice rasped.

He grasped her silky smooth hands between his and raised them to his mouth. His tongue slipped through his lips ever so subtly as he kissed those dainty fingers. The sleeve of her gown slipped to her elbow, revealing the luscious white of her forearm.

Hot yearning swirled beneath his kilt while he languidly smoothed kisses along the length of that silken arm. Anne's muffled groan sent him undone. The thickening beneath his kilt shot to rigid. He stepped in and gazed down upon her lovely face. "I want to kiss ye."

Her breath quickened, but the desire in her darkened eyes expressed all. Taking her hands, he placed them on his hips. With one more step, he pressed his body against hers, molded to it as if God almighty had made them a matched pair. Calum lowered his head, and Anne's eyes stared at his mouth, hungry.

Gently, he touched his lips to hers. Anne's fingers dug into his flesh. Her breathing quickened to shallow gasps, but her lips did not move. The realization that she had never been kissed shot through the tip of his cock like lightning. Calum stroked the parting of her lips with his tongue and dove into her mouth. Sweet, feminine, Anne didn't resist. Taking her hand, he showed her how to caress his skin, how to touch him.

Gradually, Anne responded. Her hands clamped around his hips and slowly crept lower. The tops of her breasts pushed into his chest. Calum wanted to feel more of her, but the stiff stomacher of her gown forced distance. If only he could unlace it and free her from her bindings—all of her bindings.

His heart raced while he fingered an errant lace at the back of her gown. He rubbed the length of his body side-to-side in harmony with hers. She completely melted in his arms.

Heaven help him, he needed to stop. Now. His breath stuttered as he pulled away. Her eyes glazed, her cheeks red with lust, she panted. As if shamed, she released hands and cast her gaze downward. "Please forgive me, my lord." Her voice warbled.

Calum caressed her cheek. "It is I who must be forgiven. Ye are far too delectable to resist."

"I must not forget the fact that I am married."

Calum's gut clenched—must that offensive detail continue to plague him? "Of course." He took a step back wiped his palms on his kilt. "I will endeavor to practice restraint, milady."

"Yes, we must."

Anne stepped into her room. When the door closed, the lock clicked. He ran his fingers through his hair, trying to block the image of Anne undressing and releasing those breasts that had toyed with his sensibilities all night. He'd just kissed her—threw decorum out the window and had given into his lust. He was no better than Norman who tried to take advantage of every lassie in sight.

Calum raced down the stairs and grabbed a bottle of whisky.

He passed the friar, slumped in the corner with one eye open. "Where are ye going?"

"To the stables. 'Tis the only place where I can forget a temptress with golden hair and sapphire eyes."

Once outside, Calum took a long draw of the whisky and coughed. Having Anne in his chamber for a month would drive him mad. He pictured her sleeping in his bed, lying under his bedclothes—alone. He took another drink. Och, one bottle wouldn't be enough.

Chapter Seven

Calum's scent lingered on everything. Each time Anne closed her eyes, she felt his lips caress her hands, travel up her arm and claim her mouth. She'd actually kissed him, turned to butter in his arms and allowed him to show her how. The worst thing? She had wanted him to do it, prayed he would—and now she'd had him swirl his tongue inside her mouth, she craved more. Every inch of her flesh screamed for Calum MacLeod, *the pirate*, to put his hands on her and flutter kisses across her skin.

Sleep strayed from her grasp. Anne imagined him touching her with his rough hands, hands that wielded a sword and worked beside his men, hands that had shown her tenderness. She closed her eyes and saw John's hand cup Mara's breast. She brushed her fingers across her nipple. To her shock, a moist gush of yearning pooled at the most sacred apex of her body.

With a moan, Anne flung back the bedclothes and paced the cold floor. *A month? How will I endure this for a month? How can my weak flesh resist him?* She stood at the window, pulled back the furs and looked out over the bay. The outline of wooden skiffs blended into the smooth grey-brown stones of the beach.

Could she escape? What danger lay across the sound? This was northern Scotland, a land where barbarian's lurked in the mountains. Without a guide, her chances of making it to England safely seemed slim. Could she convince Bran to help? Though only two and ten, the boy was nearly as tall as a man, broad shouldered, as well. But Bran's fierce loyalty to Calum gave her pause.

Anne marched to the hearth and tossed a clump of peat onto the fire. Escape might be the only way to stop the yearning. But, did she really want to rush into Lord Wharton's arms? She could not slip away without a plan. That would be foolish.

In the interim, she needed to find something to occupy her time—and keep her mind off the devilishly handsome laird.

Brochel Castle would have the same issues as Titchfield House, and by the state of the keep, it wouldn't be difficult to find a challenging cause. She'd apply herself to the task on the morrow.

***

"Are ye awake, milady?" a female voice asked.

"Yes." Anne tied off the stitch and snipped it with her sewing shears. "I was just mending a hole in the duvet."

Mara stepped inside holding a tray. "I brought ye some porridge. I thought ye might never come down."

"I'm sorry. I thought I'd mend some of these holes before the coverlet started molting. I should have gone down to the hall."

"'Tis no problem." Mara pattered over to the table and set the tray atop. "Ye must be sick with worry, being a hostage and all."

Hostage? She hadn't thought of herself that way. Mara looked at her questioningly as if waiting for a reply. Anne slipped into the wooden chair. "I've had a lot on my mind."

"Ye must yearn for yer husband something awful."

Anne couldn't hold back her shrug. How could she yearn for a man she did not yet know?

"No?" Mara pressed.

With a sigh, Anne explained what had happened and why she'd been found alone in her stateroom. "You see, I've no idea what he looks like. He's eight and fifty. At that age, I am not convinced I want to meet him."

Mara shuddered. "I shouldna let John leave this morning."

John's gone? Already? A rock formed in the pit of Anne's stomach. "'Tis nothing that can be helped. I cannot stay here. I'd take a skiff and row down the coast if I thought it safe."

"I wouldna think twice about doing that. Ye'd be taken by Gypsies or worse."

"Gypsies? In the Highlands?"

"Aye, they're everywhere." Mara ran her hands over her linen wimple. "Are ye comfortable here?"

Anne spread her arms wide. "I'm staying in the laird's chamber. That's a situation which cannot last."

Mara took the seat across from Anne. At Titchfield House it would be unheard of for a servant to take a seat uninvited, but one look at Mara's angelic face and Anne didn't mind. Mara had an endearing air about her, and Anne needed a friend now more than ever.

The Scottish woman leaned forward with a sly grin, as if she had a secret she couldn't keep. "He likes ye."

Anne picked up her spoon and studied her porridge, praying the fire in her cheeks hadn't resulted in a brilliant blush. "My heavens. What are you talking about?"

"Calum." Mara sat up, appearing satisfied with herself. "He looks at ye the way a starvin' man eyes a leg of lamb—same way John looks at me."

Anne fought her smile by forcing the corners of her mouth into a frown. "Oh please. There must be hundreds of eligible women in the Hebrides who could win the laird's affections."

"A few have come to Raasay on their father's arm, but they always go home with long faces."

"Why would that be? Surely Calum would want an heir."

"Of course he does, but he's a difficult man to please— stubborn like all Highlanders if ye ask me." Mara sprang up and studied Anne's handiwork. "I think he wants to marry for love." Her voice trailed off, as if that were the most romantic thought she'd ever had.

"Marry for love?" Anne shook her head—that was a fantasy she could ill afford. "You must be daft."

Mara crossed to the bed and slammed her fist into a red satin pillow, giving it a hearty fluff. "Why would ye think that? I fell in love with John. Heavens, I cannot imagine being married to any other man."

Anne scooped a spoon of porridge. Calum probably hadn't chosen a wife because he was too busy privateering. "May I ask you a sensitive question?"

"Hmm. Ask it and I'll tell ye if I'm able to answer."

Anne set down her spoon and dabbed her lips with the cloth. "What's it like—ah—being married to someone you *love*?"

Mara smiled as if she'd opened a window to a field full of fragrant blooms. "Tis like sleeping with yer dearest friend every night." She lifted her hand across to her shoulder and it skimmed down to her wrist. "Except he's a brawny man, and in his arms I feel safe and protected…and loved. As if I'm queen over all the Earth."

Mara's gaze turned distant. With a turn of her head, she shook her finger at Anne. "Ye should have seen Calum when ye were dancing last night. I thought he'd go mad watching ye with the others."

Anne again frowned, fighting her urge to smile. "I'm his prisoner. Under his protection until he can deliver me to the baron. 'Tis all."

"Think what ye like. I ken what I saw." Mara bustled to the door. "I must away. I have to find somewhere to store all the food from the *Flying Swan*, see to the day's meals, change the linens, see to the sick—there's a nasty cough going 'round—Oh yes, and there's never enough time for all the housekeeping."

"You're not doing all those things yourself?"

"Aye, who else?"

"Mara, you cannot possibly think you can take on everything and still maintain your sanity."

"Well, someone's got to do it."

"You're right, someone must, but not you. I have experience as the mistress of an estate. Your job is to see the tasks done to your satisfaction." She held up her finger. "It is *not* for you to do them yourself."

"But what am I to do? Everyone is busy. They'll think me a laggard if I dunna pull me weight."

"They will not. They will respect you for your clever management. Let me dress and I'll watch you work. If the keep looks anything like it did yesterday, you could use a lesson or two from an earl's daughter."

Mara smoothed a hand down her worn kirtle. "I dunna know."

Anne threw open the lid of her trunk and found her apron. "What harm is there? Besides, I must do something rather than sit in this dank chamber waiting to be whisked back to England."

***

Calum took a skiff over to the *Flying Swan* right after John left for Applecross on the mainland.

Walking the deck with his boatswain, Robert, Calum discussed necessary changes. "We need to rid ourselves of the obvious signs, like the swan maiden on the bow."

"What shall we name her?"

The first thing that came to Calum's mind was *Lady Anne*. That wouldn't do. It would remind him of her long after the woman was gone—haunt him even. "Let's call her *The Golden Sun*." He ran his fingers along the rigging. "'Twill remind everyone of our crest, yet will no' drive anyone to suspect the MacLeod's of Raasay."

"*The Golden Sun?*" The boatswain scratched his chin. "I like it."

Calum patted Robert's back and led him to the captain's cabin, tossing his satchel on the bed. Together they went over the drawings of the ship and pointed out where the carpenters could make changes so the ship could no longer be recognized as the *Flying Swan*. It wouldn't take much—adding a cannon portal on each side, changing the shape of the bow, adding a poop deck—all subtle changes to make the ship unrecognizable.

"How much time do ye need?" Calum asked.

"Two, mayhap three months, given we have the materials."

"Good. Check the stores and get back to me with a more definite timeline. I've heard word the Spaniards are hauling loads of silver from the New World and Sir John Hawkins is the only one plundering." He leaned in. "I want a piece of that."

Robert rubbed his hands together. "Aye, captain. I'll have the carpenters start on it straight away." His eyes strayed to the satchel. "Are ye planning on staying on the ship?"

"I thought about it."

"Has it anything to do with the English lassie ye were dancing up a storm with last eve?"

Calum bristled, yanked open the satchel, and pulled out a shirt. "What of her?"

Robert ran a hand across his beard. "So you're hiding from the clan?"

"Never." Calum threw the shirt on the bed. "I'm putting a safe distance between me and what I ken I shouldn't be trifling with. Mind yer step when ye leave. The rain's made the deck slippery and a fellow can end up in the sea with no one to throw him a rope."

***

"You cannot read or write?" Anne asked and then cringed. She was well aware few had access to tutors as she had.

"Nay, milady." Mara threw up her arms and walked toward the kitchen door.

"Wait. Forgive me. I can be a muttonhead at times." Anne patted the bench beside her and motioned for Mara to resume her seat at the table. "You could draw pictures and use ticks to count the number of barrels."

"But why is it so important to record the inventory? When we run out, we're out."

"If you know how many barrels of oats you have, you can determine *when* you'll run out. It will help you plan for sowing seed—you might even have enough of something to sell." She avoided suggesting they send a ship out and steal it. After all, she wanted them to become self-sufficient so they wouldn't need to plunder English ships.

Mara opened her mouth as if to object but shut it. Leaning forward, she looked at the parchment.

Anne drew a bowl with a squiggly line across the top. "This could be your sign for oats."

"Aye, that looks like a bowl of porridge."

"Good. How many barrels did you count?"

"Ten."

"Easy, just make ten marks like this." She drew precise strikes in a row beside the picture. "When you open a new barrel, put a line through it like this—Now how many barrels of oats are left?"

Mara hesitated, but didn't need to count the tick marks. "Nine."

"Do you know how often the keep goes through a barrel of oats?"

"It takes about a fortnight."

"So how many weeks do you have in store?" Anne held her breath, praying the math wouldn't be difficult for someone with no education.

Mara looked at the paper and counted twice for every tick. "Eighteen weeks?"

Anne clapped her hands. "Exactly! You're very good at this."

"Ye think?"

"I know it. It comes natural to you."

Grinning, Mara sat a bit taller.

By the midday meal, they had all the food stores inventoried. Anne's heart swelled with pride when she watched Mara show the cooks how to mark off items when they pulled things out of the larder.

Even Friar Pat came by the kitchen and inspected the morning's work. "Calum will be pleased."

"Do you think so?"

"Aye, child."

Anne looked at his brown habit and bit her bottom lip. "I hope I won't go to hell over this."

"And why would ye say that?"

"I'm helping the enemy manage their stolen wares."

"First of all, we're no' the enemy." He grasped her shoulders. "And secondly, these people are starvin'. Aye, Calum may have taken the *Flying Swan*, but he did it for a good cause."

"Men were killed."

"He tries to spare as many lives as possible, but this is war. Do ye ken what the English have done to our lands? Do ye ken about the embargoes?" The friar dropped his hands and shook his head. "They left us with nay other choice."

Anne wanted to believe him, but sighed. She was definitely going to hell. "Will you bless me, Father?" After all, her family had secretly remained Catholic. At least she needn't hide it on Raasay.

"Aye, child." He placed his hand on Anne's head and made the sign of the cross, reciting Latin prayers.

By supper, Anne and Mara had organized a cleaning schedule and had assigned all women to specific tasks. Mara's face glowed with amazement at how much easier it would be for each person to have their own area of responsibility. No one would be overburdened, and if things went as planned, Mara would have idle time in the afternoon.

Anne sat beside Mara at the kitchen table, enjoying a cup of warm milk. Mara bit her bottom lip. "I'm a bit worried on how to go about telling everyone about it."

"I think you should do it at the evening meal—have Calum announce it. You'll have far more cooperation if he shows his support."

***

When the bell rang for supper, Anne stood along the wall and watched the clan pour into the hall. She gazed past the door, searching for Calum. Norman sauntered past, his shoulder brushing Anne's. "He'll nay be coming."

"Oh?" Anne lifted her chin, giving him her best show of indifference.

"He sent a message with Robert saying the ship needed his undivided attention for a few days." Norman grasped her elbow. "Let me escort ye to the table."

Prickles of warning fired across Anne's skin. The hold Norman had on her arm was none too gentle and he reeked of whisky. She pulled back, but he held fast.

"'Tis no proper way for a married woman to act, flaunting herself so."

Anne jerked her arm away. "Pardon me? I have done nothing of the sort."

"I saw the way he ogled ye while you gaily danced away last eve." He stopped and faced her. "Have ye forgotten you're a hostage?"

"The fact has not left my mind for one minute."

"If it were up to me, ye'd be locked in the tower, just as the English do to our kin when they're captured." He leaned close and inhaled. "Ye should smell like shite, yet ye've been treated like some sort of highborn lassie, sleeping in the laird's chamber, traipsing around the keep in all yer finery like the damnable Queen of England."

"If my presence in the hall offends you, then I shall happily retire from your sight."

Anne didn't wait for his reply. Clamping her hand over her mouth, she raced from the hall. Mara called after her, but Anne continued up the stairs. She was Calum's guest and the wife of one of his bitter enemies. Is that why he was staying away? Was he hiding from her?

Anne returned to her chamber and locked the door. She wrung her hands. Blast Calum for kissing her. He had taken advantage of her weakness and her inexperience.

For a moment, she paced her room, hands clenched tight. Tears stung the back of her eyes, welled hot and salty. She threw herself onto the bed, and beat a fist into a pillow. With every hit, she muttered, "The sooner I am gone from this place…the better!"

Anger surged hot, and ebbed, leaving her limp as a doll. Pushing her face into the pillow, she gave into the tears, her shoulders shuddering as she wept.

Chapter Eight

Calum stood on the deck of *The Golden Sun* and watched the lights of Brochel Castle burn brighter while the sunlight faded. His belly growled, complaining about his meal of bully beef and whisky. His stomach never gave him trouble at sea, but somehow it knew when he was home.

Anne would have eaten by now. He pictured her in the exquisite blue dress she'd worn the eve before. With all those trunks, she surely had a plethora of enticing gowns, but he'd be content if she wore the blue one every night He loved the way it hugged her womanly shape, and could watch her dance in that gown until the day when the stars lost their sparkle.

He groaned and looked at the vast, twinkling sky above. He'd banished himself to the ship for a reason. Visualizing a maid—no, a *matron* in lavish gowns—and wanting to run his lips over every inch of her exposed flesh, was exactly what he needed to block from his mind.

But he couldn't, unless he could find a way to avoid blinking or closing his eyes. He very well might be damned to the fires of hell the next time he got her alone. Oh how deeply he desired to cast his duty aside and show her the delights of passion. And Anne wanted it. He read it in the way her blush crawled up her face, and the longing reflected in her eyes. God, it would be sweet to guide her to a fervent passion. Calum closed his eyes and reached out his hand as if he could brush his fingers across the pliable flesh above her bodice.

A loud thud banged against the hull. Snapped from his thoughts, Calum's hackles pricked. Drawing his sword, he eased to the starboard rail and peered over.

"Ahoy the ship."

Only the white of Bran's teeth shone in the moonlight. Good thing the lad had said something. Calum would have cut the rope ladder and given him a good dousing. Sheathing his sword, he bent down and offered Bran a hand. "What the blazes are ye doing here?"

"Mara sent me."

"What's wrong?" *Is Anne ill, did she take a tumble?*

"Norman's been in his cups again." Bran stumbled over the rail. "Had words with Lady Anne, he did."

"Och, for the love of God." Norman could be an arse the size of Scotland when he dipped into the whisky—bloody swine. "Tell me lad, what did he say?"

"I dunna ken, but Lady Anne fled to her chamber without eating supper."

"Bull's ballocks. I cannot turn me head for a minute and Norman shows his beasty side."

"Aye, yer brother has never been able to hold his liquor."

Or keep his cock under his kilt. Calum froze. "Where is Norman now?"

"He had his supper in the hall with everyone else."

Blast it all. If Calum hadn't promised his father he'd teach his younger brother some refinement, he'd ship Norman back to Lewis where he could annoy Ruairi. Calum hoisted himself over the rail and skittered down the ladder to the skiff with Bran right behind.

***

After sending Mara away, Anne dashed to her trunk and snatched her shillings and jewels out of her treasure box. What had she been thinking, going along with Calum's plan to ransom her? To dally about Brochel Castle, helping them inventory stolen goods made her no better than a pirate herself.

If she escaped, Lord Wharton would not be blackmailed into paying a fortune for her release. Anne counted the silver coins. She certainly had enough to pay someone for safe passage.

She thanked the stars Norman had confronted her. It was the kick in the backside she'd needed to get out of Calum's chamber and do something about this miserable state of affairs. Kissing him and then wanting more? She must take matters into her hands and stop this nonsense.

Besides, Calum had said he would protect her. Now he'd hid himself on the *Flying Swan*. He might as well be in France for all the protection he could provide from the ship's decks.

Anne waited until the rumbles from the hall silenced. She opened the door a crack and listened, only the growl of her belly resounded against the stone walls.

Taking a candle, she pattered down the steps to the first landing. The chamber doors she could see appeared closed, their occupants tucked in for the night. Her patience in waiting had been rewarded. She descended the remaining stairs into the great hall. The embers of a fire dimly gave the immense room a ghostly dancing light. A chill hung in the air.

Anne made her way across the floor, careful not to bump into the tables. A light glowed from the kitchen, suggesting someone might be within. She nearly dropped her candle when a man's deep chuckle echoed. Was it Norman? She hesitated. She needed to gather some food before she launched a skiff, but she wasn't about to have another confrontation with Calum's brother. Anne whipped around and headed for the double oak doors. A bench caught the hem of her gown and screeched across the floor.

Behind her, footsteps clapped on the floorboards. She broke into a run.

She'd nearly made it to the door, when a voice called out. "Lady Anne?" Friar Pat leaned against a table, catching his breath. "Whatever are you doing up at this time of night?"

Stopping, she blew out a rush of relief. She rubbed her hand against the pouch in her pocket. "I was feeling a bit hungry. I apologize if I startled you." She glanced over his shoulder, toward the dim light shining from the open kitchen door.

As he approached, Anne could see his cheeks were flushed red. He hiccupped and covered his mouth. "Pardon me. I'm afraid I may have dipped into the mead a bit much. I brew me own and I only have use of the kitchen well past supper."

Anne rubbed her arms. "The keep takes on a chill at night."

"That it does." He took another step closer. "And how are ye finding it here amongst us wayward souls?"

"Everyone has been quite pleasant. Mostly."

The friar gestured toward the bench. "It seems our laird has taken a liking to ye."

She was not going to slip away without a polite chat. "Oh? But he's sent off a note of ransom."

"Aye. I suppose he has." The friar ran a hand over his belly. "He wouldn't have had much of a choice in the matter given you're married."

There was that "married" word again. How it followed her as if she'd been a baroness her entire life. Anne shot a hungry glance toward the kitchen and slid onto the bench across from him. "Our choices in this life are rather limited."

"But I see yer presence here as a blessing."

"You do? Why?"

"I watched ye with Mara today and studied yer ledgers when I was taking grain from the stores for me mead. Mara hasn't been the matron of the keep for long, ye ken."

"She didn't tell me."

"Well, she probably didna have time. When Calum came here, the keep was in ruins. The clan members were crofters, paying rent to the Chief of Lewis, living in long houses and hovels up in the hills. Calum spent seven years rebuilding the keep and the people love him for it, but like God's sheep, some work harder than others. Mara's ever so busy—takes too much upon herself."

"I agree and we've come up with a plan to share the work more fairly."

Friar Pat reached across and patted her hand. "Ye see what I mean. 'Tis exactly what the lassie needs." He stretched his arms out with a yawn. "I'd best find me bed afore my head drops to the table."

Anne bid him goodnight. What a sweet man, and he cared so much for the clan. Calum was lucky to have him. But she needed to continue with her plan. She inhaled deeply through her nose and let the air whistle through her lips. Picking up her candle, she headed to the kitchen.

Inside the vast room, she found a fire banked in the great hearth. Long wooden tables stood cleaned and ready for morning. Cast iron pots hung on hooks overhead. Anne opened a cupboard door and peered inside, hoping to find the breadbox.

A footstep slapped the stone floor. Expecting the friar, she glanced over her shoulder with a smile. But her heart flew to her throat.

Norman.

His voice came from behind like a rat crawling up her spine. "Why are ye sneaking about, wench?"

The sour stench of a man who'd guzzled too much whisky permeated the room. His arm clutched her waist. He wrenched the candle from her hand and pressed his lips to her ear. "Ye didna answer me."

Anne fought to pull away, but he squeezed her tighter and pressed his unwelcome body against her. "I'm seeking a bit of bread. I missed supper because of you."

"Ye missed supper because of yer own highborn pride."

Norman set the candle on the counter. Anne twisted free. He was faster and flung his arm around her waist, tugging her into his body.

"Release me!"

"And why should I? You're an English wench and a ripe one at that."

Something hard rubbed against her buttocks. Turning, she cast her gaze downward. His kilt tented. Anne's heart raced with fury. With a shot of strength, she pounded her fists against his chest. He tightened his grip. Swiftly, she cocked back her knee and slammed it into his crotch.

With a roaring bellow, Norman released her and doubled over. Anne darted for the door. Norman lurched after her, caught her arm and yanked her back.

"That was a dirty trick," he said, his voice strained. "But I'd expect no less from the likes of an English wench."

Anne twisted away, but Norman yanked her back, and struck her face with his open palm across.

Recoiling from the sharp sting, Anne stumbled into a bench. She flung out her arms, but couldn't stop the momentum and crashed to the ground.

Footsteps pounded. A tall figure burst into the kitchen.

"Ye miserable rutting bastard," Calum roared.

Anne rolled to her side. Calum leaped through the doorway and launched himself at Norman. The two brothers careened across the floor, fists flying. Norman slammed an undercut into Calum's jaw, but he caught Norman's arm and twisted. Calum laid his brother flat on the ground, locking his hand in a death grip around Norman's neck.

"Ye'll no' touch her again," Calum growled.

Anne sprang up, but the two men blocked the path to the door. She pressed her back to the wall, searching for an out.

"What is she to you?" Norman's voice strained as he choked out the words.

Calum's eyes darted toward Anne. "Ye want the English to come and blast Raasay out of the sea? That's what they'll do if ye defile Wharton's wife."

Calum released his grip and Norman slithered out from under him. He stretched his neck and coughed. "Ye are infatuated with her, ye bloody miserable sop."

Anne's mouth went dry.

"Get out of me sight. We'll have words in the morning when you're no' blinded by drink."

Norman scrambled to his feet.

Calum pointed toward the cove. "Take a skiff to *The Golden Sun* and sleep it off. If ye touch her ladyship again, I'll kill ye, brother or no."

Calum's hard, dark glare in the shadowy light told Anne he could do it. Barreling away, Norman didn't look back.

Anne pushed herself into the wall. Calum looked the deadly predator when his gaze shot to her.

Anne clenched her fists under her chin. Could she make a run for the door?

The furrow between Calum's brows eased and his eyes became human again. "Are ye all right, milady?"

Gasping, Anne nodded.

"Apologies, me brother is such an arse." He offered his hand. "Ye have me word it will no' happen again."

Anne placed her hand in his and let out a breath. She should have just slipped down to the beach without attempting to get food.

"You're trembling."

She tried to still her tremors. "I had nearly overcome him. I slammed my knee into his...ah...between his legs."

"Aye? That was very brave." Calum grimaced. "Ye could have been hurt."

"How did you know he would do this? I thought you were sleeping on the ship."

"Bran fetched me."

"You said I would be safe here."

Calum squeezed her hand. "Forgive me. 'Twas wrong for me to stay away from the keep."

"Norman is a bastard."

"Aye. He cannot hold his liquor. But I promise, he'll never touch ye again."

Anne pulled her hand away and glanced toward the door. At this moment, Norman headed to the beach. Drat—she could not hope for an escape this night.

Calum placed his arm around her shoulders. "Now tell me why ye were wandering through the hall at this time 'o night."

Oh heavens, he felt warm. "I—I missed supper, and after Norman's castigating, I decided...ah..."

"What?"

She rested her head against his shoulder and bit her lip. "Nothing."

He pressed his lips to her forehead. Anne relaxed into him, the tension cascading from her shoulders like a waterfall. She snuck her arms around his waist.

Calum held her cocooned within his embrace. He showered her forehead with feathery kisses. Heat coiled tight deep inside her—that new feeling that had become increasingly urgent since the first time she'd seen the laird's face. Anne closed her eyes and pulled him closer, powerless to deny his allure.

Calum's kisses caressed her cheek. Anne lifted her chin, her lips tingling. If only he would kiss her mouth again—just one more time. Calum's hand slid up to the back of her neck, sending waves of gooseflesh along her spine. His long lashes shuttered his eyes and he brushed his lips across hers.

Calum's tongue swept over her lips. Anne nearly exploded with the tingling. Without the barrier of a stiff stomacher, her breasts rubbed against his hard chest and her lips sought his as if growing a mind of their own. The friction of his body ignited every inch of her flesh.

When his mouth clamped over hers, she gave in to him. His powerful arms held her against his body and her knees weakened. With little licks, he parted her lips. A burst of salty-sweet flavor enticed her mouth. With languid swirls, his tongue danced. Wanting more, she squeezed him tighter, the tips of her breasts aching to rub against the steely muscles under his shirt.

With a sigh, he rested his lips against her forehead. "Forgive me. I didna mean to take advantage. But ye are so fine to me."

Anne closed her eyes and forced herself to pull back. "Please forgive my moment of indiscretion. It seems I'm having some difficulty resisting you, my lord." She brushed a lock of hair away from her face. "Though I feel safe in your arms, I wonder, who is the greater threat?"

Calum lifted her chin with his pointer finger, his eyes dark, serious. "I promise ye are safe with me." He placed his hand in the small of her back. "Now let's go see if we can find ye a morsel."

***

Calum couldn't look her in the face. Again he'd kissed the wife of Lord Wharton. Did he want a death sentence? Worse, she had turned to jelly in his arms. Her supple body sent his mind into a frenzy of blind passion. When the softness of her breasts plied his chest, his erection jutted against her abdomen. So strong his lust, he clutched her skirts and tugged, but the blasted voice of reason bellowed at the back of his head. No matter how much he wanted to bed her, he could not take advantage. He had a responsibility to protect Lady Anne. His very own flesh could not betray him.

Though married, Anne was as innocent as a maid. He would not ruin her. It couldn't be. In her moment of distress, she needed a strong arm for comfort. That was all.

She watched him, her ravaged lips plump and red. He used her candle to light the torch on the wall. He found a stack of oatcakes under a cloth on the sideboard and reached for two. "One of these ought to hold ye till morning."

Anne gave him an apologetic smile and took one. He gestured to the table and they sat.

"I missed you at supper." Lady Anne kept her eyes on her oatcake.

"Apologies. There's a great deal of work to do on the ship."

"I see." She shifted on the bench as if she had something she was holding back.

"Did I miss anything?"

"No, not really. I spent the day with Mara." She pinched a morsel from the cake. "I helped her inventory the stores."

"'Tis a good idea. We've never had much of note, but with a bounty this great, we should keep track of it."

"Mara picked up well. We're using a system of pictures and tick marks since she cannot read."

Calum frowned. Most of his clansmen were illiterate—another thing he wanted to address, especially with the children. Lady Anne could help him in so many ways but she wouldn't be there long enough. She took his hand and led him into the musty larder. With a dirt floor and solid stone walls, it had always reminded him of a cave.

She held the candle to the ledger. "See, she'll keep track of the inventory here."

"Och, ye have been busy."

"And that's not all. Mara told me how unbalanced the work is, and we came up with a schedule to even out the duties." She studied what looked like a line of little porridge bowls on the ledger. "We thought it would be best if you could announce it and show your support."

He rubbed his chin. "I do ask a lot of her, but I named her matron of the keep. The women should be following her lead without question."

"*Should be*, but the friar tells me she hasn't been matron for long. A few words from you would be an enormous help."

"Very well, if you think it necessary, I'll do it on the morrow." His eyes drifted to the swollen lips he'd kissed moments ago. He caressed her cheek. It took his every ounce of strength to resist kissing her again. God help him.

Calum led her back to the kitchen and again sat at the long table.

Anne delicately chewed on a bite of oatcake. Calum's hand grew a mind of its own and slid over the top of hers. "I'm thankful for yer help."

She looked at his huge hand covering her smaller one, but showed no sign of disapproval. "I was accustomed to running my family's estate. I need something to occupy my time. Idleness does not suit me."

Calum stroked the back of her hand with his fingertips. "Helping Mara is a great service. What else do ye like to do?"

"At Titchfield House we had little time for amusement, but I like falconry and picnics."

"Falconry? A keen sport of skill. Did ye train your own falcons?"

"An earl's daughter?" She sucked in her cheeks like an old biddy and shook her head. "My father would never allow his daughters to partake in such common work—that was for George, a servant employed solely for the purpose. Before my father's death, I spent many a summer's afternoon following old Master George." Her eyes lit up. "He was a Scot. He's the one who taught me a bit of Gaelic."

"Ah. That explains it."

"I'm not fluent, though."

He drummed his fingers. "Do ye think ye can do it?"

"Train a falcon?"

Calum nodded.

"Perhaps. If I found a fledgling I might have success, but I'd never be able to tame a fully grown raptor. They're much too large."

"A fledgling, aye? What, do ye take it from a nest?"

"Yes—about this time of year."

"We might be able to arrange that. What about a golden eagle—would ye be able to work with a larger bird?"

Anne sat up with wide eyes. "An eagle? They're among the best specimens for falconry—if you can handle one. My father used a golden eagle. They can fly higher and faster than hawks. Father often caught large prey such as geese."

"Aye?" Calum loved the way her dimples darted into her cheeks when something caught her interest. "We have a great many golden eagles nesting on the north of the island. And as ye said, now's the season for fledglings." Calum gave her hand a light squeeze. He'd like to hold her dainty hand through the entire night, but he forced himself to let go. "Picnics are aplenty, too. If the weather is fine, we could ride up there on the morrow."

"'Twould be lovely." Anne's hand covered her lips. "Mayhap we should have a chaperone."

An intense urge spread beneath Calum's sporran and he shifted his seat. A chaperone was the last thing on his mind. Heat still radiated where her unbound breasts had pressed against his chest. If only he could reach across the table and pull her onto his lap. Oh, to feel her round buttocks grind atop his cock while he suckled her.

Christ. Calum shoved the heel of his hand against his forehead. Had he lost his mind?

If he could rewind time and find a way to void her marriage, he'd not hesitate to do it. Would she want him if she were not wed? *No highborn English lass will want the likes of Calum MacLeod. Why must me mind continue to dwell on it?*

Anne finished her oatcake and pointed at his. "Are you not hungry?"

"What?" He hadn't touched it. "Would ye like it?"

"I'd best not, but thank you."

Calum shoved the whole dry cake in his mouth, chewed a few times and swallowed. "'Tis time to retire, milady."

Anne nodded. Calum rose and offered his elbow. "I shall see you to yer chamber."

"Thank you, my lord."

"My lord?"

"You *are* a laird."

"Aye, but ye are a higher born lady. Calum will do."

"Very well. Thank you, Calum."

Och, why did me name have to sound so...so intoxicating when she spoke it? When they reached her door, Calum rested his hand on the latch. "Is there anything else ye will be needing, milady?"

"No." Anne's eyes trailed down the length of his body. "But I would prefer it if you would find another chamber for me. I cannot continue to displace you."

Calum looked around the curved corridor and pointed to the next door. "That chamber is in need of refurbishment. I haven't given it much thought, but 'tis intended for the lady of the keep. Mayhap I'll have the carpenters determine how much work is needed."

"Queen's knees, I don't want to create more work for you. E-especially when I will soon be gone."

Calum leaned against the door jamb, wanting to prolong the moment. "We-ell make up yer mind, milady."

Her bow-shaped lips formed a darling pout. "You'll not reconsider moving me, will you?"

An errant finger reached out and brushed her silken cheek. "Nay." Forcing his voice to take on an unhurried lilt, he said, "Ye are me guest. And besides, I dunna want to move all those trunks again."

"You can be a stubborn laird, Calum."

"I suppose 'tis me right as clan chief."

Lady Anne rose up on her tiptoes and lightly kissed him on the cheek. Calum's insides flipped. He grasped her shoulder and focused on her succulent lips. The inebriating scent of her inflamed the burning deep in his gut.

Her tongue slipped out and moistened her lips as her lashes lowered. Her hot breath quickened against his mouth. "Though I know I should not, I like kissing you, Calum."

Air rushed from his lungs when she spoke his name. His heart thundered against his chest. "Kissing could be no sin."

She narrowed the gap to a hair's breadth from touching him. "But it can when your body aches for more." Her breathy voice could charm the dead.

Calum covered her mouth and pulled her into him. Sweet as honey, she welcomed him. Groaning, Anne molded to his body while her hips gently rocked. Calum's breath ragged, the pleasure from her friction nearly unmanned him. It took every bit of control not to follow her into *his* chamber and throw her down on *his* bed. God, he wanted her.

Anne cupped his head with both hands and kissed him softly. "I thank you for your gallant rescue," she whispered, her voice faint, not half as assured as her actions. She took a feeble step away. "Sleep well, my lord."

Closing the door, she left him standing alone, holding a candle with a wicked ache under his kilt. Her lock clicked. Calum groaned and slid down the stone wall. A month with Lady Anne in the keep would send him into complete lunacy.

Chapter Nine

Before breaking her fast, Anne opened her trunk, pulled out her sewing basket and fished for a piece of linen. Her escape attempt thwarted, she mulled over whether to try again. Calum had now reassured her safety—and never in her life did she think kissing would be that enjoyable. Heaven help her.

Why should she risk her life to flee back to England and Grandfather Wharton? What lay in England for her? The Countess of Southampton, her mother, had ignored her pleas to refuse the baron's proposal.

...This is a man of great esteem who will provide for you...Do you have any idea how difficult it is to find worthy peers for five daughters? No, Anne, this is an alliance that will bring riches to the family. It is your responsibility to honor your uncle's proxy agreement...

Anne shuddered. *Sharing a bed with a gouty, wrinkled old man? Curses. Why should I be anxious to join him?*

She held up her assortment of thread. A bright yellow strand peeked over the top. She glanced back at the tapestry on the wall. Would Calum like a kerchief with the MacLeod of Raasay crest? She rolled her eyes and admonished herself for thinking of him yet again.

Her wayward hand snatched the yellow thread. She sat in a chair beside the fire and started in on the kerchief. Whether she would give it to Calum or not was yet to be decided. She'd probably be united with Lord Wharton by the time she finished it. Calum MacLeod would then be but a memory along with his late night kisses. She pushed a round hoop over the linen and threaded a bone needle. It didn't take long to outline a perfect circle with even stitches.

Anne held it up to the light. If she kept it for herself, the kerchief would always remind her of this time. Never again would she be captured by pirates and held in their keep while they awaited her ransom. Anne heaved a heavy sigh.

She touched her fingers to her lips, savoring the memory of Calum's kiss. Such a ruggedly handsome man, but ever so gentle and affectionate. When he ran his hands down her back, her insides had turned to mush. Oh, how she wished she didn't have to resist him, but she mustn't shirk her duty.

Plunging her needle in for another stitch, she bit her lower lip. A scuffle outside the door stopped her.

Mara's muffled voice carried through the timbers. "Calum MacLeod, now just what are ye doing sleeping out here in the passageway?"

"I had a mind to guard her ladyship with Norman so deep in his cups last eve."

Anne set down her sewing and tiptoed to the door.

"Ye slept out here just because Norman barked at her before supper?"

"Nay, I caught him trying to force himself on her after ye sent Bran to fetch me."

"Bloody bastard."

"That's me brother you're referring to."

"I don't care if he's the brother of Saint Francis, he's a bastard. What are ye going to do about him?"

"I'll have the carpenters mend the floorboards in the next room for starters. She's my responsibility. I'll be the one watching out for her."

"Aye? What else? 'Tis just a matter of time and Norman will cross the line—if not with her, with one of our own lassies."

"He already has if ye ask me. I'll have him work on *The Golden Sun* in my stead. That'll occupy him for a time."

After a moment of silence Anne placed her hand on the latch and pressed her ear to the door.

"She's no' like the others is she?" Mara said.

"Whatever are ye on about, woman?"

"Lady Anne. Ye like her."

"Ye mean the *Baroness* of Wharton? I cannot afford to like her."

Anne gasped at his use of her formal name. No one had called her "baroness" since she'd arrived on Raasay. She hated how the sound curled off his tongue.

"Her title doesna matter. Ye are in love with her."

"Silence, woman," Calum bellowed. Anne could scarcely breathe. Was there any truth to Mara's words? No. Calum shushed

Mara with such ferocity in his tone that Anne could hardly believe him as the same man who'd kissed her so tenderly the night before.

Anne took a step back and released her hand from the latch. It clicked. Complete silence swelled from the passageway, and Anne froze as if she were a child caught pinching a sugared date.

"Milady?" Mara's voice resounded through the door.

"A…a moment." Anne's voice came out in a much higher pitch than she would have liked.

She took a few deep breaths and opened the door, effecting her most noble, passive expression. Calum and Mara stood shoulder to shoulder with wide eyes, looking as if *they* were the culprits who'd pinched the sugared dates.

She forced a pleasant smile and lifted her chin. "Is it time to break our fast?"

"Aye," Mara said, reaching for Anne's arm.

Calum bowed. "If you'll excuse me, I must cleanse the sleep from me eyes before heading to the hall."

Mara waited for Calum to take his leave and then squeezed Anne's hand. "Ye heard us, did ye not?"

Anne shrugged. "And what of it?"

"What are yer feelings for the laird?"

"He said it himself. I am a married baroness. I cannot have feelings for his lordship."

Mara leaned in and waggled her eyebrows. "Aye, but ye do."

Anne hoped Mara would soon forget this nonsense. Things were difficult enough, stealing kisses from Calum in the shadows without Mara meddling.

They walked to the great hall where Mara served up two bowls of porridge and led Anne to the far end, away from the others.

Anne studied the young matron. She seemed happy, content to live out her life in the keep, married to John. "You are so fortunate."

Mara looked up with a spoon in her mouth. "Why do ye say that?"

"Being married to the man you love."

"Aye." A satisfied smile crossed her face. "I couldna imagine being married to anyone else." She contemplated that for a minute, staring at something, or nothing in the distance. Mara focused her gaze upon Anne and shook her spoon. "But dunna take me wrong, he can be as stubborn as an ox."

"Stubbornness seems to be a common trait among Scotsmen."

Mara laughed and scooped another spoon of porridge. "Aye, ye are observant."

***

By late morning, Anne had seen nothing further of Calum and opted to take a walk. Daybreak's fog still shrouded the castle grounds with a drizzle that cast a slippery dampness over everything. Anne pulled her cloak closed and raised the hood.

Outside the main door of the great hall, the enormous gates to the shore propped open. With people bustling around her, she stopped at the head of the trail that led to the beach and looked out over the Sound of Raasay. Blurred by the mist, the *Sea Dragon* moored in the bay alongside the *Flying Swan*—she'd been told the name had been changed to *The Golden Sun*. Anne pressed her fingers against her temples. That ship stood as a reminder of Calum's privateering activities.

She did not want to contemplate all the reasons why she should abhor the ship and turned to observe the day's activities in the courtyard. People, most too thin, scurried about with their daily work. Hammers cracked in the workshop. The clang from the blacksmith rang out above the stir. Two men laden with a load of lumber passed on their way to the beach. "Good morn, milady."

She bid them good morning and noted the drizzle hadn't affected them at all. They worked in their linen shirts and kilts just as if it were a summer's day.

Anne made her way across the courtyard and around the back of the tower. She stopped at the sound of swords clashing.

"Is that all ye've got, Ian?" Calum's voice echoed between the bailey walls. "Ye'll no' last against an English army if ye tire so easily."

"Nay, m'laird, I was just afeared I'd hurt ye."

"Come again and this time, fight like a man."

Anne peered around the corner. The MacLeod guard was sparring with Calum in the middle, wielding his massive claymore against a burly man. Not only Calum, but all the men were shirtless, their red and black kilts low around their hips.

Every muscle in Calum's back rippled as he brandished his weapon with deadly precision. His arms flexed and strained when his opponent, Ian, locked swords. Calum lunged against the strain, his calf muscles swelled as he pushed into his attacker.

Circling, Calum shoved Ian away and swung his sword in an arc with a victorious grin. "Better, but come again. Use yer heart this time."

Calum crouched with legs spread wide, ready for another bout. His chest heaved and the tang of male sweat hung in the air, not entirely unpleasant—just different. His skin had a light tawny glow as if he practiced shirtless often, and his abdominal muscles rolled in concert with the massive claymore swinging in his hands.

Anne could not pull her gaze away from the magnificent masculine form that sparred with potent strength. Calum whipped around and his kilt flicked up, showing Anne a peek of alabaster thigh. Tilting her head, she strained to see more.

When Ian again broke away, Calum glanced her way. Anne stepped behind the corner and fanned her face. She turned to leave, but his deep voice spoke softly behind her. "Lady Anne."

Still heaving, his chest glistened with sweat—and he grinned at her. His clean shaven face left his bare chin looking even bolder than before—smooth and ever so kissable. Anne averted her eyes. She would not ogle the bulging muscles across his stomach. "Yes, my lord?" She glanced back at him.

He looked toward the drizzly sky. "I'm afraid the weather has no' complied with our plans to picnic."

She watched a bead of sweat trickle down the center of his chest, all the way until it disappeared under his kilt. Her heart stuttered. He hadn't forgotten. "Perhaps the weather will improve on the morrow."

"I've been thinking about it all morning and I believe I know the perfect spot to find your fledgling."

Training a fledgling golden eagle would certainly help her mind focus on things far less disturbing than the laird's well-muscled chest. "I shall look forward to it, then."

He grinned, his blue eyes dancing, and her heart squeezed tight. With a quick bow, he strode back to his men. Anne clutched her cloak tighter, as if she could hide the heavy tingling in her breasts. She headed to the gardens, praying for the mist to cool the fire in her cheeks.

***

Days later, Anne held up her work to study it in the light. She'd finished sewing the circular belt of the crest and now used different shades of gold and yellow to bring out the brilliance of the sun.

The hammering in the adjoining room stopped, and Mara's voice carried through the walls. "Ye've done fine work on the bed. The laird will be very comfortable indeed."

The bed was finished? When would Calum start occupying it? She looked at the adjoining door. Truly, she'd best keep it locked, given her inability to control her impossible urges.

The door opened, and Anne jolted in her seat. Mara stepped in, smiling as always. "I thought I'd find ye here, milady."

Anne covered the stitching of the sun with her hand. "I thought I'd spend some time perfecting my needlepoint."

"'Tis a worthy pastime." Mara walked in and sat opposite her. "What are ye working on?"

Anne fidgeted with the silk thread. "Just trying some new colors I purchased in Portsmouth."

Mara leaned forward. "Well, give me a look."

Anne moved her hand and scrunched her nose. "The tapestry is the only picture in the room."

"Ooo. 'Tis beautiful." Mara sat back and chuckled. "But I dunna think the baron will admire it."

"No. I daresay he'll burn it and chastise me firmly."

"Are ye going to give it to *him*, then?"

"The baron?"

"Nay, silly. Calum."

From the fire beneath her cheeks, Anne knew she was blushing—radiantly. Mara had the most maddening way of pulling secrets from her—the few she had. "If you must know, I thought I'd give it to him to remember the woman he captured and held *hostage*."

"It doesna sound so romantic when ye put it like that."

"Good. 'Twas not meant to be romantic." *Well, mayhap a little romantic.* Anne looked at the kerchief. She had used painstakingly tiny stitches to achieve the desired texture. "Besides, I needed something to keep my hands busy."

Mara stood. "I've got to get on with me chores."

Anne held up her hand. "Let this be our secret." The last thing she needed was for the entire clan to be gossiping about her making a keepsake for the laird.

***

Calum had become accustomed to having Anne beside him during the evening meal, but tonight he clamped his fingers around his tankard and ground his teeth. Mara had invited the lady to sit in John's stead, and the two women leaned their heads together, chatting like a pair of hens. Mara's glance shot toward him time and time again. They had to be talking about him, damn them. Why the pair just couldn't sit up on the dais and talk about him to his face was confounding.

He kneaded the knot in the back of his neck. John would arrive soon then things would return to normal. At least the work had been completed on his chamber—temporary chamber. He wondered if Lady Anne had any idea he'd spent the past week sleeping on the floor outside her door. He hoped not.

Working with Mara and the children, the lady had already endeared herself to the clan in so many ways. Losing her would leave a void. Of that he had no doubt. Was his unmitigated attraction because he could never have her? Calum shook his head at his stubbornness—always wanting that which could never be.

Friar Pat blocked his view of the lady with his brown robes. He held up a ewer. "Would ye care for a tot of me potent mead, m'laird?"

A slow smile spread across Calum's lips. He would indeed enjoy a tot of the friar's fine drink and he held up his tankard. "Ye are a saint among men."

"Ye overestimate me talents." Pat glanced over his shoulder. "It seems ye are a tad fixated on the baroness."

Calum ran his fingers through his hair. "She's distracting— and she's in me care. I'll not have one of our young bucks touching her."

"'Tis a slippery spot you're in." The friar saluted with the ewer. "But, God willing, 'twill all work out in the end."

Calum toasted him with his tankard and took a long swig. The honeyed liquid slid like cream down his throat. His eyes returned to Anne but she was no longer there. He took quick inventory of the hall. Many had headed for their beds, but Mara remained talking and laughing as always. He caught her eye and beckoned her to the dais with a wave of his hand.

Mara skipped across the floor. "Yes, m'laird?"

"Has Lady Anne retired?"

"Aye."

"Who saw that she made it safely to her chamber?"

"Oh come now, Calum. Ye ken she's safe with Norman on *The Golden Sun*. My oath. She comes and goes all day, but after supper yer fretting over the lass like a mother hen, ye are."

"Och, woman, you're too trusting." Calum stood. "The lady is under *my* care. Not yers."

Calum pushed past her with a curl to his upper lip. Mara trusted everyone to a fault—except Norman. Nonetheless, she shouldn't have allowed Anne to leave the hall without an escort. Not at night. Sure, Raasay was an island, but one easily accessed by a small boat. And now the galleon had been plundered, his clan had more enemies than ever before.

He bounded up the stone stairs of the tower. In moments, he rounded the corner and stood outside her door. Should he knock? There was rustling within. "Lady Anne?"

"A moment." Her voice sounded clipped. It seemed an eternity before she opened the door, her dressing gown clutched closed under her chin. "Is everything well, my lord?"

She obviously was going to continue to address him as lord and Calum had stopped correcting her. "I wanted to ensure ye made it to yer chamber without incident."

"As you can see, I am here."

Calum looked beyond her to the bed. If only he could lead her there now.

Lady Anne eyed him with a demure smile. Did she have to bless him with those irresistible dimples? Again? She lowered her lashes and moved to close the door. "If there is nothing else…"

Holding out his hand, he pushed the door open and walked inside. "Work on the other chamber is complete." He didn't want to bid her goodnight. Not yet.

Lady Anne hesitated a moment, but she closed the door behind her, leaving them alone in her chamber. "My lord, 'tis late."

He strode to the adjoining door and opened it. "Ye see." He gestured to the newly appointed room. "We'll have to keep this locked to ensure I don't sleepwalk and end up in bed beside ye."

Calum nearly stepped on her when he turned.

Anne's eyes opened wide, round as shillings. "You sleepwalk?"

"Nay, but it could happen." Improvising, he snuck his hand around her waist and pulled her into his body. Warm, unbound woman molded against him. Though her arms remained at her sides, she had the most delectable way of arousing him.

Calum buried his face in her hair and inhaled. "Ye smell of honeysuckle and roses. 'Tis more than a lonely laird can bear." He reached for her hands and placed them on his waist. "Kiss me, Lady Anne."

Her arms slid to his back. She kneaded his aching muscles as their lips met with a searching passion. This was a far cry from the timid maid he'd first kissed only days ago. A raging fire ignited across every inch of his skin. Calum ran his hand up to the neckline of her dressing gown as Anne arched against him. Their lips intertwined, he slid his fingers under the soft red wool and found a velvety smooth breast that yielded to his plying fingers. Her nipple erect, Calum fingered it, longing to suckle her. His knee pressed against the bed. It would be so easy to lay her down and slip between her legs.

Anne threw her head back and emitted a throaty moan of pleasure. So seductive the sound, in a blink of an eye, he was fully erect. But then she opened her sultry eyes and grasped his wrist. "We mustn't."

Not trusting his voice, Calum tried to breathe normally and then nodded. He glanced at the bed. God, he'd never in his life desired a woman this much.

"We should not be alone together. I cannot trust my flesh."

Calum closed his eyes and wrapped her in his embrace. "It appears ye were right. We need a chaperone at all times."

She raised her face to him, those tempting eyes posing an unintended challenge—one he dared not take now he'd returned to some level of sanity. He savored those rose petal lips one last time and slipped into his new chamber, locking the door behind him. Calum leaned against the warm wood and inhaled.

Where was John? Calum picked up the poker and stirred the fire.

He then slid his claymore from his belt and released the heavy silver buckle. In an instant he'd undressed and filled the bowl with water. Standing in front of the warm hearth, he lathered a bit of rosemary soap in his hands and made quick work of washing the stench of the day's work from his body.

Gooseflesh rose across his skin as the cold cloth brushed over his flesh. His cock bounced straight up when he swiped the cloth across its head. As of late, he was hard more often than not. Calum closed his eyes. She slept so close, he could practically smell her through the walls.

Forcing his mind to think about anything but Anne, he ran the drying cloth across his body, tossed it aside and slipped under the bedclothes. He loved the feel of crisp linen sheets against his bare skin. It reminded him of his boyhood, of climbing into bed without a care.

Something thudded against the wall. Calum sat up. Holding his breath, he listened intently. His—Anne's bed creaked. Realizing the head of his bed butted up against hers with only a wall between them, Calum groaned. He dropped onto the pillows and stared at the ceiling.

What is she wearing? Did she strip naked as did he? Calum slapped his hand to his forehead. Of course a lady would never sleep raw, especially the daughter of an earl. But imagining her that way sent shivers across his skin. He could never resist the urge to picture her bare breasts as they teased him from under the square necklines of her dresses. The touch he'd stolen this evening proved her breasts to be generous and rounded. Calum imagined their taut rosy tips. A familiar thickening lifted the bedclothes, torturing him.

Anne's bed creaked again. Had she rolled over? Was she on her side—on her back? Was she thinking of him? Did those thoughts send a yearning deep inside, so hot that it rained fire on her soul?

Calum arched his back and willed his thoughts to focus on anything but Lady Anne, but with every creak of her bed, his hunger returned. He vowed to exhaust himself on the morrow with more work. He'd spar with his men, not with his own lust.

Chapter Ten

From his study, Thomas Wharton watched the messenger's horse trot up the path to the manor. The clench in his gut told him the man either bore news from Master Denton, still in London, or news as to the whereabouts of his bride.

Samuel entered and cleared his throat. "A missive has arrived, my lord."

"Good God, man. Don't hover. Show the messenger in."

"Right away, my lord." Samuel beckoned with a wave of his hand. "Mr. Elliot from Edinburgh."

Wearing a pair of leather breeches with a matching doublet and feathered cap, Elliot looked to be an aspiring gentleman. "I was told to deliver this with haste, my lord."

Wharton snatched the parchment and examined the note. By the crumpled edges, the missive was well traveled. He held the seal up to the light. *Damn, a blank.* "How did you come by this?"

"A rather gruff Highlander paid me quite handsomely. Said I was to return with your reply."

"You hail from Edinburgh?"

"Aye."

Wharton ran his thumb under the seal and stared at the black scrawl—the terms of his wife's ransom. "Blast the bastards to hell." He slammed the missive on his desk and eyed the messenger.

Mr. Elliot removed his cap and held it in both hands. "The...the Highlander told me to pay an Englishman to deliver it to you, but I thought it would be expedient to deliver it myself."

Wharton smirked. *A Lowlander, eh?* He'd probably pocketed the money intended for the English runner. But that didn't matter. Aside from a few shillings, he'd have no loyalty to the man who paid him. Wharton moved to his sideboard. "Would you care for a tot of brandy?"

"That would be too kind, milord."

"Not at all." Wharton gestured to the red velvet divan. "Please, have a seat. I've a business proposition for you."

***

Isabelle, the little girl who Anne had picked up and carried into the keep the first day she arrived, hung on Anne's every word. She and a handful of other children sat wide eyed at a table in the hall while Anne pointed to a parchment upon which she'd drawn the alphabet.

"Repeat after me. A is for apple."

The children repeated with a lilting Scottish burr.

"B is for ball, and what does C stand for?"

"Calum!"

Bran pushed through the oak doors and ran up to Anne, his brown curls jostling. "Lady Anne, are ye ready to go falconing with the laird?"

"Bran? You should be attending these lessons. It is important for a young squire to read."

Bran glanced at the parchment. "Och aye, but no' today. Calum's waiting for ye in the stable."

"He's finally ready to go find a fledgling?"

"Aye, and I'll be yer chaperone." His hands flew to his hips as freckles bunched around his nose with his grin.

Anne smiled at the boy's exuberance. She wondered if he understood the importance of his role. "Will you protect me from evil lurkers?"

"Evil what?" Bran furrowed his brow. "I don't think we've any evil lookers on Raasay."

She opened her mouth to correct him, but changed her mind. "Very well, I'll fetch my cloak and be down momentarily."

Anne dismissed the children and skipped up the stairs, thrilled to be getting out of the keep and into some fresh air. She bundled her hair into a forest green snood which matched her dress, and donned a pair of brown leather gloves. At last she would be able to see more of this isle in the wild north.

Calum met them outside the stables with a devilish grin lighting up his face. "Would ye like to see me island, milady?"

She clapped her hands together. "I could think of nothing more invigorating on this lovely day."

He even had a sorrel mare fitted with a sidesaddle, bridled and waiting. He stepped up and placed a hand upon her waist. With a gasp, Anne scooted back. The touch of his fingers sent sparks across her skin—right there in broad daylight.

"Apologies, milady. May I assist ye to mount yer pony?"

She looked for Bran. The lad was already in his saddle and had started up the trail. Fine chaperone he would be. "Yes, of course, but I'd prefer to use the mounting block."

Calum held out his hand and she climbed the two steps. Once they were both mounted, Calum led her to the trail head at a slow walk.

"What about Bran? He's lengths ahead."

"The lad kens where we're going. If he doesna hold up, we'll see him at the loch."

She should insist they catch up with him, but she wanted to enjoy the day. Following Calum at a leisurely gait, Anne walked her pony up the rocky path that led north and west of Brochel Castle. "My, 'tis rugged country."

"Aye. The growing season is short and we've no' much in the way of good soil for crops, but we're making a go of it."

Anne thought of the *Flying Swan*. "Do you think there will come a time when you no longer need to plunder English ships?"

"English? Aye." Calum arched an eyebrow. "I hope we dunna have to do that again, honestly."

"'Tis good to hear."

"I'll no' give a promise for the Spaniards, though. Word has it Captain Hawkins is the only one plundering the silver Spain's taking from the Americas. I wouldn't mind a piece of that."

Anne smirked. "Is that the way of the world? The natives mine the silver, Spain steals it, and England takes it from them?"

"Perhaps so. Even the crusades were more about conquering people and pillaging their lands than it was about freeing the Holy Land."

"Hmm. My father had a silver urn handed down through generations. He said our ancestors brought it back from Tunis during the crusades."

"It must be something—growing up under the roof of an earl."

"I suppose. We never wanted for anything." Anne ran the reins through her gloved hands. "But Father's death was a tragedy all the same."

"I'm sure it was."

"A year after I was born, King Henry appointed father principal secretary of state. After, Mother said she would conceive every time he came home from court. He was rarely around, but Mother always managed to be with child."

"So you have a large family?"

"Three brothers and four sisters, though two of the boys died in infancy. I'm the second sister. Elizabeth, the eldest, wed Thomas Radcliffe." Anne looked at Calum to see if he recognized the name. "He's the third Earl of Sussex."

Calum let out a high-pitched whistle. "An earl for yer sister and a baron for you, aye?"

The same old musket hole stretched Anne's heart again. "Elizabeth actually had the pleasure of being courted."

"And why no' you? Were ye no' presented at court?"

"Alas, no. Father passed before I came of age and then I was needed in Southampton. Aside from Elizabeth, I am the eldest living child. My brother, Henry, was sent to my uncle for his fostering and I remained behind to ensure the estate prospered."

"Was that the same uncle who arranged yer marriage?"

A lump stuck in her throat. "Yes." Anne tapped her heel against the pony, urging the mare into a canter. With the wind in her face she let herself laugh. For the first time in months, she felt free. She didn't want to think about the future and she didn't want to think about pirates or barons or a sister who had married a fetching young earl.

Calum cantered up beside her. "Ye handle your mount well."

"Did you think I would not?"

"Nay. Being born on the mainland, ye would have had a need to ride." He pointed. "Bran's up ahead. There's a clearing that looks over an inland loch."

"I'll race you." Anne grasped her riding crop and slapped it against the mare's hindquarters. She laughed as her mount lurched forward, giving her a head start. Calum dashed up beside her on his bay stallion, but slowed his pace to match hers. They pulled the ponies to a stop. "You let me win."

Calum ran his hand along the coarse neck of his Highland steed. "Did I?"

She now understood why Bran had ridden ahead. He'd spread a blanket over the grass and in the center sat a lovely basket, a flagon and three brass goblets. Beyond it, the slope opened to a pool of water, edged by ferns and willow trees.

Calum jumped down from his mount and raised his arms up to Anne. "May I help ye dismount?"

His eyes sparkled like blue crystals in the sunlight. Her tongue flicked out and tapped her teeth. With a stutter of her heart, she reached out and placed her hands on his shoulders.

Calum's fingers clamped around her waist and he drew her to him. Anne gasped when her breasts pressed against his hard chest. He held her there for a moment while he took in a deep breath, then slid her down his body until Anne's feet touched ground.

She slipped her hands to his upper arms, as firm as granite under her grasp. Wanting to touch more of him, she squeezed his muscles tighter.

Calum's hands tightened around her waist.

She glanced at the blanket and food awaiting them. "If I didn't know better, I would guess you sent young Bran ahead so the luncheon would be ready when we arrived."

"Aye, of course he did milady," Bran said before Calum could defend himself.

Calum released her and stepped back. "It made sense to me to have the picnic all ready when ye got here—and who better to prepare it than the chaperone?"

Rather than take issue with his specious reasoning, Anne sat on the blanket. It would have been inconvenient for Calum to ask someone appropriate, such as Friar Pat, to escort them. The friar wouldn't bend to Calum's whims. But Bran, on the other hand, would do anything to find favor with his laird.

"How old were you when you came to Raasay?" Anne asked.

Calum reclined on his elbow while Bran found a seat on a nearby rock. "One and twenty."

"What was it like? Did you strut onto the beach, stick your pennant into the ground, and tell the clan you were their chieftain?"

"Something like that, but I had an entourage from Lewis. Me da and me older brother were with me."

"Did the people accept you or did you have to earn their trust?"

"Och, I had to earn it right enough." Calum uncorked the flagon and poured a goblet of for Anne and then one for Bran and another for himself. "But me da's gift of the *Sea Dragon* softened them a bit. Once we started rebuilding the keep, everyone came 'round."

Anne pulled the cloth off the basket, reached in for a parcel and unwrapped it. Smoked herring—a staple for the MacLeod's. She broke the bread and they ate.

As daintily as possible, she swirled the herring in her mouth and muted the fishy taste with a bite of bread. Anne fidgeted as

Calum's gaze never strayed from her face. She needed a diversion from the yearning his attentions stirred.

Looking up at the sky, she searched for birds and heard the screech before she spotted its source. A magnificent golden eagle soared over the rocky terrain. "Look—there's an eagle."

Calum sat up and followed her line of sight. "I kent we'd see them." He flicked his wrist at Bran. "Go follow it lad, and see if ye can find its nest."

Bran's face fell. "But I haven't finished me luncheon."

"Ye can take it along."

Bran groused under his breath as he shoved a handful of herring in his mouth and washed it down with a hearty gulp of ale. Then he headed off.

"There's a good lad," Calum called after him.

Anne tapped a finger to her lips. "You drive the boy awfully hard."

"Aye? With his da gone, someone has to ensure he grows up to be a MacLeod. No milk-livered men will last in *this* clan."

Anne eyed his firm jawline and trailed her gaze down Calum's sturdy neck. She had little doubt his words rang true. Raasay was no place for the faint of heart.

He inched toward her and ran a finger over the back of her hand. Anne's skin tingled. How could the hands of such a vigorous man be so gentle? She'd watched him wield his claymore with forceful power, and no man on the island could best him, yet with her he could be so tender. She closed her eyes, giving in to the thrill of his touch. How she wished she'd never attended the queen's coronation.

"How did yer uncle become mixed up with the likes of Wharton?" Calum asked, as if he'd heard her thoughts.

Anne's eyes flew open. "I don't pretend to know what goes on between the dealings of men, but they're both members of the House of Lords. I imagine they met there."

Calum straightened the blanket, and gazed to the dark blue loch that pooled at the bottom of the hill.

Anne leaned into him. "I thought Uncle had forgotten about me—at least I hoped he had. I assumed myself too valuable to the estate. And Mother needed me. I-I could have died when I was called to the parlor and he presented me with the decree."

"Ye weren't even consulted?"

"No. Upon my father's death, the king granted my uncle full power over me—all the children. The same plight could befall my younger sisters."

"But couldna ye say no?"

"And suffer the wrath of my queen…Put in jeopardy my family's name?"

His finger resumed its light caressing. "'Tis an unsettled world in which we live."

Anne bent forward and pressed the heel of her free hand against her forehead. "Yes, and it seems a mere maid is of no significance in it."

Calum sat up and cupped her face in his hands. "Ye cannot say that. Ye are no *mere* lass. Ye are tender hearted—Look how ye've helped with the keep and the children. You're the most beautiful and caring woman I have ever laid eyes upon."

His gaze bore through to her soul, the connection so intense, a yearning swelled from her breasts to her core. In a blink, Calum's eyes lowered to her lips.

Anne's breath quickened. Oh how deeply she wished to feel his mouth over hers. "I cannot sleep at night, for the memory of your lips upon mine is burned into my heart."

Calum brushed his lips across hers. Anne moaned as his tongue entered her mouth. Tasting spicy male, her heart raced. She laced her fingers through his silken hair, and Calum leaned into her. Heart thundering in her ears, Anne pushed into his kisses with unbridled passion. This could be the only chance she would ever have to feel the caress of a young, virile man, to be held by conditioned arms that could fight for her, protect her.

With his hand supporting her back, he laid her down. "Nor can I sleep for the memory of ye, milady."

Anne relaxed into the blanket. Calum's feathery kisses cascaded down the length of her neck. Then lower. Anne arched her back. He parted her cloak and swirled his tongue over the flesh above her bodice. Her breathing ragged, her heart racing, all that existed was Calum's seducing lips. Her breasts filled with longing, then his finger dipped below her bodice and stroked a taut nipple. She wanted to cry out with the tingling that rippled across her skin.

"No, Calum." Somehow she forced an ill-timed, throaty whisper.

An unwanted tickle in the back of her mind chimed a warning. Kissing, yes, but she should not allow *this*. She took in a deep breath and pressed against his chest. "We cannot."

Calum pulled away, his brow furrowed and his eyes dark and drawn as if she'd plunged her father's dagger into his heart. "But why? I ken ye like it by the way ye respond."

She sat up and scooted away. "'Tis not a question of how my body responds." If only he would understand. "I want to kiss you and lock away the memory in my heart for all the years I'll be cloistered with a man old enough to be my grandfather."

He fingered her veil. "I promise I will no' take your innocence, but let me show you love."

Anne stared into his eyes. The honesty there assured her his words were true. She wanted this—wanted him more than she'd ever wanted anything in her life. She let him pull her into his embrace and met his lips while the raging storm in her loins coiled with a fire so intense, she feared restlessness had taken up permanent residence.

Bran crashed through the woods and skidded onto the blanket. "I found the nest—but we'll have a difficult time reaching it. I think we need wings."

Calum quickly pulled away, and Anne brushed her fingers across her mouth looking anywhere but at their chaperone. The memory of Calum's lips singed her flesh as if they were still upon her. She closed her eyes and wished they did not have to stop. Whatever it was that continually sparked between them stirred a desire neither could resist. But Calum had vowed not to take her innocence, and she fully trusted the laird to honor his word.

***

Calum never should have kissed her breasts. Every time they were alone, he lost control. If Bran had not arrived when he did, Calum would have had Anne's skirts up around her waist. His wayward urgings be damned. How often did he need to remind himself she was never meant to be his?

"Bran—Help Lady Anne mount her pony."

Both the lad and Anne gaped at him, but Calum turned his attention to adjusting his stallion's girth. "Me saddle was slipping a bit." It was a fib, but a necessary one to regain his composure.

Calum couldn't bring himself to place his hands on the lady's waist just now. Images of her stuttered breathing and flushed skin beneath his lips were too vivid and raw. His lips still burned with the sensation of her silken skin, ripe and yielding to his kisses.

He watched Bran try to lift her by the waist. Though a strapping lad, he had nowhere near enough strength, and Anne caught herself on his shoulders before they both sprawled over backwards. Calum resisted his urge to dash to her side and sweep her into his arms. Red as a cherry, Bran brushed himself off. He resorted to cupping his hands while he bent down to give her a leg up—like he should have done in the first place.

Once in the saddle, Anne shot Calum a look that cut his heartstrings. She snapped her head forward and whipped her cloak over her shoulder. Calum clamped his fist around his reins and held his pony back. "Lead on, Bran." He'd bring up the rear for a time until his blood cooled.

With the wind at his face, it wasn't long before the lump in his stomach eased. He hoped they would find this fledgling. It would provide amusement for Lady Anne, and with so many birds nesting on the island, using raptors to hunt would offer yet another source of food for his clan.

Bran trotted his horse faster and pointed to a rocky crag. "Up there."

The rock was high and jagged. Calum could see the white excrement staining the cliff, a telltale sign of a nesting bird. He rode in beside Bran and studied the cliff. "If we can climb to that ledge, ye might be able to reach it if ye stand on me shoulders."

Anne let out a soft whistle. "It looks rather dangerous to me."

"Bran and I can do it, but ye'll need to stay with the ponies."

"What if you fall?"

Calum couldn't resist a wink. "Well now, I'll no longer have cause to be dragging meself through a bog of guilt every time me wayward eyes glance yer way."

Bran gave him a crooked smile. Anne looked at her hands. He didn't think she'd come up with a quick rebuke—but she did. "I'll not have you risk your neck for me or for a fledgling."

"Very well, I'll risk my neck for *me* then." Calum hopped off his mount and took a step to help Anne, but she slid off her mare on her own. He hobbled the ponies and started up toward crag. "Come, Bran."

With Calum's first step, rocks crumbled beneath his foot. He stood back and examined his intended path. "Mayhap if we circle around the side, we'll find better footing."

They hiked over to the spot Calum had seen. Unfortunately, the ancient rock crumbled there too. He glanced down the hill toward Anne. She shaded her eyes with her hand and watched them.

Calum ground his back molars. He was going to climb this rock if it took the rest of the afternoon.

Once they got started, Calum found footholds with relative ease but they ran into an impasse once they climbed to the ledge. The lip jutted out, feet from his grasp. Calum drummed his fingers as he teetered on a boulder. He reached for his dirk. "The rock's soft enough, I can chip out a few notches for me feet. I'll climb the wall and hoist meself up on the ledge, then I'll hang over and pull ye up."

"Are ye sure, Calum?" Bran looked up at him from below, his face smudged with dirt. "Ye could fall."

Calum palmed his dirk. "Yer like a fat, lazy MacKenzie with yer bellyaching. Och, ye climb the rigging up to the crow's nest. 'Tis no' much different to this bit 'o rock."

"Beg yer pardon. The stone just doesna seem as forgiving as a netted rope."

Calum slammed the dirk into the stone. "Silence yer tongue. I'll catch that fledgling if I have to do it alone."

"Given all this effort, I hope the wee bird hasn't flown the nest."

Calum shot the boy a glare. With the little naysayer below and the sharp-tongued lassie watching, he must find a way up to that ledge, no question.

Chapter Eleven

When Calum jumped for the ledge and missed, Anne squeezed her arms tight against her body. Far above his head, there was no chance they'd reach it. She wished she'd never mentioned falconry. It took months to train a fledgling. What would happen to the bird once she left? Would Calum assign someone to care for it? Perhaps—yes, if she asked and *if* he was serious about hunting with raptors.

Anne looked at the sky. Teaming with birds, falconry would be another way the clan could help stave off hunger.

Calum had left his claymore sheathed to his saddle, but he pulled out his dirk and started chipping at the rock. Was he actually going to attempt to mount the ledge? Anne paced, wishing the men would just come down and forget this whole thing.

An eternity passed while Calum chipped and Bran clung to the rock below him. Finally, Calum put away his dirk and motioned to the boy. Anne held her breath. Calum looked like a spider climbing up a vertical wall. He launched himself onto the ledge and held on with his arms, his legs dangling over the side. Her feet tingled as if she were hanging in the sky along with Calum.

He swung his leg over the edge and pulled himself up. Anne clapped her hand over her mouth. The man must be part squirrel.

He motioned to Bran. Oh no, he couldn't expect the boy to do the same. But Calum lay on his stomach and reached his arms over the side. Bran balanced on a rock and jumped up, grasping Calum's hands.

Bran swung there for a moment, and Calum used brute strength to pull the lad over the ledge. Anne held her hands against her chest and exhaled. They were safe. She had no idea how they'd get down, but at the moment, both appeared unscathed.

An eagle screeched overhead. Calum knelt and Bran climbed on his shoulders. They teetered a bit while Calum stood. The eagle swooped at Bran's head. He swatted it away and wobbled. Anne drew in a gasp, but Bran reached out his hands and steadied himself against the rock wall. Calum eased closer to the cliff. Reaching up, Bran seemed to catch something. He drew his hands back to his chest. Did he have a fledgling? The eagle dove, but Bran slid his legs down and sat between Calum's shoulders. He waved at her. He *did* have one.

Anne glanced at his pony. Drat. Bran had left the cage behind. She dashed over and untied it from his saddle. She could climb up and meet them half way. She only hoped Bran wouldn't crush the bird before she reached them.

Anne held up the cage so they could see it. Calum hollered something, but she couldn't discern it. No matter, he'd tell her just as soon as she could reach them. She made her way around to the place where Calum had started to climb and stepped up. Steadying herself on a rock, she pulled up her heavy skirts. Women's clothing could be ridiculously cumbersome. But, the men's climb had looked as if it had been easy until they reached the ledge.

Anne held up the cage while she slid her doeskin boots over the big rocks. Unaccustomed to climbing, her legs burned. The weight of her riding skirts made the ascent all the more difficult. But she could see them now. Looking up the hill, straining to see Calum, she took a step. The stone beneath her foot crumbled. She flung out her foot to find traction. It dropped into a hole and twisted. Anne fell to her knees. The rubble below her gave way. Out of control, she tumbled down the crag with a landslide of rock and dirt in her wake.

***

When the rubble gave way and sent Anne careening down the hill, Calum forgot the bird and barreled after her. He feared the worst when she lay in a heap against a huge boulder. His heart flew to his throat, but then she moved. Anne had her back to him when she first tried to stand. She wobbled and dropped back down. His heart beat faster. Just as he reached her, she looked up, blood streaming down her face.

His gut seized. "Lord in heaven, you're bleeding."

She shaded her eyes then studied the blood on her hand. "'Tis my ankle that hurts. It twisted a bit."

"Just yer ankle?" He tore a makeshift bandage from the hem of his shirt and held it to her head. "Ye've had a nasty blow." He bent down and inspected the gash, just under her hairline.

"I dropped the cage. I hope I didn't break it."

Calum held the cloth to her head. "Ye cannot be serious. Ye've just tumbled down a rocky crag and you're worried about a wee cage?"

Bran skidded to a halt behind him. "Lady Anne, are ye all right?" Bran took one look at her bloody face. "Och, you're bleedin' like a stuck pig."

She pushed Calum's hand away. "'Tis only a scratch. How about my fledgling? Did the poor thing make it down the hill?"

Calum reapplied the bandage, slipping his arm around her back to give her support. "Hold still. That fly-bitten bird is the least of our concern."

Anne persisted. "Bran?"

The lad stepped forward and revealed the eagle cradled in his hands. "'Tis still a chick—no' quite ready to fledge."

Anne's face lit up with an enormous smile. "Oh, look at that sweet little thing. He's beautiful. Thank you, Bran. Thank you both."

It was as if the bird was all that mattered to her. She rested against Calum's arm and closed her eyes. "I'm afraid I need some help getting back to the ponies. My ankle's awfully sore."

Calum raised the hem of her dress and revealed the swelling. She wouldn't be walking anywhere. "Dunna ye worry, milady. We'll have Friar Pat to tend ye." In one motion, he stood with Anne cradled tight in his arms. "Bran, put the bird in the cage. We've got to take Lady Anne back to Brochel quickly."

He hated to see her bleeding. This was his fault. He should have brought Mara so Anne wouldn't have had to stand alone while he and Bran climbed the crag. How could he have bounded up there just to impress her?

With one arm, he cradled Anne against his chest, led the horse to a boulder and mounted. Her tiny frame felt so small, so vulnerable. "Lead the mare," he called over his shoulder.

Anne's eyes opened and closed as he rode, as if she were having trouble staying awake.

He gave her a squeeze with his fingers. "Are ye all right? Am I holding ye too tight?"

She turned her head toward him and closed her eyes again, mumbling something he couldn't understand.

He rode hard and fast, supporting her so she would not jostle overmuch. "We're nearly there. 'Twill be all right."

His gut twisted in knots, Calum cantered the pony through the bailey and headed straight for the great hall. The arm supporting Anne burned, but he tightened his grip and held her steady while he kicked free of his stirrups and slid off. In the blink of an eye, he was surrounded by worried faces. He pushed his way into the hall. "Someone call the friar. Mara! I need ye now!"

He cradled Anne against his chest and bounded up the steps.

"Calum?" Anne's sweet voice asked.

"We're nearly there, love." Did he just say "love"? He hoped she hadn't noticed. His emotions had run on the edge of raw for too long. He repeated "milady" in his head until he reached the second landing.

Her fingers brushed against his chest. "Why are you so beautiful?"

Now he knew the knock to her head had made her delusional. Him? Beautiful? He'd been called a lot of things, but never beautiful. But Calum's heart fluttered when he glanced at her eyes. They were half cast, her lips parted, as if she were dreaming. Even with blood caked in her hair, she looked an angel.

He pushed through the door and propped her against the pillows on the bed. Heaving a sigh, he pressed his lips to her forehead. "How are ye feeling, milady?"

"Better. My head's throbbing a bit."

"And your ankle?"

"I think it will be fine."

She tried to lean forward to look at it, but Calum placed his hand on her shoulder and encouraged her to lie back. "Rest."

Friar Pat barreled through the door with Mara right behind. She carried a basket full of bandages and bottles of herbs.

The friar rushed to Anne's bedside, wheezing from exertion. "What happened?"

"She had a nasty fall." Pat shot him an accusing look and Calum spread his palms. "I told her to stay by the ponies."

"I wanted to help. 'Twas very clumsy of me," Anne said, again trying to sit up. "I'm so sorry to cause such a stir."

The friar patted her shoulder. "There, there, lass. Ye mustn't exert yerself until I've had a chance to look at ye." He turned to Calum. "Ye best take yer leave while we see to the baroness."

Calum moved to the end of the bed. He wasn't about to depart the chamber until he knew Anne would be well.

Friar Pat and Mara paid him no notice. The holy man leaned over and inspected the gash on her head. "And how are ye feeling now, milady?"

"My head hurts, but otherwise, I think I'm well."

He stretched the skin of her temple with his fingers. "It doesna look too bad."

"Her ankle is swollen too," Calum said, grasping the footboard and leaning forward.

The friar's brows formed a straight line across his forehead. His gaze darted toward Calum with a silent admonishment. Calum pursed his lips and folded his arms. If he didn't keep his mouth shut, Pat would usher him out and lock the door.

"We'll apply a honey poultice to keep the head wound from turning putrid, and then I'll have a look at yer ankle." The friar patted her hand and smiled. "How does that sound?"

"Just give me a moment to rest, and I'll be up and around."

Calum ran his fingers through his hair. "Ye were unconscious. Ye cannot just spring up out of bed and traipse around the keep as if nothing happened."

Anne pushed herself forward, a flush rising to her face. "Pardon me, but I know my own body." She swung her legs over the side of the bed and swooned.

Mara caught her before she fell forward and helped her back upon the bed.

The friar pointed at the door. "Calum MacLeod, ye need to let us tend to the lady in peace. Go stable yer pony and I'll send word as soon as she's ready to see you."

He headed for the door, but Anne's voice stopped him. "I want to see the eagle."

He glanced over his shoulder. She looked so frail resting atop the huge bed. His heart twisted into a knot. This was his fault. If only he could hold her in his arms while the friar tended to her. He could protect her, mayhap even take some of the pain away. "I'll bring him shortly, milady."

***

Anne choked back the pain as Friar Pat gently flexed her ankle and determined nothing was broken. She examined it over her skirts. The swelling had already gone down some and aside from a little bruising, it didn't look too bad. After applying a honey poultice to her head and rubbing a soothing salve into her ankle, the friar offered Anne a warm cup of willow bark tea. "This will help the pain. I'll have Mara bring up a draught to help ye sleep, but ye must rest for three days."

She cupped the tea in her hands. "Three days? That will drive me mad. I should be fine by the morrow."

"We cannot take any chances with yer health, milady. Do as I say and ye'll be walking on your ankle pain free in no time."

Anne bit down upon her objection. There was no use arguing, but she would give it a fair test once she was alone. *Stay in bed for three days? He must be daft.*

As Mara and the friar took their leave, Calum tapped on the door and cracked it open. "I have the fledgling, milady."

Thank heavens he'd returned so quickly. Calum's brows pinched together and he held up the eagle. Sitting up, the bedclothes neatly tucked around her waist, Anne beckoned him forward. "Thank you, thank you. Bring him here, please."

Calum grinned like a boy on Christmas morn. The downy eagle chirped and stretched its wings. Anne held out her arms. "Aw, what a sweet little biscuit."

Calum set the cage beside her and dragged a chair over to the bed. "I think he's hungry."

"We must feed him. Have the cook grind up some meat and mix it with a bit of water." Anne made kissing sounds. "Hello, little darling. We're going to turn you into a fierce hunter." He chirped back at her as if he liked the idea. Anne opened the cage and stroked his feathers.

"What should we call him?" Calum asked.

"It could be a girl."

"Can ye tell?"

Anne lifted one of its little legs. "Not yet." She smiled at Calum. "How about Swan, since we met on the *Flying Swan?*"

"I wouldn't think ye'd want to be reminded of that."

"Why not?" She studied his face and smiled at his worried frown. The feared laird was not so fierce now she'd come to know him. The thought that their time together would not last tugged on her heart. She allowed her eyes drift down with a sigh.

Calum sprang to his feet. "Are ye in pain?"

Anne forced a smile. "No. I'm sorry. I was just thinking how difficult it will be when it comes time for me to leave." She shook her head. "Isn't that daft? Here I'm your prisoner and I am ever so enjoying learning about life in the far reaches of Scotland. You must think me a fool."

Calum resumed his seat and grasped her hand. "Nay, milady. It has been very pleasant to have ye here. Everyone thinks so."

"Aside from Norman."

"Aye, well perhaps no' me brother, but he'll come around."

"Probably not before I leave." Anne returned her attention to the fledgling and reached her hand into the cage. "Come here, darling. You'll feel safer if you nestle with me." She cupped the baby raptor to her bosom and Calum watched her with a faraway glint to his eye. "Would you be able to bring his food, please? I'd like to give it to him and start the bond."

In no time, Calum returned with the soupy meat mixture, and Anne ladled it into Swan's mouth with her fingernail.

"'Tis a bit tedious."

"Yes, but I've nothing better to do." She cradled the bird like a babe. "And he needs a gentle hand to care for him." When she stopped feeding the bird, Swan gave her a peck on the wrist. Anne jerked her hand away. "He's nearly ready to eat on his own this one—almost drew blood."

"Perhaps ye should wear falconing gloves." Calum leaned in and examined her hand. He rubbed the spot where Swan had nipped her then held it to his lips. "I never want to see ye hurt again, milady."

Their stares connected and held. He cared. The swelling in Anne's heart could not possibly be love. But this man had come to mean so much to her. How had she let that happen? She ached to bring Calum's head to her breast and hold it there too. And though Swan settled into the crook of her arm and slept, she wanted more from Calum. Riding back to Brochel, he'd held her in his arms and she never had really lost consciousness. It felt heavenly to be surrounded by his powerful frame. She'd closed her eyes and wished she could stay there forever.

Anne clamped her fists to her head when the hole in her heart jerked her back to her plight. The daughter of the Earl of Southampton do as she pleased? Never. Her life had never been hers and never would be.

Mara entered the chamber with a goblet. "I have the draught the friar prepared."

"Must I drink it?"

Calum reached out and grasped her hand. "It will help ye sleep."

Anne closed her eyes—her life would be hers in this moment. "Set it beside the bed. I shall take it when I'm ready to sleep."

Mara pursed her lips, but did as Anne asked.

"Thank you." It was a small win, but one she needed.

Calum stayed beside her bed. In the chamber where no one watched, he was tender and gentle. Anne saw none of the hardened pirate who sparred with his men every morning and plundered ships to bring back food for his people. Next to her was a strong man with crystal blue eyes that looked at her as if she were the most beautiful woman on earth. She would take this moment and lock it in her heart for all eternity.

Chapter Twelve

For a moment, Calum wondered if he'd gone to heaven during the night, but when he opened his eye, Anne was singing. He listened to her sweet, bell-like voice. She reached for a high note and hit it with such clarity, the back of his neck tingled.

Rolling to his side, he pulled a pillow over his head. Did she have to sing like an angel too? He knew he'd spent far too long beside her bed last night. Mother Mary, the reaction he'd had when she fell was not normal, no matter how he rationalized it. How had he allowed himself to become enraptured with the baroness? Lady Anne had bewitched him with her charm.

Calum dressed, berating himself for lusting after his prisoner. What kind of low beasty man did that make him?

He had to get away from the keep. It was time he paid a visit to *The Golden Sun*.

After Calum rowed out to the ship, Norman stood with his fists on his hips and watched him climb aboard. "Come to visit me in exile?"

"Come to see the progress ye've made on the rebuilding, little brother," Calum grumbled.

Norman swept his arm and gestured across the deck. "Behold. The damage from the cannon blasts has been fully repaired."

Calum walked over and stomped on the new decking. It held fast. "You're a good hand when yer sober."

"Aye? I've been thinking about that a bit."

"Oh?"

"The first few nights on the ship, I drank everything in sight. One morning Robert came aboard while I puked me guts over the rail."

"That's a common enough sight."

"It's no' the fact he saw that got me riled. It's what he mumbled under his breath." Norman's hands fell to his side. "He said every family's got to have a parasite—a failure."

Calum reached out his hand, but Norman batted it away. "No. I dunna need yer sympathy. Since that day, me lips haven't touched a dram of whisky and I'll be damned if they ever will again." Norman looked him in the eye. "I dunna like the man I become when I drink, and neither does anyone else."

Blinking, Calum forced back the sting rimming his eyes. He hadn't shed a tear since he was a babe and he wasn't about to now. "'Tis good to hear." Everywhere he looked, he saw signs of repairs. "And with what ye've achieved, I imagine ye'll make a fine sea captain."

Norman nodded toward the captain's cabin. "Come, I want to show ye something."

Calum stepped inside and noted the MacLeod tartan covering the bed—a fine improvement over the English quilt. A drawing on the table caught his eye. He lifted it and studied the artwork. "This is remarkable." Norman had sketched the ship with its new additions.

"Do ye like the lettering for *The Golden Sun*?"

"Aye. I think ye missed yer calling. Ye should have been an artist."

"Baa. But Robert says 'tis easier to work with me prints than with the original drawings."

"I'll have to remember that."

"So what news have you?"

Calum set the drawing on the table. "We've finished the work on the chamber beside mine."

Norman ran his finger along his plaid. "I suppose ye had to fashion a place to sleep—so the lady's still here?"

"Aye."

"The sooner we're rid of her, the better."

The hackles on the back of Calum's neck pricked. "Ye ken, she could have acted like a spoiled heiress and hidden in me chamber, but no, she's worked with Mara and the children. The keep has never looked so fine with everything in its place. She's organized the women too, and there's no more bellyaching."

"Listen to yerself speak. Ye defend her like she's yer missus." Norman threw his hands up. "She embodies our vilest enemy."

Calum clenched his fist and pulled it back. Norman flinched. Hell. He didn't want to hit him, but Norman's words struck a chord. Worse, Calum knew he was right. He'd ask Lady Anne to marry him on the morrow if she weren't already wed. Calum dropped his hand and stretched his fingers. "I worry about what this ransom business will bring on our heads. But John will return and the lady will be gone soon enough."

"That will be a blessing."

Calum raised his chin. "Until then, I expect ye to treat her with respect—if and when ye see her."

Norman gave an exaggerated bow. "Aye, yer lairdship."

***

John Urquhart sat in the shadows of the Sheep Heid Inn and nursed a tankard of ale. His uncle, Sir Tomas, had recommended Malcolm Elliot, but John felt uneasy trusting a Lowlander to deliver the missive. The man had never looked at him straight in the eye. John hated trusting such a man.

If he'd had it his way, John would have delivered the missive himself. He could have played the part of an Englishman, and Calum knew it. John loved Calum like a brother, but the laird's only weakness was his love for his people and reluctance to risk their lives.

Calum didn't want John riding into England because of the danger. Now he'd been waiting for Elliot's return for a week. If he didn't come soon, the galley John had waiting in the Firth of Forth would set sail for Inverness without him. Then he'd be in Edinburgh with no plan for a quick escape. That was every bit as dangerous as riding into Wharton's lair and playacting the part of a country messenger.

A buxom barmaid brushed up against him. "Ye've been holding up here for days. What do ye say ye take me up to yer room and I'll ease the tension under the laces of your trews?"

He nudged her away. "I've a bonny wife at home who keeps me fires warm. Run along, wench." John adjusted the damnable trews. He didn't dare wear his colors in Edinburgh, but he'd be mighty glad when he could throw off the itchy leather trousers he'd been wearing since he arrived.

The barmaid huffed away, clearing John's view of the door. He sat erect.

Elliot's dark eyes stared at him from across the room. Eye contact. John knew something was amiss. He reached under the table and slid the dirk from his belt.

John stood and headed toward the back door, but Elliot raced up and caught him by the arm. "Where are you going? I've a missive for you."

Elliot shoved the note into John's gut and took off at a run.

The door of the inn burst open and a heavyset man barreled through, aiming a musket at John's head. John dove under the table just as the slow match fired. Mayhem erupted. Tables toppled to the shouts and screams of the patrons. John drew his sword and fled toward the bar. The big man ran forward and slammed the gun barrel into the wood within inches of John's head.

He ducked aside and rolled up over the top of the bar.

"What have you done with my wife?"

Wharton.

John eyed the cowering bartender who inclined his head toward the back room. Wharton drew his sword. John dashed into the room, praying he'd find a door.

Two barmaids hovered in the corner, next to the servant's entrance. Shoving a table aside, John bolted for the rear door. His hand reached the knob when the table scraped the floor behind him. John swung back, his blade hissing through the air, but Wharton deflected the strike.

Wharton lunged. John pulled the latch, and the two careened out into the alley. The stench of rotten food and piss swamped John's senses. Falling, his back jarred against the cobblestones. Wharton's bulk crushed atop him.

"Where is she?" the baron growled.

John wrenched his arm free and slammed his dirk into Wharton's shoulder. The big man reeled back, squealing like a pig. Footsteps slapped the pavement. *Soldiers.* John slipped out from under Wharton and jumped the fence, landing on a stone terrace. He scanned for his options. Only one door—he pushed inside and ran across someone's kitchen, then the parlor. Servants squawked. John eyed the door opposite him. In three steps, he crashed through it and dashed onto the street.

A pony pulling a cart laden with barrels trotted past. John jumped onto it.

Over his shoulder, the driver shouted, "You can't do that. Get off, ye maggot."

John leapt over the barrels and pressed his dirk under the driver's chin. "Take me to the pier and I'll spare ye. And if you're fast about it I may even give ye some coin."

The driver bobbed his head. John spotted a blanket stuffed at the back of the seat and wrapped it over his shoulders and head.

He took a chance and peered down the street behind. Foot soldiers crisscrossed the lane, but they hadn't spotted him. Not yet.

***

During Anne's confinement, Calum had a mews built in the garden—an aviary of quiet solitude where Swan would feel safe. After three day's rest, her headache had eased. Anne's ankle was nearly healed and she could step without limping, thank heavens. If she showed any sign it still pained her, Friar Pat would have restricted her to quarters for yet another unbearable three days.

Since Bran had helped Calum find Swan, the lad would learn to train him and Bran met Anne beside the mews. Anne slid her hand into the falconry glove and reached for the leather jesses she'd secured around Swan's ankles. The bird latched his claws around her finger and she fed him a small piece of meat, humming her lullaby.

Wide-eyed, Bran watched the bird. "He likes it."

"Yes, but you must sing to him. Your song is your call." She ran her hand along Swan's back. "Do you know the Gaelic lullaby, *Sofi Linge Valdal?*"

"Aye, what Highlander doesna, but I'm surprised ye do."

"My family's falconer was Scottish born. 'Twas his falconry lullaby, and 'tis what I've been singing to Swan." Anne swallowed back her tears. She was already attached to the eagle, blast it all.

"Why so sad, milady?"

She gave the bird another morsel. "When I leave, you'll have to carry on with his training."

"Ye need to teach me."

"Yes." Anne's whisper was barely audible. If she had to pick anyone on the island to work with Swan, it would be Bran. He had a gentle and optimistic nature. "Come, let's see if he's ready to fly."

Bran sang Anne's lullaby with a clear tenor as they walked down to the beach. Anne's spirits soared. Bran would indeed make a good substitute. She fastened the leash to Swan's jesses. "Are you ready?"

Bran studied the bird. "I think ye should ask *him*...Do ye think he's ready?"

"We'll find out." One reason she wanted to train on the beach was the bird's lead wouldn't catch in anything if he failed to fly. Swan's wings had developed enough he could glide down from her arm, but she would never forgive herself if he got hurt during his first flying lesson.

She held up her arm and looked at Bran. The boy grimaced as if something terrible were about to happen. Anne laughed and tossed her hand to the wind. Swan flapped his wings and squawked like an adolescent boy, but the breeze caught his wings and he soared upward with Anne holding the ten foot lead.

"I cannot believe it." Bran ran beneath Swan's flapping wings and watched the bird with amazement.

Anne sang the lullaby then Swan resumed his perch on her forearm.

"How'd ye do that?"

"'Tis the song. Associate it with food and he'll come to it every time."

Anne let Swan fly a few more times and then cast her eyes to Bran. No matter how much she wanted the eagle to be hers, she knew it was best for the bird if she trained another to be his falconer.

"Swan comes to the song, to you, because he associates you with food, but once he can hunt his own prey, he'll come to you because you represent his home. You will be his lord, Bran, and he will feel safe with you."

Anne took off her glove and handed it to the boy. "You give it a try."

**

By the time a month passed, dark circles had taken up residence under Calum's eyes and Friar Pat kept trying to give him a tincture to "help with that digestive problem." The kindhearted holy man finally stopped needling when Calum told him the problem was a wee bit lower than his gut.

Lady Anne had become more irresistible by the day. The only thing keeping his temper in check was his daily sparring session with his guard. At least he could work off the tension he built during the night without drawing suspicion to his misplaced yearnings.

The rain stayed at bay for the Beltane Fire Festival and Calum's spirits soared. All candles and lamps in the castle had been snuffed and Calum would have the honor of lighting the bonfire of fertility.

On the beach, Calum supervised the men raising the maypole and the women adorned the wreath of flowers that encircled it. Of all the holidays, this was his favorite. The haddock had been running strong in the sound. They would feast on good fish, mussels and crab.

Mara looked up from her work at the wreath then scurried over to him. "The wood's dry, ready for the bonfire. The fish are cleaned and soaking in the hold, m'laird." She pointed to the net off the shore used to keep the seafood fresh.

Calum patted her shoulder. "Excellent. Ye have everything organized."

"Lady Anne has taught me well."

"Then it has been a blessing to have her with us."

"I miss John so terribly." Mara frowned. "But I dunna want her to leave us. She is such a fine lady and a pleasure to be around. I never thought an English woman could be as sweet as she."

"We will all miss her, I'm afraid."

Calum looked up the hill. With the day's work done, the clan men and women were clamoring down to the beach. Bran had hold of Lady Anne's hand, hurrying her along as if they were late for a wedding. Friar Pat scuttled down the hill after them with his robes flapping in the wind. Calum and Mara chuckled and moved to greet them.

Calum reached for Anne's hand. She blessed him with a brilliant smile. "Bran, 'tis a wonder the lady made it down the hill in one piece with ye dragging her. Did ye no' remember she's recovering from a twisted ankle?"

The boy gaped and looked at Anne. "Are ye all right milady? I didna mean to rush ye."

"I'm quite invigorated. This must be a special celebration indeed."

The friar waddled in beside them. "Aye. Beltane used to be a pagan tradition, but we Scottish Christians have embraced it as the celebration of rebirth." He clasped his hands together and looked toward the heavens. "Praise God, winter is behind us."

Calum gestured to the crowd gathering around the fire. "Come milady. I would be honored if ye would stand beside me as I light the fire to commence the festival."

"Aye, 'tis nearly dusk," Mara said.

***

Anne's insides fluttered when Calum strode across the stony beach to meet her. Dressed in his finest kilt and doublet, his powerful frame made all the lords at court pale in comparison. She closed her eyes and cemented the memory in her mind. She never wanted to forget her gallant captor or her time on Raasay.

Anne allowed Calum pull her toward the enormous pile of wood and sticks as the clan watched. He struck the flint to light the torch, but the wind from the sound snuffed it before the flame took hold. Anne cupped her hands around the ironwork. "Try again."

Calum struck again and the torch burned bright. He gave her a wink and held it high. "With this flame I light the Beltane fire. May God favor us and make our women and our crops fertile. With this flame we will relight the fires of Brochel!"

The crowd roared a raucous cheer. Calum circled the stack of wood, lighting the kindling around the bottom.

Bagpipes and fiddling filled the air, while children chased each other around the maypole. Calum placed his hand in the small of Anne's back. "We let the wee ones dance first. The real dancing starts after we sup."

She loved the way his eyes sparkled, reflecting firelight. "Oh? That sounds intriguing."

"It is." Calum spread his tartan over the smooth stones. "Will ye share me plaid?"

Warmed by the raging fire, Anne sat beside him. "Tell me more about Beltane. The friar said it has pagan roots."

"Aye. 'Twas the most important ritual to our ancestors. It honored the sun god, and if he was pleased there would be a bountiful harvest. When the fire burns down, unmarried couples seal a promise by jumping over the coals together." He looked away and fingered the fringe of his plaid.

"Pardon?"

"They say on Beltane all marital restraints were lifted and women could lay with whomever they wished for the night."

The flesh on Anne's entire body prickled with heat. Did she just hear him correctly? "I'll wager that caused a great many problems."

Calum picked up a smooth stone and rubbed his thumb across it. "I'm sure it did. 'Tis why it is only a legend." He looked at her with a crooked smile. "If me wife ever lay with anyone but me, I think I would kill her, and the rutting bastard too."

Anne cleared her throat. "Well, 'tis a good thing the Scots have done away with that practice."

Norman strolled over carrying three tankards of ale. "What do ye think of Beltane, Lady Anne?"

She accepted the tankard, but scooted a tad closer to Calum, eyeing Norman with uncertainty. "'Tis a merry festival indeed."

Norman looked at her for a moment, his expression puzzling, but then he bowed and sat on the opposite side of Calum. "I think it is time for me to take a wife."

Anne's attention piqued.

"Have ye someone in mind?" Calum asked.

"Nay. I would like leave to visit Ruairi on Lewis."

Calum narrowed his eyes. "Ye think you can behave yerself? I'll never live it down if ye sail over there and fall into yer cups."

Norman hung his head. "Ye ken. As I said before, sleeping on *The Golden Sun* has given me time to think." He held up his tankard. "From now on, ale will be the strongest spirit that passes me lips."

"Very well. After John returns, we will make arrangements."

Anne watched Calum swirl his fingertips over the rounded stones. They would see John any day now. She closed her eyes, but the bonfire still blazed behind her lids. She wanted to imagine what her new life would be like, but all she could see were the rugged lands of Raasay and the stone walls of Brochel Castle with its handsome laird presiding in the courtyard. The vibrant laird who had just told her on this single eve in ancient Scotland, the laws of matrimony could be cast aside. From the depths of her soul, Anne wished it could be so....but alas...

What would the baron do when he received word of Anne's ransom? Would he pay? Would he pursue Calum ruthlessly until he and his entire clan were wiped from the island? Would Lord Wharton accept her now she'd spent weeks among the "barbarians"?

Calum didn't give Anne much time to mull over her unanswered questions. He jumped up as the games began. "I must toss the caber."

"And what is that, do tell?" Anne asked, standing as well.

"'Tis a one-hundred-fifty pound log, or there abouts. The man who tosses it the farthest wins."

She chuckled. "You mean tosses it without squashing himself?"

"Aye, well there's that, too."

She clapped a hand to her chest. "Don't tell me men have been killed?"

"I've only seen it once, when I was a lad." He shook his head. "'Twas a very poor harvest that year."

Anne glanced at the friar who'd moved in beside her. "They take this festival seriously, yes?"

"Aye, milady, they do." He pulled her into the crowd. "Come stand here with me where ye'll be out of harm's way."

Anne thought Calum would birth a calf, he bellowed so loudly when he tossed the log. It looked to be as long as one of the rafters in the keep—as big around, too.

As he predicted, Calum won the caber toss and the stone throw. His team also won the tug-o-war, but he was bested by William in the test for the swiftest. William had long, slender legs, and ran like he was fleeing a mob of archers bent on skewering him.

"He's very fast," Anne said, applauding the victor.

"He's Calum's runner in battle. None faster than William," the friar agreed.

Anne gaped when the women stepped up and had a go with the bow and arrows. Though Calum won that contest, too, she had never seen women included in any sort of competitions. They were quite adept. *Must have had practice at some time.*

As the games ended, Mara stood on the driftwood and clanged the supper bell. The feast laid out rivaled some Anne had seen at court, at least for the sheer quantity of food.

"It all comes from the Sound of Raasay," Calum said, stepping behind her.

"I thought you told me your people were starving."

"We eat well in late spring when the fish are running. Winter's the worst—and pickled herring gets awfully dreary by February."

Anne reclined against a large log of driftwood and watched. People sat in groups, some large with children and grandparents, and others small. The beat of excitement touched everyone. The snow had gone, and the promise of warmer weather swirled on the breeze. With Calum stretched out beside her, she felt like she belonged. Of course, she'd had her home at Titchfield House, and belonged to the Wriothesley family by birth, but never had she experienced a bond as strong as the one that wrapped around her this night.

The pipers started again and she wanted to dance. Calum must have sensed her eagerness and reached for her hand. "Will ye dance the maypole with me?"

"Yes, my lord."

Calum flashed a toothy, wicked grin and led her toward the ring of dancers. He leaned in and whispered in her ear, "The pole signifies male forces and the wreath beneath is female. The men dance the reel after the women. When the music ends, they choose if they want to be caught—'tis the lassie's choice."

Anne hesitated. Would he tempt her? God, she hoped so. Anne shook her head, queen's knees, she must hope *not*. Since her injury, she had lasted this long fighting her urges to wrap her arms around his masculine shoulders and kiss him. She would turn to jelly if he kissed her again. She knew it, and what would old Lord Wharton think if he discovered she had lusted after her captor?

The high-stepping reel interrupted Anne's worries. She looked to the side and saw Mara sitting with Friar Pat. They both watched her. Anne gulped and studied the feet of the other dancers. She moved hers in kind, jumping in the air, pointing her toes and leaping sideways around the pole of masculinity.

Calum danced directly across the circle with the men. He focused on her, dancing with grace, unlike the bearish force he'd shown earlier in the games. His eyes did not stray from her. Anne's breathing quickened. His powerful legs expertly executed the steps, and Anne was glad her skirts covered her wayward feet. She merely had to keep up with the beat bellowed by the bagpipes. Calum turned his back to her and leapt high. His kilt flicked up. Anne blinked. She couldn't deny it, she'd seen the white alabaster of a rock-solid bum cheek. Her heart thundered in her ears. She could no longer hear the music.

In her mind only she and Calum existed, dancing together on the beach. His kilt flicked again, enticing her to see more of what lay beneath. His eyes seduced her, begging Anne to give in to her curiosity.

The pace changed and the woman next to her lightly tapped Anne's shoulder. "We dance to the right now."

Anne followed the crowd, the tune of the pipes resounding in her ears. The men leapt forward, mixing with the women. Calum's masculine scent—spicy, laced with sweat—electrified her and his hot breath caressed her neck. This was the most seductive dance in which she had ever partaken. When his hands grasped her waist, shivers coursed over her skin. "Ye can run from me now, lass."

Anne's head spun. Run? She didn't want to run, she wanted to turn and press her body against him. "I…"

She tried to pull away, but her heart would not allow it. With a snap of her head, she whipped around and faced him. With the most stirring grin she'd ever seen cross his face, Calum lifted her in his arms and twirled around the maypole. Together they spun in complete union. Anne threw her head back and closed her eyes. If only she could stay there in his arms the entire night. If she had not been wearing layers of heavy skirts, she would have wrapped her legs around him and cradled his head to her breast.

The music stopped. Calum's chest heaved as he squeezed her against his body, gazing into her eyes with a longing that made her feel as if she were the only woman on the beach. His eyes filled with hunger, suggesting he wanted to kiss her and more. Anne's breath stuttered, her body molded against his. His tongue shot out and wet his bottom lip. He slid her down his muscular chest. And then she felt it. Her mons slowly slid over his rigid manhood. A hot gush of longing coiled tight between her hips.

Calum lowered his head as if he would kiss her. But he leaned down to her ear, his breath fluttering through her hair. "Mayhap we should make our way back to the plaid."

Anne didn't trust herself to speak. She froze when her bottom brushed against his manhood. He let out an audible groan. The crowd applauded as Calum looped his arm through Anne's elbow and led her to his blanket.

Fanning her face, Anne willed her heart to resume a more sedate cadence. "That was far more vigorous than a volta."

"Aye, milady. I think we'd best remain spectators for the duration of the night."

A pang of disappointment needled at her, but she knew Calum was right. Neither one of them could control their urges.

Norman filled their tankards with ale. Anne overheard him whisper in Calum's ear, "'Tis a good thing John will be here soon. Her ladyship has ye enchanted."

Anne pretended not to hear and reached for her cup. Perhaps a few tots of ale would do them both good. She practically guzzled the potent liquid and reached for the pitcher. She offered some to Calum and he held up his tankard. "There's a good lass, I mean lady."

He smelled delicious as she leaned over him and poured. "I think a bit of ale will be good for the both of us this night."

His eyes trailed down the length of her body. He raised the tankard to his lips and drank. Wiping his mouth with the back of his sleeve, he watched the dancers. Anne watched him. He seemed much more subdued than before. Had she caused him to lose his enthusiasm? She wanted him to have a good time—it was his festival. She thought to ask Bran to escort her back to the castle, but Calum's hand inched across the tartan. His rough fingers brushed hers.

Anne glanced at him, but he kept his eyes averted. He clasped his fingers over hers and leaned toward her. "I wish we lived in another time."

"As do I." She lowered her voice. "Would you like me to retire so you can dance with the others?"

Pain filled his eyes. "I want ye to stay put. I'll escort ye to your chamber when 'tis time."

Smiling, Anne spread her skirts over her legs and nestled against his warm chest. He wanted her beside him. There was no place on earth she'd rather be.

Chapter Thirteen

The bonfire ebbed to coals, sending columns of sparks into the sky. The night smelled of wood smoke and sea air. Calum slipped his arm around Anne's shoulders and rubbed. "Ye are shivering."

"A bit, but you radiate enough heat for us both." She lowered her head and nestled into him.

He wanted to draw her onto his lap, but the accusing looks coming from Friar Pat across the fire told him his actions had already stretched beyond appropriate. Calum strengthened his grip upon her shoulders. He could sit there with Anne in his arms until morning.

They watched unmarried couples jump across the pit with laughs and giggles. He ached to take Anne's hand and pledge his adoration by jumping across the coals with her. But it couldn't be. Calum could not allow himself to forget she was married. *Married but still innocent.* The throbbing under his kilt continuously reminded him of that fact. No amount of ale could drown the longing.

Anne had made it worse—unintentionally, of course. She looked a goddess, dancing the reel with her long skirts swishing, her cheeks rosy. He'd lost control when he'd placed his hands on her waist and heard her gasp. If they had been alone, he would have thrown her down right there and shown her the extent of his affection. But like a responsible laird, he forced himself to lead her back to his plaid, rather than into the shadows where he could have had his way. Damned be to hell his responsibility. This was Beltane—the one night when he might cast aside caution and surrender to his passion.

Calum inclined his head toward Anne. Like the other clanswomen, she wore her tresses loose for the gathering and the vigor of the dancing had tousled it, giving her a raw appeal that enticed his deepest urges. A wisp of silken hair with the honeysuckle scent tickled his cheek. Why must every fiber of her being entice him? Should he forget about the future and enjoy the moments he had until he turned her over to Wharton? His gut clenched. He would never be able to forget she belonged to the devil.

Anne glanced at him and tensed beneath his grasp. "Is something amiss?"

"Nay. Just thinking of the future."

Anne bit her bottom lip and shuttered her eyes. She knew what he meant.

Across the coals, Mara squealed. Dread crept up Calum's neck. He slid his hand from Anne's shoulders and followed Mara's line of sight. A skiff glided up onto the beach.

Mara dashed toward it. "John. Praise the heavens, you're home!"

Calum loved John as a brother, but his arrival cast a black shadow across the celebration.

John splashed onto the shore and hefted Mara into his arms. She wrapped her legs around him and they twirled across the beach. Calum wanted to hit something. Hard. God on the cross, how he wished Anne would wrap her legs around him like that—but now his days with her would be few.

Pushing his sudden gloom aside, Calum rose to greet his cousin. Standing on his plaid, he waited for John to finish kissing his wife. He glanced at Anne who watched, open mouthed, while John put on a display of mad passion, his lips locked with Mara's, their bodies clinging together. It must have been the longest kiss in the history of Scotland when John finally came up for air.

He set Mara down and held his hand out to Calum. "'Tis good to be home."

"Welcome John, ye've been sorely missed."

The friar waddled up and slammed John's shoulder with a hearty whack. "'Tis good luck to arrive on Beltane." He winked at Mara. "I'll bet God will bless ye with a bairn this very night."

Mara turned a brilliant shade of scarlet.

Calum stepped up to John's ear. "Before ye go, did ye get a response?"

"Aye. Do ye want it now?"

Calum pulled him aside. "Give me the short version."

"The bastard nearly shot me dead in Edinburgh—betrayed by the runner I was." John pulled Wharton's missive from his sporran. "But this says he agrees to terms."

Calum slipped the note away and clapped John's shoulder. "We'll talk more in the morning. Go enjoy yerself."

John grinned and cast his eyes toward his wife. "That I will, m'laird."

Anne moved in beside Calum and touched him on the shoulder. "They look so happy."

He tapped a stone with the toe of his boot. "They do."

"Wouldn't it be divine if all marriages could be carved of such love?"

Calum watched John lead Mara up the hill—up to their marriage bed. A burning void swelled across his chest. He'd most likely never marry, never have a loving woman to hold in the night. He turned to Anne and tried to smile. "Aye, a marriage without love is a woeful tragedy, but we live in a time when it happens all too often."

He offered his elbow. "Would ye like to retire, milady?"

They didn't speak as Calum walked with Anne up the hill and into the keep. Her nearness, her hand upon his arm, tore his insides to shreds. John had returned and she must soon leave.

Entering the keep, the bell-like timbre of Anne's voice broke the silence. "Thank you for allowing me to celebrate the festival with the clan."

"Do they have a May Day festival in Southampton?"

"Nothing as invigorating as Beltane. My family does not encourage such—ah—displays of exuberance."

Calum ran his fingers along the rough stone walls. "The ever so proper English."

"I'm afraid so."

Calum wondered how the English ever actually got married with their code of proper conduct. But then there was Anne's plight. She had been wed by proxy, without the enjoyment of being courted.

They stopped outside her chamber door and Calum took her hands in his. "Lady Anne, I…" So many conflicting emotions boiled under his skin and tied his tongue.

"Yes?" She swayed slightly as if tipsy.

"Ye are a beautiful woman, both inside and out."

She plopped her head against Calum's chest. It hit him a bit hard, though he could understand the gesture, if half his frustration also coursed through her.

"I'll be leaving soon."

He brushed her cheek with his forefinger. "Aye."

"Staying here hasn't been anything I could have imagined."

"Oh? Did ye expect us to be hostile?"

"After plundering the ship? Yes." Anne swayed and leaned against the door. With her eyes half cast, she looked a woman ready to be ravished. "How could you do that and live with it on your conscience?"

"How can ye marry a man ye dunna know, and cannot love?" He reached out and clasped her fist to his heart. "We'll no' be pirating again, as long as we can sustain ourselves."

Anne slid her arms around his waist. Calum's heart thudded against his chest. He clasped his hands around her back. Ferocious, demanding heat spread under his kilt. Anne raised her chin, lips parted. "I've tried, but I cannot block your kisses from my mind."

Calum needed no more coaxing. This was Beltane. He would think on the future tomorrow. He bent his head and brushed his lips across her lovely silken mouth. Pulling her body against his, Anne's breasts molded to his chest. He licked the tip of her tongue. Groaning, he increased the pressure and swirled her tongue with his. She rubbed her hips against him, and his manhood hardened with a deep searing heat.

He could no longer resist the fire burning for her. Christ, what was he protecting her from? He was saving the lady's virtue for a tyrant. Calum's hand slipped down to her round buttock and pulled her closer. Her pliable flesh gave way to his touch, but when a prolonged and satisfying moan escaped her lips, he ground his manhood against her and nearly spilled his seed.

Squeezing his eyes closed, desperate to regain control, he pulled his lips away and tasted her sweetness with the tip of his tongue. He wanted to savor her, to hold this moment forever close. He showered kisses along her neck and inhaled her luscious scent. Calum lifted his finger and ran it across the surging flesh above her bodice that had so often teased him. With a gasp, she shuddered in his arms. All he had to do was pick her up and carry her to the bed—*his* bed. He slipped his finger under the fabric of her gown and found a taut nipple straining against her stays, every bit as erect as his cock.

Anne stared at him, her breasts heaving.

He slid his fingers toward her cleavage, but she clamped her hand around them. Meeting her eyes, she raised his hand to her lips and kissed it. She rested her head on his chest—gently this time. "Thank you."

His hope sank like lead. "The pleasure is mine, milady." Calum pulled down on the latch and opened her door.

Anne took a step inside and staggered. Calum darted to her. "Are ye ill?"

She put a hand to her forehead. "My head is spinning." She sucked in a deep breath. "I want you so badly, I cannot breathe."

Merely flesh and blood, Calum could take no more. He lifted her into his arms and kicked the door closed behind them.

Anne jerked. "We cannot."

"I'll see ye to the bed."

With all the flames snuffed for Beltane, only the sliver of moon glow shone through the window.

Anne wrapped her arms around his neck and leaned into him, closing her eyes. "I wish I could hold you always." Her voice sounded far away and dreamy.

He gently sat her atop the duvet and removed her slippers. Kneeling before her, he held her hands to his lips. "Lady Anne, it would be unfair of me to confess my love, but I want nothing more this Beltane Eve than to bring ye pleasure."

"But…"

Calum held up his hand. "I have vowed I will no' take yer innocence, but a man and a woman can find pleasure together without consummation."

"They can?"

"Aye."

Anne cupped his face with her palm. "I trust you." Her voice was but a throaty whisper.

Calum's hands trembled. He had won her trust. At one time she'd thought him a merciless pirate, and there she sat, completely vulnerable, sapphire eyes boring into his, declaring her belief in his ability to control his urges. God help him.

He ran his finger along her low cut bodice, savoring her yielding flesh beneath. "May I remove yer gown and yer stays?"

Without a word, Anne stood and held out her arms. He realized she had done that many times and it dawned on him, an earl's daughter would have had a serving maid—most likely a great number of them.

Calum's hands trembled as he unlaced her bodice and pulled away her gown. Her breasts blossomed over the top of her stays, and he sucked in a ragged breath. She wore her laces in front—the only way she would have been able to tie them by herself. He tugged on the satiny string, slowly tugging the laces from each eyelet.

Pulling it away, Anne's breasts sprang free and pushed against her shift. Calum stood back, clasping the stays in his hands, salivating. The pink buds of her nipples strained into the white cloth, highlighted by a ray of moonlight. The good Lord had endowed her with ample bosoms indeed. His own knees buckled. He could barely control his desire, gazing upon the shadow of her form. How would his body respond if she stood naked before him?

He placed her garments on the chair. Anne moved in behind him, running her hands over his chest. Calum rolled his head and groaned at the pleasure from the silky smooth touch of her fingertips.

"Now you," she said.

Anne skimmed her hand around his waist and crossed in front of him. She unlaced his shirt and tugged it from his kilt. He helped her pull it over his head. Her fingers went to his belt, but he grasped them. "If ye unbuckle it, the only thing I'll be wearing is me hose and me boots." He loved the shadowy blush that rose up her cheeks. "But if ye want to…"

"I do want to."

"I may no' be able to stop meself." Anne bit her lip and released her hand. Leaving his kilt in place, Calum kicked off his foot gear and led her to the bed. "I want to savor this moment forever."

"I do as well."

Sitting on the bed, Calum pulled her between his legs. He placed his hands on her hips and pulled her mons against his erection. Groaning, he kissed her. With his hands, he showed her how to rock her hips against him with only his kilt and her thin shift between them. "Does this feel good for you?"

"Unbelievably so, but my insides are screaming for more."

He ran his hands over her breasts, kneading round, firm flesh. Watching him, she reached up and pulled the bow to open the front of her shift. Calum pushed the material aside and licked her nipple. Anne's moan ignited his lust. He covered the tip of her breast with his mouth and suckled. Her entire body shuddered.

Anne smoothed her hands over Calum's hair. "Oh God. Please."

In one motion, he pulled her onto the bed and lay beside her. "I want to touch you." Tugging up the hem of her shift, he exposed her white skin. Though he could scarcely see in the dark, the flowery bouquet from her sex made his head spin. Calum slid his fingers up her thigh. A gasp caught in Anne's throat. She tensed.

"Open yer legs for me."

"Are you certain?"

"I will respect ye. I promise."

Slowly, she eased her legs apart. With a feathery touch, he slid his hand into the hot moist core of her womanhood. She was so wet, he could slip into her in one thrust. His cock throbbed, pressing her hip.

Anne tensed again and tried to sit up but Calum coaxed her back down. "Relax and let me show ye pleasure."

"Yes."

Anne eased against the pillows and he swirled his finger around the tiny nub just above her opening. Yielding to his touch, she rocked her hips. Her moans drove his pulse and passion to thrum faster. Calum rubbed his erection against her hip, teetering on the edge of losing control. He slid his finger inside her, and she clamped tight around him. A bit of seed leaked from his cock. If he could only enter her, claim her for his own. But he wanted to show her pleasure, wanted her to know what it was like to come. He worked his finger faster, slipping it over and around her sex until Anne arched her back and cried out, clutching him and panting. Kissing her hair, Calum held her to his chest until her breathing eased.

"W-what was that?"

"'Twas only a sampling of what could be between a man and a woman."

Anne kissed him and brushed her hand over his sex. "You said a woman can pleasure a man."

Calum's cock throbbed. "Aye. But I wouldna expect a lady to lower herself."

"I want to." Anne pushed up onto her elbow. "Will you show me?"

He guided her hand under his kilt and wrapped her fingers around his shaft. Holding his hand over hers, Calum showed her how to stroke it. "No' too fast, but steady."

"I wish I could see it, but 'tis too dark."

Anne milked him with her soft touch, and he drew her mouth to his. Calum pushed into her hold, hips bucking faster. Anne instinctively sped her stroke. He could only think of her core, that hot opening which had yielded to his touch. His mind lost control as she worked him. With one final thrust, he roared, "Anne!" He spilled his seed, his cock pulsing over and over again until they both fell back against the pillows.

Calum pressed his lips against her forehead. "Ye are the fairest lass in all the Earth." *But only mine this night.*

After a languid kiss, Anne curled up beside him and fell asleep in his arms. He watched her peaceful countenance in the moonlight. Never before had he seen a woman so beautiful. Never before had he wanted a woman so much that the need consumed him. Calum brushed a lock of hair from her face.

He must take Anne to her husband soon, else they'd be damned forever.

***

Lord Wharton studied the map of Scotland strewn atop his parlor table. Master Denton hovered across from him, his arms folded. "Fortescue said they wore red and black plaid."

"Large checks or small?"

"He didn't say."

Wharton looked at his beady-eyed henchman, and the scrambled eggs from his breakfast roiled in his gut. "He didn't say or you didn't ask?"

"Oh I asked—right before I sliced off the tip of his finger."

"And?"

Denton studied his gnawed fingernails. "I honestly believe he did not know."

"Stupid Londoner. Doesn't know a Stewart from a MacGregor, I'd wager." Thomas studied the map. "Where does that leave us?"

"My guess is they're from the Hebrides. In London, I learned MacNeil is making a name for himself pillaging English ships. Word has it his lair is on the Isle of Barra."

Wharton slid his finger across the map and found it, a small island in the Outer Hebrides. He reached for his cup of peppermint tea. "Out of the way, is it not?"

"And well-fortified I've heard."

"Bastards," Wharton growled under his breath. "Are you certain it's them?"

Denton shook his mop of straight black hair. "No. Lawlessness permeates the Hebrides. Their allegiance is to the clans. They scarcely recognize the throne of Scotland and *despise* England."

"I can raise an army, but to fight a war on the sea…" He drummed his fingers on the table. "I would need to appeal to Her Majesty."

"That *woman?*"

Wharton frowned. Denton was right. It would take a year or more of petitioning before Her Majesty would grant him warships to find his wife—if she ever did. War with the Spaniards was imminent. He could possibly seek Northumberland's assistance.

"Exactly what did the missive say?" Denton asked.

Gritting his teeth, Thomas snatched it from his ornately carved mahogany desk and read aloud. "At dusk on the seventeenth of May, launch a thousand pounds in an unmanned skiff at the mouth of the Firth of Solway. Do not follow the skiff. Do not hide in the skiff. After payment is received, Lady Anne will be found outside the citadel of Carlisle. If payment is not received in full, the lady will be executed."

Wharton slammed his fist on the desk and drew his sword. "I will gut the miserable bastard and destroy his clan." He pointed the blade at Denton's heart. "I will have my vengeance."

Denton waited for him to sheathe his sword before he reached for the missive. "'Tis not signed."

"Motherless tit-sucking swine."

"We must formulate a plan."

Denton always had to be the voice of reason. Wharton didn't care to be reasonable right now. "I won't let them steal away with a thousand of *my* pounds. They can eat my shite. Her dowry wasn't even half that."

Denton tossed the missive on the desk. "What is worth more, the money or the baroness?"

"You overstep your station." Wharton pursed his lips. "They will not murder my wife. We will sail the skiff as they request and once Lady Anne is in our grasp, we will hunt them down like the savages they are. They may have my coin in their hands for a time, but it will not make it to their coffers."

Denton grinned, his yellow teeth making his appearance even less formidable. "We should be able to slip over to Maryport to hire a ship, if need be."

"Yes, and raise an army. I'm sure there are still loyal men from my days as sheriff. We shall leave on the morrow. I'll need rooms there and a physician to examine…" Wharton stopped himself. It was no concern of Denton's that he planned to have Anne examined before taking her to his marriage bed. He didn't trust the rutting Scots, and if they had touched her, it would be a greater disgrace to his name than he could bear.

"With some planning we should be able to capture them outside the citadel."

"My thought exactly." Thomas plodded to the hearth and snatched up a piece of coal with cast iron tongs. "I will see them all hanged, drawn and quartered."

"We shall line the bailey of Carlisle with their heads."

"No." Wharton pointed at Denton's sternum. "We will ship their heads back to their mothers and wives and show those bloody Scots who is the superior race."

Chapter Fourteen

Calum rose early and met John and Norman in the solar behind closed doors. "I was worried ye wouldn't return in time, John. The missive instructed Wharton to launch the ransom in an unmanned skiff in the Firth of Solway on the seventeenth of May."

"The seventeenth? Are we sailing, then?" John asked.

"Nay, we'll ride."

Norman leaned in. "Ride all the way to Carlisle with a woman in tow?"

"Aye, a proper English lass at that. She'll no' last a day," John added with a shake of his head.

Calum sliced his hands through the air. "Hear me out afore ye start yer bellowing." He eyed the two men. "We'll ride to Carlisle with Lady Anne. It should take a fortnight, give or take. Norman, ye'll set sail in the *Sea Dragon* a week after we leave and moor in the north cove of the Firth of Solway—ye ken the place."

Norman nodded. "Aye."

"Once we recover the skiff, I'll have Bran head to the cove with the ransom. I'll take Lady Anne to the citadel. With some luck, she'll cooperate and I'll be out of there by the time Wharton and his men realize it is she."

John scratched his chin. "Ye dunna think the baron will recognize her?"

"Nay." Calum grinned. "I'll dress her in trews and tie her hair under a bonnet."

"Ye best ensure the cap's no' made of Raasay plaid," Norman said.

"I've asked Betha to fashion me one of grey wool."

John looked worried behind his dark eyes. "Ye think the lady will betray us?"

Calum sucked in a ragged breath. His actions from last eve had not been carried out with a mind to coax her into going along with his scheme. This whole business had torn his insides to shreds. The only positive thing about it was it would soon be done. Hell, if Anne stayed at Brochel any longer, he'd betray his honor—he nearly had already. "Nay."

Norman shot John a sideways glance. "She won't. She's grown a fondness for our laird whilst ye've been away."

John sat back and folded his arms. "Good. 'Twill help aid our escape if she doesna start screaming outside the citadel of Carlisle."

Calum pushed away from the table and stood. "Now I've got to go tell her we cannot take all those blasted trunks with us."

The two men exchanged frowns and Calum lowered his voice. "I'll no' tell her about the *Sea Dragon*. 'Tis best she doesn't ken our plans to return to Raasay."

"And what about after?" Norman asked. "Wharton will come hunting us with guns blazing."

"Aye, 'tis another reason why I want to sail home. We'll need to prepare for battle by land or by sea."

Calum strode out of the solar and headed up the winding stairs to Anne's chamber. "Lady Anne?" He rapped on the door. "Are ye within?"

"A moment."

After an inordinate amount of rustling, she opened the door, smiling with those dimples that made his heart pound against his chest. She dropped into his arms, and Calum's resolve turned to butter. If he could only pick her up and take her to bed—but last night had been a mistake. He never should have been so forward. It made what he had to do all the more difficult.

Squeezing his eyes shut, Calum kissed her forehead then held her at arm's length. "We need to speak."

From the crease on her brow, she knew why he was there. She gestured toward the table.

Calum's stomach turned over—twice—and he took the seat opposite her. It had all seemed so easy when he'd left the solar—walk up to her and tell her they were leaving on the morrow. Now, staring into those fathomless pools of Icelandic water, his mouth went dry. If only she had not married the bastard. "Och, damn it all."

Her arms folded. "I beg your pardon?"

"We should not have—I should not have..." Calum bent his head and spread his palms to his sides. "We must leave on the morrow. Yer letter of ransom has been answered, and I must take ye to Carlisle."

Anne frowned. "Carlisle? But Lord Wharton is in Alnwick."

"The terms are the baron will meet ye there." Calum couldn't look at her face. He glanced to the five trunks lining the wall. "We'll be on horseback and cannot take yer things. Pack a satchel with yer keepsakes. I'll see yer trunks delivered to Alnwick when things settle."

Anne covered her face with her hands as if pressing away tears. "What of Swan? His training has only begun."

He'd just told her they were going back to England, and she was worried about a damned bird? "Bran will look after the eagle. We cannot tow a squawking fledgling with us." Calum cringed. He sounded far less sympathetic than he had intended, but the eagle could not make this trip. Not with so much at stake.

He stole a peek at Anne. She stared at her hands, folded tight in her lap. Her knuckles blanched white. "So that's it, then?"

His heart told him to kneel before her and beg her not to leave. She could seek an annulment, falsify her death, anything so she could stay at Brochel. But she was a lady, born into nobility. She was too refined for a life on a frigid island in the north of Scotland. She deserved the comfortable life of a Baroness, planning fetes and luncheons, fretting over the penmanship on her invitations. Besides, the longer she remained at Brochel, the more dangerous it was for his entire clan.

"'Tis time to join yer husband." His voice sounded strange to his own ears, the words constricted in his throat. He could not tell her how he felt. It would only make things worse.

***

Anne hid her emotions behind a stoic façade and listened to the news. She waited until Calum walked out of her chamber and closed the door. A tear slipped from the corner of her eye and trickled down her cheek. Pulling a kerchief from her dressing gown pocket, she held it to her eyes.

That sickly, hollow feeling came over her as it had the first day on the *Flying Swan*. Last night had been a delusion—she had allowed him to take advantage. Her feelings of belonging had been the musings of a lonely woman who would be an old maid if it weren't for a baron who had spied her from across Westminster Abbey. How foolish she'd been to allow herself feelings for Calum MacLeod, pirate laird of Raasay. His rugged good looks and charming manner had captivated her and betrayed her heart.

Anne doubled over and wailed into her kerchief. Her *fantasy* was over. Now she must leave her things behind—and Swan. The bird had become her tie to Raasay, he brought her hope, gave her a piece of something of which she so desperately wanted to be a part. What could she pack in a satchel? Her head still throbbing, she threw herself on the bed and wept into the pillow. She didn't care who heard.

Mara's voice chimed from the passageway. "Milady?"

"Go away."

"But I have a parcel for you."

Anne wiped her tears and opened the door. "You do realize I have no room for a parcel of any sorts."

Mara held up a bundle of clothing and stepped inside. "Trews, a shirt and boots to make the journey more comfortable, milady."

"Whose idea was that?"

"Calum's"

"He must be daft." Anne held up the trousers. "Have you ever heard of sumptuary laws decreed by King Henry VIII?"

"Och, no milady."

"If I'm seen in England wearing men's clothing, I could be thrown into prison or worse."

Mara pushed inside, the door closing behind her. "That makes no sense at all."

"Tell that to the magistrate. The laws were enacted to keep the different classes separate, and distinguish men from women, no doubt. Dress as a man? 'Tis absurd." Anne massaged her temples and closed her eyes. "Besides, I'm only allowed a satchel, and I must have a gown when I meet my h-h…" she couldn't say it. "Lord Wharton."

Mara took back the trews and set the clothing on the table. "Tell you what. I think ye should wear the trews under yer skirts. 'Twill stop the chafing from the saddle and will be warmer when yer sleeping on the trail—and ye'll need the boots, regardless. Ye cannot ride a pack horse in satin slippers."

Anne pursed her lips. Mara's argument had merit. She could wear a day dress over those wretched man-trousers, and roll up one of her finer gowns for her satchel. Anne walked over and unclasped a trunk. She rifled to the bottom and pulled out a brown, linen gown with an embroidered square-necked bodice. She used the dress for falconry. On the top lay one of her favorite gowns, a red silk she only wore during fine weather. But summer months approached. Surely, Calum would ship her things before winter.

"Can I help ye, milady?" Mara asked.

Anne's eyes shot to the smaller trunk, which held her most precious keepsakes.

"I understand if ye dunna want me here," Mara offered.

Anne studied the kind face that reflected so much concern. In the short time the she had been at Brochel Castle, Mara had become as dear to her as Hanna. Anne tried to smile. "Stay. You can help lift my spirits."

Anne pulled out a satchel from the small trunk. When she opened it, she also pulled out her box of keepsakes and set it on the table.

Mara ran her finger over the woodwork inlaid with ivory. "'Tis beautiful. I've never seen anything like it."

"My mother gave it to me on my sixteenth birthday. I've always kept my cherished possessions in it." Anne opened the lid, and Mara gasped. She didn't have a lot of jewels, but the ruby necklace alone was enough to cause a stir. A golden locket with a small portrait of her father, a pearl ring, and a dozen or so necklaces glinted within the box. All had been purchased to match her gowns. They were beautiful, but not inordinately expensive. Anne put the jewels into a leather pouch and removed the false bottom of the box.

Mara leaned closer. "Look at the fine green velvet inside. What else do ye have in there?"

Anne pulled out the marriage decree and held it up. "Just this." She unfolded it and remembered Mara couldn't read. "'Tis proof of my marriage to Lord Wharton. I may need it if he doesn't recognize me."

Mara laughed. "I'll bet he'd recognize ye from a hundred paces. Ye are too bonny to forget."

"You cannot mean that." Mara had a knack for lightening her heart. Anne refolded the document and slipped it into the pouch. She tossed her shillings on top and tied it closed. It would be the first thing in her satchel to ensure she wouldn't lose it.

Mara helped her roll the red gown carefully to avoid wrinkling it, though silk was prone to creases. "Whatever will become of all yer fine things?"

"Calum said he would ship them to me later, though I can't help but fear I'll never see them again."

"If Laird Calum MacLeod makes a promise, he'll see it kept. On that ye have me word."

"But what if…" Anne busied herself with folding a spare shift. "What if?"

"What if the baron chases after him? What if he has an army waiting in Carlisle? What if he...Calum is killed?"

Mara placed her hand on Anne's shoulder. "There, there, ye cannot be letting thoughts of doom cloud yer mind. Ye'll drive yerself mad afore ye get there." Mara led her to the chair and massaged Anne's shoulders. "I always say when ye have a choice between a good thought and a bad, pick the good. What use is the bad? It only serves to make ye feel worse."

Anne leaned into Mara's magic hands and closed her eyes. "I wish it were that easy."

Mara twirled around her. "It is, milady. It is."

Anne reached for her keepsake box and held it out. "Since I cannot take this with me, I'd like you to have it."

"Me? Och no, I couldna accept. It looks awful expensive and 'twas a present from yer ma."

Anne pushed the box into Mara's hands. "It is mine to give. You have shown me kindness when there was no motivation for you to do so. Take it and remember me."

"Oh, milady, ye are too kind. And to look at you. Ye are the one who helped me organize the keep. There's plenty here to remember ye by."

Anne smiled. "Good. That's how I want it."

Chapter Fifteen

With her satchel packed, Anne wished she could make this journey without Calum MacLeod. Her breeding would never allow her to clench her fists and stomp across the floor, but that's exactly what she wanted to do. How could he just walk into her chamber and completely ignore the intense passion they had shared the night before?

The stone walls closed in on her. Anne whirled in a circle. She would never hold Calum like a lover again. Mercy, the next time she'd touch a man, it would be Lord Wharton. She needed some fresh air, but it was still morning. Calum would be in the courtyard sparing with his men. Perhaps if she snuck through the kitchen, she could make it to the garden without catching his eye.

She pattered down the steps, pushed out the door, and headed toward the garden at the side of the tower. She caught a glimpse of Calum, clashing swords with three at once, his shirt off. She held a hand to her eye to block the sight of his rippling muscles. How dare he display himself in the courtyard half-naked? The sight of him would put impure thoughts in any maiden's mind. There should be a law against it.

Anne dashed to the solitude of the gardens and the privacy the hedge provided. With a heavy sigh, she lowered her hand and slowed her pace. She needed to regain control of her anger. She detested it when she teetered on the brink of losing control. A few deep breaths of the crisp island air and she'd come around. Her fists loosened and the blood flowed back to her fingertips. Anne walked along the hedge and fought to reason with her feelings. Calum had been a pleasant diversion during her *captivity*. He could never be more than that and they both were painfully aware of it. She had no choice but to face her responsibilities.

Rounding the corner, Anne nearly tripped over Friar Pat. "Oh my, pardon me, Father."

He stood and brushed his hands on his robes. "Ah, Lady Anne, 'tis good to see ye out this morning. Do ye take an interest in gardening?"

"Yes, well I admire a well-kept garden."

He gestured toward a recently sewn plot. "This is a bit o' land the Laird gave me to grow healing herbs for the clan."

"'Tis good you cultivate your own herbs. Do you get much chance to gather in the forest?"

"Aye, I collect willow bark, that sort of thing."

"I see." Anne hung her head and continued on her path.

The friar hurried beside her. "It looks as if something is ailing ye, milady."

She hesitated.

He gestured to a nearby bench. "Would ye care to talk to an old friar about it?" Anne cast a glance at him. His careworn eyes twinkled in the sunlight. "It never did a soul a bit o' good to hold its worries inside."

She nodded and sat on the bench. He took her hand between his warm palms. "Now tell me, what ails ye?"

"Calum's ransom note has been delivered to Lord Wharton, and John has delivered the baron's reply."

"Ah, so ye'll be leaving us?"

"On the morrow." She took in a deep breath. "There are a great many things weighing on my heart."

He ran a hand across his mouth as if trying to collect his thoughts. "Ye've formed a fondness for the laird."

Anne's cheeks burned. "'Tis humiliating to admit I have, and since I've never met my husband, I harbor no such feelings for him as of yet." She pressed her free hand to her face. "I am so ashamed. I feel like I've betrayed Lord Wharton, yet I have always been uneasy about meeting him."

"And why is that, lass?"

"He is eight and fifty."

The friar grimaced. "I can see where that would bring ye some concern."

"Aside from his age, I'm aware of his conquests in Scotland. And news of his atrocious actions as High Sheriff of Cumberland reached as far as Titchfield House." She squeezed her fingers around the friar's hand. "What if he's a tyrant?"

He patted her hand. "What do ye feel in yer heart? Would Lord Wharton have gone to the trouble to arrange this marriage if all he wanted to do was mistreat ye?"

Anne bit her lip. "What if he did?"

"Then I'll be the first to lead an army to send the baron to his grave." He shook his head. "I do not believe a wife should endure living under a tyrant's roof, but ye should no' be thinking of that now. Ye are going to meet yer husband at long last. A marriage in the eyes of God is a very holy thing. Ye should be a happy bride."

Anne looked up and watched a wisp of cloud sail through the fathomless blue sky. "Thank you, Father. Your words bring my mind peace."

As they stood, the friar rested his hand on Anne's shoulder. Just like the cloud above, she had no control over her destiny. Her time on Raasay had been a distraction which had postponed the inevitable.

"I hope ye will always remember us fondly."

Anne tried to put on a brave smile. "I will."

She headed back toward the keep when the friar called after her. "Calum is a good laird and a good man. He will keep ye safe until ye are in yer husband's arms."

***

Calum watched Anne from across the hall, laughing and bright. She had declined to dine with him on this, her last night at Brochel Castle. She sat beside Mara and John carrying on as if they had been the best of friends since birth. She had not so much as glanced his way since he'd visited her chamber and gave her the news. Had last night meant nothing to her? It had been the most erotic experience in his life. If only he could share this last eve with her in his arms. But it was done—Anne would probably prefer to skewer him with her father's knife than cradle him against her breast.

Calum's edgy frustration was further incensed by Norman who would not cease yammering into his ear. "The men will start work adding the poop deck tomorrow."

"Good."

"Are ye sure ye want the work to continue once ye set off to Carlisle?"

"Why should it not? The longer it takes, the more likely an English ship will spy her."

"But won't Robert have charge of the keep?"

Anne's laughter twisted Calum's gut. "He'll manage for a few days."

"I don't know. He should have his eyes on the women and children," Norman pressed.

Calum snapped his head around and raised his voice. "The carpenters will tend the ship while Robert tends the keep. Where's yer brain, brother?"

Norman held up his hands. "I'm no' the one who's fallen for the wife of Scotland's greatest adversary. Ye need to pull yer head out of *yer* stubborn arse."

Calum sprang to his feet, toppling his chair. He pounded his fist on the table. "Are ye challenging me? 'Cause if ye are, I'd like nothing better than a good sparring match this night."

Norman thrust his nose an inch from Calum's. "I dunna want me face broken by a raging bull. But ye need to set yer priorities and get yer mind off that English wench." Sneering, he leaned in. "Ye cannot have the lass, and the sooner we're rid of her, the sooner ye'll be back to yer old self."

Calum eyed his brother. He snapped his jaw shut. The noise of the crowd had lowered to a hum and he didn't need to look to know everyone watched. He pushed past Norman's shoulder and shoved through the big doors of the great hall.

The cool air provided a welcome chill to the sweat on his brow. Norman was right. How could he have allowed an English woman to slip under his defense? Her tentacles had wrapped around his heart, and it was his own fault for permitting it. What an idiot he'd been, treating her as a guest and letting her sleep in his chamber because of her blasted highborn status. He was a *laird*, by all the saints. He should never have allowed her to sleep in his bed. *Fool.*

Calum ran down to the beach. He kicked stones over the remnants of last night's bonfire. Images of Anne's hypnotic eyes, gazing at him across the maypole attacked. He could still see her breasts as they strained against her bodice with every breath. He roared aloud. Falling to his knees, he pressed the heels of his hands against his eyes, but visions of Anne were burned into his soul. God, did she know what she did to a man simply by looking at him?

She was so innocent, yet so desirable, so consuming. Had the queen of the fairies sent Anne to Raasay to torture him? Did he need to send up an offering and pay to remove this vise from his heart?

Calum threw back his head and wailed, "Yes, brother, I admit it. Ye are right. She tortures me every waking moment and she *cannot* be mine!"

***

The next morning, Anne stood beside Swan's mews and slid her hands into her falconry gloves. At least the eagle would have a permanent home. Friar Pat had agreed to look after Swan until Bran returned to resume the eagle's training. She reached in with a morsel, and the bird plucked it from her fingers. He jumped onto her outstretched hand, and she stroked the long, brown-gold feathers. They had all come in now, and he was a remarkably powerful specimen in full plumage. "I shall miss you more than anything." Though that wasn't completely true, she would miss Swan terribly nonetheless. "I will always sing to you, and mayhap one day you'll fly far away and will hear my song on the wind. We're two of a kind, we are—free spirits who will always be held captive." Her voice warbled and she bit down to stop her trembling chin.

Mara walked up the path, carrying Anne's satchel. "Are ye ready, milady?"

Anne returned Swan to his perch, ran her hand over his feathers one more time and closed the door. Hanging her gloves on a peg, she turned to Mara and nodded, wiping a tear from her eye.

For the last time, Anne walked the winding trail to the beach. At one time it had seemed such a long path, but now it only took moments to reach the bottom. Two skiffs sat cradled on the rocks as the men loaded them with provisions. When they approached, Calum straightened. "Where are yer trews?" he demanded, his tone far from his usual polite tenor.

"She's wearing them, m'laird." Mara lifted the hem of Anne's skirt all the way to the knee so Calum could see the boots and the hem of the trousers. Anne batted her skirts down.

His hands flew to his hips. "The whole purpose was to travel in disguise."

"I'll not be breaking sumptuary laws." She wouldn't back down on this. In a few hours, Calum MacLeod had torn down and taken away everything she'd grown to love. He'd shown her she was no more important than the ransom he aimed to collect. She had become a pawn for him, just as she had been for her uncle.

"Aye, but if anyone recognizes you, we'll all be dead." Calum snatched Anne's satchel from Mara's grasp.

The back of Anne's neck burned. "Dead, you say? That is an outrageous assumption. Who would possibly recognize *me* in the Highlands?"

"I provided the clothing I expected ye to wear on this journey. I am chieftain of this clan, and while ye are under my protection, me word is final." He sliced his hand through the air. "I would have ye no' forget it."

The burn from her neck spread up her cheeks. Anne clenched her fists. Her nostrils flared with each puff of air she drew in. The heartless pirate stood before her, setting off to collect his ransom. At last he had shown his true form.

Mara touched Anne's elbow and peered at her with a smile that looked more like a grimace. "We gave it a try." She threw her arms around Anne and hugged. "I'm going to miss ye, milady."

Anne closed her eyes and returned the squeeze, her throat closing. "Ah, Mara, you have become like a sister to me." She held her at arm's length and looked upon her warm brown eyes. "Remember to keep track of the stores."

"Aye, milady."

"And don't let anyone slack off in their cleaning."

"No, milady."

"Of course you won't." Anne hugged her again. "I'll miss you enormously."

"And I will you."

Friar Pat reached out and placed his hands on Anne's shoulders. "Go with God, milady. He always provides an answer to prayer."

"Yes, he does."

Norman stood next to the friar, a smug grin fixed across his pinched face. She gave him a clipped nod. Calum offered his hand to help her into the boat. Anne reached for it, but pulled her hand away. Her gaze trailed across to the second skiff where Bran coiled a rope. "Master Bran, would you please help me aboard?"

"Aye, milady. But I thought ye'd be riding in the boat with Calum."

"I believe I trust the strong arms of your crew this morning." She stole a glance at Calum out of the corner of her eye. He frowned like the rough brigand who'd kicked in her stateroom door. She wished he would have looked at her like that during her entire stay on Raasay. If he had, her insides wouldn't be tearing her apart right now.

She took a seat at the back of the boat. Bran and Ian clamored in after her, and the men on the shore pushed them into the Sound of Raasay. Fast approaching deep water, Anne's stomach lurched. She looked down at the dark waves beneath the skiff and clamped her fingers on the sides of the boat. How small she seemed compared to this large expanse of water. Anne looked across to the mainland and tightened her grip. They had a long way to row and the boat rocked and listed in the wind.

Swallowing hard, Anne tried not to think of the icy waves beneath her. This was the party that would accompany her to Carlisle—three men and a boy? And what had Calum meant by traveling in disguise? Was she putting them in danger? She did not want to see anyone hurt, and would try to discuss it with Calum when things settled. Besides, if the wind blustered any harder, they might not even make it to Applecross.

Grasping the side of the boat, Anne turned and looked over her shoulder. Mara and the clansmen stood on the shore and waved. The hole in her heart stretched. She had enjoyed every moment with these hard-working, unpretentious souls. She would miss them.

As Brochel Castle became a tiny fortress in the distance, the bottom of the boats scraped onto the sands of Applecross—the mainland. The lead sinking to the pit of Anne's stomach did nothing to lift her spirits at this first stop of a trudging journey.

Calum and John quickly pulled their skiff ashore then Calum splashed through the water. He lifted Anne out of the boat without a word.

"I could have stepped out on my own."

"I didna want ye to wet yer skirts, milady." He kept his eyes forward and scowled as he trudged to the beach. Before he set her down, he whispered in her ear, "Let me do the talking. The English have spies everywhere. If they hear ye speak, ye'll put us in harm's way. Do ye ken?"

Anne nodded her head. Calum held his back straighter. There was no swagger to his step. Though she wasn't completely blind to the danger of traveling in the far reaches of the country, she honestly had not considered she'd be in peril. John had gone to Edinburgh and returned safely, but he hadn't been travelling with an English lady in his company.

Calum led them through the windblown sea grass to a set of stables. The men had made quick work of saddling the horses when a big Scot appeared in the doorway, a sword in hand. "Calum MacLeod, ye'll not be taking those horses until ye pay yer rent."

Calum whipped around and faced him, the two men standing eye-to-eye.

Bran leaned over and whispered in Anne's ear, "That's Dougal MacKenzie—they sort of have an *arrangement.*"

"Och, MacKenzie, 'tis always a pleasure to see yer bonny smile." Calum slid his hand into his sporran without taking his eyes off the Scot. "I've got it right here for ye." He pulled out a pouch of coins and handed it to the man.

Dougal weighed it with a bounce and slipped the pouch into his sporran. "Yer brother's causing me kin some consternation to the north."

"What Ruairi does is nay concern of mine. Raasay no longer answers to Lewis."

"When next ye see him, remind him to keep his arse in Lewis and off MacKenzie land."

Calum bowed his head. "I'll send him a missive upon me return."

Dougal's gaze strayed to Anne. He assessed her from head to toe. "And where are ye off to with a fine lassie in tow?"

Wearing her day gown, Anne thought she looked the part of a commoner, but her embroidered dress was a far cry from that of a Scottish woman's plain kirtle. Her cheeks prickled with heat as Dougal's glare raked across her body yet again.

"Returning me cousin to her family in Edinburgh," Calum lied.

"Lowlander, aye? It seems they're taking on more of the English customs all the time."

"Aye," said Calum, motioning for the others to mount.

Bran slipped over and gave Anne a lift. Though a man's saddle, she tried to sit aside, but Bran shook his head and whispered, "astride."

Anne had never ridden with her legs either side of the horse. Thank heavens she had worn the trews. Her mother would be horrified to see it. Bran helped her adjust her skirts so they rested across the horse's rump in the back and gathered in the front, but as they set out, her seat felt decidedly more secure.

Chapter Sixteen

Anne had never seen land so rugged. She wondered how anyone could grow a thistle, let alone crops in the rocky terrain. On the first day, she saw neither towns nor farms and when Calum led them into a copse of trees to make camp she asked, "Is there no inn?"

All the men chuckled, and Calum shook his head. "We'll nay see an inn until we reach Fort William three days hence."

Anne surveyed the clearing. She'd never slept in the wild before—or in the company of a band of Scotsmen. With no other option, she dismounted. Her legs nearly gave way beneath her and she leaned against her horse with a pained grunt.

"Not used to riding, milady?" Bran asked.

"Most certainly not all day, especially astride." She tried to walk a few steps. Her legs were wobbly, as if her ankles and knees would no longer function. They all watched her. Afraid she'd look like a ninny, Anne put her hand in the small of her back and stretched. That actually helped. She took a few more steps and the pain in her legs eased.

"It always takes me a few minutes to find me legs after a day of hard riding," Calum said, gesturing to a clump of grass. "Would ye like to rest while we make camp?"

Though her bones ached and she longed to plop down on the grass and curl into a ball, she declined. "I'd prefer to help." All the men had been set to task. She wouldn't sit by and simply watch. "I shall gather some firewood. Besides, my legs still need some stretching."

"Very well." Calum loosened the girth and pulled the saddle of Anne's horse. Calum's gaze flicked toward her. The pain in his eyes was unmistakable. Anne reached out her hand, but Calum had already turned away. Were they to act as mere acquaintances this entire journey?

She wanted to scream and weep at the same time. But instead, the exercise did much to help Anne to regain her composure and her legs. She made countless trips, hauling in branches and twigs and by the time she dumped the last armload on the heap, darkness had shrouded the camp.

They dined on bully beef and oatcakes. Calum passed a flagon of whisky—another of Friar Pat's hobbies. Anne took a swig. It burned her throat going down. She sputtered and gasped, trying not to make a show of her discomfort.

From across the fire, Calum chuckled. "Ye better go easy on that. They don't call the friar's whisky potent for naught."

He seemed more relaxed now, though his gaze still darted between the shadows surrounding them. Anne longed to have Calum wander around the fire and sit beside her, wrap his arm over her shoulders and tell her things would be all right. The last time they'd sat at a fire had been only two nights ago at Beltane. She'd been alive with desire for him. And now she had no hope she'd ever feel such passion again.

Anne stared into the leaping flames and let them mesmerize her. Her entire body ached but the whisky spread welcomed warmth through her insides.

"What is it like to be wed by proxy?" Bran asked.

Calum shook his finger at the lad. "'Tis no question to ask a lady."

Anne stirred the fire with a stick. "There's not much to tell really." She glanced up to see four pairs of eyes focused on her, popped wide with great curiosity. She took in a deep breath. "My uncle rode to Titchfield House and bounded into the hall with great purpose. He called us all together—my mother, my sisters and me. Then he said…" Anne swung her fists to her hips and mimicked a deep masculine voice. "Lady Anne, I have found you a husband at last. By royal proxy, I have signed and witnessed a marriage decree that formally weds you to the Baron of Wharton."

Anne looked across the stunned faces, illuminated by the firelight and dropped her hands to her sides. "I could have died. And once I learned his age, I think a part of me did."

"How could he do that without yer consent?" John asked.

"When my father passed, young King Edward appointed my uncle guardian. Uncle More left the daily operations to me and took my brother, the heir, to his estate in Loseley Park for his fostering." She shook her head. "I digress. The king entrusted my uncle with complete power until my brother came of age." Anne stared into the fire. "I imagine he negotiated quite a good settlement for my hand, otherwise he would not have been so anxious for me to leave Titchfield. The coffers were doing quite well, you see."

A silent pall hung over the campfire, and Anne stared into the flames. The crackling took her back to the dreaded day when her life had been swept out from under her. She didn't want to look up and see the pity in their eyes—especially Calum's eyes.

After a time, Bran tossed a stick of wood on the fire. "Do ye ken *My Bonnie Lass She Smileth?*"

Anne's heart squeezed. The boy had a way of changing the mood toward the better. "Yes. 'Tis an English madrigal. How do you know it?"

Bran shot an insecure glance at Calum who nodded. "I heard it in an English alehouse when we were…"

"That's enough." Calum stopped him.

"Will ye sing it with me?"

Bran started the melody. Anne matched his voice with her soprano. On the second verse they broke into harmony. Anne's gaze drifted across the fire and caught Calum staring at her, his eyes dark and intense, hungry—starving. His full lips parted, and her heart lurched, making her voice warble. She wanted to walk over and let him cradle her in his lap, but she turned her away so his gaze could no longer affect her.

When the song finished, the men applauded. Anne stole a glance at Calum. His gaze had not changed. *Why does he have to look at me so? Does he not know it ignites a fire inside my breast?*

The flagon of whisky went around again. Anne took a healthy swig and licked her lips, pleased she didn't cough. Before passing it to Bran, she tilted it back one more time. She needed something to numb the ache in her heart.

When they unrolled their plaids around the fire, Calum placed his beside Anne. "Laird? You cannot."

Calum rested his claymore between them. "Ye are under me protection and mine's the strongest sword. I will see to yer safety, milady." His voice no longer had the harsh tone from earlier in the day.

It was bad enough watching him from across the fire. Now he lay so close, she could feel the heat radiate from his back. The smell of wood smoke and horse mixed with his own spicy scent tortured her. If only she could reach out and touch him—reach out and place her hand on his muscled back—apologize for her tirade on the beach—ask him to cradle her in his arms and tell her all would be well.

***

Calum rolled onto his back and watched the stars. Every night on the trail could not be as draining as this one or else he would be worn to a splinter by the time they reached Carlisle. Did Anne have to challenge him at every turn? Why she could not wear the trews was an act of pure stubbornness. Wearing them under her skirts—what good did that do? Besides, if she didn't eventually dress as a man, he'd have to come up with another plan. *Dammit all.*

Calum glanced at her. He shouldn't have looked. Anne's hair glistened like gold against the fire. If only he could reach out and draw her into his embrace—protect her from the night and the chill that comes with darkness. But she had become cool toward him since he'd visited her chamber with news of the ransom. He couldn't hold her aloofness against her. 'Twas the truth that he sought payment for her, and he hated himself for it. Again and again, he wished he could will away her proxy marriage. It seemed false, yet it was a lawful union.

In two weeks' time, this would all be a painful memory. He couldn't bring himself to think about what it would be like without Anne at the keep, sleeping in the adjoining chamber. Her smiles, those subtle glances from under her long eyelashes, would all haunt him forever.

Why had he not made love to her on Beltane? Damn his needling, chivalrous streak. He owed nothing to Wharton or the English. Though he could not put his clan in jeopardy—before Anne, the clan had been his only care. Calum looked to Anne and watched her in slumber. Perfection. She was born to be a queen, or near enough to it. His heart formed a lump in his throat. He would do anything to see her happy.

Calum closed his eyes and tried to ignore the rock beneath his back. Sleep teased him throughout the night and he lay on the ground neither asleep nor awake but aware of every nighttime sound echoing around them.

Dawn had turned the sky to violet when Calum heard a rustle in the trees. He grasped his sword, rose to a crouch and peered through the leaves. A buck with a hearty rack of antlers foraged a mere twenty feet away. The camp must be downwind. Without a sound, Calum sheathed his sword and reached for his bow and quiver of arrows.

The deer moved out of sight, but he could still hear the leaves rustling. Easing forward, he crouched in the clearing and waited until his senses were absolutely sure of the beast's location. Springing up, Calum raced into the wood, his bow at the ready. Behind a tree, the stag's head snapped up.

Calum let his arrow fly. It hit, embedding into the animal's shoulder. The deer spun and bolted. Running after it, Calum snatched another arrow. A trail of blood guided him toward the wounded stag. Calum had to finish him. Not only did they need the meat, he would not leave the animal to suffer a lengthy death.

The beast fought against the pain but Calum could tell he was slowing. Calum's lungs burned and his thighs ached but he pushed up the steep incline. With every step, he gained a bit. He could hear the deer's breathing crackle. It wouldn't be long now. The stag turned and faced him with black soulful eyes, as if wanting to see his killer. Calum's gut twisted but he had his shot. Without hesitation, he released the arrow, hitting his mark with a swift kill. The magnificent beast's knees buckled and he dropped.

Gritting his teeth, Calum circled the deer. He tapped him with his foot to ensure the stag was dead. Only then did he kneel down and cut out the innards to lighten his load and keep the meat fresh. He hefted the stag over his shoulders. He could hear the camp stirring as he barreled into the clearing and dropped the carcass to the ground. "We'll have a good meal of venison tonight. Tie him to the pack mule."

***

The venison was a nice addition to their diet of bully beef and oatcakes and helped to sustain them over the next three days. Anne's body longed for a soft bed and the warm water of a bath. They rode into Fort William. It wasn't much of a town, with a single inn situated along a dirt cart path. By this stage, Anne didn't mind. It was the first likeness of a road she'd seen since leaving Portsmouth. Anne waited with the others while Calum went inside to make arrangements.

When Calum finally came out, he didn't look happy. "They have one room available." He looked at Anne. "You cannot stay in there alone. Ye'll take the bed and the rest of us will sleep on the floor. Apologies, but 'tis the best I could do."

There went her imaginings of a bath.

Calum grasped her elbow and whispered, "Stay close to me. I dunna trust a single scrapper inside. They'd sooner slit me neck and spirit away with ye draped across the pommel."

He placed his hand in the small of her back and spoke so all could hear. "The mistress of the inn will serve us a warm meal. Watch yer backs and dunna drink too much." He locked eyes with John who fell in at Anne's other elbow.

When the door opened, the racket of men telling tales and the stench of sour ale wafted around them. Inside a candelabra, encrusted with years of wax and dust, dimly lit the room. Rickety wooden tables huddled in the center of the room with the bar at the back. Calum led them to a dark corner where they would attract little attention.

He held out a chair for Anne and then sat with his back to the wall. This was a side of Calum she'd never seen. Very cautious, trusting of no one, his face deadly, his eyes shifted across the room with watchful vigilance. A buxom woman set a loaf of bread and a carving knife on the table in front of them, behind her was a greasy-haired man toting a black pot and five bowls. The stew splashed over the sides as he ladled it up. Anne tried not to cringe. Luncheon had been a quick bite of bully beef on the trail and she was starving.

Calum divided the bread and Anne looked at her bowl. She didn't dare ask what was in it. Bran dove in, dunking his bread and chewing. Anne carefully dipped a corner of her bread and nibbled. Finding it palatable, she dipped in for another taste. The matron tossed a handful of spoons on the table and brought a pitcher and five tankards.

Anne rubbed the knot in her shoulder and let out a long breath. The men at the bar had left them alone. She sipped her ale and looked back over her shoulder. A big Scot, possibly larger than Calum, stared back. She could smell him from where she sat. She averted her eyes, the knot in her shoulder seizing up as if she needed it to tell her to be careful.

Calum's guarded frown transformed into a scowl and she didn't need to turn around to know why. The big oaf had wandered up behind her, his stench nearly rancid. Calum's hand disappeared under the table and he tipped his chin up. "What can we do for ye, friend?" He drew out the word friend as if to emphasize its importance.

"I'll pay ye coin for a toss with yer wench."

"She's no wench." The chair clattered against the wall as Calum stood with his fingers wrapped around the hilt of his sword. "I suggest ye go 'bout yer business afore ye insult the lady further."

Anne glanced between the others. The unspoken expressions and nods around the table were unmistakable. She fingered the little dagger in her pocket and tried to swallow down the lump in her throat. She knew she was no match for a soul in the room, including the buxom matron of the inn.

Chairs scraped across the floor and she stole a glance over her shoulder. A half-dozen men walked up behind the big Scot. She stiffened when he reached out and grabbed a lock of her hair. "Me thinks I want a turn with the lass."

Anne's hands shot up to protect her head when he pulled. Her knife flew out of her hand and skidded across the wooden planks. Faster than she could blink, Calum drew his sword. With an inhuman roar, he leapt forward. One foot tapped on the table and he launched himself over Anne's head. Feet first, he thrust his full weight into the brute's chest. Careening backward, the Scot thudded hard against the floorboards. Anne shrieked when he jumped to his feet and scrambled to pull his long claymore from its scabbard.

Anne dropped to her knees and scurried to the wall as the room erupted in a full on brawl. She eyed her knife. Crawling under the table, her hand was inches from it when a booted foot kicked it across the room.

She scurried back against the wall and she hugged herself as Calum and his men stood back to back in a circle in the center of the room. Drunken, barbarous savages lunged in, swinging claymores and battleaxes. Calum's relentless sparring sessions sprang into action. The MacLeod men wielded their swords with expert finesse. Even Bran held his own. Bloodied, the attackers began to ease away, but the big Scot advanced on Calum with fire in his eye. He swung his sword over his head and Calum stopped him with a swipe of his dirk across his exposed under arm. The brute staggered back, mouth agape. He raised his sword and charged in for another clash of iron.

Anne shrieked. A thick, hairy arm grabbed her around the waist and hefted her over his shoulder.

"Help!" Anne kicked her legs as the pungent swine hauled her out the door. She slammed her fists against his back and the heathen mocked her, howling with a hacking laugh.

He pushed through the stable doors and into a vacant stall. Throwing her down on a musty pile of straw, he slid the door shut behind him. The moonlight shone through the barred window and cast a shadow across his black bearded face.

He glared down at her and cackled while he unclasped his sword belt. "You're a pretty morsel to be traveling around these parts."

"Keep your filthy hands off me."

His eyes popped wide. "Why you're an *English* lass."

"Lowlander." She hedged, trying to affect a Scottish accent. Calum had warned her to keep her mouth shut. The feral beast took a step toward her and Anne shoved her back against the wall, her hands blindly feeling for anything she could use as a weapon.

"It doesna matter to me, wench, as long as you're warm."

Discarding his belt, in one move he crouched over her. His hands either side of her head, he trapped her with a low chuckle. Anne swallowed hard and crossed her legs tight. The stench of him made her wretch. She shrieked when he grabbed at her, his hands everywhere. Her dress ripped. He seized her leg. Anne twisted against his brutal fingers. He pressed her to the ground and forced her legs apart with his knees, pinning her shoulders down with his hands.

"Friggin' boar's bullocks. Trews?"

Anne kicked and gasped for air. His face was an inch from hers and he licked her mouth while one hand fumbled with her trouser laces. Unable to break from under his crushing weight, she raised her head and bit his cheek. Her mouth filled with vile beard and the taste of salt and dirt but she didn't release. She sank her teeth deeper until he yanked his head away.

He bellowed like a bull being castrated and jerked his palm back. Anne tried to shield her face, but the speed of his hand ripped through her defenses and slapped across her face. Her teeth crunched and the stinging pain seared her skin. Anne struggled to pull her legs together against his weight. He crushed his body atop her. She could scarcely breathe. With all her strength, she shoved his heavy chest, unable to make him budge. Hot prickles attacked her skin as she wheezed. His weight would soon suffocate her.

Chapter Seventeen

In a flash, the rutting bastard's heavy body lifted. Anne sucked in a gulp of God given musty air and recoiled at a thud crashing across the stall.

"I'll cut off yer cock and stuff it down yer neck!" Calum crouched low and brandished his claymore as the moonbeams shot rays across his deadly sneer. A savage growl erupted from Calum's throat as he circled the filthy animal.

The rogue's eyes darted toward his sword. Anne saw it glimmer in the hay beside her leg. She snatched up the hilt and bolted for the far wall.

"Ask forgiveness for yer sins 'cause I'm sending ye straight to hell."

The brute bent down to pull a dirk from his hose. Calum didn't hesitate. He lunged and sliced his blade across the stunned man's neck. The Scot's mouth gaped and his hands flew up to stop the bleeding but there was little he could do. He flopped down to the hay and lay in a lifeless heap, his vacant eyes staring at nothing.

Calum dropped his sword and pulled Anne into his embrace. "Are ye all right, milady?"

She buried her head in Calum's shoulder and shuddered. "I-I don't know." Tears streamed down her face. With every nerve trembling, she tried to be strong. "I-I'm a b-bit shaken." Anne wanted to nestle against his warm chest and stay there.

His lips caressed her forehead. "Of course ye are. A woman as fine as ye should not be traveling these lawless lands—'tis no place for any lassie."

Anne wrapped her arms around his waist and he grimaced. Her hand touched something hot and wet. She held up her hand to the streaming moonlight. Blood. "You're injured."

"Tis just a scratch, but we need to get back to the men." He led her out of the stall. "'Twas only a drunken barney but I want to be sure it's over."

Mopping up a substantial puddle of blood, the inn's matron shot them a heated look when they returned. Calum dug in his sporran. "I'll pay ye for the damages."

"Aye, ye will." She held out her hand while Calum counted out the shillings.

Ian and John walked in through the back door. "The big fella didna make it," John said.

Calum faced them. "I'll take me *cousin* upstairs. Give me a minute to get her settled, then bring a basin of hot water."

Anne let Calum take her arm and lead her up the creaking steps. Her hands still trembled, but so did his. He closed the door behind them and faced her. "I shouldna brought ye overland but now 'tis too late to turn back. Ye do not look like a Scottish lassie and I cannot figure how we'll make it all the way to Carlisle with ye in that dress and yer highborn English accent."

"I'm sorry." Anne studied the toes of her boots. "If you had only explained the danger—queen's knees, you just said your word is law and I'd better go along with it or else."

"I'm a *laird*. The care of the clan is in me hands." Calum stretched his side with a grimace. "'Tis no' just that. Do ye ken how beautiful ye are?" He raked his fingers through his hair. "I've never seen a woman with half yer beauty. Ye have it all—hair of spun gold, rosy lips like an archer's bow and eyes that look as if they were forged of sapphire. 'Tis too much for a Highland scrapper to resist."

"How could you exaggerate so?"

Calum grasped her shoulders. "What I'm saying is you're very pleasing to the eye—very. Every heathen from here to Carlisle will want to lay with ye."

Anne bit her bottom lip. "I'll wear the trews on the morrow."

"Thank ye."

"Can the pack mule carry my day gown?"

"Aye." He cupped his hand against her cheek. "All yer fine things left behind. Is that why you're fighting me so?"

Anne wrapped her arms around her body. Her things? Is that what he thought? What about leaving Raasay and Mara and Bran and Friar Pat, Swan…and *him*? Did he have no clue how she felt? How much this ransom tore her apart?

"Anne?"

"We both knew this was coming." She swallowed the words she so desperately wanted to speak. Calum had made it clear—he cannot love her. "But that does not make it more palatable."

She dropped her gaze and studied the blood caked on the side of his linen shirt. It ran down over his kilt. He looked as if he was still bleeding. He needed tending. "Remove your shirt and I shall inspect your wound."

"'Tis nothing."

She tapped her foot. "I'll be the judge of that. Now let me have a look."

With a groan, he cast his eyes toward the rafters. "Do ye ken anything about stitching up wounds?"

"I'm adept at needlepoint."

Calum tugged his shirt out from his kilt and pulled it over his head. The sight of Calum standing bare chested right in front of her sapped every ounce of her resolve. A shock of heat coiled between her hips. Her knees buckled and her mouth went dry. The muscles on his chest stood proud and square, leading to a rippled stomach. His kilt sat low on his hips, exposing his naval—and below it, a silky trail of tantalizing coppery hair. Anne couldn't breathe, and this time there was no smelly brute crushing her.

Calum chuckled and pointed to his side. "Me wound's over here."

With a blink, Anne tore her eyes away. The heat rising to her cheeks felt like a blast from a flame. She stared at the oozing cut just above Calum's hip—a sobering sight.

"I told ye 'twas just a scratch."

Anne placed her fingers on either side of the gash. He gasped when her cold fingers touched his warm skin and gently inspected the wound. Blood gushed out, and Calum pressed his shirt against it.

Anne grasped the shirt and held the compress in place. "It needs to be stitched."

Reaching down, Calum lifted her chin and tilted it up toward him. His chest heaved with every breath. His tongue slowly ran across his top lip. She'd kissed him enough to know he wanted to taste her—even with his wound bleeding. Events in this God forsaken place had rekindled the spark they shared. Anne realized it had never been snuffed.

John burst through the door with Ian and Bran behind him, carrying ewers of water. They all stood in the doorway with gaping mouths.

"What?" Calum threw a hand out to his side. "She needs to stitch me wound."

They all nodded with nervous laughs, and the tension in the room eased. John, Ian and Bran gathered around her, showing their battle wounds. Fortunately, none had anything else that needed to be stitched.

Anne had Calum sit on the lone chair and she knelt beside him. She removed a bone needle and catgut thread from the kit Friar Pat had insisted they carry along. Careful not to cause more bleeding, she closely examined Calum's flesh. It seemed so human, so vulnerable. Yet he had fought with the heart of a lion. He smelled of wood smoke and the spicy musk that made him not just any man, but Calum MacLeod, Laird of Raasay.

He had always said he would protect her and this night he had not hesitated to act on his promise. A pink scar under his arm caught her eye.

"How did you come by that?"

"Fighting the English with the Sutherlands, protecting Dornoch Castle in forty-seven."

Anne did the math. "You were but a boy."

"Aye."

His eyes darkened, and Anne realized he'd been in the midst of battle against Lord Wharton's sword. "He was there. Was he not?"

"We chased him all the way back to Carlisle."

"Why were you helping the Sutherlands?"

"That's what any honorable Scot would do when their ally is plundered by a…"

"Murdering bastard?" The curse spilled from Anne's mouth. *Is the baron truly thus?*

Calum ran his hand over her hair. "Aye."

"I'm sorry," she whispered.

Beside her sat a man who would defend his clan against any foe and fight for her virtue, the virtue of his enemy's *wife*. Calum was a man of honor. She brushed her fingers across his warm skin. This would hurt him. She looked at the bone needle and gritted her teeth. Deftly, she pushed it through and tied off the first stitch. Calum made not a sound but took a draw from his flagon.

She kept her eyes on her work. "He's a good man, your friar. 'Tis nice to see someone looks after you."

Calum took another swig of whisky. "Aye. He does what he can."

She needed to take another stitch. Examining at the wound, Anne's stays pushed against her ribs as if constricting her to the point of swooning. She swallowed and willed herself to keep her wits. Her hand trembled when she held up the needle.

Calum reached down and wrapped his fingers around her wrist. "Would ye rather John do it?"

She dared rake her eyes up his torso and met his gold-flecked gaze. With a swallow, she shook her head. "I'll be fine." Anne steadied her hand. He took in a breath, drawing her attention to the line of copper hair below his navel. If only she could run her hand across the rock-hard muscles of his abdomen.

He cleared his throat and she again focused on the task at hand. Though he showed no outward sign of discomfort, the needle had to hurt. She must work quickly for him. After the first piercing of flesh, Anne tied off five stitches. She blew on the gash to cool the burn, just like Hanna would have done back at Titchfield House.

Calum took a long draw from his flagon and gave her a cockeyed grin. "Ye done well, milady." His voice sounded low and husky. He reached down and traced his finger from her ear, along her jaw. He stopped at her lips. Her tongue snuck out and tapped it. Eyes locked, Anne wondered if it was the whisky or if he, too, felt the surge of their unbridled attraction.

Chapter Eighteen

Calum and his men had the horses saddled and the mule packed. The feisty English woman had locked herself in the room right after they'd broken their fast. She'd insisted on privacy and four ewers of hot water. Calum warned her they had no time for a bath, but of course she wouldn't listen. *Why does someone need four ewers of hot water to wash their face and hands? At this rate, we willna reach Carlisle until Christmas.*

He didn't care if she was bare arsed naked. Heading toward the inn to fetch her, he didn't make it far. Anne walked out the door wearing her trews. The only problem, she looked nothing like a man. Calum rubbed his hands across his eyes and gaped again.

"What?" she asked.

Anne's trews fit snugly, and she'd belted the linen shirt around the waist so it clung to her bosoms. He could tell she'd wrapped them, but she had far too much on top to be wearing a shirt snug against her body. Anne managed to stuff all of her hair under the bonnet, but she had the cap cocked halfway atop her head like one of her fancy coronets.

Her eyes had that spark behind them—told him he'd better tread lightly. "Ye look—ah—too pretty. I think we need to roughen ye up a bit."

Bran trotted round the corner on his horse. "Milady? Dunna tell me you're going to wear that? Ye'll have every single man within a hundred miles on their knees beggin' for a kiss."

The lad was obviously coming of age. "Get back in the stable and check the mule," Calum barked.

"But I've already checked him ten times."

"Do it again." Calum returned his gaze to Anne.

"And just how do you think you'll turn this." She gestured to her chest. "Into something that looks like a man? I've been at it all morning."

Calum tried not to stare and pushed her back into the inn. He started to reach for her belt, but pulled his hands away. "May I?"

"If you must."

"First thing, yer shirt needs to hang loose." Calum pulled off her belt. "Looks better already." He removed his plaid. "Ye can wear me colors." He draped it across her shoulder, ensuring it covered her breasts.

She examined his work. "I say, that is an improvement."

"Next we need to set yer bonnet to rights—I'm sorry, but you're wearing it like a lassie."

"My tresses are too thick. I even braided them and pinned them to my head."

"Ye did a grand job. Ye haven't a single strand of hair showing." He reached up and tilted the hat to the side. A braid tumbled from beneath.

"You see?"

Calum stepped back and frowned. "What if ye wear a single braid down yer back and tuck it into yer shirt?"

"Do you think that will work?"

"'Tis worth a try."

It was a mistake when Calum placed his hand on her shoulder to help her re-braid her silken hair and stuff it down the back of her shirt. Attacked by the heady scent of delicious woman and rose soap, his eyes trailed to her collar. He caught a glimpse of the pearly smooth skin of her nape. If only he could slip his hand down and touch her. And then push his hand under the waistband of those trews and fill his palm with sleek, creamy buttock.

"Does it look all right?" she asked over her shoulder.

"'Tis better." He hoped she didn't notice the crack in his voice. She turned to face him, and he bit back his yearning. He positioned the bonnet tipped over her right ear as a man would wear it and stepped back, allowing his senses a brief reprieve from her feminine scent. She was still far too beautiful. He ran his hands across the floor and smudged her cheeks with dirt.

Anne sneezed. "Queen's knees, next you'll be having me roll in a swine's bog."

"Is there one nearby?" Calum laughed, but it might dampen the scent of woman who drove him to the brink of madness.

He knew he'd overstepped decorum when she cuffed him on the shoulder. He didn't mind. She wore her trews as he requested, and since the mishap last night, the wall of ice she'd thrown up between them had melted a bit. Though he could never make her his, he wanted to part on good terms. Not only so she would represent him well to Lord Wharton, but also because he valued her friendship and wanted her to remember him with fondness. He would always cherish her memory.

With a twinge of remorse, Calum grasped her elbow and led her toward the door. Anne stopped and faced him. "I wanted to thank you for last night."

"Baa, 'twas just a wee skirmish."

"It may have been to you, but things could have turned out very badly for me." Shuttering her eyes, she stepped in and kissed him on the cheek.

Again, the achingly familiar scent of roses and woman attacked him. A rogue wave of desire crashed through his mind. All the emotion from the past month came flooding back. He grasped her shoulders. She lifted her chin, her eyes dark, lustful. He cast his gaze to her mouth and brushed his lips across hers. When her tongue flicked out and caressed him, he nearly came undone. If only he could take her upstairs and claim her for himself. But if this was all he could steal, he would savor every moment until forced to say goodbye.

He opened his mouth and welcomed her tongue. She tasted of fresh mint. Anne's arms slipped around his neck and pulled him close.

"Calum," John called from the doorway.

His heart sank as he pulled away. They'd already lost too much time. Calum bit his lip and stared into Anne's fathomless sapphire eyes. They reflected the same torture branded into his heart. Unable to look away, he held her gaze, silently telling the lady how much he loved her. He could not say it, but he would make the memories from the past months last a lifetime.

***

Lord Wharton set up his command at the King's Head Inn at Carlisle. It took little effort to raise an army, especially with the promise of quick payment. He placed an extra guard on the battlements of the citadel with instructions to watch for Scots, particularly those wearing red and black tartan. With any luck, the bastards who had his wife would pay a visit before they delivered Lady Anne and he'd have Denton track them to their camp.

He rubbed the spot where the outlaw had cut his arm. The pain of it constantly reminded him he'd nearly had the bastard in his clutches. But he'd slipped away like a rat in a sewer, leaving no trace, not even a clue to lead Wharton to the clan's lair.

Since the kidnapper was a pirate, the baron stationed sentries at the mouth of the Firth of Solway and at Bowness-on-Solway, a half-day's ride from Carlisle, it held the greatest vantage point of the entire waterway.

Lord Wharton ran his fingers over the small chest on the table in his room. It held one thousand gold sovereigns—the price of Lady Anne's ransom. He hated being in this position. This was no longer about his wife. It had become an insult to his reputation. Wharton could not bear the thought of failure in the eyes of England.

Yes, Lady Anne had piqued his interest at the coronation. Thoughts of her had consumed him—to feel the taut flesh of a maiden beneath him after years of marriage. She had looked so pure, so ripe, so fuckable the first time he glimpsed her from across the hall of Westminster. For months he could think of little else but his desire to bed Lady Anne Wriothesley, daughter of the Earl of Southampton. Forcing his cock through her maidenhead would empower him, show all he was a powerful lord to be feared. To hell with established noble families and their "old" blood. The name of Wharton would be respected throughout Christendom. Though Lady Anne was not the earl's firstborn daughter, her breeding was impeccable, and her status on his arm would bolster his reputation—unless a scandal erupted.

Wharton had tried to keep news of his wife's disappearance confidential, but it had been nearly impossible with the loss of the *Flying Swan*. A plundered ship created gossip in London, especially with the new galleon having been taken so close to England's shores. He must move quickly to ensure his reputation suffered no ill consequences.

The baron shook his head. His need to take Lady Anne to his marriage bed must wait until he was sure she remained pure. He would not have his name sullied by a whore nor would he have a bastard child foisted upon him.

A rap at the door pulled him from his thoughts. Master Denton stepped inside.

"Any word?" Wharton demanded.

Denton hissed a breath of air through his bottom teeth. "No. I think they're smart enough not to come near Carlisle until they deliver the baroness."

"What of my money? Someone must intercept an unmanned skiff with a thousand pounds with haste once she's launched."

"We'll have lookouts posted." Denton ran his finger across the top of the treasure box. "Have you changed your mind? We could still try to intercept them before the lady is delivered."

Wharton nudged the box out from under Denton's touch. "No. Proceed as planned, but we *will* recover the ransom after she's safe. You have my word." He shook his finger under Denton's nose. "I want you on the bastard's trail as soon as she's spotted and I want a full out public display of horror for him and his men, understand?"

Denton grinned. It was not a smile anyone would care to meet in a dark alley.

***

As Calum expected, once Anne dressed in the disguise, no more skirmishes like the one at Fort William detained them. The remainder of their two-week journey south continued smoothly, aside from the rain, mud, and the increasing misery which lay siege to his heart.

Calum timed it perfectly and on the sixteenth of May they arrived outside Gretna, a small village on the north inlet of the Firth of Solway. He chose to avoid contact with humanity and they found a clearing in which to camp. Calum would not chance lighting a fire—not this close to Carlisle.

He asked Anne to take inventory of the food stores and pulled his men into a tight huddle. "At dusk on the morrow, Wharton will launch the skiff with a thousand pounds."

"Have ye given any thought to how we'll intercept it?" Bran asked.

"That's what I was just going to tell ye." Calum nudged the lad with his elbow. "John and Ian—rub Bran down with fat mixed with coal to turn his skin black and protect him from the cold. Wait until the dark of night. With any luck, we'll have a cover of cloud." Calum grasped Bran by the shoulders. "Swim to the skiff with four bladders filled with air and a butcher's hook."

Bran grinned. "Then I'll reach over the side of the boat and nab the coin."

"Aye. Hook the ransom to the bladders and swim with it back to the north shore. Ye'll need to shove the skiff on a path toward the southern shore. They'll be watching it. I want the skiff as far off course as ye can manage." Calum looked to the older men. "Once ye have the coin, ride west until ye reach the cove. Do not stop for anything. Ride hard."

"Are ye planning to take Lady Anne to Carlisle alone?" John asked.

"I recon they'll no' be expecting two men dressed in trews to be riding into the citadel. I'll take her as far as I can and then high tail it to the cove. If I'm not there by dawn the next morning, set sail without me."

"I dunna like that. Wouldna ye rather have one of us up a tree to cover yer back when ye cross the border?" John asked.

Calum sliced his hand through the air. "The fewer of us there are, the less curiosity we'll attract." *And the fewer of us will die.*

Calum knew his cousin wouldn't like it, but there was no use putting more good men in danger. If there was a skirmish, Calum could slip out easier on his own. And if he was caught, Wharton would most likely forget about chasing after the others. His men could return home safely and Brochel Castle might be spared an English attack.

John pulled him aside. "If ye dunna return is Norman in charge?"

"Nay, ye are, John. Just as I wrote into the charter. Ye'll need to make the decisions until I make it back to Raasay."

Anne came up beside Calum. "We've only enough food for two more days. You'll need to do some hunting before you head home."

"'Tis what I thought." Calum hated misleading her, but it was best she remained unaware of their plans. One slip of the tongue and Wharton could engage the *Sea Dragon* in battle before it reached the protection of Brochel Cove.

Calum inclined his head down the path. "Will ye walk with me?"

"Of course, my lord." Anne placed her hand in the crux of his elbow—a comfortable gesture—one that had become all too accustomed. But his insides churned. If only he could grovel at her feet and beg her to turn tail and ride back to Raasay with him.

Once out of earshot from his men, Calum stopped and steeled his resolve. "Tomorrow night I will take ye to Carlisle."

Anne said nothing.

He faced her and clasped her hands between his. "I wish I didna have to do this, but ye belong to another man."

Anne dropped her gaze and stared at their intertwined hands. "I understand. I must honor my family's wishes."

"I need to ask ye to dress in yer trews one last time."

Anne shook her head. "In England, such a thing is illegal, a crime punishable…"

Calum held up his hand. "Lord Wharton will protect ye from that, and ye can say I forced ye. We'll be riding straight into the lion's den. If ye care anything for me, ye will do as I ask."

She raised her chin and looked him in the eye. "Very well. If it will help you, my lord."

He knew she was hurting by her clipped speech—and the way she refrained from using his name. Calum's heart skipped a beat. She cared. Though from the outset, he'd wanted to earn Lady Anne's respect, it made parting so much more bittersweet.

She stepped closer. "When we reach Carlisle, there will be no time to say goodbye, will there?"

He cupped her face with his hands. "No, lass."

She rested her hands on his shoulders. His entire being turned molten. She closed the gap and met his gaze. Her warm body touched his. Calum laced his arms around her waist and squeezed his eyes shut. Anne pressed her lips to his, her mouth sweet and moist. The heat rising beneath his kilt liquefied his knees.

During this journey, his erections had grown harder and more painful. She rubbed her mons against him and he groaned. Heat spiked and hit him low in the gut. He rocked his hips with the need to enter her. The friction of her movement made his eyes roll back. She would unman him right there in the woods if he did not ease the pressure.

His thighs shuddered and his ballocks ached like hellfire and brimstone. It took every ounce of control Calum could muster to restrain himself to a kiss. Right now, this very moment, he should lead her into the brush and rip off those damnable trews. Thank God he'd been riding in front of her this whole trip, because the view from behind rendered him dumb as well as mute. He'd been a fool to think he could make her look masculine. Everything about her, from her nose, to her tiny waist, to her womanly hips, and her heady smell that invaded his senses whenever she was within his grasp, drove him to the very edge of insanity.

Anne slid her hand down the length of his back and around the front of his waist. She rested her palm on his abdomen and stroked him. He tried to breathe. Calum knew he should move her hand away, but it felt too good.

"When I stitched you up, I wanted to brush my fingers over the coppery curls below your navel."

A rush of heat blasted through the tip of his cock and a moist bead pooled where it tapped his kilt. He pulled his shirt out and guided her hand across flesh that screamed for her touch. Her fingers tickled him, teased him, but it wasn't low enough.

Watching her eyes, Calum slid his hand down and untied her trews. Damn his soul to the devil, he could not resist her.

***

Anne could scarcely breathe as Calum thumbed her laces loose and slid his hand into the front of her trousers. The entire journey she had ached for him to touch her again. When they lay beside the campfire at night, it took all of her willpower not to reach out and wrap her arms around him, even with the other men present.

"I've wanted this so much—wanted you."

Calum covered her mouth and pulled her against him with unbridled force, as if he'd been holding in as much longing as she had.

Anne yanked his shirt over his head and unfastened the buckle of his kilt. She looked him square in the eye and dropped the plaid. Oh Holy Mother, he was beautiful. Standing naked in the shadows, the outline of his erection stood proud. He bent his knees and rubbed it between her legs.

Anne threw her head back and moaned. She shoved down her trews, yanking them over her boots. Pulling him with her, she lay back on the mossy ground.

Calum kneeled over her, kissing her, eating her as if he'd been starved. Anne reached between them and wrapped her fingers around his manhood and stroked. Calum's groan inflamed her core. She didn't know how to do it, but he was right over the sacred spot where he could claim her.

"I want to feel you inside me."

Calum pulled back so she could see his eyes. "We cannot. Do ye ken what he'll do if I take yer innocence?"

"I no longer care."

"Ye would be ruined…I cannot…"

Anne stroked him, arched her back and touched his manhood to her sex. Her thighs shuddered with the longing heat that spun tight inside her.

Calum eased his body over her. His manhood brushed along her opening. Anne's hips rocked, mimicking his motion. "I must pleasure ye without entering yer core."

"Then do so."

Anne closed her eyes and clamped her fingers on Calum's buttocks as he built the friction, rubbing his cock against her. Moisture from her sex spread over him and she thrust her hips up, bucking out of control. The tension mounting, she would explode at any moment. Calum's mouth demanded more from her, exploring, sucking. And then it happened—sweet release that took her over the top and gave reprieve to the coiled tension which had built for days. Straining against the need to cry out, Anne subdued her voice to a throaty rasp.

Calum rose to his knees and ran his lips down her neck and across her bound breasts. His manhood rested on her belly, still hard. Anne gently rolled him to the side and stroked him. He moaned and moved with her motion, sliding his hand down to tickle the sack just beneath. Anne increased her friction in concert with Calum's thrusting hips. Oh, how she wished she could straddle him and feel his manhood slip inside.

With a muffled groan that grated in his throat, Calum pulled her lips to him and found his release.

"Is there no end to your treasures?" Anne rested her head against his chest. "I don't know whether to love you or despise you."

Calum ran his hand across her hair. "Why would ye despise me, lass?"

"Because you have shown me a world I can never have." She ran a finger down the center of his chest. "And a potent man who will never be mine."

"I ken what ye say."

"If this were another time and place, I'd ask you to run away with me. But you have your clan, and I my family honor. We must follow our duty."

They lay in each other's arms until John called for them.

***

As Calum watched Anne retie her trews, his hate for Wharton dove to new depths. Calum cursed his weakness for understanding Lady Anne's duty. And he was all too aware he must return to Raasay in one piece. For the first time in his life, he resented it.

She pulled a piece of fabric from her pocket and stared at it. Looking closer, Calum could see it bore the crest of the MacLeod of Raasay. She beamed at him with those adorable dimples. "I imagine this is the best time to give this to you. I stitched it to resemble the tapestry in your chamber."

Calum's mouth went dry. He accepted the gift and studied it in the moonlight. How intricate the needlework. Anne had taken the time to make this for him, the sign of his clan? "'Tis perfect." He held the kerchief to his lips, closed his eyes and kissed it, his heart squeezing as if encased in a vise. "Made by yer fine hands. I will cherish it always."

Anne smiled—a naughty grin he'd only seen a few times. "I hoped you'd like it. I wanted you to have something to remember me by."

Calum had thought he could steel his heart against the agony, but this pushed him too far. He gathered Anne's hands and held them to his thundering chest. "I cannot let ye go. All ye need to do is say the word and we'll turn around."

She froze. Her mouth opened and closed. "We agreed to this at Brochel…" She looked away. "The ransom…"

Calum tightened his grip. "I care nothing for Wharton's coin."

Anne trembled violently beneath his palms, the whites of her eyes round in the moonlight. "We've come this far…my family honor…And Friar Pat said…"

Honor? That is the only word she need utter. Calum lowered her hands and released them. "Enough."

What was love without honor? Their love had been doomed before it began.

"We've no recourse but to see the plan through." Calum rested his lips upon her forehead and grimaced against the stabbing pain in his heart. "I will nay forget ye, Lady Anne. Yer bonny face is burned into me soul forever."

***

Anne lay on her side and listened to Calum's breathing. She didn't think he was asleep but there was nothing left to say or do. They had agreed. She was doing the right thing. *Truly?* Friar Pat had cemented her conviction. Holy in the eyes of God, she must honor her marriage vows.

Calum rolled to his side, and Anne stared at his broad back. Earlier, she'd run her fingers along the solid muscles of that back. If only she could touch it now. She shouldn't have been so forward, but God help her, she wanted him. Without thinking, she had yanked down her trews and cast aside nine and ten years of noble breeding, giving into the desire which consumed her. If it weren't for Calum's restraint, she would have been compromised. She inclined her head toward him. They had shared intimate passion, yet no guilt crept up her spine. He'd given her a gift she could lock in her heart and treasure until her death.

When she'd exposed his manhood, her thighs had shuddered. She'd lost her sense of reason. He'd shown her delights she could never have possibly imagined. The flesh between her legs still tingled. She'd never felt the pull of longing as powerfully as she did in that moment. Anne opened and closed her palm. She had held his manhood in it and had milked him as he had milked her. Together they had reached the pinnacle of passion. He said it was but a sampling of what could be. How could anything be better? She had wanted to pull the shirt over her head and unbind her breasts. If only Calum could hold her breasts in his hands and suckle them one last time.

She took in a deep breath. She recalled catching him ogling them a time or two at Brochel Castle. Of all her womanly parts, she thought he liked her bosoms the best.

Anne balled her fists. On the morrow she would face Lord Wharton, and he would expect the same things from her she'd shared with Calum. How could she give herself to a wrinkled old grandfather—open her legs and let him touch her? She shuddered at the thought of Wharton's mouth over hers with the rotten taste of decaying teeth. She loved Calum. Sharing such intimacy with any other man was unthinkable—as if she were a courtesan to her soul. *Sold to the highest bidder.*

This path would take her back to England to resume her life where she had left it when the big Scot had raided her ship like a pirate. She knew differently now. He'd secured the food and grain for the livelihood of the clan. She might have done the same thing, faced with sick children and nothing but pickled herring and seaweed to eat. He hadn't lied. They were all far too thin, living on that piece of rock they called an island.

She'd grown a fondness for the MacLeods of Raasay whom she would not forget. Aside from Hanna, she'd never had a friend like Mara, nor known a young man as full of vitality as Bran. Life at Titchfield House had been a bore in comparison, with everything so utterly proper and so utterly dull.

She closed her eyes and prayed life with Lord Wharton would at least harbor some kindness. Anne rolled to her back and gazed at the stars. *Please make him compassionate toward your servant, Calum.* She steepled her fingers against her lips. If Lord Wharton was anything like his reputation, her prayers might be mere whispers in the wind.

Chapter Nineteen

Anne and the men dawdled a bit the next morning. They changed into trews and linen shirts, opting to stuff their plaids into their satchels. Calum folded the tartan sash he'd given Anne to wear and packed it as well. He wanted nothing to identify the clan. They mounted their horses later than usual, this time in silence, as if they all had an unsavory task to perform. Even Bran frowned and watched the trail in front of him.

The sun had moved to the western sky when Calum looked at his men. "This is the path. Go with God."

Bran looked at Anne and raised his hand, as did the others. Yet, they said nothing. Anne realized they were in enemy territory now. If spies were lurking about, they'd pick up on any unusual movement.

She reined her mount beside Calum and kept her voice low. "Where are they going?"

"'Tis best ye dunna ken."

They continued on in silence until the sun set and then Calum spoke. "I will take ye to the citadel of Carlisle. Once there, I ask ye to wait and allow me some time to ride away."

"Will the baron be there?"

"Aye. 'Tis also why I didna want ye in yer gown. He'd recognize ye straight away. Dressed as a man, 'twill take them some time and I'll be able to ride nearer the citadel with you."

"Do you think it safe?"

"I cannot leave ye to ride alone. I must see ye arrive unharmed."

Anne reached her hand out but he shied away.

"Guaranteed, the baron has spies lurking in every dark corner." His gaze shot to her with a look of longing and defeat. "We said our goodbyes last eve."

Anne ground her teeth and turned her attention to the dark path ahead. She wanted to turn her mare around and gallop back to Scotland. Lord Wharton was an old man. What would his skin feel like beneath her hands? Would his lips be as tender and caring as Calum's?

Her stomach clenched. She loved Calum MacLeod. Blast the proxy marriage. How could it be upheld in a court of law when she had not given her consent? Her family was powerful. Surely a botched marriage would be a minor blemish on the Wriothesley name that would soon be forgotten. But what about ruining her younger sister's chances? Could she stage her death? She moved to rein her horse around when Calum pointed.

"Ye can see the flames atop the battlements of the citadel."

The nape of Anne's neck pricked. Could that be the light of her doom?

Calum led her to the edge of the town and stopped in the shadows. "This is where we must part ways."

Her mouth went dry and Anne swallowed. She didn't want to say goodbye. Could she change her mind now? "I wish..."

"Ye'll be fine, lass."

"How will you get back?"

"Ride like hellfire." Calum leaned toward her. "I'll never forget ye, Lady Anne."

He reached back and slapped her horse's rump. Before she could object, the mare took off toward the gates. Anne steadied herself against the sudden jolt and slowed the horse to a trot. Looking ahead, her skin crawled as if she approached an executioner. It didn't help when a rider neared, wearing black, with a gaunt face. Passing, the dark rider eyed her like she was a thief. A group of soldiers clomped behind him.

She gazed at the two rounded towers, joined by a sharp-toothed portcullis. The tall curtain walls around Carlisle reminded her of a prison. She reined her horse outside the black gate. What should she do next? Merchants and people swarmed around her, but no one appeared to be stationed at the wall, waiting for a baroness to arrive. Should she dismount? She wanted to give Calum plenty of time to make good his escape.

Her questions were answered when the gaunt man reined his horse beside her. "What business have you in Carlisle?" he demanded.

Anne jolted in her seat. Hadn't she seen him leave? She bit her lip and glanced back over her shoulder. She thought to run, but the man grabbed her reins. "I asked you a question."

"I-I'm looking for Lord Wharton." She removed her bonnet and pulled the braid out from under her shirt. "I am the Baroness of Wharton."

Fury flashed in his eyes. He pointed to two men. "Take the baroness to his lordship." With a thudding into his horse's ribs, he charged away at a gallop, a dozen men behind him.

A cool breeze swept through loose wisps of her hair, but perspiration stung the creases of Anne's arms. With a sharp breath, she wanted to flee, but a soldier had hold of her reins. *Run, Calum, for hell has just made chase.*

A foot soldier grabbed her horse's bridle. He led her into the city. The world spun. More soldiers surrounded her. Leading her to a lime-washed inn, they pulled Anne from her mount. With a guard on either side, Anne followed them inside and up the stairs. A sentry opened the door and someone shouted, "Lord Wharton, the baroness has arrived."

Perspiration sullied her palms. The soldiers ushered her through a chamber door and closed it behind her. A bald man dressed in red velvet with white hose peered at her through squinted eyes. His chubby jowls jostled around his chin and he folded his arms across his rotund frame.

He eyed her with a dour frown. "You could not possibly be the beautiful maid I watched from across the aisle at Westminster Abbey."

Anne curtseyed and swallowed her revulsion. "Lord Wharton. I've been traveling on horseback for weeks. I have a gown in my satchel. Please allow me a moment to compose my person."

He walked around her with an appraising glower. "You certainly don't sound like a guttersnipe." He sniffed. "Though you smell as foul as one."

Anne dug in the pouch tied to her waist. "I have the decree of marriage if you do not believe me." She held it out, wondering if she should have excused herself and said it was a hoax. No. He would undoubtedly throw her in gaol for breaking sumptuary laws.

Wharton snatched the paper from her hand and held it to the light. When he lowered it, he pursed his lips and faced her. "Well, wife. We meet at last." He tossed the decree on the table and rang a bell.

A grey-haired servant appeared from a side door. "Simon, show the baroness to her quarters, and see Mrs. Crabapple draws her bath."

"Yes, my lord."

The servant beckoned to Anne, but Lord Wharton stopped her before she reached the door. "Remain in your dressing gown. I will have the physician attend you."

Anne turned. "I am in good health, my lord."

"We shall let the doctor attest to that." He folded his arms. "And when you next address me, I expect to see a woman fitting for the title of Baroness."

He did not have the decency to ask about her person, or how she had been treated during her captivity. Of all the pompous old men she'd met, he had to be the most insufferable. She cringed. He also had to be the most unpleasant to the eye.

***

When Calum saw the man reach for Anne's reins, he knew she would have no choice but to reveal her identity. Watching her go, a part of him died.

He galloped his horse northward, but he'd cut the timing too close. The man on the black steed chased after him, a parcel of soldiers in tow. Calum's mount was tired from a full day of riding but he spurred him on, running for his life.

He got his wish and clouds shrouded the sky with darkness. Trees whipped his face, and he could not see far. Calum's mind raced. If he turned west toward the ship, they'd send scouts to trail him for certain. If he stayed on his course to the north, with fresh horses, the English would eventually catch him, unless he encountered a miracle.

Calum glanced over his shoulder. Their outlines neared closer against the dark sky. If he rode all night, he might reach Lockerbie. There, he could ask for protection from the Douglas. As far as he knew, Ruairi hadn't done anything to land on their bad side. The Douglas Clan had been hit hard in the battle of Solway Moss as well. They hated Wharton even more than the MacLeods.

The thundering of a dozen horses neared from behind. Calum leaned further forward in his saddle. He could not stop. He would not look back again.

He galloped into a forest and darkness enveloped him. Heels dug deep, he pushed harder. The horse under him lurched and stumbled. Calum flew from his saddle. Instinctively, he tucked his body and prepared for the crushing fall. His back hit first. Air whooshed from his lungs. Straining to gasp a breath, he looked back to see a gaping hole dug in the path. *A trap*. His horse lay across from him, rocking and trying to rise. *His leg is broken*.

The soldiers surrounded him. Calum panted, still struggling to reclaim his breath. A gaunt, darkly clad man walked up beside him with a tsk of the tongue. He swung his foot back and kicked Calum in the gut. With sharp gasps, Calum curled into a ball to protect his innards from another assault.

The ugly man crouched down beside him. "You thought you could escape from the likes of Baron Wharton?" He drew his fist back and slammed it into Calum's jaw. "I'd kill you now, but that would spoil the baron's fun."

The iron taste of blood spilled across Calum's tongue. Rolling to his knees, he surveyed the copse around him, seeking his best chance of escape.

A boot to the arse laid him out flat. A soldier hopped down and tied his wrists with hemp rope—so tight the bindings cut into his skin.

The darkly clad man stood, drew his knife and ran his blade across the lame horse's throat. "Drag this traitor back to Carlisle, but make sure he stays alive. The baron will want a word before we hang him."

Calum focused on controlling his breathing. His jaw throbbed but he steeled his mind against the pain. A mounted soldier yanked on the rope. Calum had no choice but to run to keep up with the fast trot. If he fell, they would drag him for certain. The more they battered his body now, the less his chances were he'd survive once they got him inside.

***

Though Anne had longed for a bath, this one was anything but soothing. She wondered where Lord Wharton had found the crotchety old matron with a cadaverous face who scrubbed her down with the roughest piece of sackcloth imaginable. "I'm quite capable of bathing myself."

"I beg to differ. I could smell you from the passageway." Mrs. Crabapple took one more turn, scrubbing Anne's back. "My lady."

"I've been traveling for weeks. There was little opportunity for a bath."

Mrs. Crabapple stood back and inspected her work. "How could you appear before the baron in a pair of trews? He will not soon forget that. His status is of utmost importance."

"I didn't have much choice in the matter. After all, I was a *hostage*."

"You should have begged for a bath before you were presented to him."

Anne glowered into the water. As she remembered it, she was pulled off her horse and marshaled up to Lord Wharton's chamber without so much as a word.

Mrs. Crabapple ground soap into her hair. "You'll be lucky if he doesn't request an annulment."

Anne folded her arms across her breasts. If Lord Wharton wanted an annulment, he was welcome to proceed. But she wasn't going to say another word to the old biddy. Anne had tried to explain, but the nasty woman countered everything she said—as if Anne had kidnapped herself. She would send for Hanna at her first opportunity.

Once she had scrubbed Anne's skin raw, Crabapple held up a drying cloth. Anne snatched it from her hands. "I'll do it myself. I'd like to keep the skin that remains."

"His lordship is displeased." The old woman wrung her hands. "Very displeased indeed. He instructed me to insure you were cleansed of all Scottish filth."

Anne reached for the dressing gown the woman had brought in with the wooden bath and tied the sash around her waist.

Mrs. Crabapple picked up Anne's clothes and headed for the hearth.

"You burn them and I will tell his lordship of your deplorable mistreatment of my person." Two could play at her game.

The woman dropped the clothes in heap and shook her hands nervously. "Please do not disparage my actions before his lordship."

Anne stepped forward. "Has he been unkind to you?"

"Ah, no." Mrs. Crabapple's eyes shot to the door. "Dear blessed Jesus, spare me his wrath…But those clothes should be burned."

"They need to be washed."

"Heaven help us all." She cowered from the pile of clothing as if it were alive. "Are you planning to wear them again?"

"Presently, they are the only set of clothes I have aside from the dress in my satchel. The Scot kept my trunks." She didn't want to speak too harshly against Calum and honestly, she had no idea why she didn't want Mrs. Crabapple tossing her trews in the fire, aside from the fact they were hers and they had been Calum's. Her heart squeezed. They were the only things she possessed to remind her of him.

A sharp rap sounded at the door.

A creaky voice resounded from the corridor. "Doctor Smallwood at your service, my lady."

Crabapple scurried to open the door. Stepping aside, she let him pass. Holding a candle, his black robes whooshed against the floorboards. Pulled low over his brow sat the black coif of a physician. He turned to the matron. "If you don't mind, I am to examine Lady Anne in private."

Crabapple frowned, and Anne inclined her head toward the door. She hoped she'd never see the dour servant again. But she swallowed hard when she faced the physician.

He gave her a nervous smile and cleared his throat. "The baron has asked me to validate your virginity."

Anne felt the blood drain from her face. "You can do that?"

"With some level of effectiveness, I have read it has been done."

"But you've never done it yourself?"

He pushed up his sleeves. "No. However, that shouldn't worry you. I've read extensively on the subject."

Anne pulled the dressing gown tighter across her body. "I can assure you, I have been touched by no man."

The physician's eyes dropped to her midsection. "I would dearly love to take your word for it, but his lordship is paying me quite handsomely to perform the test." He glanced back toward the door. "I could ask the matron to come back in if you prefer."

"Absolutely not. She'd wallow in my humiliation, that one."

The doctor chuckled, as if he understood exactly. In other circumstances, Anne might have found a fondness for the man.

"I'll need you to recline on the bed."

Anne looked toward the canopy bed with green silk drapes. She rubbed the back of her neck. If she refused, Crabapple would no doubt be overjoyed to come in and hold her down. Worse, if she refused, it would be reported to the baron. What would he do? Seek an annulment? She could live with that. However, the thought of the matron, and possibly a soldier or two muscling her down cemented her decision.

She clenched her fists and walked to the bed. "I cannot believe the extent of my degradation." She faced the physician. "I'm the one who endured a terrifying attack with cannons blasting the ship upon which I was a passenger because the baron had not the time to accompany me. I'm the one who was forced to live as a captive amongst the barbarians."

Doctor Smallwood bowed his head. "I understand you must have experienced a terrible ordeal."

Anne sat on the edge of the bed. "You are the only person who has made any such sympathetic comment since I arrived."

"I'm sure his lordship is occupied with the urgent pursuit of your captors."

Anne put her hands up to her face and pressed cold fingers to her hot cheeks. The physician would not know she feared for Calum more than she feared his exam. Let him think what he liked. *Run for your life, Calum.*

"Please recline."

Anne exhaled and scooted back against the pillows.

The physician tottered up to her and set his candle on the bedside table. He had her sit forward and removed two pillows from behind her back. "Now if you'll be so kind as to allow me to slide these under your hips."

Anne pushed her heels into the bed and raised her bottom while holding her dressing gown closed. She'd longed for the comfort of a bed but never had imagined this.

"If you'll spread your legs, I need to shine a light between them to make an examination."

"You cannot be serious. I have never…"

"I'm sure you have not. None the less, I am conducting this procedure exactly as it was written by the royal physicians." Smallwood cleared his throat and lifted the candle.

Anne opened her legs and stared at the green canopy above. She gripped her arms tightly across her chest. She would *never* forgive Lord Wharton for this. The man hadn't even inquired as to her health. Had he no compassion? Was she to be treated as chattel for the rest of her life?

Doctor Smallwood bent down. His icy hand pushed her thigh open wider. She clutched the edge of her robe, desperately wanting to pull it across her exposed and very private parts. A tear leaked from the corner of her eye and slid to her ear. The heat from the candle started to burn. She inched back with a gasp. The doctor straightened, taking the candle away. Anne slammed her legs closed and tucked them beneath her. "I believe you are quite finished here."

He pursed his lips, as if he needed to gawk at her privates for a moment longer, but Anne would have none of it. He'd had the look he requested, and she'd be damned if she'd let him peer at her a moment longer.

He set the candle back on the bedside table and pushed down his sleeves. "You said the barbarians didn't touch you improperly. How was their treatment otherwise?"

Anne bit the inside of her cheek. She must be careful. "They were rather taken aback when they found me on the ship—unsure what to do with me, actually. I was well fed and given a comfortable chamber until they could arrange my ransom."

The doctor nodded. "Smart of them, though I don't know if that will make any difference when they're caught."

Anne rubbed her shoulders as if a cold wind burst through the chamber and she watched the doctor take his leave. Once the door clicked shut behind him, the tears trapped in her eyes drained down her cheeks. Through bleary vision, she glimpsed her shirt and trews, crumpled in the corner. Staggering across the room, she doused them in the tepid bath water. Her hands still trembled as she wrung them out and then draped them over the fire screen. She would wake early and hide them someplace where Crabapple would keep her meddlesome hands off them.

Once they returned to Alnwick, Anne would insist Lord Wharton send for Hanna. Yes, Hanna would help her to forget both these past weeks *and* her bleak future.

Chapter Twenty

Though the hour was late, Wharton sat beside the hearth with his hand clenched around the handle of a tall tankard. His wife had come to him wearing men's clothing. He could send her to the executioner for breaking sumptuary laws. A woman of Lady Anne's breeding should be well aware of the penalty. Had they stripped her naked and forced her? He closed his eyes and focused on a conjured image of Scottish barbarians hiking up their kilts and taking turns with her.

He stood and threw the tankard into the fire. He didn't doubt his imaginings. He had led raids himself and used the women of the vanquished to satisfy his own raging appetite. War had a way of bringing out the savage in every man. Only a well-bred noble could walk away from such violence and return to behavior suitable to his social standing.

He plodded to the sideboard and reached for a flagon of brandy. He poured himself a goblet, needing something stronger to cool his blood. Wharton tossed it back when a light rap sounded on the door. *Finally.*

"Come."

The physician stepped inside, clutching his black bag.

"Is it done?"

"Yes, my lord. The lady needs rest. She has been under considerable stress."

Of course she would need rest, but that's not what Wharton wanted. "Is she...Is she *intact?*"

"I believe so."

"What on earth do you mean? Is she a virgin or not?"

"As I said, I believe so. The lighting in her chamber was very dim, I could not see up inside, though she is quite small." Doctor

Smallwood straightened and shook his finger. "As I said before, the only sure test is to examine the sheets after copulation."

Wharton threw up his hands. "I am paying for an *I believe so*? If she has been compromised, I do not want to soil my person, damned you. I need an answer."

Smallwood reached for the latch. "There is no evidence she has been compromised. If there is nothing else, my lord, I shall seek my bed."

Wharton waived him away. The doctor departed with a bow as Master Denton strode into the room. "We've caught the bastard."

Wharton frowned. "Only one?"

"He was alone."

"What of my money?"

"My men are still chasing it, my lord. We found the skiff empty. It appears one accompanied Lady Anne while others intercepted the ransom."

He slammed his fist on the table. "You mean to say you've lost a *thousand* pounds?"

"I did not say it was lost. 'Tis simply detained."

Wharton cracked his thumb knuckles. He needed his coin returned. "And where is the traitor now?"

"Enjoying your hospitality on the rack, my lord."

"Good." Wharton poured two goblets of brandy and handed one to his henchman.

Denton bowed. "Serving me with your own hand, my lord?"

"This once, for bringing in the bastard."

"Gratitude."

Wharton took a sip and swirled it over his tongue. "Stretch him until his eyes bulge and then leave him. Let him think about his plight during the night." He rubbed his chin. "We shall invite Lady Anne to attend the flogging in the morning."

Denton tossed down his drink and placed the cup on the sideboard. His dark eyes bore through the baron as they always did. "Very well, my lord." Denton strode out, his spurs jingling across the floorboards.

Wharton shivered. Though the man always made him feel uneasy, he knew his orders would be heeded. He licked his lips. He had caught the Scot—at least one of them. This would be yet another test for her ladyship. His hand wandered down and rubbed across his flaccid groin. Anne's appearance had done nothing to stir him and the drink had benumbed him enough he knew he wouldn't get a rise from the damnable thing even if he forced her to take him into her mouth.

After one last goblet of brandy, he headed to his bed. Tomorrow he'd send for Lady Anne. If the sheets were not bloody by the time he finished with her, she'd hang beside that plundering Highland rogue.

***

Calum tried to withhold his cries of pain, but the last turn of the crank wrenched a bellow from his gut that echoed across the dank dungeon. Stripped naked, one eye swollen shut, he lay atop a wooden rack, his hands and legs bound to the ratchets. They rotated the wheel, stretching the ropes tighter around his wrists and ankles. The last turn popped his wrist. The pain shot down his arm and roiled in his gut. Calum's head spun and bile burned the back of his throat as he struggled to gasp a breath of air.

The evil man in black had returned and probed his broken wrist with a poker. Calum swallowed his grunt.

The man's black eyes raked across his body. "You're a rugged blighter, are you not?" He walked around the rack, poking at Calum's legs and arms, studying him intently. "This will do. Leave him. We'll resume in the morning."

Calum's eyes rolled to the back of his head. They intended to keep him suspended taut on the rack? He'd be dead by morning, his arms ripped from their sockets. He tried to swallow and keep his breathing shallow and even. They had yet to ask him a single question. No matter. He would die before he betrayed his clan.

They snuffed the torches and left him alone with the rats. His mouth so dry, he would give his beloved *Sea Dragon* for a sip of water. Every muscle in his body trembled. He flicked out his tongue and licked parched lips. He prayed it would soon be over. His clan would make good use of the thousand pounds and he had named John his successor.

Calum closed his eyes and prayed Anne was safely asleep in her bed. He nearly heaved again when he thought of the tyrant Baron claiming her. With a pained swallow, he focused his mind on the *Sea Dragon*, standing on the forward deck, the wind in his hair. How he loved the open sea, the smell of salty air and the flapping of the sails above. He would send his mind far away on a new journey, chasing after silver from the Americas. The pain ebbed as he dreamed of sailing to warmer seas—consciousness slipped from his grasp.

***

When a bucket of water splashed across his face, terror seized Calum's gut. Opening his eyes, Calum became aware of a cold, hard touch on his private parts. He sputtered and blinked in quick succession to clear his vision. Every sinew in his body screamed in agony.

A rotund man, dressed in a fine leather doublet topped with a white ruff stood over him and raised his manhood with a dagger. "Did you put this in my wife?"

Acrid bile churned up Calum's throat. His thighs involuntarily shuddered and his eyes bugged open. He forced his voice to croak out the words. "No. Never."

The fat man—*Wharton*—pressed his knife into Calum's most tender flesh and looked behind him. "What do you think, Master Denton, is he telling the truth?"

Calum blinked rapidly, panting, straining for every breath. Sweat streamed down his forehead and clouded his vision.

The man wearing black stepped into Calum's view and surveyed him from head to toe. "Hmm. I'm surprised he's still alive."

Wharton smirked and slowly ran the knife across the base of Calum's manhood, making a sharp cut. He pulled away the knife and turned the blade in his hand. "Where are you from, Scot?"

Calum raised his chin, but couldn't see the extent of the damage Wharton had inflicted. His entire body convulsed with the effort to move.

"It looks as if he's not experienced enough of our hospitality, yet." Wharton chuckled. "Very well. Take him to the courtyard and tie him to the post."

When they released the tension of the rack, Calum's muscles burned as if seared by hot coals. His broken wrist dangled, swollen and blue. Before he could stretch out the stiffness, guards grabbed him under the arms and hauled him to the courtyard.

Blinded by the light, his eyes barely registered the shocked faces around him or the people who darted out of his path. He tried to work his legs beneath him, but they wobbled. "Water."

"You won't be needing a drink where you're going," a guard growled.

Calum tried to slide his good hand across his body to cover his manhood, but the jerking motion of the guards dragging him made it impossible. Hot blood streamed between his thighs from where Wharton had cut him. Calum dropped his gaze and let out a breath. Everything appeared to be still intact. He all but collapsed against the guards, who muscled him forward. A woman gasped.

His mind sharpened. His eyes darted across the dozens of horrified faces until he saw her.

Anne stood behind two soldiers who guarded her with crossed battleaxes. She wore a gown of red silk. Topped with a matching wimple, she looked like an angel from heaven. Calum closed his eyes. He would take her image to the grave.

***

Anne nearly vomited when they dragged Calum into the courtyard. She knew they were watching for her reaction, but she could not hide the shock and horror of seeing Calum beaten and stripped naked. With one eye half closed by an angry purple bruise, she barely recognized his face. Blood and dirt smudged his entire body.

She covered her mouth with her hand. Wharton and his henchman didn't even have the decency to cover his manhood, and blood streamed between his legs as if he were a woman with her menses. Was this the baron's idea of humiliation? The gruesome sight of seeing Calum in such abominable pain sent shivers needling up her spine. Clenching her fists and pressing them to her stomach, she had to cast her gaze away.

The stench of lavender mixed with male sweat invaded her senses. Wharton ran an uninvited hand down her back. "Your new attire is pleasing, my lady." He used his pointer finger to force her face toward Calum. The guardsmen tied him to the whipping post. "You must watch this, wife. I'm sure it will please you that your pirate is getting his due punishment."

Anne jerked her head away from Wharton's touch but her eyes remained fixed on Calum. The muscles in his back bulged beneath taut, dirty skin. She stole a glance at Wharton. He watched her, his large belly protruding beneath his doublet and hanging over his velvet breeches. *No wonder he's subjected Calum to such humiliation. He cannot stand to gaze upon the powerful and lean back of a younger man.*

Hands clenched at her sides, Anne lifted her chin. Denton stepped behind Calum with a cat 'o nine tails. The hideous man actually grinned when he snapped his arm back and hurled it forward with brutish force. The biting tongues of leather sliced through Calum's skin. He arched his back, but uttered not a grunt of pain. Nine streaks of blood oozed down his back and ran in streams over his buttocks.

"Where are your men holed up?" Denton growled.

"Stop this," Anne said through clenched teeth.

Denton recoiled his arm to issue another lash. The whip snapped out and bloody lines crisscrossed Calum's back.

As if her own skin had been sliced open, Anne spun her head toward Wharton. "Raasay. He's from Raasay. Now stop this. Can you not see you've nearly killed him?"

Wharton's mouth formed a thin line. His face tightened, giving a squint to his eye. He nodded at Denton who delivered another savage blow. Anne suppressed a heave. Had she betrayed Calum? *No.* She would do anything so he might live. And why hadn't they simply asked her? Could this public display of brutality have been avoided?

Wharton grabbed her arm and dragged her up to Calum. He took her by the shoulders and pressed his mouth against her ear. "Did you lay with this man?"

Anne's ears blazed with a fire roaring inside them. "Are you mad?" She wrenched her shoulders out from under his grasp, but kept her voice low so as not to be heard by the surrounding crowd. "Your physician verified the fact I remain untouched last night. I'll not have my virtue sullied in this public forum."

Wharton whipped his hand back so fast Anne didn't see the slap coming. She nearly fell into Calum from the force of the blow. Her hand flew to her cheek. The sting prickled like a thousand needles. Gasps and cackles erupted from the crowd.

Calum growled through his teeth. "Leave her be."

Wharton stepped up to him. "What is she to you?"

"Nothing. She's done nothing." His voice filled with agony, ripping out Anne's heart. She eyed Wharton's dagger. If only she could snatch it from his belt and cut Calum's bindings. She scanned the courtyard. Guards surrounded them. There was no chance for escape. Not from here.

Wharton threw his head back and laughed. "A chivalrous pirate? Do you fancy *my* wife?"

Panting, Calum said not a word, his blood splattering the ground around him.

Wharton yanked Anne to his side. "This man is guilty of treason and pirating on the high seas. He will be hanged, drawn and quartered at dawn on the morrow. His head will be spiked on the citadel as a warning to all who think to cross me."

"No," Anne croaked. The world around her began to spin out of control. She couldn't breathe under her constricting stays. Wharton pulled her into the crowd. She reached out her hand but guards surrounded Calum.

Without a word, the baron dragged her into the inn and up to her chamber. He pushed her inside and slammed the door behind him. "I watched you. You have feelings for that traitorous cur."

He sauntered toward her, and Anne clutched her hands against her chest. "He means naught to me."

"What happened during the time you were away? Did he touch you like this?" Wharton yanked her into his body and ran a chubby hand across her breast. It felt grating, sick, for it was nothing gentle and nothing like Calum's touch.

"Of course not. Calum didn't know I was aboard the *Flying Swan*. He worked as quickly as he could to return me to England." Anne gritted her teeth and feigned her best adoring gaze upon her unsightly husband. "To you, my lord."

"Do not seek to placate me, woman. I can see through your pretty exterior."

"You must stop this insanity. I was abducted en route to you. I have done nothing wrong."

He raked his eyes down her body and stepped toward her. "So you say."

Anne's fists flew to her hips. She stood her ground and faced him.

Wharton wrapped his fingers around the back of her neck and tightened his grasp. She wanted to cry out, but he shoved his mouth onto hers. Anne tried to pull away but he held her fast. It took every effort to remain calm and allow Wharton to thrust his tongue in her mouth, but she could not bring herself to respond. She wanted to bite down. No. That would be a costly mistake.

When he finished, Anne backed away. He advanced with revulsion in his eyes, rubbing his hands. "I'll not have my wife looking at another man. Do you understand?" With a quick step, he drew his arm back and slammed his fist into her gut.

Anne doubled over, and he shoved her to the floor.

"Answer me!"

Sucking in air, tears burned her eyes. "I-I understand."

With a step, he drove the tip of his shoe into her side and pushed her hip into the hardwood. Anne cowered, cradling her head with her hand. He bent down, picked her up and tossed her onto the bed.

She grasped a pillow for protection. "Stop. Please."

Wharton untied the front of his breeches and climbed on top of her. Anne pulled her knees up and wrapped her arms around them. She screamed as he fought to open her arms and straighten her legs. He lay forward and pinned her under his weight. Anne struggled, gasping for breath. Her mind flooded with images of the brute in the stable, forcing her. Calum wasn't here to fight for her. Wharton tugged up her gown. Holding her down, he fondled himself. Anne cried out, writhing beneath him, barely able to breathe.

She glanced down. He yanked on his manhood with rapid strokes, but it remained flaccid. He lifted his face to her, his eyes hard. He shoved himself back into his breeches. "We'll resume this later when my blood has cooled."

Anne rolled out from under him and curled into a ball. The door slammed. He would be back. *When?*

Tears welled in her eyes and her throat burned with inaudible screams. *They're going to kill Calum. They cannot. They cannot.*

Gathering her wits, Anne rose and tiptoed across the room. She pressed her ear to the door. Everything remained silent. She cracked it open. Two battleaxes crossed before her. She closed the door, turned the lock, and drew in a ragged breath. As she feared, she had married a monster. Anne held her head with her hands and staggered to the bed. She needed her wits. How could she escape this nightmare, and save Calum from the gallows?

Chapter Twenty-one

Calum lay upon a musty bed of straw in the corner of a dank cell. Stone walls encased him, a small wooden door the only portal to freedom. Still without water, he ran his rough tongue across cracked lips. And without food, he had lost control of his wits. His hands shook. *Hanged, drawn and quartered.* He shuddered, completely aware Wharton would ensure a man wasn't killed by the hanging. The bastard would want to watch as the executioner cut Calum open and pull out his innards. It was the most hideous death imaginable.

Devoid of light, Calum lost track of time. In and out of consciousness, pain controlled his mind. He tried to remember how beautiful Anne had looked. His good hand dropped to the straw, his finger brushed something soft—cloth. He reached out and brought it to his nose. Anne's scent. His mind flashed back to the night she'd given him the kerchief. She'd said she wanted him to have something to remember her by. Could he ever forget her? No, not even if he lived to be ninety. He crumpled the kerchief into his fist. He would die with it there.

The lash marks on his back throbbed with knife-like sting. Anne had revealed his home, told them he was from Raasay to stop the lashings. Didn't she know he'd rather meet his end than give away his clan? Though she had done it for him, he needed to warn them. *What was she thinking?* Trembling, he raised to his elbow and peered across his cell. His stomach convulsed with dry heaves when he tried to push himself to his knees and his broken wrist gave way. He traced his good hand over the swelling. He heaved at the agony of a mere light touch and swallowed back the bile.

Footsteps approached his cell. They scuffed across the dirt floor as if creeping. A lock clicked. The door opened and closed quickly. Two soldiers stood over Calum, holding a torch. "Ye look like ye've been through the fires of hell."

"John?"

"Aye, and Ian."

"I told ye to sail back to Raasay. Is the ship lost?"

"Nay. Norman has the ship hidden on the Scottish side of the Firth." They eased him to his feet. "Put on this uniform. We need to move fast."

Calum reached for the trews, but his knees gave out and he stumbled. "I've no use of me left hand." John helped on his left and Ian on his right.

"Can ye walk?"

"Not sure—The rack."

"Christ," John swore. "Ye'll have to bear it until we can get ye to a horse."

Calum gritted his teeth and hissed against the pain of a shirt scraping over his open wounds, but he held in his bellow. John helped him into his trews and Ian pushed a helmet onto his head and draped a cloak across his shoulders. Supporting him under his armpits, the two men helped him past two dead guards and up the stairs.

Calum barely maintained consciousness as John and Ian led him through the back corridors of Carlisle. When the smell of fresh hay wafted to his nose, he knew they'd arrived at the stables. John pushed a mounting block in front of him—something only used by women and old men. Calum didn't balk, but leaned into them as they helped him step up and throw a leg over a horse.

He reached for the reins and stopped. He opened his palm, holding the kerchief. "Anne."

"She's with her *husband* now," John said.

Her husband? That evil monster? She'll die. Calum slid her gift into his pocket. His head spun. "We need to save her."

"She's lost to us."

Calum tried to argue but everything faded. His consciousness blurred in and out. The pain nearly skewered him but Calum grit his teeth and wrapped his good hand around the reins. With cloaks pulled close about them, they headed for the citadel gates. Barred, a soldier stopped them and asked their purpose.

Calum pulled the helmet down over his face and crouched behind Ian, out of the soldier's line of sight.

John leaned forward in his saddle. "By order of Lord Wharton, we are in pursuit of the enemy's men." John delivered his response with a practiced English accent.

The soldier leaned around Ian and eyed Calum. John spurred his horse and pulled on the reins. The steed reared. "Open the gate now, soldier," John bellowed with unmistakable command.

The iron gates groaned as the guards winched them up. The horses' shod hooves stuttered on the cobblestones, anxiously anticipating their chance to run beyond the town gates. Calum's gut lurched as the gate raised high enough for them to duck under and ride through. Following John's lead, Calum and Ian barreled out, and turned their horses north, fleeing to Scotland.

Calum grabbed a fistful of mane to keep his seat. Blinded by pain, he fought to keep his wits. If he survived this, he would kill Thomas Wharton and free Anne from the demon's wicked grasp. But now he had no choice but to flee for his life. He must regain his strength. Without it, he would be of no use to her.

***

Anne used an eating knife from her luncheon tray to pry open the immobile window. At the sound of thumping down the corridor, she turned her head and froze for an instant. Heart pounding, she dashed to the door and pressed her ear against it. Rapid knocks beat not far away.

A door creaked. "What the devil?" Wharton's voice bellowed.

"The prisoner's escaped." Denton's gravelly voice delivered the curt response.

"That's not possible. The man hung on the precipice of death."

"He had accomplices."

Anne's mind raced. *Calum has escaped? Praise God.*

Doors slammed, footsteps thundered back through the corridor and down the wooden steps. She ran to the window and pulled aside the drapes. Nearly nightfall, the courtyard amassed in a flurry of turmoil through the distorted view from the diamond-shaped sections of glass. Her breath fogged the widow as she waited and watched the scene below. Using the drapes to wipe away the condensation, she craned her neck. His lordship and a cache of soldiers cantered toward the gates. Citizens scurried in every direction to avoid being trampled. She glanced to the ground below her window. It was a bit of a drop, but not so far the jump would kill her.

The baron, clad in a coat of shiny armor, disappeared through the citadel gates. A mass of helmeted heads and blue tunics bobbed, as the soldiers trotted behind him. How long had Calum been gone before Wharton and the guards discovered him missing? John must have doubled back. Calum was too weak to escape on his own. She wondered if he even had the strength to flee but knew the answer. Calum would hang on. He had far too much to live for.

Anne whipped around, pulled her trews out from under her mattress and held them up. She reached back to untie the laces of her bodice when a rap came at her door. "Your supper, my lady."

Crabapple.

"A moment." Anne stuffed the clothes back under the bed. She'd need food. It would be madness to flee until the sun had lost all its light, and the townspeople had shuttered themselves inside.

Anne opened the door, and Mrs. Crabapple stepped in. Her stare shifted across the room as if she suspected Anne of having a hand in Calum's escape. She tromped to the table and set down a tray. "Full supper for you. You must have found favor with his lordship."

Anne looked at the slab of roast beef overlapping the pewter plate. A slice of bread sat on a cloth, and a tankard of ale beside it. With a tsk of her tongue, Anne asked, "How long do you think I should be punished for my own kidnapping?"

Crabapple folded her arms and raised her chin. "'Tis not the kidnapping. 'Tis the way you embarrassed the baron by appearing at the citadel wearing those abominable breeches."

"I'll hope you tell that to the murderous Scot when my husband brings him back to serve his sentence." Anne's skin crawled at her own words, but she needed Crabapple to think she had accepted her fate, else soldiers would be guarding her window as well as her door.

Crabapple cackled. "I'll watch his execution with great satisfaction."

Anne sat at the table and picked up the eating knife. "As will I."

When the door closed, Anne shoveled in a few bites of meat and a hunk of bread. Guzzling the ale, she darted to the washbasin and snatched up the drying cloth. She wrapped up the remaining food and pushed it into her satchel.

Working loose her laces, she slipped out of her gown and braided her hair. By the time she finished dressing in her shirt and trews, nightfall blanketed the town. Anne glanced across the room and stared at the bed. She pattered over and arranged the pillows under the bedclothes to give the illusion of a sleeping form beneath. Hopefully, Crabapple wouldn't notice her disappearance until morning—and Wharton would not return this night.

She snuffed her candles and tried to open the window. The cursed thing still wouldn't budge. Anne bore down and used all her weight to force it up. With a creak that could have awakened the dead, it cracked an inch. Anne snapped her head around, certain the guards would barrel through her door, but it remained closed. Now the window was started, it took less effort to push it up far enough to slip through.

Anne secured her satchel across her shoulder. It still had her shillings and her keepsakes. She pulled the bonnet low over her head so it shadowed her face. She poked her head out and surveyed the courtyard. The hum of the crowd from the alehoue buzzed through the air. In the distance, horses clomped across cobblestones. She heard a voice and cast her gaze to the battlements. Guards chatted with their backs turned, watching the scene beyond the walls.

Anne slipped her legs over the sill and slid down until she hung by her fingertips. Closing her eyes, she released her grip. Her knees burned as she landed in a crouch, but the pain eased when she straightened. Hugging the brick walls, she tiptoed through the shadows toward the gates. Soldiers inside the guardhouse chatted. Holding her breath, Anne slipped past their open door and hid in a recess alongside the iron gates which barred her from freedom.

Anne waited, worried her white shirt would pick up the light. She bent down and swiped her hands over the dirty cobblestones and rubbed the muck across her clothes and face. Why hadn't she thought to sully herself with ash from her chamber hearth?

The clomp of hooves approached. Anne pressed against the stone wall and held perfectly still.

The deep bass of a soldier's voice echoed through the archway. "Night patrol. Open the gate."

The chain creaked as the gate cranked up. Anne remained frozen in place. The soldiers rode through. She waited for the last man to ride clear before she slipped out the gates. She hugged the outer bailey walls until she came to a copse of trees. Motionless, Anne listened. Footsteps on the battlements above walked toward her and stopped. Trembling, she tried to mold her body into the wall. After an eternity, the footsteps started again. She waited until the sound faded and then ran for the cover of the trees.

Her foot squished into mud, and she crouched down and rolled in it. Holding her hands up, her fair skin was barely discernible.

Anne ran until a stitch in her side screamed for her to stop. Panting, she leaned forward with her hands on her knees. She looked across the shadowy lea around her, now peppered with trees. Though she must stay away from the path, she had a good sense of north from the stars overhead and the moon's position. She gazed toward the black horizon. She hated the dark, but it was the best time to move unnoticed. Shoving her satchel tighter over her shoulder, Anne trudged ahead.

***

Calum had no idea how he got in the skiff, but he welcomed the sight of the *Sea Dragon*. John and Ian rowed toward the ship with strong strokes. Calum scanned the shoreline for the enemy and exhaled a long breath when he saw no one.

The skiff thudded against the ship and John hauled in the harness. "I'll help you put this on."

"I can do it." Calum stood, but his head spun the world upside down. The next thing he knew, he was on his arse in the bottom of the boat.

"Stubborn Scot." Ian braced his feet either side of him and lifted. Calum couldn't stop the bellow roaring from his gut. Shards of pain shot through the welts on his back and his eyes rolled back. Calum nearly lost consciousness as John slipped Calum's legs through the ropes and shouted, "Pull him up."

Nausea clamped his gut. He gripped the ropes with his little remaining strength as the men hoisted him up the hull of the ship. Calum had nothing left, no fluid. Nothing. Hands reached over the rail and pulled him onto the deck.

"Holy Christ, Mother Mary and all the saints. Ye look like ye've been to hell and have no' made it back yet."

Calum couldn't focus, but he'd recognize Norman's voice anywhere.

The men carried him aft. His head dropped. Sails above clapped, billowing in the wind, demanding to be set loose.

"Weigh anchor," John yelled.

Calum's eyes lost focus when they placed him on the bed. They were safe. For now. Blackness enveloped his mind.

Chapter Twenty-two

The damned horse beneath him continued to lose speed, and the arm wielding his crop burned. Wharton's strength waned. He swapped hands and still could not whip the horse hard enough to drive it to a faster pace.

The trees opened up and a steep slope dove toward the sandy shore. The water glistened black, reflecting the moon with silver streaks. Wharton reined the horse to a stop on the beach. He scanned the firth's dark outline.

"There." Denton pointed out to sea.

Following the henchman's gloved hand, Wharton spotted a carrack in full sail, heading for the Irish Sea. The bastard had quite a lead. Wharton's eyes narrowed. "The pox-ridden whoreson." He whipped his head back toward the mob of pathetic soldiers who only now filed onto the shore. "Someone fire a musket shot, damn you all!"

Wharton rode into the surf as a lead ball screeched, rolling into the barrel of the damnable weapon. Though inaccurate, a blast from a musket would tell the blighter Lord Wharton was coming. Wharton's insides roiled with the click and earsplitting peal.

He glanced down at the froth streaming from his horse's neck. *Pathetic beast.*

Denton rode in beside him. "We'll cut them down on Raasay."

Wharton slapped the crop across his knee. "I should have let you whip him to death."

"That would have been enjoyable. But I like the chase."

"Let him think he has won. We'll strike him when he least expects it, and wipe out his entire clan." A flame of rage spread through Wharton's chest. "Ride to Maryport. Commandeer a navy ship under my seal."

"Yes, my lord."

Wharton shook his finger. "We need heavy cannon. Don't come back with a measly pinnace laden only with one or two guns. Did you see the size of their cannons? I want a warship."

Denton took two soldiers and headed out. Wharton eyed a skinny soldier who sat on a spirited nag. "I'll ride your mount on the return journey."

"My lord?"

"You heard me. Dismount, you ignorant buffoon."

Wharton hefted his leg over the fresh steed. It was time to return to Carlisle and lay claim to his wife. How beautiful she'd looked this morning when she stood and watched the Scot receive his lashings. He may have had a tad of preoccupation troubling him after the excitement of demonstrating the extent of his power. But his cock would not betray him again.

***

Anne had never imagined trudging across the rolling hills and lush leas would sap her strength in such a short amount of time. A smooth trail would be much easier to cross, but someone might see her. She marched on, using the stars as her guide.

Had her empty bed been discovered? Had the baron returned? Had he caught Calum? No. Calum could not be caught. Not this time. She shook her head and blocked all doubt from her mind. John and the men would save Calum. Somehow.

In no way could she have remained locked in her chamber, waiting for the baron's return. He might decide to rip her clothes from her body and tie *her* to the whipping post—make a public spectacle while she stood naked in the town square. She could still feel his unforgiving fist in her stomach and the image of him opening his breeches and exposing himself made her want to scream. She would find Calum and beg for his forgiveness. The baron was capable of anything.

Cold chills ran up her spine with the thought that kept returning, no matter how hard she tried to thwart it. What if his lordship caught Calum? Surely Calum and his men had a plan of escape. They had been so careful to avoid attention on their journey south—and Carlisle bordered with Scotland. Once they crossed over, he would be among his folk. But the MacLeod's were Highlanders. Did they have allies with Lowland clans? Had Calum chosen the region of Solway because of the damage Lord Wharton had done when he raided and burned their homes?

Surely any Scot within fifty miles would take Calum in, purely because he was running from the baron.

Once she found Calum, she would tell him the words she had held in. She would tell him she cared *not* about her marriage, or riches. Anne longed for a life on Raasay—a life with people who loved the rocky dirt God had given them. She wanted to be a part of the clan who would not back down in the face of adversity, even if they had to stand and face Wharton's army. She knew in her mind he would chase after them, regardless. The time had come to fight.

Would Calum even look at her now she'd revealed she hailed from Raasay? But Denton would have killed Calum if she hadn't stopped it. *Oh, God.*

Calum must understand she had done it for him. He needed to get back to Raasay and send out a call for assistance from the other clans. Calum's brother in Lewis would help, would he not? What Scotsman wouldn't give his right arm to send Wharton to hell?

Anne's mind swirled with creeping doubt. If only she could catch up to Calum. If only she could feel the strength of his embrace, she'd be reassured she had done the right thing.

Her feet throbbed with each step. As the night passed, she forced her eyes to open wide and push up her heavy lids. In the east, a sliver of cobalt glimmered along the horizon of the black sky. The sun would rise soon.

With her attention drawn away, Anne's toe caught on a rock. Her foot twisting, she stumbled forward with a sharp cry. Reaching out her hands, she crashed to the dirt. A knifelike jab shot from her ankle up her leg. She wrapped her fingers around her throbbing ankle and rubbed. *Dear God, I cannot be injured.* It was the same ankle she twisted the day they had found Swan.

She scanned her surroundings, now growing a bit clearer in the early dawn. Smoke from the chimney of a stone farmhouse sailed sideways in the wind. Could she risk stopping to ask for help? No.

Anne tried to stand. She tested her ankle. It burned under her weight but she could bear the pain. She hobbled away from the house until she heard trickling. *Water.* Violets and oranges now illuminated the sky, with the sun promising to make a speedy appearance. She slipped into a grove of trees and found a brook. Anne dropped to her knees and scooped up in handfuls of water. Ice cold, it tasted fresh as rain, and she guzzled greedily until her stomach sloshed.

Dawn had arrived. She spied a rock formation with an overhang. Crawling underneath, she pulled brush around her. Too tired to eat, Anne curled upon her side and rested her head on her satchel.

***

Lord Wharton dismissed the guards and used his key to open the door to Anne's chamber. He strode to her bed, his erection straining against his breeches. He was more than ready to bed his bride.

It had been very late when he returned from the hunt, his body tired from giving chase. Though he had stopped outside Anne's door, he chose to let her sleep. Besides, he didn't want the embarrassment of a flaccid cock to plague him again. No. It was preferable to consummate the marriage when he was rested and in better humor.

She still slept soundly beneath the green duvet. At least he thought she did, until he pulled back the bedclothes and found her bed padded with pillows.

Wharton glanced toward the door to ensure it was closed. He wanted no one to see him looking so completely foolish. A tick twitched above his eye. He should have known a woman as beautiful as Anne Wriothesely would be a whore.

When news came the Scot had escaped, he had barreled past her door and made chase, not giving her a second thought. Drapes billowing from the window caught his eye. He marched over, yanked them aside and peered through the open window. To jump from that height would hurt, but it wouldn't kill her.

His fingers shook as he clamped them on the frame and pulled it shut. Grinding his teeth, Wharton burst into the corridor and barreled straight to the citadel. He marched up the stairs to the pie-shaped chamber of the captain of the guard. Uniformed in a blue surcoat sporting a white cross, the man stood at once. "My lord?"

"Summon everyone who guarded the baroness. I want to speak to them immediately."

"Is something wrong, my lord?"

"The pirates have taken her." How could she have jumped from the window on her own? The Scot and his accomplices must have abducted her. Wharton hunched over, his arms tight against his body as if he'd been punched in the gut. *The bastards negotiated her return for the ransom with no intent of leaving her behind. Dammit all, their ship was within my sights.*

Within minutes, six guards lined the captain's office. Wharton paced, glowering at them all. "Did you hear rustling, struggling of any sort?" No one said a word. Wharton threw up his hands. "Come, men. She just floated out the window like a bird?"

"I did hear a noise right after her supper was delivered—sort of sounded like she dropped something."

Wharton looked at the soldier, but didn't see his face. The news of the Scot's escape came before he'd eaten. Had the sailing ship been a decoy? Surely not, they'd picked up the trail outside Carlisle—but had she been taken, or did that pretty head of hers devise her own escape?

He narrowed his eyes. "Are you sure of what you heard?"

The soldier scratched his head. "I think so. Mistress Crabapple delivered the tray and came out straight away. I-it could have come from below—I guess."

Wharton looked at the floor. His blood boiled. *Imbecile.* In one swift move, he snatched his dagger from his belt, pinned the soldier against the wall and held it to his throat. "What was it?"

"B-below. I-I'm sure it came from below."

Wharton backed away and pointed the dagger toward the door. "Out, the lot of you and I'll not pay you a farthing!" Wharton whipped around to face the captain. "What kind of lowlife soldiers have you recruited since I left my post as sheriff?"

The man spread his palms, but a female voice from the doorway interrupted. "I've just come from her chamber, my lord." Mrs. Crabapple stepped inside, wringing her hands. A shrewd, trusted servant who had nursed his own children, Wharton had brought her from Alnwick to attend his new bride.

"Did you serve supper to her ladyship?"

"Yes, my lord."

"Did you serve her *after* the prisoner had been discovered missing?"

"Yes."

"Approximately how much time had passed after the escape?"

"Not long. She seemed content you were going to catch him—said she was looking forward to watching his execution."

"Did she?" Wharton scratched his chin. After witnessing Anne's discomfort during the lashings, he did not believe a word.

Mistress Crabapple's hands worked over each other, her fingers clenching and unclenching on gnarled knuckles. "Yes, but I didn't trust the baroness from the moment I saw her—She's aloof and full of her own importance, that one."

He slammed his fist on the desk. "I do not believe I asked your opinion." He cared not for a servant's impertinence. "What did her ladyship confide to you?"

Mrs. Crabapple cowered over her trembling hands. "She spoke little—said she was forced to wear the breeches." She righted and held up a finger as if remembering something. "But she wouldn't let me burn the filthy things. Said they were all the clothes she had aside from one gown."

"Very well. You are dismissed, but speak not a word of this outside my company." He flicked a dismissive hand her way and turned his attention to the captain. "She might not be on the ship."

"She would have been behind us." The captain examined a map of the area on his wall. "That doesn't make sense."

"But did she have an accomplice?"

The captain shrugged. "If she did, it wasn't the man you stretched on the rack and whipped. He hovered so close to death, he could not have mounted an escape on his own and overpowered two guards, let alone climb into the baroness's window to spirit her away."

Wharton glared out the window of the circular tower. "I'll lead a scouting party."

The captain folded his arms. "With all due respect, my lord, if you are caught in this part of Scotland, you'll dead within minutes."

Wharton frowned. The captain spoke true, but Master Denton was off commandeering a ship—which he would soon board to blast the tiny island of Raasay out of the sea. Considering the choice between a hunt overland or a battle at sea, where he'd have a comfortable bed to sleep in each night, he chose the battle. "Go. Pick up her trail and bring her back to me within the week."

"Yes, my lord."

Wharton reached for the door latch. "If you catch her in the company of those rutting Scottish bastards, kill her."

Chapter Twenty-three

Calum lay curled on his side. He could not control the shaking. "Light a fire in the hearth, ye miserly bastards." He tried to shout through his arid voice box, but all that came out sounded like a garbled croak.

A damp cloth draped across his forehead. Calum's teeth chattered as if frost covered his body. He attempted to reach his hand up to pull the cloth away, but something held him down.

A voice echoed down the passage of a narrow cave. What was he doing in a cave? The voice called to him again. "Calum."

"Mara?"

The voice came closer. "Yes, 'tis me."

Calum tried to open his eyes, but something weighed down his lids. Why could he not move? Did they think him dead? But she spoke to him. He heard her speak his name again, further away this time—almost a whisper.

"Anne? Come back."

His mind took him to the dark dungeon. Calum tried to focus. John and Ian had helped him flee. He tried to move, but the dungeon walls closed around him. Soldiers burst through the door and dragged him to the torture chamber. Calum cried out when he spied the rack. They would not strap him to it. Not again.

Something ice cold touched his wrists. Shaking ripped through his body.

He heard a crack. Lashes of a bullwhip cut his skin. A soft voice gasped. Could it be Anne? Yes, she was beside him—but her arms were bound over her head. He heard the crack of a whip and steeled himself against the sting he knew would cut through his flesh. But Anne shrieked in pain. Anne? They could not lash her. She had done nothing wrong. Anne's face contorted until it faded into the blackness.

Dark shadows surrounded him. He shivered again. "Anne. Where are you? Anne! I will save you."

Mumbled voices came from afar...

"Has he awakened?"

"Still delirious—but I thought he recognized my voice for a moment."

"'Tis a good sign. Help me remove his bandages. I've mixed a fresh poultice."

"I dunna ken what the clan would do without ye, friar."

Something cool pressed against Calum's shoulder—and then there was nothing.

***

The drastic change in her sleeping pattern made Anne's head spin as if suffering from the latent effects of poppy essence. She tried to straighten out her legs and her muscles screamed. Her limbs weighed her down as if tied to bricks. How far had she walked? Further than ever before in all her days. She wasn't prepared for such exertion. The only thing that ached more than her muscles was her empty stomach.

She reached for her satchel and pulled out the parcel of food. Since she'd lost her knife in Fort William, she tore into the meat with her teeth. She leaned her head back and salivated. Never had a piece of beef tasted so good. She ate half and forced herself to stop. She'd need it for her next meal—and then who knew where she'd find food.

Anne shoved her hand deep into her satchel and found the leather pouch that contained her precious possessions. She worked it to the top and shook it. Good. Her shillings glinted silver against the worn leather. Once she traveled further into Scotland, she'd find a guide to take her to Applecross—someone trustworthy. Her quandary was who? Calum had been careful to stay away from others on their journey south. Anne quaked at the thought of finding a mob of drunken Scots like those at the inn in Fort William. Perhaps if she came across a well-kept manor or a keep, she would find someone with a thread of kindness.

She slipped her shillings back and retied the pouch. If she told someone she had fled from the baron, they might help her—as long as she kept it silent that she was his wife. She loosened the thong again and fished inside. Yes. Lord Wharton had kept her copy of the marriage decree. Otherwise, she'd tear it to shreds and bury it.

Anne slid out from under her rock ledge and stood. Putting weight on her left foot shot daggers of pain up her leg. She crouched down and rubbed it. The flesh beneath her boot had swollen during the night.

"Curses, curses, curses." She would not let a few sore muscles and a swollen ankle stop her. She scanned the ground and found an old staff of the perfect height, knarred by nature, the bark stripped at the thick end. With her satchel over her shoulder, she took several practice steps. With each one, she became more surefooted—at least that's what she told herself.

The ankle strained under her weight, but her muscles did loosen a bit with the exercise. She hobbled to the edge of the trees. With summer coming, the sun stayed out longer, and she wondered if she could chance setting out during daylight. Green hills rolled as far as the eye could see. She had no idea where to find the main path north. Surely she had veered far from it.

Without a soul in sight, Anne headed north, the sun her only guide.

***

Two nights had passed since she camped under the rock overhang, and Anne had not seen so much as a hovel. Thus far, she had been fortunate enough to find water but she hadn't eaten in over a day now. Certain she'd crossed the border into Scotland, she needed to find a compassionate soul soon.

Her ankle had gone past hurting and a dull ache reverberated up her leg with each step. At least the hunger had dulled the pain. She prayed the kind soul would also have a horse. She must have been daft to think she could walk all the way back to Raasay.

It was still light when Anne dragged herself to the top of a crag. How many more of these hills would she have to climb before she found a horse? She climbed onto a boulder and turned full circle. From her breathtaking vantage point, she could see hills of green rolling for miles in every direction. The vastness of the world around her was daunting.

She spied movement in the distance and a tremor shot through her fingers. Anne drew in a quick breath and crouched behind a clump of heather. Down in the valley, a contingent of soldiers in blue tunics rode with purpose. *English*. Were they looking for her? Was the baron with them? She squinted against the glaring sun and strained to discern if his large form was amongst them, but she couldn't tell. She slid down the north side of the rock where she would be less obvious. With the sun shaded, she blinked twice. On the horizon, loomed the grey battlements of a stronghold.

At last, an ally. She would see Calum again. She would declare her love and beg for his forgiveness. The needles of guilt pricked at her neck yet again. But she'd had no other choice. If she hadn't told the baron about Raasay, Calum would be dead and she would be lost forever. Anne clutched her arms tightly around her ribs. Calum lived. She would find him.

Filled with renewed energy, Anne watched as the soldiers turned west—away from her. She leaned on her walking stick and hurried down the hill as fast as her ankle would allow. Once at the bottom, she could no longer see the keep. That didn't stop her. Spurred on by what she had seen, Anne climbed and clenched her teeth against each jarring step. She had to find a way to Calum. She had to kneel at his feet and kiss them. Even if he forced her to be a servant, her life would be more fulfilled on Raasay—she could train his eagles and teach the children to read—she could help Mara manage the keep.

She stepped faster, dragging herself up with her walking stick. *Nearly there.* When she reached the crest of the next hill, her shoulders sagged. She had thought this would be the last one. Anne took in a deep breath and stood tall. One more slope and she would be there. Her head swooned and she pressed her palms against her temples. She would *not* succumb to her hunger. Sucking in a labored breath, she lumbered ahead.

Anne could barely focus her eyes, but the keep was in reach at last. Massive grey walls towered above, but the lines seemed jagged. She blinked. A portion of the battlements had crumbled as if hit by cannon shot. She limped to the archway. No gates secured it. She turned full circle, listening. No voices, no horse hooves, no clang of a blacksmith—she heard nothing but the call of a willow warbler on the breeze.

A lead ball sank to the pit of her stomach, but she proceeded through the gates. The sun had set and little light remained. She could not go on without food. A burnt out shell of a once great stronghold enveloped her. Anne clutched her arms across her chest. Had Wharton driven all good Scots away from this place?

Her entire body ached. A sharp pain jarred her ankle. With a cry of utter helplessness, she dropped to the ground. She had to reach to Raasay. She must find food, but she had no weapon and no trained falcon to pluck a pigeon from the air.

Anne crouched on her knees and cradled her head in her hands. With every sob, Anne fell deeper into despair. She had been traveling for days. *Dear God in Heaven, help me.*

***

Calum opened his eyes. He rested upon the comfort of a familiar bed and ran his fingers along the crisp clean sheets. He pushed up with a shaky arm. This bed was not only familiar, it was his. How had he gotten here? His arm gave way and he tried to roll onto his back. Sharp pain brought back the memory of the angry tongues of a cat 'o nine tails tearing into his flesh.

Hunger clawed at his gut. He licked his lips with a gritty tongue. *Water.* He heard a rustle by the hearth. "Water." The word grated like a rasp in his throat.

"Are ye awake, laird?" Friar Pat's deep voice held a note of fear.

"Water," Calum said, louder this time.

In seconds, the friar held a goblet to his lips. Calum gulped the liquid—not water but mead.

"This is me own brew. 'Twill help ye come round, m'laird."

Thick sweetness coated his tongue and throat. Calum nodded toward the empty goblet. "More."

The friar held up his hand. "Ye must go slow. Ye've been fevered for days."

"Food."

"I'll bring ye some broth."

"Broth?" With the mead coating his throat, his voice became clearer. Calum struggled to sit but his limbs trembled. "I want food—meat."

The friar patted his exposed shoulder. "We'll start with broth. If ye can keep that down, we'll add some porridge."

Left alone, Calum grumbled and muscled himself to a sitting position. He tugged up the pillows behind him and lay against them. Hissing through his teeth, he tested the tender flesh on his back. A hundred knives sliced angrily, but once he settled on the goose down, the pain dulled.

Friar Pat bounded through the door, clutching a bowl, with wide-eyed John and Mara behind him.

"Calum, you're sitting up?" Mara dashed to the bedside. "How is yer back?"

"Feels like a nest of stinging honey bees have taken up residence." Calum barely recognized his own voice.

The friar held up a spoon of broth.

Calum grabbed it. "I can feed meself."

The three exchanged exasperated shrugs, and Pat handed Calum a spoon, but held the bowl. Calum's hand shook and ladled the broth into his mouth as if he hadn't eaten in days. For all he knew, he hadn't. "How long have I been abed?"

John stepped in beside the friar. "It has been three days since the ship dropped anchor in the bay."

Calum rubbed his head. "Six days since we left the firth?"

"Aye."

"Any word of Wharton?"

"Nay. But blue tunics lined the shore as the wind picked up the sails in Solway."

Calum swallowed his last spoonful of broth. "Wharton will come after us. Anne gave away the keep to spare me."

Mara gasped. "She told them of Raasay?"

Calum pushed his hair back from his face. "She did it to save me from the lash."

"Little good that did," John said.

"I'm alive, am I no'?" He sliced his hand through the air. "Dunna think ill of her. She is in her own hell, living under the roof of a monster. I never should have ransomed her."

Calum looked at the solemn faces of his closest clansmen. "Have ye sent out the spies?"

"Aye."

"Have ye called for reinforcements?"

"Do ye think we need them?"

"If I ken Wharton, he will attack us with a fleet of English warships." Calum leaned forward and grimaced. Mara adjusted his pillows. "Send Norman to Lewis. Have him tell Ruairi all of the Hebrides are in peril. If we do not stop Wharton, he will take all until we all fall under his tyranny."

John nodded and took his leave. With a grunt, Calum leaned back and closed his eyes. "I need me strength. Bring me meat."

"Aye, we will but first must check yer dressing." The friar tugged on Calum's shoulder and pulled him forward. "Tis a miracle ye are sitting up, m'laird. I thought it would be days yet afore ye could do that."

"It must be yer potent mead." Calum grimaced as the bandages pulled against his tender flesh. "How is it looking?"

"I think yer wounds need to air a bit. Have another tot of me mead and I'll bring ye some porridge."

"Porridge and a slab of *meat*."

Calum guzzled another goblet of mead and lay on his side with the bedclothes around his hips. The cool air on his back eased the sting and the friar's mead numbed his head. Mara and Pat closed the door but Mara's voice drifted through the wood. "'Tis a good sign he's being cantankerous."

He'd be a fair bit more cantankerous if they kept treating him like an invalid. He needed to heal quickly. He closed his eyes and saw Anne looking like a goddess in her red dress, her long tresses glistening gold in the sun. With vivid clarity he recalled the slap Wharton had delivered across her face. If only his hands had not been bound to the post, Calum would have murdered the bastard right there in the town square. Wharton's slap was no tap, but a vicious hit that had echoed across the bailey walls—and in a public forum. What was that man capable of behind closed doors? *Anything.*

Calum pressed the heels of his hands against his eyes, blocking the unwanted images of the brutish man forcing himself upon Lady Anne. With a grunt, he pushed up and swung his feet over the side of the bed. He took his weight onto his feet. Wobbling, his legs gave out. He fell back onto the bed and roared as his bare back swiped against the woolen blanket. *Where is my meat? I cannot lie here like a sickly old man. Our very existence is in peril.*

Chapter Twenty-four

The clamor of horse hooves roused Anne from her bout of self-pity. Long shadows in the abandoned keep stretched across the open courtyard. Anne wanted to rush out and cry for help, but remembering the English patrol, she scrambled for the protection of the cavernous walls.

"Fresh tracks," A bass voice echoed through the archway.

"Looks like he's injured—he's using a staff."

Anne tensed at the singing hiss of swords sliding from their scabbards. Her staff lay in the center of the courtyard. She hid behind a crumbling column. Metal horseshoes clanged against the cobblestones. She held her breath. The first rider appeared with his sword at the ready. Anne squinted. With a grey beard, he wore a blue and dark green kilt. *A Scot.*

Taking a deep breath, she rose limped into the light, holding her hands up in surrender. "I am seeking sanctuary."

Five stout men rode in behind the old man, who reined his horse to a stop. He gaped down at her as if he'd never seen a woman before. Anne pulled off her bonnet and released her braid. The man wrapped his fingers around his beard and tugged.

Anne surveyed the astonished faces and swallowed. "This *is* Scotland, is it not?"

"Aye."

How fortunate the big fellow had found his tongue. Anne took a step forward. "Can you help me?"

"That depends." He sheathed his sword and dismounted, sizing her up as he walked near. Anne kept her hands out. With a weathered face, dark circles sagged under the Scot's guarded grey eyes. When he got within a few feet of her, he stopped and folded his arms. "You're English *and* a woman."

Anne's fingers began to tremble and she clasped her hands together. "Yes. I need to find Calum MacLeod on the isle of Raasay." Her stomach growled and she clenched her hands tighter.

"Raasay, 'tis up near Skye, no?"

"Yes."

"You're a fair bit off course." He scratched his beard. "What do ye want with the likes of a MacLeod?"

"I'm running from the English—he's running from the English. They captured him in Carlisle and nearly killed him—sentenced him to be hanged, drawn and quartered—and then he escaped. I'm trying to find him." Anne's mind raced ahead. She sounded flippant as if her story were contrived.

The Scot waved his hands across his body. "You're speaking gibberish. Are ye running from those English scouts we saw yonder?"

Anne hung her head. "I think so."

The big man knitted his brows and to took another step toward her when a voice called from the archway. "English soldiers approach."

In one motion, the Scot drew his sword and pointed toward the remains of a small building. "Hide in the chapel."

Anne nodded and touched the old man's elbow. "What is your name, friend?"

"Rorie Douglas. Now be gone with ye."

Anne hobbled into the chapel and found a narrow window that opened to the courtyard. Rorie and his men scattered into the shadows as the last sliver of sunshine fell to the west and the moon cast an eerie glow over the ruin.

Horse hooves echoed outside the keep, but this time they scraped and grated in an unwelcomed screech. A dozen or more soldiers cautiously walked their horses through the archway.

"That's far enough, Sassenach." Rorie's voice echoed between the stone walls, but Anne couldn't be sure where it came from. The soldiers stopped, their helmeted heads turning with wary, searching eyes.

Anne recognized the captain of the guard—she'd seen him in Carlisle. He held up his hand. "We mean you no harm. We're searching for an Englishwoman."

Anne held her breath. *Please do not repeat my title.*

"She could be dressed as a man," the captain continued. "We found tracks leading this way…"

An uneasy silence pealed through the air. Would Rorie reveal her presence?

"What is she to you?" Rorie delivered the words with an unmistakable lilt of curiosity.

"She's wanted for treason against Lord Wharton."

A fireball ignited in Anne's gut. *Treason? For what? For jumping out a window?*

The captain spun his horse in a circle. "You wouldn't want to cross Lord Wharton—not after what he did to your keep."

Anne gasped. The baron was responsible for this burnt-out shell? With not another moment to think, Rorie and his men sprang from the shadows, bellowing like wild animals.

The English captain reached for his sword but an arrow skewered him in the chest. Anne looked up to the wall walk and spotted an archer. He made swift work of leveling the odds while Rorie and his men met the English in a mounted battle of swords. Rorie rode his horse into the center of the skirmish, fighting two at once. Blood spewed, a hand severed, the helmeted head of a soldier flew to the turf and rolled. The dead man's stunned horse galloped wildly out the stronghold archway.

Anne clutched her satchel against her chest as she watched the deadly mayhem in the moonlight. She clenched her chattering teeth. A fallen sword lay twenty feet from the chapel. She inched toward the door and peeked around.

Rorie's booming voice exploded over her. "They're fleeing lads. Give chase!"

In seconds, the Scots raced through the archway and Anne was left alone with nearly a dozen dead men. She tiptoed out of the chapel and grasped the sword. Much heavier than it looked, the weapon scraped across the cobblestones. The captain moaned. She snapped her head up and stared. The arrow pierced through his chest and he gurgled as if air escaped through the wound.

Dragging the sword, Anne moved toward him, wary. He inclined his head toward her. "I knew y-you were here."

Something in his throat caught as if he had more to say. Anne took another step toward him and bent closer.

"Whore."

Anne stood motionless. Is that what he thought, or did he speak the baron's words? He was a pawn to a tyrant, a paid soldier carrying out his duty—dying for it.

She didn't want anyone killed for her sake, even if they did take Lord Wharton's blood money. She kneeled beside him and bowed her head. "In the name of the Father, Son and Holy Ghost…"

The soldier's eyes went vacant. A trickle of blood leaked from the corner of his mouth. Anne finished her prayer and choked back a dry heave burning her throat. She doubled over as the retch she'd strained to swallow racked her body with burning convulsions of yellow bile.

Her shoulders tensed as the clap of shod horse hooves clicked on the cobblestones.

"Finished him for me, did ye?"

Anne jerked up to meet the old man's battle worn glare.

He reined his horse beside her. "We need to have a talk, you and I."

Anne wiped her hand across her mouth and drew in a heavy breath. "As you wish."

He dismounted and reached in his saddlebag. "When was the last time ye ate?"

Her hand shook as she brushed a strand of hair out of her face. "One…no, two days."

"Come, sit with me."

Anne looked into his eyes. They weren't the dark predator eyes she had seen at the inn in Fort William. Yes, in the moonlight they were dark and stern, but she saw something else, something gentler, and prayed it was kindness.

She followed him to a fallen stone column and sat. He opened a parcel of cloth and pulled out an oatcake. "Eat."

Anne salivated at the smell of oats and a hint of bacon fat. Her eyes drifted to the parcel and caught sight of a few rashers before he folded the cloth again. She bit off a chunk, trying to be as ladylike as possible.

"What is your name?"

"Anne Wriothesley." She used her maiden name. That wasn't a lie.

Rorie drummed his fingers, repeating the name and then appeared to realize who she was. "You're the daughter of an earl? Southampton, no?"

"A younger, insignificant daughter."

"What are ye doing all the way up here in man's clothing, accused of treason?"

"'Tis a long story."

Rorie spread his big palms. "I'm no' going anywhere."

She'd tell him everything except the part about being married to Baron Wharton. Her mind raced. How was she going to leave that out? "If you consider jumping out of a window treason, then I am guilty. If not, a very nasty man thinks he can ruin everyone's lives including yours and mine."

"That would be Thomas Wharton?"

"Yes." She began with the *Flying Swan* with the twist being she had boarded the ship to *wed* Wharton, not that she was already legally married. A weight lifted from her shoulders as she told it all, the time on Raasay, the fact Calum didn't want to take her to Carlisle, but would not lay claim to another man's contract to wed.

Rorie removed his bonnet and scratched his head. "I'd have staked me claim with a lassie as beautiful as you."

"Calum thought he was doing the right thing—until they captured him and stretched him on the rack." She shuddered. "They stripped him naked, took him to the square and lashed him until his back streamed with blood."

Rorie grimaced and Anne continued with the story—her near rape by Wharton and Calum's escape.

"I guarantee if Calum MacLeod is on the run from the baron, there will be many more Englishmen than these." He gestured to the poor souls his men were hauling out for burial. "Ye say his keep's on Raasay?"

"Yes, and Wharton will stop at nothing to see him dead."

"Wharton is a smart man. 'Tis why me home's in such a shambles. But if I were he with the House of Lords behind me, I'd no' ride to Raasay. I'd sail."

A twinge of hope made Anne's heart stutter. "Would you like to see Wharton dead?"

"Aye, I dream every night of sending that bastard to his grave. He earned his bloody barony at me family's expense." Rorie cleared his throat. "Excuse me for the course language, milady."

Anne pointed to her trews. "If you will excuse me for my unladylike dress."

"I now understand your need for discretion."

Anne stood and faced him. "If you take me to Applecross, we can row a skiff to Raasay, and when Wharton shoots English cannons at Brochel Castle, we shall be there to send him to his death."

He scratched his beard and shook his head. "It sounds bloody tempting. The lady wife might throw up a bit of a fuss though."

Anne reached for her satchel. "I can pay you for my passage—and a horse. I'm afraid I've injured my ankle and it's in sore need of rest." Careful not to let him see her pouch, she searched inside with her fingers and pulled out two silver shillings.

"Now why didna ye say ye could pay in coin?" Chuckling, he grasped her hand and folded her fingers over the money. "Ye keep it, lass. I'd pay *you* just for a chance to bury me claymore in that thieving bastard's heart."

***

Wharton stood at his window and watched Master Denton canter toward the citadel with a line of mounted soldiers following. With sharp tugs on each finger, the baron cracked his knuckles. The discomfort it caused cemented his obsession. He lay awake at night imagining new ways he could torture the Scot. Wharton licked his lips. He should have sliced off the thieving bastard's manhood when he had the chance.

Thomas yanked so hard, his thumb slipped out of the socket. With a rub, he slid it back into place. Anne would still be here if Wharton hadn't toyed with the Scot—Calum she'd called him. But Wharton had wanted to draw out the bastard's pain, show his new wife no one crossed him. Ever. Then the bitch had escaped and made a mockery of their marriage. He would have filed for an annulment, but that wasn't necessary. He'd be free when she was dead.

Where was the damnable Captain of the Guard? They'd set out days ago and still hadn't returned with her. Wharton could not believe the incompetence surrounding him. Must he do everything himself? That onion-eyed Captain had convinced him to stay behind. *Fool.*

Wharton clenched his fists. Did the Scot have men waiting to spirit her away? The bastard had tricked him, taken his money— and now stolen and debauched his wife. The soldiers could follow her trail all the way to Raasay. Good. There would be more Englishmen up there to fight when he arrived. Yes, he would sail into the frigid hell they called Scotland and take back what was rightfully his and more.

A black cavern swelled in his chest and he rubbed his fingers across the pommel of his sword. Killing them both would bring him satisfaction. Once they were dead, the hate which consumed him would ebb. He could then return to Alnwick and enjoy the comfort of Northumberland's hospitality—and a serving wench or two.

He stared out the window. Denton had yet to fail him, but this was unacceptable. The man should have returned days ago.

Wharton would severely dock his pay. He blamed Denton for the Scot's escape. How could he allow the enemy to walk into Carlisle, overcome the guard and ride out the gates?

Approaching from the citadel, Denton slowed his cohort to a trot and pulled to the halt in front of the King's Head Inn. Wharton barreled out to confront him.

"What the blazes took you so long?"

Denton's gaunt scowl did nothing to intimidate. He was the Baron of Wharton with the House of Lords behind him. The ass dismounted and sauntered toward him. "Shall we discuss this in your rooms?"

"I want an answer now. You've been gone for ten days. It should have taken you no more than two."

Denton removed his feathered cap and slid his hand across his black hair. "Would you have preferred to mount your attack in a land-hugging pinnace, sporting a single cannon at her stern, or wait for an eighteen-gun racing galleon fresh out of the Maryport dockyard?"

Wharton narrowed his gaze. He would not be made into a fool.

Denton gestured to a sizable man in a velvet cloak. By his embroidered velvet doublet, he had to be a knight or higher, else Thomas would take him into custody for breaking sumptuary laws. He squinted at the man. A hanging on the morrow might satisfy his thirst for blood.

"May I introduce Sir Edward Gilman, captain of the *White Lion*."

Wharton ran his gaze over *Sir Edward* from head to toe. The public hanging would have to wait. "A knighted captain?"

Sir Edward bowed. "Yes, my lord. May I be the first to offer my condolences for this act of abomination against your person. Rest assured the queen's navy stands behind her peers."

Wharton scratched the stubble on his chin. "Your ship is manned with eighteen cannons, did you say?"

"Correct. A fighting vessel. The entire crew is trained to wield cutlasses. My men are fighters, none better."

Wharton grinned. Ten days might not have been all that long to wait, especially if he had a new ship outfitted to blast that pillaging Scot and his entire clan off his miserable island. "Well then, shall we discuss this further in my rooms?"

Denton flashed his thinned-lipped smile, the smug bastard. If the man had returned with anything less, Wharton would have not hesitated to humiliate him right there in the square. Sometimes the dark sneer on that man's face needed a good slap and Wharton would have liked nothing more than to deliver it.

He plodded up the stairs of the inn to the less-than-adequate rooms he'd let for the duration of his stay in Carlisle. They'd sail north with an army. He'd have his chance to unleash the violent storm that raced through his blood and the target of his ire would be the damnable woman he'd so foolishly wed, and her Scot.

***

Wharton closed his eyes against the lurching of his gut as sailors hoisted him up the side of the *White Lion*. His size reflected the importance of his station but the strain of the ropes and the creaking of the winch had him praying the contraption would haul him safely to the deck.

Boarding from a skiff in the Firth of Solway saved them a day's ride to Maryport to use their pier. He was no milk-livered weakling who needed the security of a gangway to board a ship, as if for a pleasure cruise.

Six sets of hands reached across the rail and pulled him over. The leather soles of his shoes slipped and he tumbled into the sailors and lay sprawled across the deck, belly up. "You careless dolts." He rolled to his side. A sailor offered his hand. "I do not need *your* help."

Wharton pulled himself up using the rail, and scanned the deck for the captain. He found him standing at the helm, watching the activities from the quarterdeck. Wharton pattered up the stairs. "Ah, Captain Gilman. Have my things taken to your stateroom. I will commandeer your cabin for this journey."

The captain snapped his fingers at the tar. "Mister Winter. You heard his lordship. Take Lord Wharton's valise to the captain's cabin and see to it he's made comfortable."

Wharton brushed off his breeches and doublet. His less than elegant entrance notwithstanding, the lowlife sailors now knew he was master of the ship, and their captain was his to command.

Chapter Twenty-five

Calum wasted no time building his strength. Once his body gained some real sustenance, he could stand without swooning and now most of his stamina had returned. Boars ballocks, if anyone had seen him collapse on the bed, Mara and the friar would have tied him down and forced him to rest for a week or more. But this was no time to lie abed and nurse his wounds.

He'd been up for near two weeks and had resumed practicing in the courtyard with his men. The unsavory expectation of battle hung heavy in the air. All must be in peak condition. Though the lash marks on his back were still weeping, Calum would not let them cripple him. He sparred with John, willing the pain to seep into his blood and empower him.

The strength in his injured wrist had all but returned. He grasped his claymore with both hands as they circled. John lunged first. Calum darted aside and spun, whacking his opponent in the arse with the flat side of his weapon. "Bloody hell, Urquhart, don't ye be going easy on me. We've a war to fight."

John whipped around with his sword over his head and sped in with a downward blow. Calum raised his claymore and blocked it. He shifted his weight and swung his foot into John's path. The big man's feet flew up and he landed on his back. "Blessed Mary, Calum. We're just sparring."

"Aye." Calum pointed his sword across the courtyard, eyeing his men. "This will be a battle to the death and every man must fight for his home and his womenfolk—'cause if ye do not, that thieving bastard will take it all. He'll cut everyone's throat and laugh whilst ye bleed out."

Calum's eyes snapped back to John. "Now fight me like you're defending Mara."

"And me unborn child."

Calum lowered his sword. "What?"

John grinned and thumped his chest. "Me wife's with child."

"Thank the heavens and all the stars. Congratulations, John." But he'd make a toast later. Calum eyed him and reassumed his defensive stance, knees bent, sword ready. "Now, cousin, fight me as if yer wife's and yer unborn child's lives are at stake."

Fire flashed behind John's eyes. Bellowing like a bull, he barreled in and swung his claymore. His wrist not quite fully healed, Calum struggled to defend the jarring blows and brandished his sword with both hands. The iron weapons clashed and screeched as the blades slid down their shafts with neither swordsman willing to back down. In a battle of muscle, the two men met face to face as their hilts touched. Sweat streamed into Calum's eyes as he tried to push John away, but his cousin planted his foot into his gut and shoved. Calum stumbled and tripped, landing on his back.

A million sharp knives drove into his flesh like the teeth of a shark. Calum bellowed. His eyes rolled to the back of his head. How could his body be so bloody weak? His feeble flesh betrayed him.

"Calum?" John kneeled at his side. "Are ye hurt?"

"Of course I'm no' hurt," Calum yelled. He shook his head and tried to clear his vision. Blast it all, he would not show his weakness to his men. Calum lumbered to his feet and swayed, but he held up his sword, challenging John for another bout.

John tapped the tip of his blade against a rock. "I think ye need to coach the guard. They're looking a bit scraggly, they are."

Calum glanced over his shoulder at the lines of sparring partners. John's suggestion did have merit. "Ye aren't going easy on me, 'cause if ye are, I'll kick yer arse all the way to Applecross."

"No, m'laird. Ye've plum tuckered me out."

Calum jutted out his chin. "All right then." He sheathed his sword and strode through his troop of fighting men. He picked apart each man's technique with a discerning eye until the sentry sounded the trumpet from atop the wall walk.

Running out the gate with his men, Calum looked toward the sound. William MacLeod stood in a galley and waved his arms. Calum raced down to the beach as the mid-sized boat sailed into the shore. William jumped over the side and splashed his way through the surf. "A bloody English galleon just rounded the isle of Mull."

Calum's gaze shot to John. As they'd thought, Wharton had commandeered the big guns. "We have a day, mayhap two."

"And ye can bet she'll be laden with fighting men."

"Gather round, lads." Calum turned and faced his men with the surf pounding behind. "With a galleon, they'll have to sail round the Isle of Skye. When they reach Trotternish, let them think they've caught us unawares."

Bran held up his hand. "How will we do that with two ships moored in the bay?"

"First, we'll sail *The Golden Sun* to the cove at Applecross. She'll be hidden from sight—they won't even see her from our cove. We'll keep her sails unfurled and when they attack, we'll flank them at full speed."

"And what of the *Sea Dragon*?" Ian asked.

Calum's stomach clenched at the name of his most beloved ship. "She'll be asleep in our bay. Her sails will be furled tight and we'll no' light the lamps, but the cannons will be manned." He wrapped his fingers around the hilt of his sword. "The bastards will nay make it to our shore."

Calum knew the sea and knew his plan was sound, but he needed his brother's reinforcements. He held his hand to his forehead to shield the sun from his eyes and looked northward. *Where is that blasted Ruairi? Norman should have returned by now. I need him at the helm on The Golden Sun.*

Calum had eighty fighting men. He could use twice that and Ruairi had hundreds.

Cheering, the men punched their fists in the air and bounded up the hill to share the news with their families.

John hung back with Calum. "How do ye want to divide the men?"

Calum drew the heel of his boot across the stony beach. "With Norman away, ye'll have to sail *The Golden Sun* to Applecross."

John's lips thinned, but he nodded. Calum knew his cousin would want to stay close to Mara, especially now she was carrying their first child, but Calum needed him on *The Golden Sun* more. He placed his hand on his cousin's shoulder. "Ye'll be safer on the galleon."

"'Tis no' my safety that concerns me."

"Mara will be tucked away in the keep. They'll no' come near her."

John ground his fist into his palm. "If they touch her, I'll cut off their ballocks and make the varlets eat them."

"As will I, cousin." Calum started up the beach. "Go. Choose yer crew. I want ye to sail at dusk."

Calum's breath labored as he climbed the steep slope to the keep. He hated the weakness that invaded his muscles. It could not sap his strength, not now when he needed to defend his clan. On the other side of Skye, a galleon approached and he knew Wharton was aboard that ship. The man was too full of hate and selfish pride to recline while others blasted cannons at Raasay.

Yes. Wharton would be there so he could claim another victory against Scotland. Calum would not allow the baron to succeed. He would send the bastard to his grave and then find a way to make amends with Lady Anne. He'd win her even if it took a decade.

Calum found Friar Pat tending his plot of dirt.

The friar dusted his hands as he rose. "Ye look like ye've been bludgeoned to within an inch of yer life."

"How easily ye forget. I have."

"Ye need rest."

"'Twill have to wait until we blast the English out of the Sound of Raasay."

"They've been spotted, then?"

"Aye." Calum rubbed the back of his neck. "I need ye to mix a tincture for the pain—something that will no' sap me wits. Can ye do it?"

"There aren't many options—willow bark tea."

"That's a start."

"The best option's a honey poultice wrapped with damp cloths."

Calum hated the sticky, slimy feel of the friar's poultices but he knew Patrick was right. "Prepare enough mixture for two applications. I'll take it on the ship with me."

"Should I come along? I can look after ye then."

"Nay. The women need ye here." Calum drew in a deep breath and grasped the friar's shoulders. "If we should fail, take the women and children to the north of the island and wait for Ruairi. Me brother will come—he may miss the battle—but he'll be here."

"Ye will nay fail."

"I will no', but I need ye to promise me ye'll care for the families should something go awry."

"Of course ye have me word." Patrick stepped in and grasped Calum's shoulder. "I've listened to yer moans for near three days. If any of what ye said is true—and by the state of yer back I

believe it is—that man is nay fit to live. Send the English murderer
to his maker, and then bring back our Lady Anne."

The hair on the back of Calum's neck tingled as if brushed by
an eagle feather. "I intend to."

Anne remained ever present in his mind. He would never
forget how the baron had slapped her, nor would he forget her
strength when she stood there and took it without so much as a
whimper.

If he had only given in to his heart when she'd asked him to
claim her on their last night in the forest. He'd wanted to enter her
and make her his, but his prideful heart would not allow him. He
should have feigned her death and dealt with Wharton's ire after.
At least she would be beside him now.

If Calum could only have the chance to see her again, he
would take her in his arms and cover her mouth with his. He'd
knead his fingers into her back and when she begged for more,
he'd slip his hand around and caress those milky white breasts that
strained so proudly against her bodice.

Calum's entire body went rigid when he pictured himself
tasting her, running his tongue around the dark pink skin at the tip
of her breast. He wanted to make her moan with pleasure again
and again. He wanted to be the one to take her to the pinnacle of
passion between a man and a woman. Why had they been destined
to meet? Their souls screamed to be together, yet all the forces in
the world kept them apart.

Calum closed the door to his chamber and latched it. Her
trunks still lined the wall. Traces of Anne were everywhere. He
opened his hand and revealed the kerchief and his heart squeezed.
Taking in a deep breath, he pictured her standing by the hearth
completely naked.

When they'd danced at the Beltane festival the length of her
body had slid down his, igniting every inch of his skin. His body
had responded with a raging fire beneath his kilt. In the wood
before she'd ridden into Carlisle, she had turned to jelly in his
arms, stripped away her highborn demeanor and had revealed the
depths of her own passion. She loved him and he desired her with
every fiber of his being. He ached with a desperate need for
release. Frantic passion pushed through his swollen, rigid flesh. He
could not ignore his burning desire.

Calum unbuckled his kilt and let it drop to the floor. His
manhood jutted against his linen shirt. He imagined Anne's perfect
breasts as his fingers brushed the length of his cock. He gasped
and his head dropped back. He wrapped his hand around his

manhood and closed his eyes, envisioning Anne with her gown dropping to the floor as his kilt just had. Her ivory skin would glow amber in the firelight. With breasts and shapely hips swaying, she would reach out to him. He would eagerly step in to meet her. Anne would shutter her eyes, lift her chin and part her rosy lips for him. She would seduce him with her every movement.

His hand milked his cock back and forth as he pictured the triangle that concealed her treasure. He had put his fingers there, slid them up into the hot, wet core of her body. She'd parted her legs for him and gave in to her basest needs. Calum worked his hand faster. He could feel himself inside her, thrusting. A cry caught in the back of his throat. In seconds his body shuddered with his release, spilling his seed onto the floorboards.

Panting, he dropped his hand. Yet again he had succumbed to the weakness of his flesh. He needed to win Anne's heart, to prove worthy of her love. Would she return to Raasay after she'd watched the soldiers drag him to the whipping post, stripped bare, humiliated for all to see?

Calum pressed his palms against his face and raked his fingers through his hair. He could not live knowing she suffered under that tyrant's roof. He must see her at least one more time. He bent down and picked up the kerchief she had made. He held it to his nose and inhaled. Closing his eyes, a trace of her scent remained. If she wouldn't have him, so be it, but he had to offer her a chance to escape Wharton.

***

Riding with Rorie and his band of ten Douglas men, Anne could now travel during daylight hours. With a little coaching from the older man, Anne had her Scottish bonnet pulled down over her forehead and pasted on a venomous scowl whenever riders came near.

Though the sun had not yet set, the horses needed rest and they stopped to make camp at Loch Long. Surrounded by rolling hills, the Eilean Donan Castle stood guard in the distance at the confluence of three great sea lochs. Anne remembered passing it when she had traveled south with Calum and his men. He'd told her the castle was a MacKenzie seat and it was best to give them a wide berth. Remembering that Dougal MacKenzie had not been overly accommodating when they took the horses at Applecross, she understood Calum's reasoning.

Anne dismounted and tested her ankle. Stepping on it, a dull ache spread from her calf to her knee—definitely an improvement.

Fortunately, Rorie had caught one of the fallen English soldier's horses for her to ride and several days in the saddle had provided needed relief. She had also taken an English sword from the battle site. Smaller and lighter than a claymore, she pulled it from the scabbard she'd tied to her saddle.

Anne turned the weapon over in her hand and sliced a practice swing through the air. The iron hissed with the downward blow. Never having wielded a sword in her life, she thought her first attempt showed promise, until Rorie eyed her with his fists on his hips. "What do ye think you're doing with an Englishman's weapon?"

"I took it at the castle. I need to be able to defend myself."

"Well, ye'll no' be able to fend off much with that. A rabbit, perhaps."

Anne swung it again, trying to make her effort look like Calum in the courtyard. "Why? 'Tis the same weapon the cavalry use throughout England."

"Aye, but they're men."

"You think I cannot learn to wield a sword because I am a woman?"

He chuckled. "Ye can learn to wield it, aye. But ye'll no' be able to hold onto it in a fight. Yer bones are too fine." He drew his long claymore from his belt. "Let me show ye what I mean. Now come at me."

"You're not serious. I could hurt you."

He shook his head and beckoned her with his fingers. "Ye've surely seen men spar before, come now, lass."

Anne looked at her sword and recalled how easily Calum had wrenched the dagger out of her hand when he burst through her stateroom door. That quick twist of her wrist had hurt. She wouldn't let that happen this time. Grasping the sword with both hands, she raised it over her head and lunged at him with a downward slash.

Rorie deflected the blow with an effortless swing of his arm. The sword flew out of her hands and somersaulted through the air. To the laughs of the guards, Anne snapped her head around and narrowed her eyes at Rorie's smug smirk.

At least the sword hadn't hit anyone, or the horses. The muscles in her shoulders tensed as Rorie's son, Hamish, retrieved her sword and playacted her pathetic attempt to attack. The men roared with laughter. Anne clenched her fists. This was nothing to laugh about. More than once her life had been threatened. It made good sense for her to learn to use a weapon.

"Silence!" Rorie shoved his son aside and wrenched the sword from his hand. "What are ye standing around for? Build a fire and hunt us down some supper."

He turned to Anne with an apologetic frown, but tossed the sword aside. "If ye are hell bent on carrying a weapon, ye need something a bit less cumbersome." He bent down and pulled the dirk from the sheath worn outside his knee-length hose. "Ye need the deadly blade all men use when locked in battle, and being a lassie, a dirk isn't hard to hide or carry."

Anne nodded and accepted the knife. She rolled her fingers over the iron basket weave hilt. "Will you show me how to use it?"

"If you're attacked, the first thing ye need to do is center yer weight." He demonstrated by spreading his legs and bending his knees. Anne followed. He chuckled. "Tis a good thing I'm a married gentleman. The sight of ye in those snug fitting trews is enough to boil any man's blood."

"But Calum said I was safer traveling dressed this way."

"Aye, but if one were to take a good look at ye, there's no mistaking yer gender." He sliced his hands through the air. "Back to the lesson—Once yer weight is centered, hold the dirk in yer fist with the blade pointing down. That gives the greatest leverage for a downward strike."

Anne copied Rorie's movement and slashed the knife through the air. He showed her the tender spots on a man and how to kill a soldier wearing armor. By the end of the lesson, Anne's confidence had grown tenfold.

Rorie led her to his horse and reached inside his saddlebag. "I always carry a spare. If ye ask me, a dirk's the most important weapon in a man's arsenal." He handed it to her with a leather thong. "Tie it to yer leg."

"Thank you. I hope I never have to use it but I'll be forever grateful to you for helping me." She looked up and smiled. "Both for the dirk and taking me back to Calum."

"Baa—'tis no trouble." He looked at her and squinted his weathered eyes. "What do ye plan to do once ye reach Raasay?"

Anne took a deep breath. She had thought of little else during the ride north. "The first thing I must do is ask Calum's forgiveness. I never meant to betray his clan, I only wanted to spare him further torture."

"Any reasonable man will understand."

"I hope so. I cannot live with myself, thinking he hates me."

"'Twould be very difficult indeed to go through life and hate a lassie as fair as you. Look at all ye're risking to go after him." He pulled his saddle off his horse and set it down. Anne did the same. "What will ye do after ye see him?"

Of course she had considered Calum might not easily forgive her, but she'd do everything she could to make herself worthy of his love. But what if Calum banished her? "I cannot go back to England as long as Wharton is alive."

"What about yer family?"

"Mother would insist I go back to the baron. My sister, Elizabeth is a countess—married to the Earl of Sussex."

"Right near royalty, aye? That's a possibility."

Anne unrolled the tartan blanket Rorie had loaned her. "No. The earl is active in the House of Lords. I doubt he'd offer me sanctuary."

Rorie patted her saddle. "Sit. If Calum MacLeod won't pull his head out of his arse, I'll take ye back to the Douglas and see what me lady wife can think to do with ye."

Anne tried to smile. She could imagine no other life except one on Raasay. She closed her eyes and pictured Calum dancing with her from across the maypole. His dark gaze had focused only on her almost as if he were hungry, starving—but not for food— for her. When they danced together, his eyes had strayed to her breasts and remained there. And yet they had shared so much more than lust for flesh. An unwelcomed doubt splayed across the back of her neck. She couldn't forget he had not fought for her when it came time to collect the ransom. But Rorie wouldn't even accept a few shillings to escort her to Raasay.

Calum had never shown her a greedy side, but he could spurn her, cast her aside now he had the baron's money. Something deep inside told her to stop. She would not be the one to let go without a fight.

I want a life where I can make a difference, like I had on Raasay. Wharton wanted me to be used like a stuffed deer head to mount on his wall. At Brochel Castle, no one cared what I looked like or how I dressed. The clan opened up to me because I worked beside them, taught the children, and helped them inventory their stolen goods…which they so desperately needed.

I love Calum with every fiber of my soul, and I will do everything to make him fall in love with me.

Chapter Twenty-six

Being the laird and protector of Raasay, Calum had an understanding of the heightened emotional state of women when they were with child, but the way Mara carried on exceeded the limits of his imagination. Her wails rang through the hall as if her husband had already been skewered by an enemy blade.

John didn't help matters. He grasped her by the shoulders and gave her a firm shake. "I'll be back in no time. Ye need to tend to the keep, and nay think of me."

"How can I do anything with ye out in the night with English ships sailing about?"

John's face turned to panic as he looked toward the rafters as if in search of the right words.

Calum stepped in to lend a hand to his tongue-tied cousin. "He's needed to protect the clan. If he stays here like a milk-livered coward, he'll be no use to the lot of us."

Mara shifted her gaze to him, and red-hot pokers shot from her baleful stare. "'Tis all yer fault, turning to piracy and leading the murdering English to our home."

"Mara!" John swooped behind her and lifted her into a bear hug.

Calum rubbed his jaw. "John will be safer on *The Golden Sun* than any other place."

John hauled his kicking bride up the stone staircase and her voice echoed through the cavernous walls. "He should be with his wife and unborn child. Blast the lot of ye."

Sometime after supper, John descended the stairs smoothing out his shirt and kilt. "There's just no placating her."

Ian, who had three bairns of his own shook his head. "Ye've got several more months of it too—and it doesna get better."

"John, ye must keep yer mind focused." Calum had no time to worry about what to do with a matron who had lost her mind. He took charge and stationed a trumpeter on the high point lookout and climbed down to the shore, leading his men. John's sailors boarded *The Golden Sun* and Calum decided his crew would sleep on the *Sea Dragon*. There was much needed preparation ensuring the cannons and ammunition was stocked and ready for battle. Besides, he couldn't listen to Mara carry on as if all the menfolk were going to die—and if he couldn't take it, neither could his men. No one needed the bellyaching of a naysayer the eve before a battle. They loaded up provisions and headed for the ships.

Friar Pat opted to row across with Calum for the night. He said his prayers might be better received by the Holy Father if chanted from the deck of the *Sea Dragon*. Honestly, Calum thought the friar needed to slip away from Mara's grousing too. The entire keep was in for a very long summer.

After making his rounds and discussing strategy with his men, Calum retired to the captain's cabin. Though not as extravagant as his cabin on *The Golden Sun*, this chamber had been his seafaring home for near seven years now and served his needs. His father had given him the carrack with the lairdship, and Calum had loved the ship as much as any human—except Anne. Perhaps that was why no lassie on the isle had turned his head. Of course he had a fond taste for women—but none under his watch. The wenching he'd done was away from the clan and away from scandal.

Calum removed his shirt and unwrapped his dressing. In the mirror, he eyed the marks on his back. Pink skin peeked out from under the scabs which had formed on the outer edges. The deeper lashings in the center of his back still oozed.

He answered the rap on his door, and the friar came in holding a pot of poultice.

"I'd like to let it air for the night."

The friar placed the stoneware pot on the sideboard. "Very well. Shall I return in the morning then?"

"Aye, but first come in and have a tot of whisky with me."

"I've never been one to turn down a fine sip of distilled spirit."

"Ah, Father, you're a holy man of keen sensibilities. 'Tis what I like most about ye." Calum filled two goblets with his flagon and gestured to the table with four rickety wooden chairs. "Sit."

Patrick held the liquor to his nose and inhaled the aroma before he sipped. "Do ye really think the baron is aboard the English ship?"

"I have no doubt. That man is a hater, that one. He and his black-hearted henchman are both hewn from the same cloth. Their hate feeds them."

"'Tis a sad thing they cannot leave well enough alone."

"Aye, but the English would have been after us sooner or later, looking for the *Flying Swan*."

"They wouldna have found it."

Calum tossed the whisky down his throat. The smooth amber liquid slid down with scarcely a burn. "They would have suspected *The Golden Sun* and blasted their cannons at us anyway. This just hurried them along."

The friar reached for the flagon and poured two more goblets. "Ye will kill him?"

"I plan to."

Friar Pat frowned and stared into his goblet.

"A man like that will no' let up, and if I dunna stop him, Lady Anne will be his next victim."

"And what will ye do once the baron is no more?"

"I'll find her."

"That's what I thought." Patrick drained his drink and set his goblet on the table. "That'll do it for me. I'll see ye in the morning."

Calum watched the friar leave and pulled Anne's kerchief from his sporran. He traced his finger around the needlework of the belt circling the sun. He held it to his nose and closed his eyes. With a deep inhale, he prayed she could hear him in her mind's eye. *Know that I love you.*

***

Lord Wharton woke before dawn, dressed and clamored out of the captain's cabin. He used the hilt of his dagger to pound on all the stateroom doors. "Wake, you lazy sots. There's a battle to be fought."

Wharton didn't wait for the officers. He strode down to the sailor's quarters and clanged the meal bell. Men suspended in hammocks griped and glared at him with murderous scowls. Wharton chuckled. He liked their spirit, but he wouldn't tolerate even a hint of insolence. "All hands on deck and wipe that evil grimace off your face sailor, or I'll have you whipped."

Wharton lumbered up to the main deck and paced. A sailor scurried past, and Wharton caught his arm. "Ready the skiffs."

"But I…"

"No argument, sailor. Ready the blasted skiffs, I say."

"Yes, my lord."

Wharton committed the man's face to memory and watched him scurry away. If the skiffs weren't ready by the time Raasay was in sight, he would make an example of that useless sailor.

Captain Gilman stepped onto the deck, adjusting his feathered cap.

"Sir Edward. 'Tis about time you showed yourself. I've asked the men to ready the skiffs."

"Why, may I ask?"

"Do you know nothing of warfare? I would expect more from a knighted captain in the queen's navy." Wharton waited for a reaction, but the captain restrained his ire well. "We shall drop foot soldiers at the north of the island. If we fail by sea, then we will conquer by land."

"Hmm. And the terrain on the north of Raasay is passable? I thought it was uninhabited."

"Of course it is passable. No obstacle can stop an English soldier."

"Very well. And will you be accompanying these troops with your keen knowledge of fighting the Scots overland?"

Wharton watched as more surly, stinking sailors swarmed to the deck. "Do not think your impertinent tone has gone unnoticed. I might think to send *you*."

With a thin-lipped nod, the captain climbed the steps to the quarterdeck. "Prepare to launch the skiffs, quartermaster."

Wharton headed back to the officer's quarters and found Master Denton. "I want you to take a contingent overland and attack from the rear."

"Very well, my lord."

Wharton ground his fist into his palm. No one would stop him from killing the Scot and blasting his keep off the island. He would take back the *Flying Swan* and shove it down Fortescue's throat. He smirked. Perhaps the queen would grant him other titles, possibly even an earldom. Then he'd be on a level playing field with Northumberland. The queen might offer him his pick of any castle in Northern England. With her permission, he would take a fortress as grand as Alnwick. Lindisfarne on the Holy Island would suit—and what an excellent stronghold from which to control the pillaging Scots.

Wharton rubbed his belly. This day his appetite was not for eggs and rashers of bacon. This day he would satisfy his hunger with victory.

Under Wharton's orders, they moored the *White Lion* off the Isle of Rona, nearly a stone's throw from the northern shore of Raasay. There, he commanded the skiffs to be launched. The *White Lion* would lie in wait until the sun set. Wharton preferred to attack under cover of darkness, to pull the Scots from their supper feast, skewer them and rape their women. Wharton could scarcely control the jittering inside his bones.

***

Late morning, the battle trumpet sounded from the north cliff, signifying Wharton had rounded the Isle of Skye and entered Raasay waters. Calum used his spyglass to locate William MacLeod. The skinny man skittered down from the lookout and headed toward the beach.

Friar Pat walked in beside Calum. "It looks as if William has news."

"Aye. And 'tis time for ye to head back to shore."

"I'll hear what William has to say and take the boat back with him."

Calum filled his lungs with the crisp salty air. Clouds blanketed the sky and he hoped the rain would stay at bay. He preferred to fight upon the sure footing of dry decks. He raised his arms over his head and stretched. With fresh air in his lungs, Calum's strength returned and his muscles twitched in anticipation of the battle to come. He flexed his wrist. Even it felt stronger.

They crossed portside to meet William as the winch hoisted him to the main deck. Bran and Calum reached out and pulled him across the rail.

"What news?" Calum asked.

"They are ferrying men to the shore. Looks like they're planning an attack by land as well as sea."

"How many have gone ashore?"

"Forty or so."

Calum stroked his chin. "They think the troops will make it to Brochel from the rocky north and be here by in time for the battle?"

"Could be done with hard marching. The ship dropped anchor off Rona. Looks like they're waiting for nightfall."

"Dropped anchor did ye say?" Calum looked across the Inner Sound to Applecross. *The Golden Sun* was hidden from sight. He could send a skiff across to bring back a few men, but they were needed to man the ship. "Blast it all, where is Norman with Ruairi? Can I no' count on me own kin?"

He searched the surrounding faces for an answer. All looked as baffled as he.

"William, take a skiff over to *The Golden Sun* and tell John half the *Sea Dragon's* crew will fight the English troops by land. I'll be severely handicapped once the battle starts. Friar—muster the women and have them patrol the battlements with long bows."

"The women, m'laird?"

"It cannot be helped. Besides, they shoot arrows in the games. They'll be safer on Brochel's wall walk than any other place on the island."

The friar crossed himself. "Heavenly Father, help us."

"Once we take charge of the English ship, we'll protect the castle. No need to worry, there are only forty foot soldiers. Brochel can withstand ten times that." Calum marched across the deck and scowled. "What can forty foot soldiers do with no catapult, no cannon?"

He split the crew, ensuring Bran stayed with him where he could protect the lad. He surveyed the twenty MacLeods who would remain on the *Sea Dragon*. All good men, all trained by Calum himself. "Follow me to the gun deck. We've got a strategy to revise."

***

They rounded Loch Carron and Anne's palms grew moist against her leather straps of her reins. If only she could fly like an eagle, she'd see the Isle of Raasay from here. By the time the sun hung low in the western sky, they approached the shores of Loch Kishorn. Rorie pointed. "She's a saltwater loch and opens up at the bottom of the Sound of Raasay."

Anne's insides fluttered. "We can reach Applecross."

"'Tis five to seven more miles of riding. It will be well past dark when we arrive. I think it would be wiser to camp here for the night and make a fresh start at dawn."

She could no sooner bed down than fight with a sword. "We cannot stop. Not when we are so close." Anne wrung her hands. "'Tis only seven miles, Rorie. Surely we can make that."

Rorie pulled up his horse, and his men gathered around. "What do ye say, lads? 'Twill be a long night if we keep going."

Hamish leaned forward in the saddle. "I've had enough of making camp on the trail. I say we push on and sleep within the walls of Brochel Castle this night."

Anne had not developed a fondness for Rorie's burly son, but she thanked him under her breath. She would have died if she had to camp a mere seven miles from Applecross. She cared not if she had to ride all night. Calum was so close, she could feel his presence on the breeze as it blew the loose strands of hair across her face.

Chapter Twenty-seven

Calum listened to the waves slap the bow of the *Sea Dragon*. He stood on the forecastle deck and peered north through his spyglass. When the bloody hell would they come? Waiting was always the worst part before a battle. In his younger days, he would have given in to his impatience and weighed anchor, meeting the English head-on at the channel between Raasay and Rona. But he knew better than that. Lying in wait in the seclusion of the bay, the *Sea Dragon* was protected on three sides and with John hidden in Applecross, his flank was covered too.

He'd wait for weeks for the English to attack if that's what it took. The high-pitched scream of a golden eagle sounded overhead. *Anne.* Calum snapped his head up and watched the bird glide across the sound toward Applecross. If only he could see the world from its vantage point, he'd be able to watch Wharton's every move.

Calum craned his neck and followed the bird's flight. Its enormous wingspan carried the raptor gliding on the wind. Thoughts of Anne flooded back. She'd been so skilled with the young eagle—and her lovely voice had lulled him. If only she would return and resume her training, Swan would make a fine raptor for hawking—even better than a falcon.

Shading his eyes, Calum gazed up at Bran in the crow's nest. He'd sent the lad up the rigging hours ago. He'd need to send up a replacement if the English didn't make an appearance within the hour.

Soon it would be dark. Would the English light their lanterns and give his cannons a clear target? Calum had ordered no fires to be lit at the castle or on the ships, except for the cannon torches. If the English took too long to mount their attack, Calum would be at a further advantage, so long as the moon remained hidden by clouds.

Calum turned full circle. The clouds showed no breaks. Mayhap God was with them this eve.

Bran blew the boatswain's whistle. Calum's stomach lurched. It had begun. The English had rounded the point of Arnish and would be upon them before the sky lost its last light. He ran his fingers across the woven pattern of his hilt. The enemy would espy both the *Sea Dragon* and the keep.

"Come down, Bran," Calum hollered. "'Tis time to man the cannons."

The English galleon approached like death, quietly skimming the calm sea. The remnants of the orange-red sunset disappeared as the ship rounded the tip of the bay. Calum had teams of two manning each cannon. The torches were hidden in huge pots of iron, casting little light. Calum raised his hand in preparation for the signal, and watched the evil hull come into sight. "Hold," he yelled.

The English ship slowed. Their sails flapped and began to furl. The loud splash of an anchor dropping twenty feet into the water told him it was time. Calum dropped his arm. "Now!"

The *Sea Dragon* lurched against the surf as eight guns fired in rapid succession. The familiar burning pall of sulfur-smoke billowed over the gun deck. Unable to see, Calum waved his hand in front of his face. He didn't need his sight to count eight splashes dunk in the water. Not one cannonball hit its target. Their decoy revealed, a flash from the English ship's porthole lit up the scene before the boom from the cannon boomed across the water. Calum's gut clamped down hard as the lead ball whistled far above his head.

"Set your distances. Raise the barrels. Fire at will!"

The second English cannonball splashed feet from the *Sea Dragon's* hull. The carrack rocked with the jarring blast. Cannons boomed from both ships. The deck above splintered and groaned as a cannonball ripped through the planks. The ship listed. Calum's heart thundered. She was taking on water.

Calum dashed below to an unmanned cannon and turned the crank. He lined up the sights with the enemy ship. He stuffed down a ladle of black powder, hefted the heavy ball into the barrel and packed it tight with the ramming iron. Peering out the portal, the smoke cleared. The English ship neared, drifting close to the starboard rail. Hand-to-hand fighting would start soon. Using his legs, a bead of sweat streamed from his temple as he rolled the cannon carriage forward. Calum rechecked his sights. He could not miss this time. Water roared below decks—he blocked it from his mind. Calum reached for the torch and ignited the match cord.

The cannon kicked back and his ears rang. Deaf, he ran up to the main deck. The blast barreled through their center mast.

Through the ringing in his ears, the hull groaned as if alive. He pulled his spyglass from his hip. *The Golden Sun's* guns blasted at the English galleon. The *Sea Dragon's* stern set lower in the water. Calum prayed she would hold.

"Prepare to board!"

The men dashed up the ladder with Bran last. Calum grasped the lad's arm. "Climb to the crow's nest with yer bow."

Bran held up his sword. "But I want to fight."

"I gave ye an order, lad. Do as I say else I'll throw yer skinny arse overboard and ye can swim home to yer ma."

The boy turned tail and scurried up the rigging where he'd be safe.

The Golden Sun's guns thundered. The English galleon pitched and visibly rose up with a direct hit to her hull. Thick smoke hung over the ships, and acrid sulfur burned the back of Calum's throat.

Peering across to the crippled ship, swarms of Englishmen lined the deck, weapons ready. Calum swallowed. His clan was far outnumbered.

Drawing his claymore, he sounded the boatswains whistle three times to signal John. The English ship continued to drift closer. He grasped the rigging and sailed across the open water. When the rail of the English ship flew under his feet, Calum released his grip and dropped to the galleon's deck. Snarling, he trained his sword across a mob of bloodthirsty sailors.

English swords surrounded him. Without hesitation, Calum launched into an attack, spinning and swinging his trusted claymore in one hand and thrusting his dirk with the other. He kept his back to the rail to prevent attack from behind. Cutlasses swung at him so fast, he could not avert his eyes to assess the battle. Venom raged through his blood and he fought like a madman. Iron clashed with iron on all sides and he knew the stakes. The MacLeod's versus the English in a fight to the death. An English sailor dropped in front of him with an arrow through his neck. *Good lad, Bran.*

***

At the sound of cannons, Anne urged her weary horse to a gallop. She headed toward the outline of the stable. Rorie raced up beside her and tugged on her rein. "Slow down. Ye'll startle the MacKenzie riding full bore like that."

Rorie was right. Dougal MacKenzie stepped out of his stone hovel, claymore in hand. "Who's riding on me lands like they're hell bent on waging war?"

Anne opened her mouth to speak, but Rorie boomed over her, "'Tis the Douglas come to help Calum MacLeod fight the English."

"English?" MacKenzie turned toward the sound of a cannon blast. "Is that what he's on about? I thought he was testing the guns of his new ship."

Anne could no longer hold her tongue. "They're trying to kill him. We must hurry."

Dougal MacKenzie's eyes narrowed. "Why you're a lass." Anne tried to scowl, but he stepped in closer and squinted his eyes. "You're the same woman who was with him weeks ago."

"Yes."

MacKenzie licked his lips. "I thought he was taking ye to Edinburgh, but you're *English*." He held up his sword, confusion furrowing his broad forehead. "Why did ye return?"

Rorie rode in between them. "She's MacLeod's woman. We need to spirit her to the keep."

Anne's stomach squeezed. Calum's woman? She'd never heard it put so brashly, but she liked it. If only Calum would accept her that way. Anne clenched her fingers around her reins. Why did she have to be married to the devil? With her husband on the attack, Calum might sooner she drown in the bay.

MacKenzie eyed her from head to toe, as if appraising a horse on the auction block. "Then why was he taking ye to Edinburgh?"

She wasn't about to allow a delay to appease this man's over-curious nature. Anne jabbed her heels into her horse. "We haven't time for idle chatter." She'd kept her marriage to Lord Wharton a secret and wasn't about to let it come out now.

Rorie followed her to the stable with MacKenzie on their heels. "Bloody Wharton's on that ship and his black henchman too, I'll bet."

"Wharton? There's not a man in all of Scotland who wouldn't want a piece of that ill-breeding bastard."

Anne slung her leg over her horse and jumped to the ground. "Then join us. Calum's clan is small. He needs every sword."

MacKenzie shoved his claymore into its scabbard. "The bloody MacLeods are causing problems with me kin in the north."

Anne knew blood ran thick among Highland kin, but this was war. She would sell her soul to save Calum. "If you help us now, you have my word Calum will speak to Ruairi and stop the raids on your family."

Dougal folded his arms and planted his feet firmly in the dirt.

Fearless, Anne walked up to him and jammed her finger into his sternum. "If you choose to tuck your tail and walk away, Calum will hear about that, too."

"I'll have a chance to skewer Wharton, ye say?"

"Yes." Anne jolted at a cannon blast. "If Calum has not already run him through."

Dougal looked to Rorie and chuckled. "She's a spirited lass, no?"

"Ye dunna ken the half of it."

Standing on the Applecross shore, fires blazed on the ships illuminating the mayhem. Swinging swords glistened in the firelight. Too far to discern carrack from galleon or English from Scots, Anne's gut flew to her throat. She ran to a skiff on the beach and pushed. "We must fight!"

Rorie grasped Anne's arm. "We cannot row a tiny skiff into that. We'll be capsized."

"I cannot stand on the shore and watch." But Anne's hands shook. If the skiff capsized, she would surely die before she saw Calum.

"Our best chance is to row round the battle and protect the keep. If the English break through MacLeod's defense, they'll burn the castle and every soul within." Rorie whipped his arm around her waist and easily lifted her into the boat. "Ye sit there like a good lass while we launch."

Anne sat on the forward bench, clutching the side of the boat and tried not to look at the water. She'd been across the sound in a skiff before. She could do it again. Her gaze focused on the raging horror before her. Calum was there. She sensed his commanding power and it heated her blood with determination. *Please Calum, fight well and live. I'm coming to you. I'll be in your arms soon.* Stones screeched against the bottom of the boat until it rocked in the water. The men jumped in beside her and something on the northern horizon caught her eye. She pointed, dread filling her veins. "Another ship."

The black outline of a three masted vessel traveling under full sail barreled straight for the battle. Rorie and the men manned the oars while Anne's eyes adjusted to the dark. She watched the ship slow. The wind whooshed from the sails like ghosts hell-bent on murder.

Though she sat tall in the skiff, her teeth clenched. Anne reached down and brushed her palm across the hilt of her dirk, tied to the outside of her leg. She would stand beside Calum and fight to the death, if that's what God intended.

***

The English sailors came at Calum in droves. He fought them back. With every kill, he scanned the deck. Blood splattered, staining the deck black-red. Smoke billowed from the fires. The ship listed, making it difficult for Calum to keep his footing. English cutlasses clashed with claymores, with no end in sight. A man ran at him with a maniacal roar. Calum dropped under the attacker's sword and rolled, but the blade skimmed the tip of his shoulder. Hot blood soaked his shirt. Calum used the momentum of his sword to spring to his feet. With an upward thrust he impaled the English tar on his blade.

The wind shifted and smoke from the burning ship filled his lungs. Sputtering with a cough, Calum ran his arm across his burning eyes. Above the ship's bow, a black-and-gold flag sailed into view. *Ruairi*. Calum raced up the narrow stairs to the forecastle deck. His brother's carrack had coasted in close enough for his men to tie to the English galleon's hull. Footsteps rattled the floorboards behind. Calum turned, swinging his sword in an arc, he faced an English sailor.

Calum fought, pushing his foe toward the narrow stairs until the man lost his footing and toppled backward. Tumbling down the steps, his neck broke with a crunch. Calum brandished his sword and blocked the passage to the deck. The English quartermaster bellowed for more men to attack the stern. Calum stood his ground and fended them off.

Planks clattered to bridge the gap between the ships. Ruairi was the first to dash across.

"I thought ye'd never arrive," Calum said without looking back. "I've nearly got them licked."

"We followed the galleon's wake down the sound."

"Aye?"

Ruairi pushed through and charged down the steps, beating down the tiring English. With a wave of fresh Scotsmen flooding across, Calum stopped and scanned the mayhem. Wharton was nowhere in sight. Calum raced along the main deck, slashing his sword as he ran toward the bow of the ship. He crashed through the portal to the officer's quarters, barreled down the corridor and pressed his ear to the captain's cabin door.

Someone moved within. Calum's gut clenched with hate. Memory of his naked body being stretched on the rack seared through his mind. A low growl erupted from the back of his throat. Calum kicked in the door.

Wharton stood behind the table, a sword in one hand and a spiked mace swinging on a chain in the other. Wharton chuckled. "You've come to allow me to carry out your sentence, have you, Scot?"

Calum crept forward. "I've come to cut yer throat."

"Before I disembowel you, tell me..." Wharton narrowed his eyes. "Where is my wife?"

Calum's heart squeezed at the mention of Anne and he blinked. Where was she? Wharton didn't know? Calum rounded the table, training his claymore on the baron's heart. "She's no' in Carlisle?"

Wharton sidestepped—a quick move for such a large man. "I assumed your men had spirited her away. *You* obviously would have been unable to do it given your physical state." Calum's eyes followed him as he scooted around the cabin. "It appears you've recovered from my hospitality. I should have finished you on the whipping post."

Wharton reached up and grasped the edge of the desk. Using his weight, he pulled it forward. Books tumbled and crashed to the floor as it toppled. Calum jumped aside and it smashed into the table.

Calum wanted blood. With a roar, he leapt over the wooden splinters and swung his sword, aiming for the heart. Wharton proved skilled with a blade and deflected the blow, following it with a slam of the mace. Bone crunched as the iron spikes imbedded in Calum's flesh. Searing pain incensed him. He swung up with his dirk. Wharton countered. They fought, swords clashing. Calum thrust his dirk for a killing blow, but the bastard had a keen eye and lithe feet. Calum slashed a cut through Wharton's arm only to be met with the iron prongs of a mace to his thigh.

Calum's muscles burned. He'd been fighting for ages while Wharton hid in the cabin. Ruairi's voice boomed from the doorway. Wharton glanced away. Calum moved in for a blow to his heart. Wharton deflected the claymore but it gashed the big man's side. He fell backward and flung the mace out. The chain wrapped around Calum's arm. Wharton crashed into the glass windows. Glass shattered, and Wharton's bulk pulled Calum through the gaping hole. Airborne, Calum twisted and wrenched his arm from the mace before he hit the water. Wharton bellowed, his hands grasped for Calum as if he could stop the baron's fall.

Ice cold water gripped Calum's lungs, ripping his breath away. The impact pulled the sword from his hand. Calum clenched his fist around his dirk. Kicking, his lungs screamed with the need to breathe as he fought his way to the surface. His mind spun and his head twitched with his need for air. Stars crossed his vision. His consciousness flicked out and in. He burst through the waves and gasped, heaving in the salty air.

His vision cleared. He spun full circle. Wharton had not yet surfaced. A piece of wood bobbed in the water, and Calum swam to it. He again scanned the waves for Wharton, but the sight of flames leaping from the castle yanked his mind from his obsession for vengeance.

Chapter Twenty-eight

Wharton broke through the frigid water, wheezing and gasping. He'd never been this cold in his life. Even the chill of chasing Highlanders through the snow had not sucked the life out of him like this frigid sea.

He'd lost his weapons when he'd slammed into the water. Hitting with his back, the water slapped him like falling onto a sheet of ice. His skin stung. The current pulled him rolling over and over. In the dark, he lost his orientation, and it was only by the grace of God his head had surfaced.

He floated on his back and let the current pull him southwards away from the ships. From what he could see, the English ship was lost, going down in a heap of flames. Denton was his last hope.

Wharton shivered. He recalled the Scot's face when he'd asked the heathen about Anne. The Highlander had looked too shocked for it to be a lie. The man knew nothing of Anne's whereabouts.

Something hit Wharton's head with a hollow wooden thud. Rubbing away the pain, he looked up. *A boat.* He reached up and pulled himself around to the side. Holding on, the skiff nearly capsized as he swung his leg up. Clutching the far side with all his strength, he rolled into the boat. Water sloshed in the bottom of the skiff and he lay there and stared at the black clouds.

If Anne was not with the Scot, where was she? Had she gone back to Southampton? Who had assisted her? Surely she could not have escaped without help. He coughed. Denton would find her if he had to force the man to spend the rest of his miserable life tracking the wench. Wharton would pay the henchman. And then Lady Anne would pay for the embarrassment she had caused him—with her lovely flesh.

***

Anne crouched in the boat, trembling as a cold wind swept across them. She shuddered. The burning English galleon sat low in the water, and the *Sea Dragon* listed to one side.

The rumble of war and fire was deadened by the scraping of the fourth ship's hull against the English. Anne gasped. Was it the enemy? If an English ship, Calum would have no chance.

Dougal MacKenzie's deep voice roared over the tumult. "'Tis Ruairi from Lewis. I'd recognize that pennant anywhere."

Anne saw the blue and white lion fluttering in the firelight. Calum's infamous brother had come. She scanned the confusion aboard the English galleon and thought she saw Calum running across the deck, claymore in hand. The skiff had traveled about half the distance to the ships and the fighting was more discernable now.

The clouds parted and streams of moonlight shone down, reflecting against the black water. Acrid smoke swirled above them, pushed by the breeze. An empty skiff bobbed in the distance—a peaceful remnant of the frantic scene on the sinking ship ahead.

Anne jolted in her seat when two men crashed through the window at the bow of the English galleon. She watched them plunge into the sea and Rorie's hand grasped her shoulder. "We're nearly across. The English ship will be lost soon and all will be adrift."

Anne nodded and looked toward the shore. The keep loomed a dark silhouette against the night sky, until a bonfire ignited the outer bailey gate. Blazing arrows soared over the bailey walls. With a wave of dread that made her teeth chatter, Anne pictured Mara and all the other women and children who were within. Soon smoke would engulf them.

"Row faster!" she shouted.

***

Calum slipped his dirk into his belt and kicked toward the shore. Sea salt burned the wounds in his side and leg, but he bore down and blocked it from his mind. The English soldiers were already upon the keep. The men he sent to guard it would need reinforcements soon. The roar of battle still raged on the English ship. He looked back over his shoulder. Ruairi's ship was launching skiffs. Good. They had seen the fires ignite up at the castle.

Calum's strength bled out of him, sapped by the frigid water. Raised island tough, he could withstand the cold longer than most, but he wasn't impervious to it. His muscles weighed him down like lead as he leaned more weight onto the wooden board under his chest and used his arms and legs to push himself to shore.

The warmer water of the shallows welcomed him. Until his ears rang from a blast. Over his shoulder, a powder keg exploded on the English ship. She was going down fast in a shower of flames. A giant wave crashed over him, sending his body in a spiral to the depths. He hit the sandy bottom and used his legs to spring up. His head shot through the surface only to be pummeled by another angry swell, but he swam into it this time.

Men swam toward the shore, bellowing for help, reaching for anything that floated to help them battle the icy cold. The clash of swords on deck transitioned to a fight for survival. Garbled cries erupted from those who could not swim and shrieks of stabbing, icy pain echoed from those who could.

Calum scanned the chaos. A skiff laden with men rowed away from the wreckage. It sat low in the water with its human cargo. But the sailors in the water saw a chance for rescue and swam to it, clamping onto the boat's edge. Calum swore he heard Dougal MacKenzie's deep bass voice bellow across the sound. "Let go, ye bastards, ye'll capsize us all!"

The freezing men paid him no mind and tried to pull their bodies over the side. The boat tipped and swung back. A high-pitched scream carried on the wind. More swimmers arrived, all trying to board. The boat flipped and a woman's scream was muffled by a dousing of icy water.

Anne.

Shards of ice cut through his gut. *I cannot swim.* Anne's words filled his head. Calum let the lifesaving piece of wood slip from under him as he swam back into a sea of utter confusion.

***

The whole sky exploded with the blast from the English galleon. Bodies sailed through the fire lit air with legs and arms flailing in futile attempts to grasp at anything that would stop them from hurling toward the sea. Blood curdling screams chilled Anne's bones as helpless men thrashed, hitting the water with painful slaps and dunking splashes as if human cannonballs had been launched.

Anne clutched her fists under her chin. Had Calum been caught in the blast? Was he one of the men now fighting for his life? Or...or was he one of the dead? She closed her eyes. *Dear God, please no.*

Rorie and the men tried to steer the skiff away from the mass of splashing men. Many had started swimming to the shore, but others were flailing, drowning. Anne turned to Rorie. "We must help them."

"The boat is already overfull. We cannot take even one more. Our best option to help them is to make the shore quickly and push the skiff back out."

Anne didn't like the answer, but could see no other choice. She gripped the edge of the skiff with determination. The fires on Brochel burned brighter. Rorie and his guard were needed there now.

The remains of the English galleon slipped into the sound with a loud groan followed by a deathly sucking rumble. A mob of swimmers advanced on the skiff. Their icy fingers grabbed for hers and Anne pulled her hands back with a shriek.

Dougal MacKenzie batted one man away with his oar. "Let go ye bastards, ye'll capsize us all."

But it was too late. Dozens of men reached for the edge of the skiff and tried to climb aboard. The boat teetered up and slapped down. Anne grabbed for Rorie's arm and screamed. The capsized swimmers grew frantic and slapped at each other to gain a hold on the tiny boat. In a flash, Anne's body hurled from the skiff. Shrieking, she curled into a ball and hit the water with a splash.

A million needles stabbed her flesh. Icy water enveloped her. She opened her mouth to cry out and salty water flooded in, burning her throat and lungs. Arms and legs lashing out, she fought for the surface. Her head shook as her body screamed with the need for air.

Blackness surrounded her. Anne strained to pull herself upward. She shot through the surface coughing up salt water. She gasped a breath of air just as her body again sank under the surface. She reached out, desperately trying to grab for anything to keep her afloat. She felt something—an arm—and grabbed it. With a jerk, the arm yanked away. A hand reached out and pushed her down.

Anne's lungs shuddered with the need for air as she sank deeper into the icy sea. Her limbs dragged against her straining muscles. She needed to see Calum. She was so close, she couldn't let the sea claim her now. With renewed effort she kicked her legs and stretched for the glowing surface above her.

Blackness clouded her vision. The more she fought, the deeper she sank into the cold depths. She reached her hands up. This could not be the end.

Something grabbed her from behind. Anne wanted to fight, but her limbs had lost their strength. She could barely move. The world spun. Then her head broke the surface. She sucked in a lifesaving gasp of air.

"You're going to be all right, lass."

Calum! He wrapped his arm around her torso. She tried to speak but only coughed up salty water.

"We're nearly there now." His soothing voice calmed her as she heaved in and out sucking in sweet air.

As her coughing ebbed, she tried to talk through her quick breaths. "Ca-lum. You…you…are alive!"

"Aye, and so are you."

"I-I…"

"Save yer breath. I've almost got ye to the shore."

Calum cradled her in his arms as he staggered onto the beach. Anne had never been so happy to be on dry land. He carried her to the pile of driftwood where the Beltane festival had been and set her down. "Hide here. I must defend the keep."

Anne's teeth chattered. "I-I want to go with you."

"Nay. No one will find ye here. We'll make quick work of the English scoundrels and I'll be back for ye."

Calum squeezed her tight and kissed her fiercely. Turning away, he sped up the hill. Anne scanned the beach. Sodden men stumbled from the surf, sputtering and coughing. Some knelt upon the smooth stones, catching their breath—others lay face down, lifeless, pushed only by the surf.

***

Calum hated to leave Anne alone, but he could not turn his back on his people. Jaw set, he pulled the dirk from his belt and called to the men who littered the beach. "Use any weapon ye can find! To the keep, men."

An English sailor looked up at him and rolled to his side. Calum planted his feet and pointed his dirk at the man's throat. "Stay down and ye'll be spared. The sailor exposed his bare palms in front of his face, signaling his surrender.

Calum hesitated and surveyed the beach. Ruairi had fought through the surf, claymore in hand. Leave it to his brother to hold onto his weapon. "Go—save yer keep. Me men will defend the beach."

"Thank you."

Pain thrumming across his skin, wet clothes clung to his skin as Calum raced for the path leading to Brochel. John fell in beside him. "I kent I should have stayed with the keep."

"I dunna want one pillager left standing."

"Aye, and as I said afore, if they touch our women, I'll cut off their ballocks and stuff them down their throats while they're still alive."

Calum ran up the hill, ignoring his wounds and the sharp burn of his muscles. He could not tire. At the top, fire still smoldered at the wooden gates. The bodies of English soldiers skewered by arrows littered the ground. His gaze darted to the bailey walls. The women were gone—he knew they would have fled to the hidden chamber behind the solar.

He crept forward and nabbed a cutlass from a dead man. John did the same. With a running leap, Calum barreled over the flames and raced to the great hall. A dim fire from the hearth illuminated the brawl of shadowed figures fighting to the death.

John and Ian shot past him and charged up the stairwell. MacLeods followed Calum, armed with wood axes, fishing nets and sturdy driftwood. Some had been lucky enough to find discarded cutlasses and knives. They poured into the hall and Calum eyed his target. Black hair, gaunt face, with his teeth bared in a murderous scowl, Denton clashed with William MacLeod, pushing the Scotsman back, clearly toying with him.

Calum's gut clamped into a rock hard ball. He could no longer feel the cold from his wet clothing nor feel the burns and stings of his wounds. With a fevered stare, he curled his lip over his teeth. Fire surged through his limbs. He roared and broke into a run.

Denton drew his sword back for the killing plunge. His blade sliced forward. Calum leapt the remaining distance and deflected the blow with the cutlass just as Denton's sword tip skimmed William's midsection.

Whipping his weapon back, Denton snapped his glare to Calum. "You? Wharton should have let me rip your limbs from your body on the rack."

Calum circled, every nerve alive. He lifted his chin and inclined his head, inviting the murderer to make the first move.

Denton chuckled and slithered around him. "Well, well. I'll take pleasure in finishing the job now."

Calum wanted to bellow and charge in for a fast kill, but the calculating glint in Denton's eye gave him pause. That was exactly what the executioner wanted him to do. He circled, waiting for the bastard to make the first move. Calum caught a flicker in Denton's eye—a warning. He tensed, anticipating the blow. Denton lunged, going for his gut. Calum darted to the side and defended the strike with a resounding clang.

Denton wielded his weapon with expert cunning and finesse. Calum adjusted to the lighter cutlass in his hand. Though easier to wield, it forced him closer to his opponent. Calum liked it. He needed to fight close to ensure a lethal cut. With each swing of the cutlass, he followed with a swipe of his sword.

Denton fought like a scoundrel, darting in for quick slashes with his blade and spinning away before Calum could sink his weapon into his heart.

Again, Denton lunged. Calum deflected and swung up his cutlass. Denton spun. The blade caught the henchman's side and blood spewed across the floor. Heaving, Denton circled, holding his sword out, narrowing his gaze. With a sudden charge, he roared, "Die, you Highland bastard!"

***

Violently shaking in her wet clothes, Anne peered over the driftwood log. Norman and Ruairi's men stood at the surf, cutting down English sailors as they dragged themselves from the frigid water.

A large man pulled himself ashore and leaned forward, his hands on his knees, heaving and straining for air. Ruairi ran toward him, sword held high.

"No!" Anne leapt from behind her hideout and raced toward Calum's brother.

Straightening, Rorie drew his claymore and bellowed. "I'm a bloody Douglas, ye crazy Scot."

Ruairi skidded and jerked his sword back. "Well, why didna ye say so in the first place?"

"'Tis good to see ye too, MacLeod." Rorie chuckled.

Anne raced in and pointed toward the castle. "Rorie! Calum's defending the keep. We must fight."

Her gaze snapped to Ruairi. He nodded at the Douglas chief. "Ye go. I'll hold the beach."

Rorie grinned. One-by-one his guardsmen emerged from the surf. He pointed his claymore to the castle. "There are English to fight, lads. Arm yerselves."

"This way," Anne yelled over the pounding surf.

Anne charged up the hill, running faster than she ever had in her life. She gasped when they found the burnt-out shell of the gate, but charged forward. English soldiers lay scattered in the courtyard, skewered by arrows.

Rorie and his men pushed ahead of her and filed into the great hall. Anne took in a deep breath at the sound of sword fighting within. She stepped up to the threshold and craned her neck. Calum swung his sword with force, embroiled in a fierce fight with that black-haired monster, Denton. Both men were bleeding. Calum's pale face was drawn, his eyes dark, and cords jutted from his neck with each swing of his blade.

Denton's black hair flicked with every sharp move. He looked like a viper darting in for his attacks and slipping away from Calum's strikes. That man had to be the blackguard who stretched Calum on the rack. Anne's insides twisted with each blow, her gaze darting across the scene seeking an opportunity to help.

Hugging the wall, Anne scooted toward the two men. She had no idea what she would do, but she needed to be close to Calum. She reached for her dirk, but before her fingers brushed the basket weave hilt, an arm slipped around her waist and yanked her back toward the massive double doors.

Anne screamed.

"Shut up, whore."

She froze.

Wharton jerked her against his chest and hauled her into the darkness.

***

Distracted by Anne's shrill scream, Calum looked away for a split second. Denton's blade slashed open his shirt with a stinging cut. A wee bit closer and Calum would have been dead. Infused with rage, he eyed his target. Denton circled, barking out a callous laugh. The bastard thought he'd made a mortal wound.

Calum knew better and turned in place, waiting for Denton to make his move. Denton raised his sword. Seeing his chance, Calum spun into him, swinging the cutlass. With an earthshaking roar, he sliced through Denton's neck. The henchman's head bowled across the floor. Denton's body stood stiff for a moment and then his knees buckled and he crashed to the ground.

Calum raced out the door and through the outer bailey gates. He'd glimpsed Wharton. The bastard must already have Anne halfway to the beach. Ruairi and his men still fought in the surf. To the south, a lone skiff waited tucked against the cliff, away from the fighting.

Calum tore after them, heedless of his injuries. He leapt across the brush to cut off the corners of the zigzagging path. Anne's cries vibrated in his ears. *There!* Wharton struggled to control her as she twisted and fought to get away.

With one more leg to go to the beach, Calum's mind clicked and he jumped over the rocky crag and skidded feet away from the boat. "Stop!"

Wharton tossed Anne into the skiff and whipped around. Snatching a dagger from his belt, he held it steady. "Stay back." He kept his eyes on Calum as he shoved the skiff into the water.

Calum charged in with the cutlass held high. Wharton dove aside and caught Calum by the waist. Falling, the two men crashed to the stones. Calum's hand smashed against a rock and his sword flew from his grip. Wharton's weight crushed his chest. Calum swung his fist into the baron's temple. The big man reached up with his knife. Calum caught his arm, the blade inches from his face. Locked in a battle of raw strength, Calum stared at the knife. His hands trembled with the pressure, his face stretched as he fought with everything he had left.

Wharton crushed his barrel chest over him. Calum could hardly breathe. He tried to shove the baron away with his trapped shoulder and shook with the strain, muscle against muscle.

Suddenly, Wharton arched up and bellowed like a skewered bull. His eyes bulged and blood oozed from his mouth. The knife slid from his hand. His body dropped forward and pinned Calum with dead weight.

With a disgusted grunt, Calum threw Wharton off and scrambled out from under the beast. Anne stood behind him, her hands bloodied and shaking. Her stunned eyes drifted to the dirk in Wharton's back.

God bless her, she'd killed him.

Calum opened his arms and Anne fell into them. Her body trembled with panicked gasps. But she was warm and *alive*. His chest fluttered with relief, He brushed his lips over her forehead and clutched her to his chest.

"'Tis over lass."

"I-I killed him."

Calum knew the mortification she'd feel at having taken a human life. Anne would be numb and she would never forget it, but in time she would reconcile herself to the fact she'd done it to save him.

"Ye saved me life."

She lifted her chin. "You saved *my* life as well."

Cradling her in his arms, he bowed his head and covered her mouth with a deep, searing, wonderfully satisfying kiss.

Chapter Twenty-nine

By the time Calum and Anne arrived at the great hall, the fighting had ended. The cold from his wet clothing chilled Calum to the bone and he'd begun to feel every cut and bruise he'd acquired this night. The others would be sore and freezing as well. Rorie and his men had started to cleaning up the carnage. Calum didn't want to release Anne from his grasp, but he set her down to meet her new friend.

Anne made the introductions. "Rorie found me half starved, hiding in his burnt out keep."

The older Scot shrugged. "I couldna just leave her there and the lass was hell bent on finding ye—Could speak of nothing else."

Calum examined Anne, his expression dubious. "Ye escaped on yer own?"

Shivering, she still blushed. "Yes."

Calum stepped forward and shook Rorie's hand. "Thank you, Douglas. Ye'll find food in the kitchen and there's plenty of room to bed down along with fresh hay in the stable loft."

Calum gazed at Anne who stood with her back to the wall, shivering, her cotton shirt plastered to her body. If her breasts had not been bound, she would have appeared completely naked under the thin cloth.

He reached for her hand. "Ye must slip out of yer wet clothes."

"There is so much work to be done. We've got to put the hall back to rights."

"Aye, and it will still be here on the morrow. We're all tired, lass."

Calum lifted her into his arms and climbed the stairs to his chamber—the laird's chamber still filled with her trunks. He turned the lock in the door and gently set her on the chair. "I'll light the fire to warm yer bones."

Anne nodded, her teeth chattering. When the flames from the peat leapt to life, Calum turned and faced her. Her lips blue, she sat with a distant look, clutching her arms against her body. He reached for her hands. "Come here." He pulled her up, wrapped her in his embrace and rubbed the cold from her shoulders.

"I feel like I've been punched right in my stomach."

"I ken, lass." He brushed his lips across her forehead. "Ye've had a terrible ordeal."

Anne took a step back, steepled her hands to her lips and closed her eyes. Calum stepped toward her, but she dropped to her knees.

"Anne?"

"No. Stay where you are." Her face strained against a grimacing pain. Was she injured? Calum took another step, but Anne held up her hand. She raised her long lashes revealing fathomless tormented pools of blue. Calum fought his urge to scoop her into his arms. Twice she'd told him to stay back.

"What is it, my love?"

Anne furrowed her brow. "Love?"

Calum reached out his arms.

Anne shook her head and crossed her hands over her chest. Tears burst from her anguished eyes and streamed down her cheeks. "I must first beg for your forgiveness, my lord."

Calum stared. She wanted him to forgive her? For what? She crouched into a ball and held her hands to her face, wailing and rocking as if life was ending. Calum dropped to his knees and wrapped his arms around her. "Anne. There is nothing to forgive."

"I gave away the keep."

"Ye did it to save me."

"I saw the venom in your eyes. I-I never meant to bring war to Raasay. I-it's all m-my fault." She curled tighter into her ball, her anguished cries wracking her slim frame.

Calum scooped her into his arms and pulled her into his lap. "I forgive ye, Anne. I love ye with all my heart and soul. I would have done the same thing if it had been you."

Every sinew in her body tensed and she muffled her wails against his chest as she leaned into him. Her warm tears dribbled down his skin and he held her tighter, rocking gently. Calum's heart wrenched with her pain. He pressed his lips against her forehead and squeezed his eyes shut—rocking.

The tension of her body eased and her sobbing ebbed into staccato breaths. The peat fire began to warm them.

"The English would have come sooner or later, Anne." He raised her chin with his finger. His lips wandered across her forehead, her eyelids, her cheekbones, her chin. "Did ye hear me? I love ye."

Calum closed his eyes and covered her lips with his. Gently, he teased open her silken mouth. He took his time—every gesture long, slow, deliberate. He wanted her to feel the love that had tortured him day and night since first time he laid eyes on her.

As he pulled away, her eyes opened wide and filled with wonder. "I love you too. With all my heart." She wrapped her arms around his neck and squeezed. "I-I jumped out the window at Carlisle. I had to find you. Rorie helped me..."

Calum put his finger to her lips. "Ye can tell me all about it in the morning. But first we need to get ye dry."

They stood, and Calum took a moment to light every candle in the room. This time he wanted nothing left to his imagination.

Moving before her, he grasped the hem of her shirt. "May I?"

Anne held her arms over her head.

Calum peeled the wet cloth from her body and cast it aside. He tried not to ogle the creamy skin of her naked belly, glowing amber in the firelight. Kneeling down, he removed her boots and stockings. He craned his neck, met her gaze and then stood and placed his hand on the edge of the cloth that bound her breasts. Anne shuddered. Heat spread through his midriff.

"Are ye all right?" he asked.

Without a hint of fear in her eyes, she held her arms out to her sides.

Calum took her cue and unfastened the knot. Three times the cloth wrapped around her body. When all but the final layer remained, the pink buds of her breasts stretched against the linen. His mouth went dry and he pulled away the cloth.

Milky white, far more beautiful in the candlelight, her breasts sprang from the bindings and stood proud. Her nipples pointed at him, demanding he suckle them. He cupped his hands over her breasts and looked to her eyes for her consent. Her tongue slipped across her upper lip.

Calum's cock strained against his kilt. He lowered his head and brushed his lips over the top of her breast. With feathery kisses, he took a pink bud in his mouth and teased it with his lips and teeth. With a guttural moan, Anne threw her head back and thrust her hips forward

"I've wanted this, wanted to love you like a woman loves a man. Fully."

"And I you." Calum teased her with his mouth until Anne grasped his head and brought him to her lips. She kissed him, her tongue searching his mouth as if desperately seeking something she could not find.

Calum matched her vigor and inhaled her sweet scent. Anne's fingers fumbled with the laces on Calum's shirt. He raised his head, ripped it over his head and cast it aside.

Anne gasped and clapped her hands over her mouth. "My God. You have so many cuts. You're still bleeding."

He chuckled. He had no mortal wounds, and no wee scrape would keep him from his beloved this night. "Ye can tend me in the morning."

Licking her lips, she nodded. He released his belt and it clattered to the floor, along with his kilt.

Anne sucked in a sharp inhale. "Oh, my...you are beautiful...it is…"

Calum's manhood jutted from his loins, a testament of how deeply he loved her…how much he must have her in this moment. He stepped forward. "I'll not hurt ye."

Anne reached out her hands. "You are the most fascinating sight I have ever seen." She stepped into him. "I want to touch you—show the depths of my love for you."

Calum gave a slow nod and she wrapped her fingers around his cock and stroked. His eyes rolled back and he groaned with pleasure—he knew he would not last long, not this time. He reached for her lithe hands and stopped her. "We must go slow. Me blood is too hot to toy with it much."

When Anne fumbled with the laces on her trews, Calum interceded and pulled the leather thong. "Let me." Anne watched him with her lips parted as he loosened the laces and slid the trews from her hips. He drew in a breath of air as they slid down far enough to reveal the blonde curls that protected her most intimate secrets. Blonde—he hadn't seen her color in the dark.

Calum tried to breathe as the musky floral bouquet of her sex floated to him. A pearl of moisture wet the tip of his manhood and he shuddered. He stood and embraced her, pressing himself against her belly. Anne's breasts brushed the cut Denton had sliced through his chest. Calum drew in a sharp breath. She pulled back. His red blood contrasted with her silken skin.

She gasped. "You're hurt."

"'Tis only a scratch."

"I should tend it."

"Ye have a lifetime to tend me, but now I need to bed you."

Anne's smile had no dimples this time. She looked like a woman filled with desire, determined to make her conquest. He lifted her with ease and placed her on the bed. Kneeling over her, he ran his tongue everywhere.

Anne's slender hands ran across his skin, igniting a flame wherever they touched. "I want you to love me like a man loves a wife."

Calum stared into her half-cast eyes. "It will hurt yer first time." Something clicked in the back of his mind. She had been with Wharton—she may already have be…

"I want it. I want you."

It didn't matter. Wharton didn't matter.

She licked her lips, looking at him as a woman gazes at her man, and yet wonder brightened her face. Her innocent eyes slipped to his cock and her breath stuttered. Yes. She remained pure. He would see to her pleasure first, make sure her sex wept for him. Calum placed his mouth over hers and kissed her, showed her how deeply his love stirred. He swirled his fingers around her breast and then trailed down past her navel and through those glorious blonde curls. She shuddered, her thighs quivering as he held his hand above the button he knew would send her wild.

"Open yer legs for me." He ran his tongue along her neck, and she obeyed. He slipped his finger further and touched her. Anne arched and cried out. He watched her come undone. He slid his fingers down to her opening and pushed inside. His cock surged at her wetness. She was ready for him.

But he would not take her so quickly. He crouched on his knees and spread her legs wider. "I want to taste ye."

Anne lifted her head, panting. "What?"

"Lie back and let me love you."

Calum flicked out his tongue and Anne gasped. He swirled it around her tiny nub and slid his finger into her. She clasped his head and again arched her back. Her hips moved with his rhythm. Calum knew she was about to burst with her release. He closed his eyes and kept the pace, while his cock strained with a sizzling need to be inside her.

Anne wrapped her legs around his shoulders and cried out. She thrust her hips up against his tongue. Her body went rigid, everything wound taut followed by an earth-shattering gasp. Breathing as if she'd sprinted up a flight of stairs, Anne sank into the pillows, wonder spreading across her face.

She reached for him. "I never thought it could be better than the night in the wood."

Calum rose to his knees and showed her his rock hard erection. "It will be even better, me love."

Her lips parted as she stared at him. She reached out her hand and stroked him with silken fingers. "I want to please you. Show me how."

"Lay back."

Calum held himself up between her legs and kissed her. He brushed his cock along her exposed, swollen womanhood. She was so wet and hot, he nearly exploded. He indulged himself for a few moments, fondling her breasts and suckling her until her breathing sped and her hips swayed against him.

Back in control, he lowered his hips and moved his cock to her opening. "Are ye ready?"

Anne rubbed her hips against him and nodded. Her eyes darkened with love, her parted lips red with passion, he could wait no longer.

He slipped inside and held still, biting his lip.

"Calum."

"Guide me in so I'll not hurt ye."

Anne sank her lithe fingers into his buttocks and pulled. She let out a sharp gasp and slid him down the length of her. Hot woman milked him, surrounded him, tight and wet. Anne strengthened her grip and moved her hips. Arching her back, her moans came rapid and swift, sending him into a maelstrom of driving need. Calum could hold back no more. He drove his cock into her again and again, the tight rippling of her inner walls taking him beyond the point of ecstasy. Throwing back his head, Calum roared with his release.

Anne's hips met his thrusts. As Calum exploded, Anne arched up and cried out.

Panting, he rested on his elbows and gazed into the dark pools of her eyes, so clear, he could glimpse into her soul. "I love ye with every thread of my being."

Anne caressed his face and drew his lips to hers. "I love you, Laird Calum MacLeod."

Kissing her, Calum swore he would never again let her go. He wanted to hold her in his embrace and protect her forever. She was his.

***

The sliver of the morning sun glowed through the tiny window, and Anne ran her hand over the place where Calum slept, but was met with cold linens. She opened her eyes. The laird had risen. The fire in the hearth had been stoked, but she saw no sign of Calum.

She closed her eyes and the nightmare of the battle raged in her mind. She had nearly drowned, but an angel saved her. *Calum*. She hugged a pillow to her chest and rocked her hips. Their lovemaking only hours ago still lingered deep within her.

Calum loved her. She closed her eyes and focused on the euphoria blossoming in her breast. She loved him with every fiber of her being. She took in a deep breath. Never in her life had she imagined being with a man would be so deliciously wonderful. Calum satiated her needs on so many levels—levels she did not even know existed.

He had given her his fascinating body. Merely the sight of him naked sent shivers coursing across her skin. They had made love over and over until they both could no longer move. She wiggled her hips and sweet pain shot through her loins. Yes, she was tender, but that had no bearing on the love swelling in her heart.

With a long stretch, she sat up. The bedclothes dropped from her breasts and she realized she was naked. If only he were here— well possibly it was better he was not. A bit sore, she might have difficulty walking.

A voice echoed in through the window. She wrapped herself in her dressing gown and walked to it. Though still afloat, the *Sea Dragon* listed in the bay. Ruairi's ship and *The Golden Sun* moored alongside it as waves slopped against their hulls, the water lit golden by the morning sun.

Bonfires burned on the beach. Calum worked beside his men, hauling dead sailors to the fire, the wind blowing the stench out to sea. But there was another line of dead where the beach met the grass. The women of the keep keened loudly, preparing their men for burial. The grief-stricken ululations screeched on the wind. Anne swallowed. *So much destruction.* Her own euphoria turned to ash. This would be a sad day indeed. She must help. Anne dashed to her trunk and pulled out a day dress. Holding it up, her gut squeezed. Her clothing was entirely inappropriate for Raasay.

"Milady?" Mara knocked at the door.

Anne welcomed her inside and Mara fell into her arms "'Tis such a relief ye are safe."

"Oh, Mara, I'm so happy to see you. But…"

Mara knit her brows. "But what, milady?"

Anne hung her head. "But are you not angry with me? I-I feel like I've brought this destruction upon you—upon all of you."

"Aye, we all thought that at first, but Calum made us realize the English would have come with or without ye."

"Oh, Mara, I love you so. I want to help." She held up her dress. "But not in this. Do you have a kirtle I can borrow until I can have some of my own made?"

"Aye, but first I need to tell ye some news."

Mara ran her hand over her somewhat flat belly, and Anne beamed. "Are you?"

Mara's face glowed with a healthy pink sheen. "With child. Aye."

"Oh, my goodness, I'm so happy for you. When will the babe come?"

"Near Christmas. Me thinks I conceived the night Calum brought ye to Brochel."

Chapter Thirty

Calum used the friar's salve and wrapped his wounds before he slipped out of the chamber at dawn. No matter how much he wanted to, he could not lay abed all morning when there was so much work to be done. He knew the battle from the night before had not passed without losses. He must lead the effort to bury the dead.

Alone, he made it to the beach and stood with his hands on his hips. Most of the dead strewn across the stones were English, though the lead shepherd, Gordon MacLeod, lay nearest his feet. Calum gritted his teeth and forced back his tears. He would show the stoic face of a warrior this day. He bent down and lifted his clansman into his arms and carried him to higher ground where the beach met grass—where they buried their dead. He knelt down and lowered his friend's body gently, ever so careful to cradle Gordon's head.

Calum closed Gordon's sightless eyes. He prayed for his friend's soul that it would be delivered into the hands of God and this fearless warrior would be accepted through the gates of Heaven and exalted for his bravery. Calum prayed for his clan, for a quick recovery, and gave thanks for those who'd come to his aid. Finally, he thanked God for Anne's safe return, and prayed for forgiveness that his love for her ran so deeply. A laird should keep himself above such heartfelt emotions, but Anne owned his mind, body and soul. She embodied his need for food, shelter, even his need to breathe the sweet air of Raasay.

When Calum raised his head, his guard had filed onto the beach. In silence they cleaned the carnage, just as they had after other battles, just as their forefathers had done before them. Then the wives came and their cries of agony sent chilled knives of remorse across Calum's skin as he dug graves beside his men.

Friar Pat led a line of women down the hill. At first he didn't recognize his Anne, but the golden blonde hair fluttering in the wind, made Calum's heart skip a beat. She wore a blue kirtle over her shift—the dress of the women of Raasay. Anne carried a wooden bucket and ladle and Mara held a basket. Each woman carried something—baskets of food, shovels, peat, oils—all things they would need to finish the day's work.

Anne stopped at each man and offered a drink, silently. No one spoke. They honored the dead. Anne stopped at Calum with her eyes lowered and offered him a ladle. His fingers brushed hers when he accepted it, and a flush spread across her cheeks. He wanted to pull her into his arms, but this was not the time. They had to care for the fallen first. Her eyes met his and her tears glistened in the sunlight. Calum wiped his mouth on his sleeve and handed her back the ladle with a nod of thanks. Anne bowed and continued on. Calum watched her. The kirtle hugged her body like a glove. Her hair hung loose down her back and swayed across her shapely bottom as she moved. Calum would speak to the friar when their work was done.

It was late afternoon when the beach was clean and the dead buried. Calum stood beside Anne as the friar chanted the funeral mass. When it was over, silence encapsulated them. The only sound was the rush of waves sliding on and off the beach—just as they had since the beginning of time. In silence, Friar Pat led the procession up the hill. They would mourn until the sun set, and then they would feast and celebrate their victory.

***

After the funeral, Anne needed time to gather her thoughts. She walked through the castle gardens, every step propelling her forward, yet the weight of two stones pressed down upon her shoulders. The terror of the battle, the intoxicating fervor of last night spent in Calum's arms, and now her heart weighed heavy in her chest with the ever familiar musket hole.

Had she done the right thing? Thomas Wharton proved to be a greater tyrant than she'd imagined. Thank heavens, now that he was dead, no ill could pass to her family.

This is where God intended her to be. Calum loved her. She wanted to be with him. Forever.

Anne stopped when she came to Swan's mews. For some reason she didn't expect the bird to be there, but he hopped onto a limb near the door. He still had jesses tied to his legs. She pulled the long falconer's gloves from the peg, and slipped them on. Reaching in, she sang her lullaby.

She grasped the short strap and Swan jumped onto her outstretched arm. The bird pecked her gloved fingers. Anne found his food in a barrel beside the cage and offered him a treat. Snatching it with his beak, he ate greedily. Anne sang, cooing to him.

The bird had now grown the full plumage of a young golden eagle, his tail and wings tipped with white. He stretched his wings and Anne marveled at the enormous span. "You are magnificent."

"I thought I would find ye here." Calum smiled, stretching the dark circles under his eyes.

"You're tired."

"I'll sleep tonight." Calum looked at the bird. "He's missed ye."

"I'm surprised he recognized me so quickly. I've been gone nearly a month."

"And I never want to see ye leave again." Calum opened the cage door and she placed Swan inside. The laird stood still and watched the bird for a moment.

When Calum turned, he grasped Anne's hands to his chest and knelt. "Lady Anne, I haven't much to offer ye, but me sword and a crumbling keep. I love ye more than life itself. I love ye more than the air I breathe, and I cannot live without ye. Would…would ye be me wife?"

Anne's insides fluttered as if tickled by the feathers of a golden eagle. Calum knelt before her, with his broad shoulders and his auburn hair streaked copper in the sun. He had forgiven her, and now he opened his life to her. She wanted nothing more. "Yes." She pulled him into her arms. "Yes. I would have it no other way. I will marry you, Calum MacLeod."

Calum squeezed her until the air whooshed from her lungs. "Thank God. I dunna ken what I would have done if ye'd said no."

"I don't know what I would have done if you hadn't asked."

"Should I send word to yer mother?"

Anne stood back. That was a sobering thought. "If you do, we may be facing a whole fleet of English ships."

"That would be no, then."

"Correct. No. At least not for some time. Possibly the word should come from me—perhaps when our first child is born."

"Child?" Calum pressed his lips against her forehead. "That would be yet another miracle." He grasped her hand. "Let us go see the friar."

***

Anne wore her Scottish kirtle to the feast and took her seat beside her betrothed. Ruairi sat to Calum's right and Rorie on Anne's left. Dougal MacKenzie also sat at the laird's table beside Norman and Friar Pat.

The smell of roasted meat wafted through the great hall and trenchers laden with food lined the tables. Calum stood and raised his tankard. "The sun has set, our dead have been mourned, 'tis now time to celebrate our victory."

The hall echoed with a resounding, "Hear, hear!"

"I toast me brother, Ruairi, and me new friend, Rorie Douglas, and his guard who brought Lady Anne back to me—back to us. And to my close friend, Dougal MacKenzie, for taking up our fight and standing beside us to beat down the English!" Calum's voice rose when he spoke the final word. Everyone stood and raised their tankards with a boisterous roar.

Calum held his hands out, asking for silence. "I have one last toast." He turned to Lady Anne and held up his tankard. "To the woman who is known to us all, who brought organization to our keep, whose smile warms our hearts. To the woman who agreed to be me wife. Lady Anne."

The hall erupted in a shout of praise and congratulations as people clapped and pounded the hilts of their dirks on the tables.

"Feast me friends and share in our success."

Anne wrapped her hands around Calum's arm and whispered in his ear, "And here's to you, the strongest sword—a man who pulled me from the depths of the sea and took me soaring to heaven all in one night."

Calum gave her a wicked grin and waggled his eyebrows with a promise of things to come.

When their bellies were full, the piper and the fiddler climbed up on the dais. Bran was the first to Anne's table. "Will ye dance with me, Lady Anne?"

Anne shot an apologetic glance at Calum, but he gestured to the floor. "After him I'll be next."

Bran had heeded his lessons and spun Anne around the dance floor with practiced precision, and she threw her head back and laughed. Calum tapped him on the shoulder, and held her hands in anticipation of a reel. No one else existed as they danced the steps, but Anne was tired, as were the others. The hall emptied early.

Calum looked over her shoulder and tugged her hand. "Come. They'll not miss us."

Anne could hardly breathe as she followed.

Inside the laird's chamber, her weariness fled. Calum bent down and kissed her neck as Anne attacked Calum's clothing. How much easier things were to remove when their clothing was dry. They stood naked in front of the hearth and Anne explored every inch of his glorious body with fluttering kisses. She had him turn and paused while she examined his scarred back. She blew cool air on his skin traced her fingers over the pink scars. "Does this hurt?"

"With yer hands on me, nothing could hurt."

His manhood stood proud from its copper curls. He took her hand and led her to the bed. She watched the pleasure in his eyes as she ran her fingers along the length of him. He reached down and brushed his fingers over her sex. "Are ye sore?"

"With you, I could never be too sore."

A husky chuckle rumbled from his throat and he laid her down. He took his time and showered her body with kisses until Anne could take no more. "I want to feel you in me."

He rolled to the side and stroked his member. "Ye want me to pleasure ye with this?"

"Aye." Anne giggled at her use of the Scottish word.

He pushed her thighs apart and covered her. The heat in Anne's loins rose so fast, she could not wait. She reached for his manhood and guided it inside, watching his eyes. They glazed and his body tensed. With a gush of air, his hips rocked. Anne latched on to his buttocks and rode their wave of ecstasy until her release burst and shuddered around him.

Three more deep thrusts and Calum cried out, his body quivering while his seed sewed inside her womb. He rested with his head on her chest and she ran her fingers through his thick hair. Calum closed his eyes and his breathing slowed. In sleep, he looked as peaceful and serene. Anne spooned her body against his and let sleep come as she floated on a cloud of happiness.

Chapter Thirty-one

Two weeks later

Mara helped Anne into her favorite dress of golden silk. She imagined this would be the last time she would wear a gown this fancy. But it was her wedding day. She wanted to look beautiful for Calum and wanted him to rake his eyes across her body with the same hungry desire that had practically stripped her naked at the Beltane Festival.

Anne sat before the mirror and Mara twisted her locks into a work of art with curls cascading down her back. Mara lifted the silk wimple and veil and settled it in place. "Ye look like an angel sent from heaven, milady."

"I could have never done it without you."

Mara gave her a hug and secured the headpiece. "I think you're ready."

"Is it time?"

"Me thinks they're all waiting on you."

With a sigh, Anne regarded herself in the mirror one last time and held her hand out to Mara. "Walk with me."

Rorie Douglas stood at the bottom of the steps. "Ye look like a vision." He chuckled. "I never would have thought the guttersnipe in a snug pair of trews could turn herself into a queen."

"Not a queen. The wife of a laird."

"And a former baroness."

Anne's gaze shot to his and her mouth fell open. Someone must have told him.

He shrugged. "'Tis all right. I would have wanted him dead if I were married to that bastard."

"How did you find out?"

"Ruairi and Norman filled Dougal and me in on the details."
He offered her the crook of his arm. "We've a wedding to go to,
milady."

"I prefer it when you call me lass."

"Aye, but ye are highborn, and the people of Raasay will
respect ye more if they ken you're good enough for their laird."

He led her around the courtyard and to the garden, alive with
summer blooms. The MacLeods in their red tartans opened a path
for Anne and her eyes trailed up to the trellis. The most beautiful
form she had ever seen waited beside Friar Pat. Calum wore his
hair tied back with a red bow, and it shone with copper streaks in
the sunlight. Turning to face her, he looked every bit the powerful
laird, wearing his finest ruffled linen shirt, with his plaid draped
across his left shoulder. His kilt rested upon his hips with a badger-
hair sporran hanging from a fine chain. Held up by black flashes,
his hose emphasized his powerful calves.

Anne could see nothing but the man with whom she would
happily spend the rest of her days. It seemed as if she floated down
an isle of roses. Rorie kissed her hand and placed it in Calum's.
Their eyes locked and they became one body, man and wife, before
the clan, and in the eyes of God. Together they would bear
children and watch them grow healthy and strong, breathing
northern island air. She had no doubt, together they would grow
old.

Anne scarcely heard Friar Pat's prayers. Calum's crystal blue
eyes shimmered and stared at her with the hunger she loved to see.
He spoke his vows, and somehow she uttered hers. When Friar Pat
pronounced them man and wife, Calum shuttered his eyes with his
long lashes and kissed her—an impassioned joining of lips that
staked his claim forever. This truly was the happiest day of her life.

The Highland Henchman Excerpt

~Book Two: The Highland Force Series~

Chapter One

Scotland. The Firth of Clyde ~ 1 April, 1568

The activity on the deck stilled when the ship turned east and entered the Firth of Clyde. All eyes cast to the inlet. Entering Lowland waters always bore a risk.

His golden eagle perched on his shoulder, Bran scanned the waterway with the bronze spyglass. "Ruairi's galley sails ahead." He strained to identify pennants on the ships beyond. "MacNeil of Barra and MacLeod of Harris as well."

Laird Calum MacLeod grasped the ship's rail beside him. "Do ye see the MacDonald pennant?"

To allay all doubt, Bran surveyed the Firth waters one more time. "Nay."

"Cannons stand down," Calum bellowed and circled his hand above his head. "Continue on, Master John."

Bran turned and leaned his backside against the galleon's hull. "I never considered I'd become a knight."

Calum smooth his hand over the eagle's brown feathers. "A Highland henchman needs a title to garner respect in the Lowlands."

Knighted by the Highland Chieftain only a few hours ago, some might view the honor as contrived, but Bran's chest swelled. He owed his life to Calum. With his father dead, the clan had considered Bran an outcast, until he turned twelve and the laird took him under his wing. Now one and twenty, Bran's dedication to the clan had been rewarded.

Griffon's claws clamped into Bran's shoulder harness as the eagle stretched his back. Bran chuckled. "I aim to win the tournament and show all the might of Raasay."

Calum's weatherworn hands grasped the rail beside him. "That's what I like to hear. I didna train ye to be me henchman for naught."

"How many contestants do ye think there'll be?"

"We'll find out soon enough. Lord Ross invited all the Hebridean clans. I'm sure there'll be quite a gathering."

"Why do ye think he's holding the tournament?" Bran slipped a piece of bully beef into Griffon's beak. "Lowlanders hate Highlanders."

The salty wind picked up and Calum tugged his feathered bonnet lower on his brow. "Me guess is he's up to something."

"Then why'd we come?"

"And miss a chance to gain respect for me clan?" Calum shook his head. "Never. Besides, Lord Ross would have anarchy on his hands if he lifted a blade against us. He wants something, mark me."

"Are ye inclined to give it—ye ken, what he wants?"

"Have I taught ye nothing since yer father passed? Ye never give something for naught, lad."

"I'd consider no less. Ye have me sword, on that there will nay be a question."

The ruddy chieftain leaned in, his warm breath skimming Bran's cheek. "Stay close. Keep yer eyes open. The tournament will be over soon enough and we'll be back in Raasay with Anne and the boys."

"Weigh anchor," shouted John Urquhart, Calum's quartermaster and right-hand man. With John on Calum's right, Bran now occupied the left—a fearsome trio they made.

Bran counted the galleys moored at the estuary of the River Clyde which flowed into the firth from the town of Glasgow—six boats, all laden with cannon, but none as impressive as Calum's *Golden Sun*. With eighteen guns, the galleon and crew would lie in wait should any skullduggery arise.

Once the skiff had been lowered, Bran stood behind his laird with Griffon perched on his shoulder. He wrapped his fingers around the basket-weave pattern of his hilt, scanning the sea and shore for suspicious activity. Instructions were to gather with Sir George Maxwell at Newark. Horses would be provided for the short ride to Halkhead House in Renfrewshire.

Bran didn't like it. Though every Hebride chief was accompanied by his henchman, they were leaving their greatest weapons behind. *The Golden Sun's* cannons would be of no use ten miles inland.

***

Enya squinted at the target. Pulling the string of the long bow even with her ear, she held her breath. The string rolled to the tips of her gloved fingers. She released.

A quick flutter of her heart accompanied her grin. "Spot on the middle."

With his breeches a tad too small and his new boots oversized for his body, Rodney ran up to the target and yanked out the arrow. "Hells bells, you should've been born a lad."

Enya walked up and stuck her finger in the hole. "Wouldn't that have been something? Instead of picking fabric for fancy dresses, I'd be on a ship sailing for the South Seas right now."

The young squire's eyes popped. "And miss the tournament?"

"Well, perhaps after the tournament. I would never be able to resist an opportunity to show up a gathering of brawny knights."

Rodney flexed his muscles. "Do you think I'll be a knight one day?"

"Of course you will. 'Tis why Robert named you squire." She squeezed the lad's scrawny arm. "You have strong bones and at two and ten, you're nearly as tall as me, I'll say."

"But not as dead-on with a bow as you."

"Yet."

Together they walked back fifty paces and Enya held out the bow. "Your turn. Let me see your best."

Rodney concentrated on the target. White lines strained around his lips as he let his arrow fly. It hit the target inches below the bull's-eye.

"Not bad." She pulled another arrow from her quiver and handed it to him. "Try again, and this time, keep your fist even with the top of your ear."

He grinned and followed her instruction. *How long would the young laddie listen to the likes of me—a mere woman?* Soon he'd be off patrolling the borders with her brother, Robert, and she'd be left behind at Halkhead while her father arranged her marriage. *Oh what a wretched parcel of miserable affairs I have to look forward to.*

Enya wanted to patrol the borders—see the world, or Scotland at least. She loved to listen to tales of Robert's travels. She dreamed of riding a white steed and saving the poor from starvation. But she was stuck at Halkhead House, the youngest of Lord Ross's six daughters.

Her mother always berated Enya for daydreaming. "You must take more interest in your embroidery, dear," Mother scolded endlessly while tearing out Enya's horrific mistakes. *Embroidery. Baa.*

"Did you see that?" Rodney asked.

Enya snapped her head toward the target. Rodney's arrow stuck in the bull's-eye—not in the middle like hers had, but close. "Excellent. See? All it takes is a little adjustment and you'll hit your mark every time."

The muffled rumble of horse hooves echoed in the distance. Rodney gaped at her as if it were Christmas morn. "They're coming."

Enya grabbed his hand and headed through the copse of trees. "Let's watch from atop the hill. They'll not see us up there."

Nearly out of breath, they reached the crest just as the long line of horses carrying robust Highlanders ambled into view. Large men rode toward them with plaids draped across their shoulders, helms on their heads, targes in one hand and pikes with deadly spearheads in the other. Some had their claymores strapped to their backs and others carried the large swords in scabbards on their belts.

"They all look so...inexplicably tough," Enya said.

Rodney peeked out from behind an enormous oak. "They look like a mob of heathens if you ask me."

With their long hair and massive exposed legs, Enya could see his point. Lowland men would never be caught baring their knees or wearing kilts. But a basal stirring swirled deep inside. These sturdy men were proud, strong and focused.

Enya watched an imposing warrior ride directly beneath her hiding place. Unable to look away, her breath caught. Even bigger than the others, his chestnut hair curled out from under his helm. On his broad shoulder perched a great golden eagle. She'd seen falconers before, but never one with a bird as impressive as an eagle.

His fist grasped the reins easily, as if he were holding a thread of wool. His plaid covered his thigh just above the knee, leading to a powerful calf which rested against the horse's barrel. Gaping at the warrior's exquisitely muscular frame, Enya bit her lip.

Riding beside a man with an ornate breastplate, Enya guessed the warrior was *An Gille-coise*—a henchman paid to protect his laird and his clan. His gaze flicked across the scene like a hunter, or the hunted. Simply looking at him made her stomach tense.

His eyes darted up the hill and Enya froze. Crouching behind the clump of gorse in full yellow bloom, no one should have seen her, but the warrior's gaze fixed on her as if she were waving a torch. In a flicker of a heartbeat, time slowed. Her mouth went dry as their eyes met. His jaw tensed and his line of sight trailed to the bow in her hand.

"That's got to be the biggest man in the entire world." Rodney's amazed voice broke through her trance.

Enya's hand flew to her chest to quash her pounding heart. "You think so?" Taking a deep breath, she wouldn't let on the warrior had affected her in any way. But her fingers trembled as she watched the parade proceed through the heavy iron gates of Halkhead House—until he turned and regarded her over his shoulder. *Does he think I'm going to pull out an arrow and shoot him in the back? Perhaps he does.*

Rodney yanked her hand. "Come. Let's go watch."

Enya hesitated and stared down at her olive-green kirtle. A plain day dress, her hem was caked with mud. She ran her hands over the simple white coif she'd slapped on top of her head that morning. She looked frightful and knew it. "You go. I'll spirit round the back. If Mother sees me like this, she'll have one of her spells."

Rodney shrugged. "Och, you look fine."

Enya feigned a smile. "You ken Mother. She ordered all that fabric for me."

The lad blew a raspberry and raced down the hill without her. A long breath whistled through Enya's lips. At eight and ten, she'd been to court on a number of occasions. Mother had always made her put on a show of finery, but she didn't care for it. She preferred simple kirtles allowing her more freedom of movement for things like archery and horseback riding.

However, that brawny warrior's eyes raking across her face and fixating on her longbow made her cheeks burn. She didn't want him or anyone else gawking at her dirty gown. Besides, Enya's mother would be furious if she raced into the courtyard with a bow and quiver of arrows slung over her shoulder. A folly to use the secret entrance in daylight, she'd skirt through the woods, head around back, go in through the kitchen and tiptoe up to her chamber.

Edging around the woods proved the easy part, but once she hit the rear side of the manse, her brother, Robert, popped in front of her. "There you are."

Caught. Enya snapped her hands to her hips and challenged him. "Why aren't you in the courtyard greeting our guests with Father?"

"Why aren't you?"

"I'm not the heir."

"Touché." Robert raked his hand through his hair. Enya was well aware he didn't approve of her father's reasons for holding the tournament. "Actually, I heard the horses and was heading there now. Must welcome the barbarians, you know."

"Don't let Father hear you say that."

"And why not? He feels the same."

"Not when we're asking them for help."

"Very well." He licked his finger and rubbed Enya's cheek. "How do you manage to turn into a guttersnipe every time you venture outside?"

Her hands flew to her cheeks. "Really?"

"You'd better not let Mother see you."

"I was just heading in to clean up."

"Hurry. Father wants us all in the great hall for supper. The Hamiltons will be here. You dare not be late."

Enya cast her gaze skyward and headed for the door. She wanted to forget about Lord Claud Hamilton and his supposed interest in her. The few times she'd seen him, he'd reminded her of a rooster strutting among a gaggle of hens.

***

Heather shook her finger under Enya's nose. "I've no idea how we'll turn you into a beauty by supper. Your mother will take it out of my hide for certain."

Enya wrapped her hands around the accusing finger and kissed it. "You worry far too much."

Though she adored Heather almost as if she were a second mother, Enya hated to be doted upon. She looked at the torturous fine-toothed comb in her serving maid's hand and took her seat at the vanity. Heather started at the ends and yanked the comb through Enya's red tresses. "You should have put your hair in a snood before you went out this morning. There wouldn't be half the knots. How you manage to mess my handiwork as soon as you leave the chamber is a mystery to me." She let out a noisy sigh. "You should have been born a boy."

"That's what Rodney said when my arrow hit the bull's-eye." Enya flashed a challenging grin in the looking glass. "Wouldn't that have been a boon? I'd be free to travel, see the world." She swung her arm through the air with an imaginary sword. "Fight duels, and win this fanciful tournament."

Heather groaned and jerked the comb harder.

"Ow."

"You'd do very well to stop your dreaming and face the fact you are a lass, and a grown one at that."

Enya folded her arms and glared at her reflection. It wasn't she didn't like being female, it's just it was so *limiting*. One by one, she'd watched her five sisters marry. Her father was close to negotiating her betrothal to that pompous Claud Hamilton. Heir to an earldom, she should be overjoyed. At least that's what her mother said.

Enya hardly knew Claud. Friends with William, he hadn't been to Halkhead since her closest brother left for his fostering a few years ago. Father had invited Claud to the tournament, just as he had every other able-bodied knight who sympathized with Queen Mary. Enya blinked at her reflection. She'd better give the young lord a chance. Besides, she was curious to see him after so much time had passed. She fidgeted with her skirt. Of course she wanted to see how he'd changed. Perhaps with time to mature, he wouldn't be so full of self-importance. After all, she might have no choice but to spend eternity with him.

Saints preserve me.

Heather pulled a small clump of hair from Enya's temple and started braiding. Nice. She loved it when Heather wove her hair through her bronze tiara. Though unpretentious, it was her favorite piece of jewelry. Enya glanced over to the bed. Heather had set out her gown. It was beautiful. Mother picked the emerald damask to match Enya's eyes. She bit the inside of her cheek. If she was to see her future husband this night, she should look her best.

End of Excerpt from The Highland Henchman

Books by Amy Jarecki

Highland Force series:
Captured by the Pirate Laird
The Highland Henchman
Beauty and the Barbarian
Return of the Highland Laird - a novella
The King's Outlaws series:
Highland Warlord
Highland Raider
Highland Beast
Lords of the Highlands series:
The Highland Duke
The Highland Commander
The Highland Guardian
The Highland Chieftain
The Highland Renegade
The Highland Earl
The Highland Rogue
The Highland Laird
Highland Defender series
The Fearless Highlander
The Valiant Highlander
The Highlander's Iron Will - a novella
Guardian of Scotland time travel series:
Rise of a Legend
In the Kingdom's Name
The Time Traveler's Christmas
Highland Dynasty series:
Knight in Highland Armor
A Highland Knight's Desire
A Highland Knight to Remember
Highland Knight of Rapture
Highland Knight of Dreams - a novella
Devilish Dukes series:
The Duke's Fallen Angel
The Duke's Untamed Desire
The Duke's Privateer

The MacGalloways Series
A Duke by Scot
Her Unconventional Earl
The Captain's Heiress

You won't want to miss
Defenseless
A stand-alone college football romance

Visit Amy's web site & sign up to receive newsletter updates
of new releases and giveaways exclusive to newsletter
followers: <u>amyjarecki.com</u>

Made in the USA
Middletown, DE
08 May 2023

30269557R00161